ABOUT THE AUTHOR

Annabelle Knight is one of the UK's most relevant sex, relationship, dating, and body language experts, a bestselling author, sex toy expert and celebrity relationship coach. She has qualifications in life coaching, couples counselling, and psychosexual therapy.

She regularly appears on television, in the press, and on-air to offer her expertise and guidance on a range of topics.

Annabelle covers everything from lust to love, and anything that's in-between.

D1642846

ANNABELLE KNIGHT

Chasing Clouds

AUSTIN MACAULEY PUBLISHERS™

LONDON • CAMBRIDGE • NEW YORK • SHARJAH

A CIP catalogue record for this title is available from the British Library.

ISBN 9781398408302 (Paperback)
ISBN 9781398408319 (ePub e-Book)

www.austinmacauley.com

First Published (2021)
Austin Macauley Publishers Ltd
25 Canada Square
Canary Wharf
London
E14 5LQ

ACKNOWLEDGEMENTS

Matt Bell

Sabrina Wagstaff

Blacksheep Management

Ryan Wilson

Lee Pretious

Jenny Gosling

Lily Doble

Roy, Matt, Laura & John

DEDICATION

This book is dedicated to my wonderful parents.

Without your continued love and support this book,
or anything else I've managed to achieve, wouldn't be
possible.

Thank you for everything, I love you both more than words
can say.

CHAPTER 1

ELODIE TAYLOR COULDN'T HAVE BEEN HAPPIER. She reclined and drank in the view before her. *'Thailand really is incredible,'* she thought to herself as the sun began to set. The lush palm trees were casting long shadows over the crisp, white sandy beach of Maya Bay and Elodie thought that this must be one of the most beautiful places on the planet. The crystal-clear water looked so inviting and with one solitary cloud lazing happily in the sky she wondered if there was any better way to spend a bank holiday. She closed her eyes and stretched, letting out a long, relaxed sigh.

If only she was actually there. Instead, Elodie Taylor was more than six thousand miles away, sat on her sofa, in a small one-bed flat, in London, flicking through a travel magazine. She tore out one of the pictures and stuck it into her scrapbook. Elodie had been collating bits and bobs from magazines into a large notepad for longer than she cared to remember. She thought of it as her personalised travel guide to the world and hoped that one day she would be able to use it. It contained everything, from places to stay in Australia, to places to eat in Iceland, and everything in between.

She laid the magazine on her lap. The sound of an ambulance siren wailed by outside, breaking her reverie. She gazed around at the place she shared with her long-term boyfriend, Tom. It wasn't as homely as she would have liked but Tom's taste was far more modern than hers, and considering he paid for pretty much everything it was his taste that mostly prevailed. However, there were a few items that had made their way in; Tom knew it didn't take a lot to make Elodie happy. If she had her own way the flat would look completely different: it would be an eclectic mix of restored second-hand furniture instead of brand new flat-pack stuff. She'd have a few choice arty prints on the walls instead of film posters and definitely more knick-knacks from her travels, if she'd ever been on any.

No matter how disagreeable she found some of the decor, the one thing that was stand-out about their home was just how spotlessly clean it was. She'd spent the day doing every household chore she could imagine, she'd even sacrificed her beautiful nails for the cause. Elodie wanted the flat to be a den of tranquillity and calm for when Tom came home from work. He'd been tense recently; a combination of sales deadlines and a potential promotion looming ahead, she had reasoned.

One item that had made its way into their flat was a pastel-coloured patchwork throw that Elodie loved. Its place within their home was draped over the back of a small armchair that was positioned in the corner of their living room. The blanket had been in Elodie's family since she was a little girl and offered her comfort, and not just the warm kind on a cold evening.

Elodie's eyes now rested on a chunky wooden photo frame and within it a photograph of herself and Tom when they had first started dating. He'd surprised her with a long weekend away in Cornwall, after she had dropped in excess of several thousand hints. The picture showed them happy, smiling and considerably younger. She'd barely turned twenty when that picture had been taken. They were clinking glasses at a beachside café in St Ives and she was tanned; even Tom's milky complexion looked a little sun-kissed. They both looked relaxed and very much in love. Elodie's eyes fell onto the rum and Coke that her younger self was holding in the photo, a drink she used to love once upon a time. Tom and Elodie had been together for a long time, longer than she'd care to admit, in fact. They were college sweethearts and he was Elodie's first and hopefully last boyfriend. He was good to her; their relationship hadn't always been plain-sailing but then again, whose relationship was?

She turned her attention back to the magazine, which had fallen from her lap and lay haphazardly on the floor by her feet. She opened it back up and took in that gorgeous view once more. She let the fantasy of seeing the furthest corners of the wider world wash over her. She knew it was a pipe dream, but since when had enjoying moments of pure escapism ever hurt anyone? On colder nights Elodie would snuggle up on the sofa with her pastel patchwork blanket wrapped around her and devour luxury travel magazines one after the other, their pages littered with fabulous destinations that she knew deep down she'd probably never get to see. Lost in her reverie, she would desperately wish that she had both the means and the money to travel. Tom was a bit of a homebody and the idea of leaving everything behind to see the world was one that he didn't like at all. Her friends had encouraged her, at times, to go by herself. Carla and Steph were both very encouraging of her dreams, but even if she could work up the courage to go, her part-time job as a waitress at Betty's Book Café meant that she could barely afford the luxury of buying travel magazines, let alone the actual trips contained within their pages.

'One day,' she promised herself.

She sighed again and pushed herself up from the sofa, leaving the magazine open on the small side table next to her. She stole a glance at the time: Tom would be back from work within the hour and with him he'd bring his usual whirlwind of chaos. When it came to keeping a home, Tom and Elodie were at opposite ends of the spectrum. He brought in the bacon while she, well, she did enough to fill her time. There was always something to be done, and to be honest it didn't bother her that they had what some of her friends described as 'unbearably traditional roles.' It was these 'traditional roles' that made their relationship work, unbearable or not. This fact was met with much disdain from some of her friends and co-workers. They couldn't quite believe that a modern woman could be happy running around after a man. But it wasn't like that. Elodie 'didn't do' running, even when she'd been forced to in PE during year seven. They both pulled their weight equally, Tom even more so in Elodie's opinion After all, without him she wouldn't even have a home to care for. After deciding to make a nice salad for tea, she absent-mindedly padded into the kitchen and opened the fridge. Something fresh and tasty would be ideal now that summer was upon them. After all, it's like her mum had always said, '*Lighter nights call for lighter meals.*' She took out her mobile and connected it to the speaker in the living room, deciding that with good music came good food.

It was less than an hour later when she heard the familiar jangle of keys in the front door. The noise kicked her into gear: if she were honest with herself, she'd have to admit that it wasn't exactly the salad that had taken up all of her time. Elodie had been daydreaming about a far-flung destination wedding for her and Tom. Of course, they weren't quite there yet, but it didn't hurt to have an idea of what she wanted for when the time came. Her friends had often called Tom mean when it came to money; he always seemed to have plenty for himself but refused to fritter his earnings on anything that didn't directly benefit him. But that was his prerogative; and, besides, Elodie knew that he was saving up for something special. Something in platinum maybe, with diamonds perhaps and that possibly came in a little turquoise box too? She shook this thought from her head quickly and finished wiping down the kitchen worktop. She threw the cloth back into the sink and gave the place a final once-over; everything had to be simply perfect for his arrival.

"Hey handsome, have you had a good day?" she chimed sunnily as she heard him walk into the living room. The happy edge to her voice faded slightly when she went to join him and saw his face. Tom looked dishevelled and extremely irritated. What she saw now was a far cry from his usual crisp appearance, his white shirt was creased and dirty and his usually coiffed hair a complete mess.

"Everything OK?" she asked tentatively.

"What does it look like, El?" Tom snapped.

Elodie took a step back, as if the brashness of his tone had a physical effect on her. He looked at her and his expression softened.

"Sorry, babe. The car's about knackered. Took me an hour to get it going after work and halfway home I realised that I'd left some important paperwork at the office. I really needed to get that shit done tonight. I need to show

Clive that I'm better than Pete if I've got any chance of getting this promotion. The interview's this week and I need to show him I'm the best." He let out an exasperated sigh and slumped onto the sofa, rubbing his temples as he did so. "What's for dinner?" he asked, sounding slightly less irritated and a little more defeated.

Elodie perked up a bit; if there was one way to cheer Tom up it was with good food.

"Follow me please, sir," she said in an over-exaggerated French accent as she took a low bow and stifled a giggle. She looked up and thought she saw the faint hint of a smile play around the corners of Tom's mouth. Like a match to an ice cube, she was beginning to thaw his frosty demeanour. Tom got up and brushed down the front of his shirt.

"Give me a minute, babe. I need to get out of these clothes," he said turning on his heel and heading to the bedroom, unbuttoning his shirt as he went.

"Just stick it all in the wash basket and I'll sort it out later for you." Elodie fussed, not wanting to add to Tom's stress levels in the slightest.

Tom grunted his acknowledgement and disappeared, closing the door behind him. Elodie spied the perfect opportunity to finish preparations for their dinner. She took out the vintage candelabra and lace tablecloth that she had found in a bric-à-brac store. Tom had bought them for her, much to his distaste. *'Why do you like crappy old things?'* he had asked her over and over again. But no matter how hard Elodie tried she could never get him to see the value in giving pre-loved items a second chance.

Elodie checked the time: it had just gone seven-thirty. Tom had been home for half an hour now and other than their brief conversation when he'd first walked in she hadn't seen him since, which was almost impossible when you considered the small size of their flat. She knocked on the bedroom door, and immediately resented having to do this. The action made her feel slightly foolish and like a stranger in her own home.

"Tom?" she called through the door. "Dinner's ready when you are," she finished proudly. Elodie hesitated, straining to hear a response. Tom hadn't called her in, nor had he answered her through the door. She knocked again, a little louder this time.

'*Maybe he's fallen asleep,*' she surmised silently. There was still no answer so she tried again, repeating herself, again turning her volume up a notch.

"Yes! I heard you the first time!" Tom barked eventually, his tone stark and uninviting. Elodie backed away, feeling a little hurt. Tom opened the door. He had on fresh clothes and was towel-drying his hair.

"I had to shower El, I told you that," he said in a matter-of-fact way as he walked past her, chucking the towel on the bed as he did so.

His tone reminded Elodie of a parent scolding a child. She racked her brain but couldn't remember him saying any-thing about having a shower, but then again maybe she'd been pre-occupied. Tom was sitting down at the table when Elodie turned around; he held his cutlery in his hands and banged them on the table in a pretty fair imitation of a king waiting to be served. Elodie smiled. If her friend Carla could see this she'd be rolling her eyes and telling Elodie off for encouraging such misogynistic behaviour. Carla was one of Elodie's best friends; she was a budding model, a fellow waitress at Betty's Book Café and a very strong, independent woman who never took any crap from anyone.

"Stop it, Tom," she reprimanded, only half-seriously. "You look like a caveman." Tom put his cutlery down and beat his chest mockingly. This resulted in an over-dramatic eye roll from Elodie who walked over to the countertop to retrieve their meals. She proudly placed the large bowl in the centre of their small table and sat down opposite Tom.

"Dig in!" she said, extending a hand in a very glamorous assistant-like way that made her giggle. Tom stared at the bowl and then looked at her, an odd expression on his pale face. Elodie assumed that the expression was gratitude; she was wrong.

"Is that it?" Tom asked bluntly. "Are you telling me that you've been at home all day and I come home to a few leaves, some balsamic vinegar and some vac-packed ham?"

"It's prosciutto and it's delicious," Elodie answered,

feeling her cheeks turn pink with a mixture of embarrassment and shame.

She really had thought Tom would enjoy the meal. She didn't understand how he could react in this way. He was lucky she'd made him anything in the first place. She simmered for a second then took a deep, calming breath. If there was one thing Elodie Taylor could do, it was to try and see things from other people's perspectives. Tom had just come back from a rough day at work, he was obviously stressed and she was sure he didn't mean to sound rude.

"We've got some nice bread too," Elodie improvised, quickly getting up and bringing back crusty bread rolls for Tom. He took them from her and grunted a thank you. Elodie was determined that his bad mood wouldn't rub off on her so she changed the subject hastily and began to chat about her day. She told him about how the tumble dryer had eaten another one of her socks and how she'd listened to a great podcast while she cleaned the flat from top to bottom, how she'd run some errands for him and, when she'd lost another nail in her cleaning frenzy, had eventually put her feet up with a magazine and a cup of green tea. She gestured to the sofa; the mug was still resting on the arm and there was a suspiciously Elodie-shaped dent in the cushions. Tom didn't so much as crack a smile as she regaled him with these stories; instead, he shovelled salad into his mouth and tore off chunks of bread at various intervals, dipping them in the balsamic vinegar before shoving them in to join the salad. Elodie grimaced; she knew he'd had a terrible day in the office, but really, there was a limit to her patience, especially when it came to bad table manners. He hadn't even said thank you, for Christ's sake. There was an uncomfortable silence between them now, which Elodie found as confusing as she did irritating.

It was then she hit upon a bright idea. Why hadn't she thought of this sooner? Tom had a big interview for an internal promotion coming up, he'd been working long hours and taken on lots of extra responsibilities to prove his worth to his boss, Clive. The bottom line was that Tom was stressed and he didn't know how to cope with it. *'What's the best way to deal with stress?'* she asked herself. *'Relax!'* she answered instantly. She didn't have to rack her brain for long to come to the conclusion that there was no better place to relax than on a beach somewhere. What Tom needed now, more than ever, was a holiday. St Ives seemed like a lifetime ago and they'd had so much fun. This way Elodie could scratch her travel bug itch and Tom could relax and unwind; it would do them, both as individuals and as a couple, the world of good. She got up and journeyed over to the magazine she'd been reading earlier and flipped it open to the page that showed the beautiful beach in Thailand.

"This is what we need," Elodie said softly, "you're so stressed and we've not been away in so long. It'd be really good for us. Don't you think?" she added hesitantly.

Tom looked at her and frowned. He shook his head and pushed the magazine away from under his nose.

"We've been over this time and time again," he said through gritted teeth. "I can't afford something like that, Elodie. You're not interested in camping with my mates or going away with my mum and dad to Spain. You want the very best but you aren't willing to work for it. Do you know how fucking annoying it is to work, all the goddamn time? No you don't, because if you do four days at a push you complain about how tired you are. Jesus, all you do is pour coffee and talk to Cara!"

"Carla," Elodie corrected him, putting emphasis on the 'L' in Carla's name. Tom waved this correction away and carried on as if she'd never said anything at all.

"Then, when I do eventually get to come home you're here, trying to make out like you've been so busy, but really all you've done is the stuff you're meant to do anyway. What makes it even worse is that to top it off, you're always asking for something." Tom sighed when he saw the crestfallen look on her face. His expression softened and he reached out to take her hand. "Look, El, You're right. I'm so completely fried with work, I barely have time to think at the moment." Elodie looked down, feeling abashed. "I'm not knocking you, El," Tom went on, "but you're such a dreamer. I just don't get why you're always so keen to jump on a plane, it's like you're not happy and you want to escape. I'm just managing your expectations; it's much better to keep your feet on the ground and your head out of the clouds. What's wrong with a staycation? England's the best country in the world, shouldn't we try and see a bit of that first?" He kissed her hand. The stubble of his short beard was scratchy against her skin so she pulled it away from him. "The bottom line is that I've got bigger and better things to save for and don't you think that's more important than a silly holiday?"

He waggled his ring finger in the air and smiled smugly. Elodie grinned. He'd hinted at this before, usually when they'd been in a similar situation. It was Tom's 'get out of jail free' card, her friends had said. But Elodie knew that that just wasn't true. They were totally on that track, she just needed reminding of it sometimes. Elodie decided then and there that she'd make more of an effort from now on. It'd be worth it in the end, especially if it got her down the aisle! She tried to nod her agreement but found that she couldn't.

"Yes, England is beautiful, but there's a lot more to the world than just this little island. We should see as much as we can and experience everything while we're still young and don't have any responsibilities," she contested, trying once again to make Tom see her point of view.

"You might not have any responsibilities, but I sure do. Experience what exactly? You tell me what it is exactly that you're so desperate to do?" he said scathingly. He stopped short and looked her dead in the eye. Elodie didn't want an argument but she was getting a bit tired of Tom and his stubborn ways.

"Food, I want to taste real Indian food, I want to sunbathe on white sands, I want to feel the atmosphere in a bazaar in Morocco and more than anything, I want to wake up to something, anything, other than beeping car horns and ambulance sirens." She took a deep breath; she could feel her cheeks flushing with annoyance. Tom noticed too and sat back down.

"This is where your argument falls flat on its face, El. You want curry, go to Curry Mile. You want a tan, the sunbed shop is just down the road and the undercover market has all those types of stalls that Morocco has. And guess what, you don't have to spend a shitload of money and sit on a cramped plane for hours to experience it all. Oh, and if you're that bothered about the city noise, buy some ear-plugs." He finished sharply, stuffing the final chunk of bread into his mouth and sauntering off to the bedroom.

'*Well, that escalated quickly.*' She thought to herself, staring at his half-eaten plate of salad. She knew she wouldn't be in line for a Michelin star anytime soon but at least she'd tried. When was the last time Tom had made a meal for her? He was so quick to judge her lifestyle; just because she hadn't really figured out what she wanted to do with her life and wasn't in line for a promotion at a used car garage, that didn't make him suddenly the most important person ever. Sometimes Tom could be so self-involved. Elodie stood there dumbstruck, wondering how on earth that had just happened. Maybe she should get a proper job and just be done with it. God knows it'd make Tom, and his parents, happy to see her in a nine-to-five; they always asked hopeful questions about her work aspirations and were always disappointed by the answers. She always felt a little ganged up on whenever they all hung out together. The truth was that Elodie had a lot she did want to do, she just didn't quite know how to do it yet. But she was young and had her whole life ahead of her; she didn't need to be stuck in a job she didn't like to pay the bills right this second. Elodie decided that the best thing to do would be to go and talk to Tom properly and not let it dissolve into another heated row. She had only been trying to suggest something to cheer him up but once again Tom had misread her and flown off the handle. Now that she thought about it he'd always been like that. Tom was one of those people who didn't like the boat rocking, a 'just get on with it' kind of guy. Elodie had admired that about him in the early days but now it seemed churlish and immature. How would they ever solve any real problems down the line if Tom resorted to name-calling and storming off? She pushed the bedroom door open a crack and peered inside. He was sat on the bed, wearing a blue striped short-sleeved shirt that Elodie had never seen before and a pair of smart dark blue jeans. She could smell the recent sprayings of his beloved aftershave, which hung heavily in the air.

"I'm off out," Tom said, sensing her presence behind him.

"Pat and Al are meeting me for a drink," he finished flatly. He stood up, brogues in hand, and walked straight past her as if she were no more than a breath of air. Elodie shuddered; that was not the first time that evening he'd done that.

"But, what about...?" Elodie trailed off. What was the point? When Tom was in this type of mood maybe it was best for him to go out, see his friends and blow off some steam. After all, it was Elodie who had told him he was stressed and needed to relax. She could hardly keep him prisoner in his own home.

"OK, babe, have a good time." She turned around just as the door shut behind him, the loud clunk of the lock faded and she was left in silence.

Elodie scraped the remains of their dinner into a Tupperware container and placed it in the fridge before pouring herself a glass of wine. She felt hollow and thought a liberal amount of rosé wine would help dissipate the still palpable tension.

Elodie padded into the bathroom and began to draw herself a bath. On her way she noticed Tom's dirty clothes from earlier strewn on the floor in the order he had taken them off. She bent down, gathered them up and popped them in the washing basket beside her dresser.

"See, it's not that hard is it?" she muttered to herself.

It was a hard balance to strike: she was expected to do everything around the house whilst Tom, quite frankly, behaved like an overgrown toddler. She tried not to be reductionist about everything, she knew Tom paid pretty much all the bills, the flat was in his name and his responsibility but she paid her share of the rent and did most of the shopping; as far as she could see most of everything they shared was fifty-fifty, so surely the housework should be too? Elodie could understand it if that's what she had chosen to do, if she'd made a decision that this was what she wanted to do. But she hadn't. She wanted a bit of fair treatment, for him to understand that life wasn't difficult and stressful just for him.

She undressed herself slowly, her mind still lingering on all the things she'd wished she'd said before Tom left.

Sometimes she felt as though she were talking to a brick wall. As she sank into the tub she exhaled deeply. There was one thing that really stuck in her craw about the whole situation. She realised that this was the fourth time Tom had used the excuse of saving for a ring to quiet her. She didn't think that Tom was lying about wanting to marry her; she now thought that it was just a convenient way to excuse his own behaviour whilst vilifying hers.

CHAPTER 2

"WILL YOU STOP DOING THAT AND HELP WRITE the specials on the chalkboard? Your writing's way nicer than mine," Steph pleaded as Carla took yet another picture of herself, this time sat in the large bay window, legs in the air and winking at the camera.

"Of course it is," Carla answered dramatically, "I'm a creative," she chuckled. "Look, I'm sure El will help when she gets here and my feet are killing me," Carla contested. She turned her phone around and snapped a picture of Steph in defiance. Seeing her stern face Carla added hastily, "Besides, you owe me big time! Don't you forget who opened up the last few days so you could spend all weekend in bed with Andy!" Carla was only half-joking. She'd taken on all of Steph's shifts in order for Steph to spend some quality time with her boyfriend Andy. Steph hardly ever got to see him as his career in the army meant that he was barely at home.

Steph rolled her eyes and tried again to write the words 'carrot cake' in a curly script that was neat enough to satisfy her own exacting standards.

Betty's Book Café, where Elodie, Carla and Steph all worked, had come into existence the year after Steph had been born. It belonged to her long-suffering mother, who had worked extremely hard to make the place a success. Betty had wanted to combine her two favourite pastimes, reading and eating cake. Roll on twenty-four years and the café was a roaring success: it was a hub for the local community and even at quieter times always had a plethora of customers coming to peruse the books and order a latte, grab a slice of cake, or both. Betty had dreamt of opening a café since she was a little girl and Steph now dreamt of running it, a dream that was soon to become a reality. Betty had sat her daughter down only a few weeks ago and told her that even though she loved every second of running the café, baking the cakes and making friends with the customers, she was getting ready to hand it all over and retire. She'd been getting more tired of late and had suffered with migraines as a result of her continued busy workload. She figured that there was more to life than just work. Betty lived above the café in a little flat that she shared with her daughter. The place was cramped and Betty longed for a place of her own in the countryside. She planned on retiring at the end of the year and had asked if Steph would take over when she did. Steph had of course accepted the challenge and although sorry to see her mother step aside knew that it would make her happy to move on to somewhere new. Betty was, after all a country girl at heart. Steph wasn't fazed by the idea of running her own business; she'd worked in the café for such a long time and knew it like the back of her hand. She was a quietly confident individual and prided herself on her sense of maturity and understated poise. Mother and daughter were like chalk and cheese, Steph was a tall, slender woman, with a quiet but strong demeanour and a sensitive, sometimes stoic disposition. Her mother, on the other hand, was the complete opposite. What Betty lacked in height she made up for in volume: she was a gregarious individual with a contagious laugh that could be heard at one end of the street from the other. She was a petite, full-figured woman who more often than not was apron-clad and covered in flour. Mother and daughter shared only two traits, their fiercely loyal nature and their fiercely fiery red hair.

All the cakes and sweet treats at Betty's Book Café were homemade and the abundance of books lining the shelves in old-fashioned oak cases meant that her customers stayed longer than at any other places nearby. Elodie had loved the café from the moment she had set foot in it. She had been traipsing the city, CV in hand, looking for a job. Her 'can do' attitude had impressed some employers but not enough for any to actually offer her a job. She had visited the café on a whim and, looking back, was extremely glad that she did. Each new customer was given a bookmark with their name on: they could choose any book they liked to enjoy with their cakes and coffees. When they were done they simply needed to mark their page with the bookmark they had been given and place the book back on the shelf, ready for the next customer. Many of the books had several bookmarks in at the same time. At the end of each day, the shelves would be rearranged so that the next day's customers could find their book easily. The café had a very homely feel to it: cosy armchairs and sofas were carefully placed around, meaning that customers were right in the mix of things but had a sense of privacy as well. Mismatched coffee tables were scattered about and the old wooden floor was covered in a selection of deeply coloured rugs. The walls were covered with various chalkboards, each one encased in a different frame. On them were displayed the numerous types of cakes available, house specials and a few inspirational and funny quotes that Betty tried to live by – her favourite being, *'No matter the question, cake is always the answer.'*

Steph stepped back from the chalkboard, a look of disdain etched on her face. She was even less happy with this attempt than with the previous three.

"Carla! I'm putting my foot down, phone away, please! I don't pay you to keep your Instagram fans happy," Steph said hotly. She opened her mouth to issue an instruction but Carla jumped in.

"Just call them Insta-fans, babe, it's much cooler. And it's not you that pays me, it's your mum," Carla replied, looking up just in time to see Steph rolling her eyes. "Besides, I'm also checking my spare room app. Bloody Dora's moved out and my dad insists I have a flatmate, he thinks it's a waste having that room just sitting there doing nothing and to be honest, even with him paying half the rent I'd struggle to manage the rest by myself. So far I've had three applicants: all men, all pervs."

Carla laughed. Despite being the same age Carla and Steph couldn't have been more different. Steph still had the same phone she'd had when they'd met several years ago and didn't have any social media accounts, she just didn't see the point. Anyone she wanted to know about her life already did. If she were being completely, maybe brutally, honest, she really didn't care about what the girl who sat behind her in Maths during Year Nine was up to nowadays, anyway.

"Can you please do your fancy curly writing for the signs now?" she sighed, holding out the chalk for Carla to take.

Carla finally relented and popped the phone into her apron pocket. She took the chalk from Steph's slender fingers and began to write the chalk signs, giggling to herself internally at Steph's poor effort. She loved the girl to the moon and back but she really didn't have a creative bone in her body. Carla noticed the time and frowned, her brow knitting together as far as the Botox would allow. The time read quarter past eight. The café would be open to the Great British Public in just fifteen minutes and there was still a fair bit to do.

"Have you seen the time?" she called to Steph who was busy counting out change for the till, the clatter of coins almost masking Carla's question.

"Of course I have," Steph answered distractedly, not wanting to lose count, "I'll give her another ten and if she's not here then I'll give her a call." She decanted the last of the copper coins into the till and headed into the back to check on how her mother was getting on with the cakes.

Elodie grabbed her bag as she headed out the door for work. She couldn't believe the bank holiday weekend was over already. She'd had a restless night's sleep and had overslept. She'd laid awake for hours, sure she could hear Tom's keys in the lock and straining for even the faintest sound to signal that he was home. As it turned out she needn't have worried. He rolled in at two am, stinking of booze and cigarettes. Elodie couldn't abide smoking and Tom knew this. He'd made no effort to be quiet as he drunkenly clattered around the bedroom. Elodie had turned on the light. He'd apologised for waking her; well, actually he'd slurred the apology and Elodie had muttered something about needing the bathroom anyway.

Once in bed, Tom had tried to seduce her. She cringed away from the acrid smoky smell that preceded him and made an excuse about having a headache. He'd complained that she always had a headache nowadays and told her that he didn't need her for a good time anyway. Elodie couldn't believe it when she looked over and saw that he was scrolling through a porn site on his phone. She seethed, a war of embarrassment and anger raging within. He was being so utterly selfish and obviously didn't care about her feelings at all. He'd left her high and dry after being a complete dick, he'd made her feel terrible and now he was going to pretend like she wasn't even there while he drunkenly wanked himself to sleep. Elodie definitely did not see the funny side. She let out a low, irked sigh and squeezed her eyes shut. He simply had to take her hint and go to sleep.

When the unmistakeable groans of an adult film started she'd decided that enough was enough. She had been about to order him to sleep on the sofa when she heard the unmistakable sound of his drunken snore. She glanced over again and saw him lying there, half-undressed with his phone lying on his chest. She took it from him, turned off the film and plugged it in to charge but not before setting an eight am alarm. He'd be late for work but at least he wouldn't miss the day entirely.

'*What would he do without me?*' Elodie thought, unable to help herself from mothering him. She had spent the rest of the night on their sofa. Tom's intoxicated snuffles were far from relaxing and as the night wore on their intensity increased. It was a little after three-thirty when she decided that that was it. Elodie whipped the covers back and marched into the living room, she grabbed her patchwork throw and settled herself on the sofa, drifting into a restless but at least quiet sleep.

Forty minutes later and Elodie rounded the corner with the café in sight, her long brown ponytail swishing as she went. Her dark mood had lightened somewhat. It really was very hard to stay so thunderous when the weather outside was so sunny.

She caught her reflection in a shop window and sighed. Elodie was average height, average weight and possessed average brown hair and average chestnut eyes. '*Average looks to go with my average job in my average life,*' she pondered dolefully and feeling very sorry for herself.

She smoothed down her T-shirt. There was no set uniform

at Betty's Book Café: the only thing that Betty insisted on was that they all wore their hair up, donned pretty spotted aprons and put on name badges. Elodie wasn't a big makeup wearer, she preferred the natural look and besides, Tom thought that a lot of makeup was trashy. He'd often told her that less is more when it came to makeup, but more is more when it came to clothes. Today she had opted for a slick of mascara and some barely-there lip balm, which she felt was more than enough makeup for a day of pouring coffee and serving cake.

Elodie paused in front of Betty's Book Café and wondered whether or not she should phone her mum for advice. The Taylor family weren't that close but Elodie had a good relationship with her parents. They were sweet people who cared immensely for each other and for their daughter; however, they always wished that she could just be happy with her lot. Tom was exactly the type of man they wanted her to end up with, steady and stable. Elodie couldn't help but feel that she was cut from a different cloth. Her parents were like calico: strong and durable but perhaps a bit on the plain side. They were the type of people who said things like *'Anything for a quiet life'* and *'Any job's better than no job.'* Elodie didn't necessarily agree with sentiments such as these but understood that her parents were from a different generation and knew that whenever they said anything like this they were doing so because they just wanted her to be happy, like them. Whenever she had phoned her mum in the past, especially with Tom troubles, she had always offered the same advice. Her parents had been together since they were sixteen and had stayed together through thick and thin. Neither of them believed in giving up on a relationship. It didn't matter what the problem was, Elodie's mum would always tell her the same thing: *'Just sit down and talk it through, love.'* Tom would realise how unfair he had been and apologise and until then, she had a job to do.

Elodie took out her phone, half-expecting a grovelling text message from Tom. There was nothing on her screen apart from her screensaver, which was a picture of her, Steph and Carla hanging out in the park. The picture was quite old: Elodie knew this from Carla's hair, which seemed to change as often as the seasons. The screensaver in front of her showed them sat in the park a couple of summers ago. Elodie remembered that day well, the weather had been absolutely glorious. Betty had closed the café for some new refrigerators to be fitted so the three friends had decided to enjoy the day together. They had drunk cider in the park, read magazines and worked on their tans. Elodie gazed at the picture fondly; Steph looked exactly the same now as she had done then. Her straight auburn hair was a little longer now, but she still had the same fringe and simple style. Carla, however, was an entirely different story. Back then her hair had been honey-blonde with a pale pink streak running through it. One side had been shaved in a fashionable undercut and the rest of her locks had been left to blow wildly in the breeze. She wore a gold nose ring and, considering they were spending the day in the park, rather heavy makeup. The picture showed them all laughing and smiling. Carla held a glass in the air, an impressive pout gracing her full lips. Elodie smiled at the memory; it seemed that they hadn't had a day like that together in such a long time. It was amazing how life got in the way of everything. It was then that she caught sight of the time. *'Shit,'* she thought to herself as she realised she was late. She shoved her phone back in her bag, deciding that she wouldn't call her mum after all.

"There you are!" Steph exclaimed with relief as Elodie emerged looking somewhat shamefaced through the back door. "I thought something bad might have happened, you don't usually cut it this fine."

"Something bad kind of did. I'm sorry Steph, I had a nightmare of an evening yesterday."

Steph wasn't one to pry, so instead offered a questioning raised eyebrow that she felt Elodie could ignore if she wanted to. Carla, on the other hand, wasn't quite so subtle. Upon hearing Elodie's brief explanation she blustered up to them, having abandoned the task of finishing the chalkboards, and demanded to know what 'he' had done now. Elodie wasn't quite able to meet their eyes and instead concentrated extra hard on tying the bow of her spotted pinafore.

"Tell us later," Steph offered sympathetically. "Let's open up first. Once we've seen the morning rush off, then we can have a proper catch-up."

Elodie nodded, thankful that she had at least one tactful friend. She turned around and began restocking the soft drinks, the bottles clinking together as she placed them in one by one and drowning out her own thoughts, for which she was thankful.

The first and last hours of the day were always the busiest for the café. People came in in droves, either desperate for a pre-work pep-me-up, or an after-work treat. This morning was just like any other. There were some familiar faces that visited and some new ones. Elodie always waited the tables, Carla did a bit of everything and Steph stood at the counter taking payments and handing out takeaway orders. When the last of the early morning rush customers had gone, they gathered around the counter and chatted whilst Steph made them all a hot drink of their own.

"So what happened last night then?" Carla asked, raising her voice over the sound of the coffee machine, her large brown eyes surveying Elodie intently. "Tom surprise you with something spectacular?" she added sarcastically, unable to help her tone.

"Carla! That's hardly nice or helpful now, is it?" Steph griped as she set three mugs down on the counter: a flat white for herself, a double espresso for Carla and a latte with one sugar for Elodie.

"Nice doesn't come into it. The idiot can't even get my name right, he called me Carara last time I saw him, so I'm sorry if I'm not his biggest fan," Carla argued, quelling herself when she saw Elodie's downcast look. "Sorry El, I'm not being hard on you. I just think he should treat you how you deserve to be treated, like the wonderful, smart and funny woman you are. It's my prerogative to make sure that any guy you're with is the absolute best."

Elodie smiled a small smile at these words.

"Well, it's funny you should say that. I mean, not funny ha-ha. More like funny, dear God my world is ending and I want to scream," Elodie said with a wry smile. She told them everything that had happened. Elodie was a fair person: she didn't embellish or exaggerate, she just told them the events exactly as they had transpired, including Tom's suggestive finger-waggle alluding to an engagement ring. She hadn't intended on airing the entirety of her dirty linen to them but as she found herself getting deeper and deeper into the story she just couldn't hold back. "And by this point, I was knackered, upset and couldn't stand the sound of his drunken snores for one more second. So, I slept on the sofa." She finished curtly, taking a deep breath and a sip from her coffee cup. The hot, smooth coffee offered some reassurance. The familiar taste comforted her and she felt a quiet calmness wash over her. After all, it was just a silly fight, wasn't it? It was no big deal; they just needed to work on their communication skills. Elodie couldn't silence that little voice at the back of her mind, though, that asked her how on earth you learnt to communicate with someone who could be so stubborn and childish.

"So was that a proposal?" Steph asked in a matter-of-fact manner that was indicative of her displeasure at the idea. She evidently wanted to get all the details clear in her head before judging or offering any sort of advice. Carla raised her hand before Elodie had a chance to answer.

"Of course it wasn't, it's just what he does when he's backed into a corner," Carla retorted. "I can't believe this, what will it take for you to see that he's no good for you, El. Look, Tom's not a bad person but you can do so much better, he's so small town and you're just not! He's pulled that proposal trick before! Remember two years ago, when he got you that iron for your birthday and he said he was saving up for something extra special. Well…" She trailed off, catching the look of hurt on Elodie's face. Carla didn't want Elodie to be upset, she just wanted her to see. It was short-term pain for long-term gain. In her opinion, Elodie would be happier without that neanderthal dragging her down.

"For your information, that iron was top of the line and makes housework so much easier," Elodie contested weakly. She was well aware that the words sounded hollow, forced and something that a dowdy 'fifties housewife might say. She despised herself for saying them but couldn't stop herself nonetheless.

Elodie stared into her cup, willing the coffee to have the answers that would satisfy her friends. The pale pink lip balm mark on the rim of the cup suddenly seemed far more interesting than answering any more of these accusatory questions.

"Have you spoken to your mum about it?" Steph probed after an uncomfortable moment of silence.

"I thought about ringing her earlier, but I know exactly what she'll say." Elodie sighed, "She'll tell me to sit down and talk with Tom and that relationships are hard and you have to work at them every day. The trouble is, she's with her soul mate so I'm pretty sure that makes all that working hard stuff a lot easier."

Her two friends glanced at each other, Carla's eyebrow raised in a questioning way.

"You know what you just said, right?" Carla said, unable to hide the glee in her voice.

"What?" Elodie asked dumbly, not understanding what she had said or what the knowing glance between her two friends meant.

"Well…" began Steph diplomatically.

"You just said that working on a relationship is easier when you're with your soul mate!" Carla interrupted eagerly. "So that means, deep down, you don't think Tom is yours."

Elodie stared at them both, stunned. She felt ambushed, as if she were being cross-examined in court rather than confiding in her best friends. She didn't think that at all, or rather she didn't think she did. She could feel her cheeks flushing. Both of her friends were staring at her now and the attention was both unwanted and, she felt, unfounded. She had to say something, she had to defend Tom, defend their relationship and defend all the years they'd been together; but no matter how hard she tried, no words would form. Elodie felt a mixture of anger and astonishment bubbling within her, both completely alien emotions to Elodie who was usually a calm and sweet person who rarely had cause to raise her voice. How dare they criticise her relationship, who were they to judge? Especially since one of them hardly ever saw her boyfriend and the other had never been in a relationship in her entire life.

"Well I don't believe in soul mates actually," Elodie countered bluntly, careful to keep her tone as even as she could despite the resentment building up inside her, "so what you two think doesn't really matter, we're happy and that's all that counts."

She took another sip of her coffee, more out of awkwardness than any real desire for the drink itself. There was an obstinate reticence between the three friends now, Steph not wanting to make the situation any worse, Carla taken aback and frustrated with Elodie's attitude and Elodie herself feeling vulnerable and attacked by her best friends. All three of them wondered who would break the silence first.

"Is someone going to get that or do I have to do everything around here?" Betty's voice called from the back. The phone was ringing and from the exasperation in her voice had been for quite a while. Steph snatched it up just as the front door opened; the bell above it tinkled a delicate sound, announcing the arrival of a customer. Or customers in this case: six suited and booted individuals walked in, all looking very busy and important with their laptops and briefcases. Elodie smiled at them as they settled themselves in the far corner by the bay window. She gave them a minute before picking up her waitress's pad and her favourite purple pen and headed over to take their order. She could almost feel the knowing look Carla and Steph were giving each other behind her back; she felt the flames of annoyance spark inside her again.

'What do they know?' she asked herself. *'Nothing at all, ignore them. You and Tom are fine; he's a great boyfriend. They just can't see that because they're not as mature as he is. He pays the bills, owns his own car and has a proper job. Hell, he's even saving up for an engagement ring! No, Tom and I are one hundred per cent great. We're really good. No, we're unquestionably perfect,'* Elodie finished, not quite able to shake the feeling that if everything really was so perfect she wouldn't have to be quite so firm with herself.

The rest of the day passed by in a blur of coffee, cake and customers. The tension between the three friends subsided as the day wore on and by the end of it they seemed to be back to normal. Elodie felt bad about snapping at them. After all, they only ever had her best interests at heart and she knew this. Carla and Steph were reading the same book as Tom, but were on a different page.

Elodie wiped the last table down and turned to the door. She rotated the 'Open' sign so that it now read 'Closed' to the outside world and slowly bolted the door. She turned to Steph and Carla, still not entirely sure whether things were OK between them all. She didn't have to worry, though; Carla had a cheeky smile on her face and a mischievous twinkle in her eye.

"What?" Elodie asked, noticing that Steph wore a look of apprehension on her face.

"Let's have a girls' night out!" Carla said excitedly, bending her knees slightly and wiggling her hips to a beat only that she could hear.

"We don't want to fall out, El," Steph added calmly, "and you're right, if Tom makes you happy then that's all we can ask for. Isn't it, Carla?" Steph nudged Carla in the ribs; she responded by nodding reluctantly.

"I'm not going to stick my nose in anymore," Carla said, an air of resignation in her voice. "Steph's right, he's your boyfriend, not ours and as long as you're OK then we're OK." She finished magnanimously although her sour expression hinted at her true feelings a little too clearly. Elodie chose to ignore Carla's disdainful look and smiled at them both, glad that the fight was now well and truly over.

"Thanks, girls," Elodie accepted. "A girls' night, you say? Sounds good to me. It's exactly what we need. I can't remember the last time we all went out together."

"I can!" Steph interjected, half-laughing, "You both got so drunk! Carla threw up into her bag in the back of the cab and you ate about a million hash browns from that dodgy fast food place in town. I had to get you both into your pyjamas, take your makeup off and put you both to bed. My God, you two were so annoying, giggling the whole time and thinking you were both absolutely hilarious when really you were an absolute nightmare."

"God, that was so long ago," Elodie exclaimed, a vague image of the evening coming back to her. She smiled, remembering that she'd only had about three drinks that night. She was such a lightweight.

"Yeah it was, I had mermaid blue hair back then!" Carla added, laughing. "What on earth was I thinking?"

"Because now your hair is so normal," Steph laughed, tugging at the end of Carla's curly lavender-coloured pony-tail. Carla waved her away.

"What can I say, I'm a trendsetter," she giggled. "So is that a yes to Friday night then?" She turned to Elodie with hands on her hips, tapping her foot impatiently in a mock-authoritative stance. Elodie smiled and nodded, excited at the prospect of a girls' night out with her two best friends.

"You guys can get ready at mine, Mum's away for the weekend. She's spending the weekend in Bakewell, she's on about moving there and wants to get a feel for the place first. Personally, I can't think of anywhere she'd be better suited. So bring all your stuff with you?" Steph said prag-matically.

Elodie nodded. Her mind automatically bounced straight to clothing: she didn't have a clue what she should wear. Luckily, she had two days to cobble together a suitable outfit and worst-case scenario she could always borrow something from Carla's extensive wardrobe. Elodie could feel excite-ment beginning to bubble inside her now, the anticipation of some much-needed quality time with her friends was almost too much to handle. Elodie was confident that a girls' night out would be just what the doctor ordered; maybe Tom would even stop taking her for granted and learn to appreciate everything that she did for him if she went out a bit more.

The commute home was hot and sweaty. The tube was crowded and Elodie found herself sandwiched between a tourist's beaten old backpack and a businessman's armpit. It seemed like the train had taken days to get to her stop. Elodie breathed a huge sigh of relief when it finally ground to a halt and the doors slid open. She poured out onto the platform along with several dozen other people and headed for the exit as quickly as her legs could carry her.

Elodie emerged into the warm evening air and stopped, her eyes falling on the sign above the pub next to the station.

She wasn't much of a weekday drinker, but something was telling her that a nice cold glass of wine was a fabulous idea. Despite checking her phone several times during the day she hadn't heard a word from Tom. Steph had said that she was being childish and if she wanted to speak to him she should just do so. Carla's advice had, predictably, been the polar opposite. *'Freeze that fucker out, babe,'* was all she had offered on the matter. Elodie's thoughts returned to the uncomfortable conversation they'd had earlier; she had been so angry with them and felt ashamed at the way she had acted. With hindsight, she knew she'd overreacted and now her mind was clearer she could see that it was stupid to get mad at her friends. They were only fighting her corner and if Elodie hadn't moaned to them about all the awful things Tom had done then they wouldn't have felt the need to get involved. It wasn't fair to expect them to listen, nod and not have an opinion. Elodie decided then and there that she'd steer clear of Tom-bashing for a while. However, Carla's advice had struck a chord with her. Maybe a little bit of the good old-fashioned silent treatment would be good for him; maybe if he came home to an empty house and no tea on the table he'd start to appreciate her a little bit more.

Elodie pushed the door of the pub open and walked inside. Despite walking past the place several times a week she had never actually been inside. She was surprised at how busy it was. Most of the tables had been taken and there were several people at the bar waiting to be served. Elodie walked over to the darkly-stained oak bar and waited her turn. The barman appeared moments later carrying a tray of freshly washed glasses, which glinted in the sunlight as he set the tray down.

"Who's next?" he asked to no one in particular. A smartly dressed guy who looked to be in his late twenties put his hand up and ordered three pints of lager, two shots of tequila and a packet of crisps. Elodie looked on in disbelief as he downed the shots in quick succession and chased them back with one of the pints. He caught Elodie's eye and grinned at her, exposing a large set of pearly white teeth.

"Celebrating," he said by way of explanation. "Fuckin' smashed it at work today! Got promoted to head of sales, my buddy and me are on a sesh. We're the kinda guys that work hard but play harder, if you know what I mean? Come join us if you want?" He grinned that large toothy grin again and gestured to a table in the far corner where a slightly older man, also in a suit, sat typing furiously on his mobile phone.

Elodie managed a small smile and congratulated him before making her excuses and quickly turning her attention to her own phone. She didn't want to spend any more time talking to him than she absolutely had to; even from their short exchange, she could tell he definitely wasn't her type of person. Thankfully, the barman saved her. He took her order and poured her a large glass of her favourite Pinot Grigio blush. Elodie took a long, satisfying drink and the cool liquid slid down her throat easily. She paid for her wine and turned around, surveying the room and hoping that there would be a free table a reasonable distance from the two salesmen. There was. She wandered over and settled herself on a small table, enjoying the immediate relief she felt as the weight was taken off her feet. She reached inside her bag and pulled out the magazine she had been reading the previous day. She couldn't help herself; it was like she was addicted to looking at things she couldn't have. She read an article about the best pizzerias in Italy, one about the most secluded beaches in Australia and a third about the top five best airlines to fly with, all the while sipping her wine and periodically checking the time. She wanted to stay out later than usual but she didn't want to push the boat out too far. Having to make his own dinner would be punishment enough; Tom found even the most basic dish a culinary challenge, he couldn't even make cheese on toast without needing guidance.

Elodie walked into their little home at a little past quarter to nine. Tom was sat in sweatpants and a hoodie playing video games in the living room; the remnants of a takeaway lay on the floor next to the sofa and from the looks of the empty beer cans on the coffee table he'd been home for quite some time. He glanced up from his game when she entered the living room. Tom barely afforded her an acknowledgement and quickly returned to the important task of shooting zombies.

"Hey," Elodie said reproachfully. She could tell from his attitude that he had no intention of offering an olive branch first. Tom grunted a reply, his gaze locked fixedly on the screen in front of him. "Have you had a good day?" Elodie asked, probing a little further.

Tom continued down the road of silence. In Elodie's opinion, his current defiance would make a five-year-old seem mature. Elodie decided not to rise to it, it just wasn't worth getting sucked into his vacuum of immaturity. Instead, she quietly slipped off her trainers, dropped her bag next to them and headed upstairs for a bath.

Elodie sank under the hot bathwater and enjoyed the feeling of the rose-scented bath bomb she'd dropped in moments earlier fizzing around her. She squeezed her eyes shut and enjoyed the brief moment of utter solace she found under the water. Her mind was all over the place: she'd had visions of coming back home to an apologetic Tom, of them making up and enjoying a lazy evening in front of the telly together. She hadn't banked on just how stubborn he could be. She had to ask herself, was taking the high ground worth it? *'Was ignoring his childish behaviour the right thing to do?'* In the quiet of the bathroom with nothing but her own thoughts for company she decided that *'no, it was not worth it.'* Elodie knew that after her bath, she would wander downstairs and apologise to Tom; she would be the one to offer an olive branch and she would be the one to make amends. She couldn't help but chuckle morosely to herself as she heard her mum's voice in her head advising her to do *'anything for a quieter life.'*

Elodie sat up and reached for the shampoo. She squeezed a decent amount into her palm and lathered it into her thick locks, enjoying the therapeutic feeling her fingers provided. She rinsed the shampoo from her hair and repeated the process with conditioner. Her chocolate-brown mane felt incredibly soft and silky to her touch. There were few aspects of her physical appearance that Elodie felt wholly positive about but her hair was one of them. She climbed out of the bathtub and reached for her towels – Elodie was the kind of girl who just couldn't function without two, one for her body and the other for her hair. She was almost ashamed to admit that these towels were almost as old as she was. They had originally belonged to her grandparents and they had gifted them to her when she'd moved away from home. As a poor student, she'd accepted them gladly. She still used them every day and considering how old they were still in really good condition. She knotted the towel around her chest and twisted the other on top of her head and winced as she felt one particular strand of hair pull a little too tightly. Elodie took a quick glance at herself in the mirror. She made eye contact with her reflection and was pleased to see that despite the tense night and long day she was looking reasonably fresh-faced and relaxed. *'Must have been that bath bomb,'* she thought as she cleaned her teeth. She carefully applied light moisturiser before pulling the towel from her head and hanging it over the rail so neatly that it wouldn't have looked out of place in a five-star hotel. She twisted her damp hair up into a tight knot and let out a big sigh. *'Time to be the bigger person,'* she thought to herself. Elodie tiptoed down the stairs, the towel wrapped tightly around her, and quietly made her way over to Tom who was still sat on the sofa, his attention firmly fixed on his game.

"Can we talk?" she asked him, placing her hand on his shoulder gently. He shrugged her away and made an almost inaudible noise that under most normal circumstances would probably have been confused for a cough. Elodie knew better. She knew Tom like the back of her hand. This was him testing her; he wouldn't win, though. She had made up her mind and had decided that she wasn't going to leave until they had made amends.

"Tom," she said, a little more forcefully, "I'm sorry, I didn't mean to make you feel that way, I'm sorry for last night. Can we just be friends again?"

Tom paused the game but didn't look at her straightaway. He did move over slightly, giving her enough space to sit down next to him. Elodie lowered herself onto the sofa and wrapped her arms around his neck. She leaned towards him and kissed his cheek gently. The faint, sweet-smelling aroma of rose petals gave way to the hoppy scent of Tom's beer.

"You're forgiven," Tom conceded, nuzzling into her kisses.

Elodie pulled away as Tom turned to face her. He reached

out and cupped her face in his hands. "You are beautiful, you know," he said sincerely.

Elodie could feel herself blush: compliments were few and far between with Tom. He wasn't the type of guy to shower praise on someone endlessly, if Tom said something nice to her she knew she'd earned it. Tom pulled her into him and their lips met. Elodie was surprised to find herself on the verge of crying; her eyes prickled, tears threatening to spill at any moment. Tom didn't notice, he parted his lips as the kiss became more intense and extended his tongue, probing the inner recesses of her mouth, all the while holding her face firmly. Elodie felt him move closer and moved herself backwards so that she was practically lying down. Tom released his grip and climbed on top of her. She felt his weight press down on her and then a hand between her legs. She parted them automatically to allow him full access to her most private area.

Tom began by stroking her. There was nothing gentle about his actions. He moved with furious purpose, eager to get to the main event. Elodie let out a small moan as his fingertips brushed over her most sensitive spot, she arched her hips, encouraging him to linger there a moment longer. He didn't. His hand had withdrawn and was now tugging at the waistband of his sweatpants. He pulled them down to his knees and Elodie saw that underneath he was naked. He was already hard, the moments he'd spent between her legs enough to turn him on. Tom reached out and in one swift motion undid the towel she was wearing, revealing her round breasts. He leant forward and took one nipple in his mouth, pinching the other between the thumb and forefinger of his left hand. He let out a moan, the sound stifled by Elodie's ample bosom. His erection pressed against her soft folds and she felt him push his hips forward and begin to invade her. Tom thrust his hips in and out of her steadily; she raised herself up to meet each and every one of his thrusts with perfect, practised timing. Tom gripped her shoulders and used her to steady himself as his movements became more and more frantic. Before long Elodie felt the tell-tale signs of climax. Tom tightened his grip and she felt his body spasm, he let out a long husky moan at the same time. After a few moments, he became still and withdrew. Sitting up and grinning, he reached for Elodie's towel and began to clean himself up.

"Thanks, babe, that was awesome," he said proudly, pulling his grey sweatpants back up and returning to his game.

Elodie sat there for a moment, not entirely sure how she felt. She was, of course, happy that she and Tom were back on speaking terms but their encounter had felt hollow and she certainly didn't feel satisfied. She pulled the towel back around herself and got up. She made an excuse about getting dressed and headed back to the bedroom. Outside she heard the rumblings of thunder and was certain that a summer storm was on the way.

CHAPTER 3

ELODIE HAD THE FOLLOWING DAY OFF WORK. SHE had gone to bed early the previous night. She hadn't ventured back downstairs after leaving Tom on the sofa playing that awful zombie game. She really couldn't understand how a grown man could become so obsessed with a video game. She had fallen asleep before Tom had come to bed and woken up after he had left for work.

Elodie stifled a yawn and hauled herself out of bed. She slipped on her comfy slippers and pulled the curtains back ready to greet the day. She had been right about the storm: angry-looking grey clouds hung overhead and fat droplets of rain fell in droves onto their small patio below. Elodie shuddered, she was glad she didn't have work to go to and could spend the day inside relatively guilt-free. After all, who on earth could possibly go out in this weather?

After a breakfast of fluffy buttermilk pancakes and fresh fruit Elodie settled herself on the sofa. The house was peaceful and quiet and Elodie took a moment to enjoy the serenity. The sound of raindrops against the windowpane gave a strangely calm soundtrack to the day. She decided on a pamper day: a quick flip through her new travel magazine followed by a face mask and a little mani-pedi would be just what the doctor ordered. As she was working the following day she reasoned that she wouldn't have time to pamper herself before the big night out. Butterflies danced in her stomach as she thought about it, she couldn't believe how excited she was. She rummaged on the dining table for her magazine but to no avail. Tom had left a fair amount of paperwork on there, which had almost covered the entirety of its surface.

'I wish he'd just pick up after himself... just once!' she thought, annoyance giving way to anger as she saw he'd left not one, but two dirty plates on the table and just covered them up with his paraphernalia.

"Ugh! Tom!" she said out loud in exasperation, unable to find her magazine and irritated beyond belief at his slobbishness.

A sudden thought struck her: she hadn't actually told Tom about her night out. 'Not that I need his permission,' she thought to herself quickly before her brain had time to argue. She fumbled for her phone, reasoning that a quick text to tell him of her plans would at least be the polite thing to do. Elodie glanced around for her mobile, she was sure she'd left it around the house somewhere. She got up and looked on the sofa, running her hands down the sides of the cushions just in case it had fallen down the side. She was interrupted by a frantic knock at the door.

"I'm coming," Elodie called out as the banging became more furious. She wondered who on earth it could possibly be. The postman had already been and unless Tom had ordered something there really was no reason why anyone should be at the door. Elodie's fingers closed around the doorknob, she twisted it clockwise, pulled the heavy front door towards her and peered through the crack.

"Are you going to let me in or what?" an absolutely soaked and obviously annoyed Carla demanded. "I'm pissed wet through!"

Elodie flung the door open and Carla shot inside, water dripping down her face and pooling on the hallway floor.

"What are you doing here and why didn't you bring an umbrella?" Elodie said, laughing at the sight before her. She was pleased to see her friend but confused as to why she would just turn up completely unannounced.

"Firstly, if you'd answered your phone you'd know I was coming and secondly, it wasn't raining last night when I left the house," she said coyly.

"What, do you mean last night..." Elodie trailed off, catching the look in Carla's eye. "Oh you dirty stop out," she said in mock horror. "Who's the lucky guy then? Or girl?" she added quickly, seeing Carla's eyebrow raise.

"Guy actually. Mark, he's really sweet, was great in bed. Don't think I'll see him again though, his flat smelled like feet and I'm sure he said he was in finance, almost killed my lady boner then and there, but thankfully I'm a pro and powered through!" she laughed mirthlessly.

"You want to be careful; if you build those walls too high they're likely to turn into a prison," Elodie said sagely.

"Look, if it doesn't feel one hundred per cent right, then it's one hundred per cent wrong. That goes for all circumstances, always. If there's an inkling of doubt, then get out," Carla replied, rolling her eyes and pushing her way inside the flat.

Elodie grabbed a pair of Tom's jogging bottoms from the clothes horse, looked at them then quickly put them back. Instead, she chose a pair of her own pyjama bottoms and a T-shirt and handed them to Carla. "Here, put these on, you're soaking. I'll hang your stuff up to dry."

Carla didn't need telling twice and began to strip on the spot almost before Elodie had finished speaking. She stepped out of her sodden jeans and pulled off her now nearly transparent white cotton top and threw them on the floor. She took the spare clothes from Elodie gratefully and slipped them on.

"Beggars can't be choosers," she said sagely as she pulled the pyjamas on. They were a couple of inches too long in the leg so Elodie bent down and rolled them up for her.

"There we go," Elodie said, satisfied with her work, "almost perfect."

Carla thanked her as she bent down to retrieve her clothes. Elodie took them from her and placed them over the now spare rail on the clotheshorse. "Coffee?" she offered.

Carla nodded fervently and rubbed her hands together, evidently still a little cold from her journey.

"Have you got anything to eat?" she asked. "I'm absolutely starving, never got round to dinner last night," she finished with a wink.

Elodie had a couple of pancakes left over so reheated them and made Carla a scaled-back version of what she had had earlier on. Carla ravenously ate the pancakes and washed them down with several swigs of the strong black coffee. When she had finished, Elodie took her plate and set it down on the kitchen counter along with her own, vowing that she would do the washing up as soon as Carla left.

"So to what do I owe the pleasure?" Elodie asked when the two women had settled themselves in the living room.

"The guy I saw last night, Mark, well his flat is literally just round the corner, I didn't realise how close it was last night, I was pretty wasted and it was dark when we got back to his," she explained.

Elodie tried her best to keep a neutral expression on her face. She loved Carla to bits but didn't like her meeting random people on dating apps and going back to theirs at the drop of a hat, especially in such an inebriated state. In her opinion, it just wasn't safe. But, as she did with most things, she kept her mouth shut; she wasn't about to try and parent Carla on the importance of personal safety. Elodie remembered all too clearly the time that Steph had tried it: Elodie recalled walking into Betty's Book Café several months ago to a frosty atmosphere that was palpable from the moment you stepped through the door. It had been as though an icy palm had slapped her around the face the second she'd pushed the door open. The atmosphere was due to Steph trying to have a well-meaning word with Carla about sexual safety. Carla did not take kindly to what she had called *'judgemental bullshit'*. Elodie knew that Steph would have meant well and wouldn't have intended to come across as disparaging but she seemed to have a natural knack for it, so Carla, in true Carla fashion, had flown off the handle in defence. Elodie had played peacemaker and it had taken every ounce of her diplomatic abilities to bring Carla round. It was with this in mind that she kept her face as still as possible.

"So what was he like then?" Elodie asked, keen to find out more about this guy. If Carla ended up with someone who lived just round the corner then maybe they could double-date. It was difficult at times having single friends. Steph had Andy, of course, but he was never here and Carla had exceptionally high standards that she wasn't willing to lower. Tom's friends Al and Pat were all coupled up, which made double-dating easier but they weren't really her cup of tea. The girlfriends were nice enough but they were cli-quey and Elodie never really felt very involved. Their con-versations circled around reality TV shows, office gossip and fashion, none of which Elodie knew of or cared for in the slightest.

"Don't do that," Carla said, a warning tone entering her voice. "I'm not going to start seeing anyone. I like being single, it suits me far better and you know it." Elodie had to agree: Carla did have a knack for the single life and for as long as they'd known each other that had always been Carla's M.O.

Changing the subject, Elodie suggested a pamper session together. Carla enthusiastically agreed as she too was work-ing the following day so would also have limited time to get ready. Elodie handed Carla the remote control for the television and told her to put a music channel on whilst she went upstairs to get some beauty supplies. She reappeared a few minutes later carrying face masks, nail varnishes and a pair of pink tweezers.

"You couldn't do my eyebrows for me?" she begged. Carla was the queen of personal grooming and Elodie wasn't about to waste a golden opportunity for some world-class treatments. Carla threw one of the sofa's grey cushions at her friend in pseudo-offence. "I'll take that as a yes, then," Elodie joked, handing the tweezers over and making herself comfortable on the sofa, her head resting in Carla's lap.

The hours passed and the two friends laughed, joked and pampered themselves to their hearts' content. By lunchtime, the rain had all but stopped and ribbons of sunlight had begun to appear, breaking through the clouded sky and dap-pling the world beneath.

"What do you think?" Elodie asked, stretching her hand out for Carla to examine her work. Carla looked up from her own nails and studied Elodie's outstretched nails.

"Wow, I see you went for something completely differ-ent," she exclaimed sarcastically. "Pale pink, eh? Was it a choice between nude, clear, pale pink or bone?"

Elodie retracted her hand, hiding it behind her back in a childlike way. "Well I like them, they're understated," she said, sounding hurt.

"I'm joking, hun; they look gorgeous, elegant and sweet, just like you," Carla said quickly, obviously feeling bad that her joke hadn't been taken in the light-hearted way that it had been intended.

Elodie smiled and looked at her nails once more, no longer uncertain about how they looked.

"What did you go for?" she asked Carla, pulling at her friend's hand in order to get a better look. "Wow, they're amazing, how did you do that?" Elodie said, impressed by the artistic and professional job Carla had managed to execute.

"Well, considering the most daring colour you own is coral I had to be creative," she said, brandishing her nails in a dramatic way that made Elodie giggle. She had managed to create a dip-dye look: the nails started bright at the bed and gradually became lighter at the tip. They looked like a fancy take on a French manicure. Elodie felt a little pang of jealousy, *'Why can't I be that creative?"* she thought self-critically.

Before long the two women had run out of ways to pamper themselves and Carla decided that it was probably time to head home. She leant over the back of the sofa and reached out towards her clothes, satisfied that they were dry enough to wear home. She took off the loaned clothes and pulled hers on. First went on her jeans which had dried a little tight and took Carla a bit more effort to do up than she would have liked. She pulled her top over her head but misjudged the armholes and ended up stuck. Elodie laughed as Carla struggled against the top: she was well and truly trapped and the sight of it made Elodie laugh harder than she had done in ages.

"Help me, then!" Carla cried through fits of laughter. Elodie walked towards her, still chuckling to herself and helped Carla back out and then into her top.

"What's going on here?" a voice said admonishingly from behind them. Elodie spun round on her heel, feeling like a child caught stealing sweets. Tom was stood in the doorway to the living room, his hands placed squarely on his hips. "Alright, Cara?" he asked. Elodie winced at the pleasure he seemed to revel in at getting Carla's name wrong.

"Good thanks, Tim," Carla combatted, a sweet smile on her face. "I'm just off actually." She turned her back to Tom and, facing Elodie, gave her a fierce hug. "Thanks, El, I've had an awesome day," she whispered into Elodie's ear before giving her friend a quick kiss on the cheek. She silently mouthed the words 'Call me' and took her leave, squeezing past Tom as she went.

"She been here all day?" Tom asked as he surveyed the flat. Elodie shook her head, not entirely sure why she couldn't just tell him the truth.

Elodie awoke early the following day with what felt like butterflies doing the conga inside her stomach. Tonight was the night. She had told Tom of her plans the previous evening over dinner. Elodie wasn't sure why, but a night out with her friends felt like way bigger news than it actually was; she had actually felt nervous about telling him. So in an effort to placate any possible fall-out she had made Tom's favourite meal, steak and chips. She needn't have worried, though. Tom wasn't exactly keen on the idea, but assured her that it was more out of fear about her safety than jealousy.

'I just worry about you, Pumpkin, you're not like the rest of them. You're too nice and people take advantage of you,' he had said. Elodie had told him not to worry and that she would be fine.

She smiled to herself as she packed her overnight bag; she genuinely couldn't remember that last time she'd done this. Without realising it, her life had become very routine. 'Not that routine's a bad thing, it's just nice to mix things up once in a while,' she thought to herself as she threw her curlers into the bag. She did a quick mental check of everything she had packed and when she was satisfied that she hadn't forgotten anything she zipped the bag up and slung it over her shoulder. It was much heavier than she had anticipated: Elodie winced as it bore down on her shoulder, the leather strap bit into her skin and she wondered whether packing three pairs of shoes really was a good idea. 'Too late now,' she thought as she stole a glance at the clock on her dresser and realised that she should have left quite a while ago.

She took one last look in the mirror. Once again she had

opted for slouchy blue jeans and a baggy T-shirt; it was after all extremely important to always put function ahead of fashion, especially in her line of work. Elodie wore no makeup, she wanted to give her skin a break, especially seeing as she knew Carla would insist on doing her makeup for their night out. Elodie would be surprised if she could still recognise herself after Carla was done with her. Elodie glanced around her bedroom, just to make double sure she hadn't forgotten anything. She felt as though she were leaving a hotel room and doing one last sweep of the place before checking out.

Elodie arrived at Betty's Book Café with barely a minute to spare. She pushed the door open and the familiar tinkle of the bell welcomed her into the café. Carla was already at her station, ready and waiting for the first flood of customers. Steph was doing one last check of the cakes and Betty could be heard in the kitchen singing along to an 'eighties song that was playing in the background. Elodie saw Steph smirk as she heard her mum try and hit the high notes of 'Love is a Battlefield'. Betty was a wonderful woman with many talents; singing, however, was definitely not one of them. Elodie saw Steph lean over and close the door between the café and the kitchen.

"I don't think we need to hear any more of that, she'll end up scaring the customers away," she said almost apologetically.

"That'll be nothing compared to us later," Carla joked, an air of excitement in her voice. "I see you've come prepared," she said, nodding towards Elodie's oversized holdall. Steph reached over and took the bag from Elodie.

"I'll pop it behind the counter," she offered. "Jesus, Elodie, I don't pack this much stuff for an entire week, let alone one night." Elodie laughed: she had totally over-packed and knew it, but she wanted to be totally prepared. She was so excited, knowing that they were going to have a great night and that they'd be dining out on whatever hilarities were to ensue for months to come.

The day passed slowly. Elodie couldn't help but check her watch constantly but every time she did so she was disappointed to see that barely a handful of minutes had passed. Lunchtime dragged around and the café picked up its pace;

it seemed busier than usual, which didn't leave the three of them much time to chat. There seemed to be a relentless tide of customers that just didn't seem to ebb. Normally this was a good thing; usually, the busier they were, the quicker the time seemed to fly, but not today. For some reason, by the time closing-time came Elodie felt as though she'd been at work for several days instead of one. All three women stared at the clock, three minutes to go, two minutes to go, one minute to… The bell above the door sounded, breaking all three of them out of their trance instantly. Elodie spun round on her heels, the smile on her face not at all reflecting the annoyance she felt inside.

"Tom?" she said questioningly, completely caught off guard by his sudden appearance. He stood there, beaming like a Cheshire cat. He wore, as far as Elodie could tell, a brand-new suit and looked like he had come straight from the barbers: his designer stubble beard and dark hair looked extremely neat and polished.

"I got it, babe, absolutely smashed it!" he said, the grin widening even further. "I'm officially H.O.C.," Tom finished, his chest puffed out like a gorilla in mating season.

"H.O.C.?" Elodie asked, immediately regretting her question.

"Head of Commercial. God, El, don't you know anything?" he answered, his lip curling. "Anyone could have worked that out."

Elodie apologised quickly, Carla opened her mouth to speak out against Tom but Steph instinctively placed a warning hand on her arm which told her to bite her lip. They knew better than to get involved.

"Sorry, of course, well done. That's amazing news," Elodie offered.

"Anyway," Tom continued, completely oblivious to the now stale atmosphere hanging in the air, "we're going out tonight to celebrate, I've booked Tony's Italian and it's going to be epic, all you can eat carbonara and cheap booze," he finished proudly. He walked over to Elodie with his arms outstretched, he gave her a massive hug and squeezed her so tightly she thought her eyes might pop out of her head.

"But, I," Elodie stammered, "I can't do tonight. I'm staying with Carla and Steph," she finished weakly.

"You can go out any time, Pumpkin, I'll only get to celebrate this promotion once."

Elodie was dumbstruck. She didn't want to let anyone down, but she'd promised Carla and Steph she'd start spending some time with them and, more to the point, she really wanted to go. She opened her mouth to speak but Tom shushed her. "It's OK, El, you do whatever you want to do. I shouldn't have presumed you'd want to celebrate with me. We can go out another time, I'll have a night to myself, order a takeaway or something," he said, looking crestfallen, his chest deflated.

"No, I want to celebrate with you, of course I do, sorry, babe. I'll re-arrange it with the girls." She turned round to Carla and Steph who were still stood by the counter, watching. "You guys don't mind, do you? Tom's just got that promotion and he's already booked a restaurant. We can go out any old time, can't we?" Elodie looked hopefully from Carla to Steph and back again. Neither of them looked impressed and after what seemed like a lifetime of silence, Steph spoke.

"You do whatever you need to do El. If you want to come with us, we'll be upstairs. If not, we'll see you next week." She congratulated Tom stiffly then turned around, taking Carla with her before anything was said that couldn't be unsaid. The two women disappeared and Elodie was left alone with Tom.

"See, they're not bothered at all and it means way more to me to have you by my side." He pulled her close to him and gave her another squeeze. Elodie untangled herself from his grasp and managed a half-hearted smile that wouldn't fool even the most gullible person. She went behind the counter and picked up her bag. Tom, already impatient, nagged at her to hurry up, he wanted to go for a celebratory drink before they went to eat.

"Give me ten minutes," Elodie said, "I need to pop a bit of makeup on and get changed. Good job I bought my going-out stuff with me."

"Nah, you don't need any makeup, you're beautiful the way you are. I prefer you without it anyway, I always think that makeup makes girls look a bit try-hard," he said, in a matter-of-fact way.

"But I've been in these clothes all day," she moaned, attempting to break away to retrieve her bag.

"El, we need to go now," Tom said, looking at his watch. "The table's booked for seven and I really want a quick drink with you first. You don't need to get changed or put makeup on, surely it only matters what I think and I think you look nice. Come on, babe, let's just go." He looked at her imploringly.

Elodie took a moment then nodded, he was right. She didn't need to wear makeup, she looked fine and after all, it was his big night. It wouldn't kill her to go out like this.

"Okay then, let's go," she said with a finality to her voice that made Tom smile.

"Brilliant," he said, grabbing her by the arm and tugging her out of the door.

It was a nice evening so they walked to the bar Tom had picked. It was extremely busy and finding a place to sit was completely impossible. Post-work revellers spilled out onto the pavement outside; Elodie and Tom had to weave through them in order to get inside. The bar was packed several people deep and they had to wait quite a while before they could order. Tom ordered himself a pint and when Elodie opened her mouth to order her own drink he interrupted her and ordered for her.

"… and a rum and Coke please, mate," he said, before producing a twenty-pound note and handing it over. "Keep the change."

The barman looked impressed and thanked Tom wholeheartedly. Elodie noticed Tom's chest puff out in that obnoxious way again. She took the drink from the bar and sipped at it. She hadn't had a rum and Coke in forever: years ago it had been her favourite drink but now, not so much. Still, it was sweet that Tom had remembered. There was no denying it, Tom was in a very good mood, and for that Elodie was very grateful. He chatted animatedly to her about what his new role would entail, who he was now in charge of and how much more money he was going to be earning.

"Of course, it's not just all about me. You stand to benefit too. I don't want to spoil anything so let's just say that I might have a little surprise for you," he said mysteriously. Elodie sipped her rum and Coke and raised an eyebrow quizzically. "All I'll say is, you better pack your flip flops."

Elodie's heart soared and she broke out into a wide grin. She couldn't believe she'd been so hard on him lately, he was actually quite sweet sometimes. She could see why sometimes people thought he was a bit arrogant or emotionally inept but they didn't see this side of him. Her mind began to wander to all the fabulous destinations she'd looked at and lusted over. She tried to remember which ones she'd mentioned to Tom, or maybe he'd stolen a peek at one of her magazines for inspiration. She didn't care either way: she was going to get to spend some quality time with the man she loved, with some sand underfoot and some sangria in her hand. *'You know what goes with sun, sand and sangria, don't you?'* a little voice in the back of her head whispered. Elodie giggled to herself but Tom didn't notice. He was too busy waving frantically over the crowds of people to someone whom Elodie couldn't see.

"Who's that?" she asked, standing on her tiptoes to get a better view.

"Al and Patrice," Tom said, waving his two friends over. Alan Hopkins, or Al as he liked to be known, was Tom's best friend from school. Despite being offered an unconditional place at a university up north Al had decided to give it a miss and stay near Tom. Where Tom went Al went too and that included work. He had claimed that anything beyond Watford was a little too far north for him anyway. Patrice was a colleague Tom and Al had met a couple of years ago when he'd started working in their department. The three of them had soon become firm friends. Patrice had been new to London and Tom had taken him under his wing, introduced him into his friendship group and shown him all the sights. Elodie knew that in Patrice's mind Tom was something of a legend. She smiled at them both as they came over. Each of them gave her a quick kiss on the cheek and then they turned their attention to Tom.

"Alright, mate," Al said, raising his hand to flag the barman down.

The barman, who had several other people to serve, rolled his eyes but came over anyway, clearly deciding which battles were worth fighting and which were not. Al ordered six pints for the lads and nothing for Elodie when he saw that she had half of her rum and Coke left. Elodie didn't exactly love Tom's friends; she thought them to be quite immature and hardly ever socialised with them. She was always pleasant to them but the fact that they had stolen her away from her own friends made her current circumstances quite a bitter pill to swallow.

The minutes dragged by, each one seemingly longer than the one that had preceded it. The boys talked about nothing other than Tom's promotion, and they talked non-stop. Elodie couldn't get a word in edgeways and after several failed attempts to join in gave up trying and sipped at her drink instead. She winced, pretty sure that her rum was a double measure. It was strong, and no matter how many sips she took it never seemed to get any nicer. She couldn't believe she actually used to enjoy this drink. Elodie glanced around. She saw people chatting animatedly, heard laughter and felt very much out of the loop; no matter how hard she tried she just couldn't get into the swing of things socially when she hung out with Tom and his friends. She would never have admitted it, not to anyone, but she was so bored she could cry.

Elodie took out her mobile phone and pressed the home button. She tensed a little when she saw she had several messages, all from either Steph or Carla. She scanned the messages: all of them were in the same vein, begging her to reconsider and reconvene their girls' night out. Elodie looked up and caught Tom's eye. He was giving her a disapproving look.

"Are we boring you, babe?" he asked, his tone a little sharper than it should have been, given her crime.

Both Al and Pat had stopped their chattering now and were looking uncomfortably at Elodie. She suddenly felt hot under their attention and embarrassment flushed her cheeks, like a schoolgirl caught behind the bike sheds when she should have been in class. She shook her head and shoved her phone into her back pocket, eager to get rid of the evidence as soon as possible.

"Carla and Steph were just…" She trailed off. Tom reached over, his eyes never leaving hers and took her hand.

"Just ignore them, babe, they're just jealous," he said, giving Elodie a knowing look, one that said *'trust me, I know exactly what I'm talking about'* and promptly returned to his conversation.

It was a good few minutes before Elodie had worked up the courage to lift her gaze from the floor. She couldn't believe Tom had reprimanded her like that. Her cheeks, previously flushed pink, had returned to their normal colour and she looked up, feeling as though taking her phone out when Tom was in the middle of a story about his meeting would be just the teeniest bit offensive. In his position she was sure she would have done the same. She tried to concentrate on what was being said and even managed to get in a few well-timed 'yeahs' and 'wows.' These seemed to satisfy Tom's ego and he grinned at her broadly. Soon enough, though, the three men returned to the type of lads' banter that just didn't hold weight with Elodie and she was once again left twiddling her thumbs. She looked around; she didn't want to appear impolite again but it was hard not to when it was almost impossible to join in with the conversation. Their lad chat seemed to be nothing more than background noise to her now. None of them had noticed the faraway look in her eyes, they were far too wrapped up in themselves now. A couple at the other end of the bar looked to be having some sort of argument. Elodie imagined what it was about. She began to narrate their conversation in her head, matching the words she imagined them saying to their actions.

'But darling, a kiss isn't cheating!' she imagined the woman saying. It was as if the woman could hear the thoughts form in Elodie's mind: her head snapped around and she fixed Elodie with a stare that instinct told her to look away from. Elodie averted her gaze immediately, pretending instead that something on the wall behind the woman was actually what was interesting to her. Her eyes settled on an old clock that hung high on the wall behind the bar. The minute hand ticked over to show that the time was now ten to seven and Elodie breathed an internal sigh of relief – it was time to go. She couldn't have been happier and downed the last dregs of her now warm drink so that there was nothing to hold her back. She put the empty glass down with probably a little more enthusiasm than was needed. The sound halted the conversation causing all three of them to look at her sharply. Elodie ignored their looks and tugged at Tom's shirt sleeve gently.

"Tom, we need to get going," she said diplomatically, not wanting to sound too overjoyed at their imminent departure. She didn't dislike his friends, exactly; they were just a bit too bland. Elodie often thought of them as Tom's fan club rather than real friends but she would never say that to Tom; after all, who was she to criticise?

Tom slid his shirt cuff to the side and checked his watch; Elodie's mouth fell open as she saw that instead of his usual Casio he wore a brand-new, glistening, and very pricey-looking timepiece. It was a leather-strapped watch with a gold face and diamonds inset underneath each Roman numeral. Elodie suspected that it was very expensive and had her suspicions confirmed when she grabbed his wrist to take a closer look and saw the word 'Gucci' glint in the light.

"Like it?" he grinned. "Thought I'd treat myself to something a bit special, you know, sort of 'well done' present."

Elodie didn't know whether to laugh or cry. The watch must have cost hundreds of pounds, hundreds of pounds that they just didn't have spare. She was well aware that with his promotion came a big pay bump but still, splashing the cash this early on and to this extent just seemed reckless.

"It's lovely," she said through gritted teeth. Tom didn't notice her tone: he was too busy lapping up the attention from Al and Patrice, both of them gushing compliments amongst the back-slapping and glad-handing.

Elodie, although irritated that Tom would make such a big purchase so impulsively, reasoned that it wasn't her place to tell him how he should spend his money and, after all, it was like he said, the watch was a treat. She also thought it would be silly to, in her mum's words, 'bite the hand that feeds her'. Tom did pay for pretty much everything;

she helped out where she could, of course, but her job at Betty's hardly meant a six-figure salary. *'Maybe it's time to figure out what I really want to do with my life,'* she pondered. It was with this thought that she remembered that she had her own treat to look forward and decided not to make the watch thing a 'thing'. She could hardly criticise him when he'd obviously gone to a lot of trouble to make her happy.

Tom knocked back the rest of his pint and picked up his suit jacket, which he'd hung on the back of a barstool for safekeeping.

"Come on then," he said, "we better get going if we're going to make the table."

Elodie picked up her bag and made her way to the exit, glad to be leaving the pub, Tom's friends and that God-awful rum. They bade farewell to Al and Patrice and after saying their goodbyes were finally alone and for the first time all evening. Elodie snaked her hand around Tom's waist and drew him in towards her; he returned her affections with a kiss on the side of the head. They walked for several minutes in relative silence, which suited Elodie down to the ground. The noise and hubbub of the pub had given her a headache. She rubbed at her eyes feverishly, her fingers making their way to her temples and massaging them in an effort to diminish the dull ache behind her eyes.

"Have you got any Paracetamol?" she asked Tom hopefully. He shook his head and patted down his jacket as if by way of proving that he was telling the truth. Elodie sighed. She knew by now not to rely on Tom for things like this; usually it was she who packed for every eventuality.

Soon enough they were walking into the restaurant, Tom gave his name and added, "Table for six."

"It's for seven, Tom," Elodie corrected. Tom's eyebrows furrowed momentarily before he broke out into a grin.

"Six *people*, you big idiot," he laughed. "It's a good job you're pretty, isn't it?"

Elodie looked at him, confusion etched on her face. Her question was answered before she had the chance to ask it. From behind her she heard the unmistakable laugh of Patrice, followed by Al's voice and after that the high-pitched giggles of Christy Goldbeck and Mimi Delaney – Al and Patrice's girlfriends. Elodie's heart sank; this was not what she had signed up for. She felt ambushed, forced into abandoning her own friends and to forgo a highly anticipated night out with them that she had been desperately looking forward to. She felt coerced, no, tricked, into spending the evening around a table where she quite frankly couldn't stand most of the people around it.

Before she was able to ask Tom what on earth he was playing at, they were upon them. Christy and Mimi descended on her like birds of prey to an unsuspecting mouse. They wrapped their arms around her in a huge, bear-like hug and squealed excitedly as they rocked her from side to side. Once she was released the onslaught of inanity started. She was bombarded with false compliments and questions that neither of them were the slightest bit interested in hearing the answers to. "You look fab, babe, love the shoes. So, how have you been? Where's that amazing bag from? Have you done something different with your hair?"

The two women were like carbon copies of one another: both tall, both thin, both with glossy, perfectly teased hair that never had a strand out of place. The only difference as far as Elodie could tell was their hair colour. Christy's hair was a deep brown, almost black, whilst Mimi's was peroxide blonde. Elodie had never seen either of them without a full face of makeup, big hair and skyscraper heels. Doing her best to hide the fact that inside she was screaming *'please kill me now'*, she smiled at them both and tried to join in the conversation, once again finding it hard to get a word in edgeways. She couldn't help but feel incredibly dowdy stood next to them. Admittedly, she would have made more of an effort had she known that the meal out was with them but still, that didn't change things now. She was in clothes she'd worn all day, she felt grubby and at that moment in time would have given anything for her fairy godmother to wave her magic wand and transform her from beast to beauty. She thought about her overnight bag bursting with appropriate attire; sadly for her, though, it was still at Steph's. Her makeup-free cheeks flushed with embarrassment for the second time that evening.

The meal passed by slowly. Elodie wondered several times

throughout it if there might be something wrong with her. The conversation seemed so dull; they only ever seemed to discuss the same topics over and over again. The boys constantly talked about work or sport, whilst Christy and Mimi giggled, gossiped and drank copious amounts of wine. Feeling as though she were constantly being left on the sidelines, Elodie wondered how on earth she could join in. She tried to make an effort, chipping in here and there but more often than not her comments went unnoticed and even when they did include her it always felt a little like they were doing it out of pity.

"I love how you're not afraid to go *au naturel*, Elodie, I could never go out like it. I just don't suit that 'stripped back' look," Mimi said as she polished off her second glass of wine.

"I know, right?" chimed in Christy. "Most people wouldn't dare go out like that, but you just don't seem to mind what people think. Good for you, you're so brave."

Elodie gritted her teeth through moments like this and let her mind take her far away. She always felt that if she stayed present during these catty conversations she'd wind up saying something she'd regret. She couldn't bear to think about what Tom would have to say if she told his best friends and their girlfriends what she really thought of them.

She took a deep breath and thought about Carla and Steph and imagined what they'd all be doing right now if Tom hadn't shown up and changed their plans. She imagined them cracking open a bottle of Prosecco, all the while chatting animatedly whilst they got ready. Her spirits sank: she'd rather be with them a million times over. If she had known that this was where the night would take her she wouldn't have gone with Tom in the first place. She'd been faced with a difficult decision and Steph and Carla had seemed so understanding. They really were great friends and she'd let them down. She made a mental note to make it up to them: perhaps she'd organise a nice meal at hers and they could have a girly night in?

A firm hand on her shoulder broke her reverie; she looked up and was surprised to see Tom staring at her.

"Babe, dessert?" he said. She looked around and quickly

apologised when she saw the waiter standing over them, pen and pad poised to take her order. She absolutely hated it when customers ignored her at work and here she was, doing the very same thing.

"Oh, sorry. I'll have the chocolate torte, please," she said, managing a smile.

"Are you sure?" Tom asked, a look of concern carved on his face. "You've had quite a lot already, haven't you? You can't still be hungry surely, especially after all that garlic bread."

Elodie was taken aback. She looked at him, then around the table.

"I'm absolutely stuffed," Mimi said, rubbing her stomach, "I couldn't manage another bite." Christy nodded along to her friend like one of those dogs you see in cars sometimes.

"Oh, yeah. Of course," Elodie answered mechanically, hardly believing the words that were coming out of her mouth. "I'll just have a latte then."

The waiter, clearly affronted on her behalf, asked her if she was sure about that. Elodie nodded and in an effort to distract everyone's attention grabbed her water glass and took a deep drink: she had suddenly become very hot and the ice-cold liquid offered a welcome reprieve. Was she going mad? Had Tom just called her out for wanting a dessert? She stole another glance around the table; no one seemed to notice her mood nosedive.

The waiter brought over their drinks. Christy and Mimi had ordered the sickly-sweet dessert wine on offer and the guys had gone for port. Tom cleared his throat: once all eyes were on him, he raised his glass in the air and put on a wide, Cheshire-cat smile.

"Now I know you guys have all rallied round to celebrate me tonight, and I do truly appreciate it," he said with a false modesty no one but Elodie could decipher, "but there's someone in my life, someone who has been with me since day one. When I had nothing. She's stuck with me through thick and thin and it's because of that I've organised something extra special." He took this moment to take a dramatic pause before turning his attention to Elodie. "El, babe. I know it's been stressful living with me lately. I also know how much you've wanted to get away. That's why I've booked us an amazing holiday."

Tom clapped a hand on Elodie's shoulder in triumph. She couldn't help but break out into a large grin. She knew this had been coming, but hearing the words out loud and knowing that her all her patience had paid off made Tom's revelation all the sweeter.

"Oh, Tom!" she squealed, leaning over to throw her arms around him, "thank you so much, I can't believe you've done this for me, you're the absolute best!"

A deep swell of emotion rose within her chest and made her feel so deliriously happy she felt like she could burst. A huge smile erupted on her face: this news had certainly made the whole evening completely worth it. How could she stay annoyed with him when he'd been so incredibly thoughtful?

"Now I hope you're not mad but I took a peek into a couple of those magazines you like."

"I thought it was weird that the ones I'd left downstairs had gone missing!" Elodie exclaimed, remembering not being able to find them amongst Tom's things on the kitchen table. The annoyance she had felt at how messy he'd left the place melted away in an instant, it was as if the sun from their soon to be holiday had already started shining down on her.

Tom smiled at her, a grin wider than before that showcased his large white teeth. He stroked his stubble and took a deep breath with a smug yet playful expression on his face.

"Well, it gets even better, babe. I had a good look through those magazines of yours and, sure, we could have gone away together to Mexico or the Bahamas, but I thought we could do something *even* better, something far more memorable."

Elodie wriggled in her seat, barely able to contain her excitement; she was unable to imagine what could possibly be better than Mexico or the Bahamas.

"I did some Maths and figured out that for the price of one of those holidays we could do something else, something you've never even dreamt of. We could *all* go away together, my treat," he finished proudly, his hand gesturing to the entire group.

There was an almighty squeal from Christy, and Mimi clapped a hand over her mouth in delight.

"I've cleared it with the lads, so, ladies, pack your bags because next week we're all going to an all-inclusive, four-star resort in Malaga! Nothing but us lot, a shit-tonne of booze and the hotel's got five different restaurants. We won't have to leave the resort once. The girls can tan all day and we can drink all night. I've cleared it with Clive, we've smashed it so hard this year that he's agreed to let us all have the week off, together! Everyone else will have to pull their weight now we won't be there to keep them afloat," he said smugly.

Al and Patrice practically roared their agreement, whilst a torrent of praise gushed from Christy and Mimi. Elodie opened her mouth to say something, closed it and then opened it again, completely amazed at how her emotional state had managed to crash and burn in less than two seconds. This couldn't be happening, Tom couldn't possibly have got this so wrong. *'Doesn't he know me at all?'* she questioned herself. She was sure he meant well, but really, what on earth was he thinking? Malaga was definitely not somewhere she was keen to go, especially with a group of people she could barely call friends. The idea of being an outcast for an entire week wasn't only daunting, it was downright terrifying.

"Tom, I... I don't know what to say," she began.

"Well, how about a little thank you, babe? This is all for you, after all." Tom cut in, a sharp tone to his voice. He was clearly miffed that Elodie's reaction wasn't in the same vein as the rest of the group's.

"Thank you, of course, sorry..." she found herself mumbling.

Elodie wasn't exactly sure what happened next. She seemed to be telling them that she needed some fresh air and amidst their high-fives and cries of adulation, she found herself silently picking up her bag and leaving the table. She slipped across the dining hall towards the exit and faltered.

She couldn't just leave. Tom had tried his best; it wasn't his fault he'd got it so wrong. Was she being ungrateful?

She needed a moment to herself. She turned on her heel and pushed the door to the ladies' room open instead, she just needed a minute to think. She slumped against the wall next to the door and steadied herself against the hand dryer. Her breathing began to calm now and she could finally begin to hear herself think. She still wasn't sure precisely what it was she should do. Should she leave? Would it be incredibly rude? What would everyone think of her? Ungrateful, that's what. Would it be worth the flack she'd get? Or should she just swallow her pride and stay, pretend to be thankful for the holiday and just get on with it? So what if the idea of an all-inclusive resort stay wasn't exactly what she had wanted and so what if the people she'd be going with weren't exactly her cup of tea? *'Everyone's different, after all,'* she told herself firmly. *'Maybe I just haven't given them enough of a chance.'*

Suddenly the door the bathroom burst open and thumped right into her, smashing her in the side. She let out a small whimper, which was drowned out by the clatter of heels on the tiled floor and the high-pitched voices of Christy and Mimi. Without so much as casting a glance around, the two women had walked straight into the cubicles before locking the doors. Elodie heard the bolts slide and thought it best to get out of there immediately.

"She thinks she's so much better than us, Meems," came Christy's voice, high-pitched and cold. Even though she was slurring slightly Elodie could hear her as clear as a bell.

"An entire week with her. Ugh, she's so, what's the word?" Mimi asked. There was a brief pause before both voices rang out at the same time.

"Boring," they both said, laughing spitefully before adding, "Snap!"

"I mean, look at what she's wearing, on her boyfriend's big night as well. She either couldn't give a shit about him, or doesn't give a shit about herself," Christy chided.

Elodie could feel her heartbeat quicken. She was sure the two women would hear it, thudding away inside her chest.

"Pathetic, isn't it? I've never been a fan. I don't know what Tom sees in her. It's like I've always said. 'Never trust a girl who wouldn't know what contouring was if it hit her in the face!" Mimi laughed.

"We should try and set him up with Tina!" Christy exclaimed.

"He's never going to dump her, babe. You heard him, right? She's been with him since day one. He feels like he owes her or something," Mimi replied.

It was at these words that Elodie felt a sharp stab of anger laced with hurt. Was Tom only with her out of pity? Because he felt like he owed it to her?

The sound of toilets flushing brought Elodie back to her senses and before either of the two women had a chance to unlock the doors and emerge from their cubicles Elodie pushed open the door and with purpose strode out of the restaurant and into the street.

CHAPTER 4

ELODIE SOON FOUND HERSELF BACK AT BETTY'S Book Café; she had gravitated there automatically, like a bird flying south for the winter. Her key turned effortlessly in the back door and she slipped inside. Maybe it wasn't too late to join Steph and Carla. *'Mind you,'* she thought to herself, *'I bet they're really pissed off with me too.'* Elodie sighed; she couldn't seem to do right for doing wrong. The gnawing feeling of knowing she'd disappointed people really weighed heavily on her heart. There was only one thing for it: she'd have to apologise, sincerely, and hope for the best.

Elodie paused. She had come in through the back door and had two options: she could turn right and head into the kitchen where there were stairs that led up to the flat that Betty and Steph shared, or she could turn left and through the swing doors that led into the café itself. She decided to try the café first, reasoning that in all probability Steph had most likely left Elodie's bag there, maybe in case she came back for it but more likely to get it out of the way. Steph's flat was incredibly small, after all. The café seemed to glow eerily in the dark: the fridges were always left on and they cast a yellow light across the place that changed the feel of the entire café. Elodie crept about, wondering whether Steph would have left her flat door open or not. She hoped that Steph had; that way, if she really hurried she could slap on a bit of makeup, get changed, slip into some heels and be on her way within half an hour.

It seemed that the quieter Elodie tried to be, the more noise she made. Her eyes struggled in the dimly-lit café. She bumped into a chair: the clattering noise it made cut through the silence and made her jump. She whirled around and in her haste managed to send a vase filled with peonies crashing down onto the floor below.

"Shit," she muttered out loud, cursing herself for being so clumsy. Elodie rarely swore, unless the situation really called for it – and this was definitely one of those situations. The vase, which Elodie knew to be one of Betty's favourites, had cracked neatly in two and lay on the floor; the water it had held now pooled on one of the rugs. Elodie bent down and picked up the broken remnants of the vase. She tossed them in the bin as she headed into the kitchen for something to mop up the mess with. She pushed through the swing door and screamed as something, or someone, jumped out from the shadows. The light flashed on and Elodie was momentarily dazzled. She instinctively raised her hands over her face to protect herself. Instead of being met with some sort of threat, she was met with laughter: hysterical, mirth-filled laughter. She lowered her hands in confusion and saw, to her delight, Steph and Carla stood there. Considering the sight in front of her it was Elodie who should have been the one laughing. Both of her friends wore thick, clay face masks. Carla now had a bright pink face and Steph's was a sickly yellow colour. They had obviously heard a disturbance and gone down to investigate, as both women had chosen a weapon to defend themselves with. Steph was brandishing one of her mum's thick, ceramic rolling pins and Carla had opted for one of her skyscraper stiletto heels. Both of them wore their pyjamas and both of them were still laughing uncontrollably.

"What on earth are you doing here?" Carla asked through stifled giggles. "We thought you were a burglar," she finished as both women lowered their weapons.

"Long story," Elodie said, before adding, "why aren't you two painting the town red?"

"Long story," Steph replied. "Despite bringing half of her wardrobe Carla couldn't find a thing to wear, then after the one millionth outfit choice, she decided that a takeaway, a bottle or two of wine and a film would be far better. Plus, you know, a night out without you just wouldn't have been as fun."

Elodie managed a half-smile. She felt incredibly guilty the

two of them had missed their night out, especially now she had turned up out of the blue.

"So go on, then," Carla began, but Elodie cut her off before she could finish.

"You won't believe what's happened to me, well you will believe it, actually I don't think either of you will even be surprised."

"Let me guess, Tom took you to McDonald's and you had to pay for your own Happy Meal?" Steph quipped; her dislike for Tom had intensified considerably over the last few hours.

"That wouldn't have been so bad, actually," Elodie conceded.

Steph took her arm and guided her now forlorn friend up the stairs with Carla following behind. Once settled back in Steph's flat Elodie began her tale, starting her story from the moment they'd left the café. Elodie realised that on past occasions, whenever she had confided in her friends she had glossed over the worst parts; she never wanted Steph or Carla to dislike Tom and as a result of that had only ever bestowed on them half-truths and inexact details that shed a more favourable light on him. Taking a moment to wonder why it was that she always felt the need to protect him, she surged on with her story. Carla and Steph never interrupted her; they simply sat there with bated breath, listening to every word that poured out of their friend's mouth.

When Elodie finished she took a deep breath. She half-expected them to ask her what the problem was, especially Steph who was extremely matter-of-fact when it came to things like this. She looked in turn at each of them, wishing that someone would say something. She felt like she had been babbling on about Tom and his horribly selfish ways for an eternity now, surely they had something to say about it all?

"Well, I just have one question," Steph eventually offered. She twisted a strand of her fiery hair around a long finger contemplatively. "What are you going to do about it?"

Elodie looked at her blankly. The whole reason she'd spent the last hour giving them a blow-by-blow account was for them to tell her what to do, or at the very least offer her some sort of opinion that would make her decision easier.

"Well, I was hoping you guys would help me with that," Elodie confessed.

Carla got up from the arm of the sofa where she had perched throughout the entirety of Elodie's tale and wandered over to the fridge.

"I'm okay for alcohol," Elodie said when she saw that Carla had taken out a half-full bottle of wine.

"You're having one and that's that," Carla replied. "We all are."

She poured all three women a glass and, making sure they all had an equal amount, passed them out before sitting back down with her own. Elodie eyed the glass dubiously: she wasn't entirely sure that drinking would solve her current dilemma. She went to set it down on the coffee table but Carla caught her hand.

"Honestly El, you'll feel better after a drink and it's only a small one. After this evening, no after the last few weeks you've had, you deserve it," Carla said.

When it was put to her that way Elodie was inclined to agree. She raised the glass to her lips and took a sip of the crisp, cool liquid. Despite being in the company of two other people she allowed herself an internal moment of calm, quiet, alone-time. She closed her eyes and exhaled, unable to help the confusion she felt. She was completely at a loss. Tom wasn't a bad person; in fact, he was exactly the same as when she'd first met him. He hadn't changed one bit, so why was he only now beginning to grate on her? She felt weirdly indifferent to Tom: she forced herself to imagine not being with him and found no emotion attached to that thought. She didn't hate him, far from it, but she had to question whether she was actually in love with him. Was their relationship based on convenience? Did they even really like each other or had they just been together so long that staying together was the easier option? Elodie thought that if she had to ask herself these questions then perhaps the answer was obvious.

"Ugggghhh," she groaned, "this is horrible, why is this happening?"

Elodie ran her fingers through her hair and sighed an exasperated sigh. Steph gave her friend a small smile and sidled closer to her. She put her arm around Elodie and drew her in nearer, Elodie sank into her friend, grateful that she had them to talk to. Steph gave her a little squeeze and Elodie found herself fighting back tears.

"It's okay," Steph said gently, "we're here for you, whatever you decide to do. Anything you need, anytime, we're here."

Carla nodded her agreement and took another sip of wine. "Why don't you get an early night?" she suggested, "things might look a little clearer in the morning."

Elodie shook her head.

"No, I need to think. Maybe I should ring him. He'll be worried sick, I just upped and left, didn't I?"

The realisation of what she had done made her feel terrible. If the shoe were on the other foot she would be so upset, so wholly disappointed and probably very angry. Elodie couldn't reconcile her feelings. On the one hand, she felt hurt that Tom could have got everything so wrong, that he didn't really know her or, if he did, he didn't really care. But, on the other hand, she had to question herself. Was she being too demanding? Should she be grateful and, despite how she felt, just put up and shut up? Her mind flashed to Mimi and Christy: what they had said about her was scathingly cruel, they were horrible girls and Elodie had no intention of giving them a second chance now. She couldn't imagine spending an entire week with them; having to smile sweetly whilst internally screaming didn't sound like her idea of a good time. But was that Tom's fault? He couldn't exactly help who his friends went out with, could he? She groaned again. Everything was a mess and this was all just too much to try and deal with. Maybe she should just go home, talk to Tom and clear the air. She pulled out her phone and scrolled to his name.

"Put it on speaker," Carla said, leaning forward.

This suggestion didn't go down well as it was met with an icy glare from Steph who shook her head fervently and told Elodie to do no such thing. Carla huffed and settled herself back on the arm of the sofa. Elodie drew the phone up to her ear and listened; her breath caught in her throat as the phone rang.

"Hi there," Tom's smooth voice said, "you've reached the voicemail of Tom Wright, leave me a short message and I will try and get back to you."

Elodie hung up. She tried again but to no avail. She imagined Tom sat at home, in silence, hurt and upset that he had such a selfish girlfriend. He was probably wondering what he'd done wrong and feeling well and truly sorry for himself. This imaginary scene tugged at Elodie's heartstrings and she let out a little whimper on his behalf. Elodie hung up and set the phone down on the coffee table. She didn't want to do this, whatever this was, over voicemail.

The three friends sat in awkward silence for a few moments, Steph and Carla unable to do much other than simply be there for their friend. A loud buzzing sound broke them from their reverie. Tom's name and picture flashed up on the screen. Elodie gasped and picked up the phone, she held it up to her face, staring at it, unable to perform the basic task of pressing the answer button. Carla, taking control, grabbed the phone out of Elodie's hands, answered the call and threw it back to her so quickly that if you had blinked at that precise moment you'd have most likely missed it.

"Hi Tom," Elodie said cautiously. There was a brief pause before she tried again. "Tom? Tom? I can't hear you," she persisted, her voice getting louder with each word. She stood up and covered her free ear with her other hand; pacing up and down, she called out to him again. Carla and Steph shared a confused look, neither one of them quite sure what exactly was going on. Elodie pointed to Steph's bedroom and Steph nodded in reply. Elodie mouthed the words 'Thank you' and let herself inside, closing the door firmly behind her as she went in.

Steph's room was exactly what you would expect. It was simplistic in style, clean, organised and a stark contrast to the rest of the flat, which Betty had decorated in vivid shades of burgundy, red and mauve. Elodie settled herself on Steph's bed: it was incredibly comfortable, and within a few moments she had found herself kicking off her shoes and reclining into the plump feather down pillows.

"Tom, are you there?" she asked again. Tom was clearly in a pub: the background noise was deafening and Elodie could barely hear him over it.

"Hold on a sec, I'm going outside," Tom said. His words were slurred slightly and Elodie could tell that he'd continued drinking, even after the copious amounts he'd consumed during the meal. This, combined with the noise, meant that Elodie was only just able to decipher what it was he had actually said. She waited; seconds ticked by, and with each one, the background noise grew more faint.

"What is it?" he asked when he eventually spoke.

"I just wanted... I just wanted to talk to you. Sorry, are you busy?" Elodie stammered, not entirely sure why she was behaving as if it were her and her alone who was in the wrong.

"Why would I be at home? I'm celebrating," Tom cut in abruptly. "I don't know what's gotten into you recently El, you're changing, getting ideas above your station, my mum reckons. You want all these finer things but expect me to go and get them for you. Well, it's about time I put my foot down El, enough is enough, you either..." He broke off.

"Put up and shut up?" Elodie asked. She knew these were the words he'd choose. She'd heard his parents use them time and time again; if it wasn't 'put up and shut up', it was 'like it or lump it.' Both amounting to the same thing: be grateful for your lot in life. *'But what if I can't do that, what if I want more of a lot?'* she thought glumly.

"Look I'm going back to join the party, you just have a nice night. Think about what I've said, El. Most women would kill to be in your shoes, you'd do well to remember that – and before you say anything, it's not just me who thinks that. All my friends think the same, everyone says you're punching above your weight."

The phone went dead and Tom was gone, presumably to continue drinking with people who thought that he was way too good for Elodie.

'How can he be friends with people like that?' she thought angrily, hot tears beginning to sting at her eyes. She took a

deep, calming breath and told herself to get a grip. Elodie hated feeling like this. She was out of control emotionally and genuinely had no clue which way she should turn. Elodie couldn't imagine not being with Tom. They had been together for so long; he had been her first and up until recently, she'd thought her only love. Now, when she tried to look towards her future she saw nothing but a big, glaring question mark hanging over her.

CHAPTER 5

"ELODIE?" STEPH SAID, GENTLY SHAKING HER
friend by the shoulder, "it's ten-thirty. I've made you some
toast and here's some water. You'll be dehydrated after last
night."

Elodie gingerly opened her eyes and squinted at Steph.
The overly bright light streaming through the open curtains
in Steph's bedroom was particularly offensive to her; she
turned her head and buried her face in the pillow before
managing a croaky muffled noise that vaguely resembled a
thank you. She wallowed in the darkness there for a few
moments before Steph attempted to wake her again.

"Okay, okay," Elodie moaned, sitting up and rubbing her
eyes sleepily. The twelve hours' sleep she had just managed
hadn't seemed to refresh her in the slightest; if anything,
she felt worse now than she did before her head had hit the
pillow.

Steph handed her a plate stacked high with toast, all with
various toppings, none of which appealed to Elodie right
then and there.

"I'm alright for the moment," she said as she waved the
plate away. "I'm not hungry, I'm just..." she trailed off, her
voice cracking slightly.

She felt completely numb. The previous night had seen
the three women do nothing but pick at the bones of Elodie's relationship. Carla and Steph had been reluctant to
get too involved at first; they didn't want a repetition of the
argument they'd had in the café. However, one hour and
two glasses of wine later, Carla had opened another bottle
and they had both offered opinions. For two people so different they were definitely on the same page when it came

71

to Elodie's relationship with Tom. As usual, Carla had done little to sugar the pill and had told Elodie exactly what she thought. Steph had been the more balanced of the two and had offered Elodie sage advice that any agony aunt would have been proud of. Between the three of them, they'd gone over every detail of Elodie and Tom's relationship; Carla and Steph quizzed Elodie on everything, not out of nosiness but rather their desire for Elodie to make the right decision.

The more Elodie talked, the more she opened up. She found herself not only opening up to her friends, but also to herself. She realised that she had changed a lot since she had first met Tom, but he had hardly changed at all. She knew she couldn't be mad at him for this: it wasn't his fault and coercing him into becoming someone else was not only unfair, it was also foolhardy and selfish. Embarking down that path would lead to tears – well, more tears, anyway. Elodie had definitely shed her fair share: she cried for the loss of her relationship, she cried for her unknown future and she cried for herself. Carla and Steph had been amazing throughout the entire evening. Between the two of them, they struck a perfect balance of tough love and comfort, both of which Elodie was in dire need of. Elodie had made her decision, or at least she thought she had. She couldn't stay with Tom: it wasn't fair on either of them.

It was a horrible idea to acknowledge that the person she had envisioned spending the rest of her life with was actually someone that she didn't really like, let alone love. She tortured herself to sleep by picturing his face: she imagined the hurt in his eyes, him begging her not to go and promising to change his ways and how devastated he'd be afterwards. These thoughts brought on fresh tears and after Steph had put her to bed she cried herself to sleep. Carla and Steph had made do in the living room, both of them wanting Elodie to get the best night's sleep she could.

"You have to eat something," Steph said with a finality to her voice that made Elodie reach out and grab a piece of jam on toast. She chewed on the corner thoughtfully, wondering exactly what her next move should be. She did feel a bit better about everything: she knew this was for the best. With Tom, her life had been mapped out, but it was like Steph had said, *'a mediocre certainty is not the type of future to aim for.'* Elodie knew that Steph was right: life with Tom wouldn't have been for her. She would have tried – in fact, she would have tried her very best – but she knew that even with her best efforts it wouldn't have been enough. She would always have had a nagging voice in the back of her mind asking, *'What if?'* Carla had pointed out that if she were to stay with Tom, not only would she be forfeiting any chance of long-term happiness for herself, she would also be forfeiting *his* chance of happiness too. So in the end, it was the idea of ruining both of their lives that spurred her decision.

"I have to do it today, don't I?" Elodie said, breaking her own train of thought. Her words were more of a factual statement than a question. Steph nodded and took a piece of toast for herself.

"The sooner the better, El," Steph replied, getting up off the bed and stretching. "I'm going to grab a shower. Carla's up and watching telly. Why don't you finish your breakfast with her and when you're done I'll drive you home?"

"Thanks, that'd be great but it'll be quicker on the tube and I don't want to put you out."

"You're not putting me out at all. Come on, I insist. It'll give you one last chance to talk things over and," she grinned, "if you burst into tears again at least you won't have to do your 'cry face' in front of the general public."

Elodie, despite feeling pretty emotionally bruised, couldn't help but offer a wry smile.

"Okay then," she said in a small voice.

Steph nodded her approval and opened the door. Elodie followed her out into the living room where Carla was sat, covered in a fleecy blanket and positively glued to a Saturday morning TV show.

"Morning," Elodie greeted her. A sleepy edge to her voice still laced her words.

Carla looked up and offered her a warm grin. She shuffled over and patted the now empty space next to her. Elodie took little convincing. She slumped down onto the sofa and pulled a corner of the blanket over her.

"How are you feeling?" Carla asked, ripping her eyes away from the screen and turning to face Elodie.

"Better," Elodie said decidedly. She was well aware that there would be nothing more damaging than re-hashing her decision over and over again and despite the enormity of her decision, she felt decidedly clear of mind. She knew she had made the right choice.

"That's good. Do you need anything, do you want me to come with you?"

Elodie shook her head. She needed to speak to Tom alone, one on one. She owed him that much.

"Steph's driving me home and other than you guys, and a stiff drink, I probably won't need anything else – well, apart from a place to live," Elodie said wanly.

"Come live with me!" Carla said, excitement creeping into her voice. "I still haven't found anyone to replace Dora and you'd be perfect. Oh go on, say yes."

Elodie thought about it for a moment: living with Carla seemed like a very easy, very obvious, very fun option. There was just one problem. Money.

"There's no way I can afford to live at yours, you live in a stupidly expensive area. It's okay, I can find somewhere, I'll flat-share, rent a room or something," Elodie said.

"El, it's London, it's all stupidly expensive," Carla combatted, laughing, "seriously, though, my dad pays for most of the flat, we just split the difference and call it quits. It's what I did with Dora. You didn't think I could afford that place on my salary from Betty's, did you? Even with the odd modelling job thrown in, I could barely afford a place half that size."

Elodie had, to be honest; she had never really thought about it before. She realised that having Tom as a financial crutch had made her pretty ignorant of how everyone else afforded things. Now she would no longer have the Bank of Tom, she would have to get a real handle on her finances. She groaned. The single life was going to be a lot of work.

"So how much are we talking?" Elodie asked, not wanting to agree to anything that might end up affecting their friendship.

"Five hundred, all in?" Carla said, the smile fading from her face when she saw Elodie's look of incredulity.

"Five hundred? I just won't be able to afford that, that's…" she counted on her fingers quickly, "almost half of my earnings, on rent!"

"El, that is a crazy good deal, you'll have a decent-sized bedroom, furniture included, a living room with a balcony. I'm telling you, you couldn't even get a studio in zone six for that money. How do you not know this?" Carla finished incredulously.

"Really?" Elodie asked dumbly; doubt was creeping up on her now and threatened to overturn her decision over Tom. '*A life of mediocre certainty doesn't sound that bad when the very realistic prospect of bankruptcy is the alternative option,*' Elodie thought to herself.

She mulled it over. It would be fun living with Carla; her flat was lovely and she'd never lived with a proper friend before. If only she earned more money, she could be more certain of what she should do. She hated that it was something as shallow as money that was steering her: she shouldn't think about money, she should think about what she wanted. It was at that precise moment that a realisation struck Elodie as hard as a hammer hitting a nail. This was the kick in the backside she needed. A sudden burst of excitement exploded in her chest. She needed a job. No, she needed a career.

Carla looked at her, a puzzled look etched across her features.

"What?" she asked, unable to read her friend's expression.

"I think I've just had an epiphany," Elodie said slowly. "I need to figure out what I want to do with my life."

"Join the club," Carla answered with a dry laugh. "I'm hardly Kate Moss yet."

"Don't be daft, you know exactly what you want and you're taking steps to get there. I'm just well, floating, I guess."

Elodie paused. She hadn't realised up until that point that when compared to the rest of her friends she was definitely bringing up the rear, career-wise. Steph was going to manage her family business, Carla was on the path to catwalk superstardom and she was, well, she was a part-time waitress.

'Not that there's anything wrong with waitressing; I just can't imagine doing it part-time for the rest of my life,' she thought.

Elodie pondered her future. She had no clue what she wanted to be. What she actually wanted to do or where she wanted to do it was a complete mystery to her. Elodie could think of no particular skills or passions that she had which would lend to any obvious career path. Unless professional holidaymaker was a job there wasn't anything that immediately stood out to her.

"What's going on in the head of yours?" Carla asked, interrupting her thoughts. Elodie was surprised to hear a note of concern in her voice.

"I just…" Elodie sighed, trailing off. "I just don't have any idea what I could do. There's nothing I'm good at – Ouch!" She squealed as Carla's punched her in the arm.

"Less of that. You absolutely rock and so what if you're not obviously a chef or scientist or whatever! Plenty of people take ages to figure out what they want to do, Christ, J. K. Rowling was in her thirties when she got published, Kristen Wiig was thirty-odd when she made it big and Vera Wang was forty when she designed her first dress. If we go by their standards you're an early bloomer," Carla offered enthusiastically.

"Hmmmm," Elodie answered, sounding less than convinced. "But they're all talented. I just wish I'd figured this out sooner."

Elodie felt a hand on her shoulder and a fleeting moment of thankfulness settled within her. She was so lucky to have such good friends and promised to repay the kindness both of them had shown her if they ever needed it. She groaned, realising that before she could start her new life, chase new dreams or even put a new load of washing on, she had to talk to Tom. After all, they were still technically together and he had no idea what was coming.

Elodie and Steph left later that morning; Elodie had showered and put on some fresh clothes that she had packed the day before. The journey back to her old home was uneventful, which didn't go down well. Elodie had been desperate for anything to go awry: a traffic jam or torrential down-pour, anything to prolong her travels and put off the inev-itable conversation she had to have with Tom. She'd gone through what she wanted to say over and over in her head, prompting different responses and coaching herself on how to react. By the time she got to her front door, she felt pre-pared and felt at one with her decision. Deep down she knew she was doing the right thing. She just hoped that in time Tom would see this too.

Elodie turned her key in the door and pushed it open. She blinked into the darkness, her eyes struggling to adjust to the new, dimly-lit surroundings. Her home presented her with an unsettling smell, somewhere between old ashtrays and cheap perfume. She stretched out a hand and felt for the light switch. The sight that met her eyes stopped her dead in her tracks. The place was a mess: empty beer cans strewn about the floor and haphazard shoes from both sexes told her that Tom must have had some sort of after-party. Elodie wrinkled her nose and let out a groan of disgust. Tom certainly hadn't mourned her absence for very long. She couldn't believe she'd felt sorry for him, imagining him all alone the previous evening. It seemed to her that he was getting on just fine without her.

Elodie jerked her head as she heard an unfamiliar noise coming from under a pile of jackets that had been piled high on the sofa. She gingerly picked up the lapel of a dark blue, pinstriped one and lifted it up. Tom's face came into view. He had lipstick stains on his cheek, his shirt was unbuttoned and his tie was no longer around his neck but now around his forehead. He looked like some sort of second-rate Rambo.

"Babe?" he croaked at her. "Fetch me some water, will you? With ice," he stipulated.

Elodie began walking to the kitchen, an automatic response to any of Tom's requests. She stopped dead in her tracks. This was exactly the sort of thing that had pushed her into the decision she had made. She'd been a doormat for almost the entirety of their relationship; she sure as hell wasn't going to continue to be one now.

"Tom, we need to talk," she said, more abruptly than she had intended. Tom waved her away.

"Water first, I'm dying here," he said, pulling the blue pinstriped jacket back over his head. "And can you turn that light off, for the love of God? Are you trying to blind me or something?"

Elodie scowled, got up and poured him a glass of water. She did this against her better judgment but knowing Tom he wouldn't give her an inch until his every whim was catered for. She pulled the jacket back from over Tom's head and handed him the glass. He slurped at the water noisily then dropped the half-empty glass onto the floor to join the beer cans and haphazard shoes. It tipped over and the remainder of its contents splashed out onto the carpet. Elodie watched the dark stain spread outwards with an interest born from procrastination and apprehension. She sighed. Her carefully chosen words evaded her now, she opened her mouth but the well-rehearsed script died on her tongue.

"Babe," Tom said, a sweet, almost girlish tone to his voice, "would you get me some breakfast from Maccers?"

Elodie grimaced at this request. What did he think she was?

"I'm not your personal waitress," she said quietly, almost to herself.

"But you're so good at it," Tom cooed, as if expecting her to be pleased.

Elodie stared at him, her eyes searching. She was almost willing him to understand what was about to happen. If he'd just get there quicker, perhaps he could do, or say, something to make everything better. She waited, but Tom did and said nothing. His eyes flickered as he began to doze back off to sleep.

"Tom, this isn't working," Elodie began, the words suddenly seeming to tumble from her lips. "I think we should break up. I've been feeling this way for a while now and, well, a few things have made me see that we're just not right for one another..." Elodie trailed off, giving Tom an imploring look that simply begged him to make this easier for her.

Tom didn't say anything for several long moments; in fact, neither of them did. They sat in what felt like a stunned silence: the force of Elodie's words seemed to have struck them both dumb. After a few minutes, Tom sat up and ran his fingers through his hair.

"You're not thinking straight, El, you can't be. Why would you want to give all this up?" he stretched out his arm and pointed.

Elodie's gaze followed his finger. Give up what, exactly? Sure, they had a nice home, she never went without and for the most part they had a stress-free, pleasant enough existence. But now, Elodie realised that just wasn't enough. She wanted, no, needed more from life. She didn't want to look back and wish she'd done things differently.

"I *am* thinking straight Tom, and I think you think the same thing. We're not suited, we want different things."

"Is this about the group holiday?" he cut across her abruptly, a nasty edge creeping into his voice. Elodie shook her head.

"That's just one thing in a long line. We're just," her mind raced trying to find the right word, "mismatched."

"This has literally come out of nowhere, you can't just up and leave me. It's humiliating." He looked at Elodie with an expression she'd seen so many times but never truly understood; disgust.

Elodie looked at him. *'So now we get down to it,'* she thought.

"Humiliating? It's not about humiliation, I'm not doing this to get back at you or hurt you. I want what's best for both of us. Tom, we don't make each other happy. At least not any more we don't. I'm so sorry but I've made up my mind. I've thought about it long and hard and as horrible as this is, we're just not..." she broke off, her voice beginning to crack with the weight of her words.

Elodie put her head in her hands and sighed; she felt awful. She questioned herself over and over again: was this the right thing to do? Should she work on being a better girlfriend for Tom and push all these negative thoughts to the back of her head? She knew what her mum would say, but that was fine for her, she'd already found her...

"Soulmates," Elodie said aloud. "You're just not my soulmate, Tom, and I'm not yours. Face it, I'm not the person you want me to be."

"You would be if you just shut up once in a while. You never do anything, El, you hardly make any effort now," he spat. "For fuck's sake, of all the days. I've got friends over, I'm hungover and now you're saying that we're over. Look at you, playing the 'holier than thou' card. I thought you were better than this, but no! God, you're so selfish sometimes. Look, just come here, you'll like the holiday when we're on it and just think, all that extra money I'll be earning will be going on something extra special."

He gave Elodie what she assumed he thought was a cheeky wink and reached out for her. She pulled her hand away from his. She didn't want him to touch her. She had thought she would feel sorry for Tom, that this whole breakup would be made even harder by his tears of pain and hurt. But here he was, making out that somehow all of this was her fault and that worse still, he would forgive her if she'd only quit her whining.

"I don't know how else to say it, Tom. This is horrible and, believe me, I've tried but we just don't fit anymore. It's no one's fault, so please don't try and make out that I'm the one to blame. I'm not and I'm certainly not shouldering the responsibility so you look better in front of your friends."

"Elodie, don't," Tom said. This was the first time during this whole conversation that she thought she heard pain in his voice, but as quickly as it arrived it had left. "You'll regret it. You've got nothing without me, you'll have nowhere to live, no money coming in, no luxuries and, I don't want to sound harsh, but you'll have no future. I can provide for you, I thought that's what you wanted."

Elodie shook her head.

"This is what I mean, I'm just not that girl. I don't want a boyfriend who doubles up as a cash dispenser, I want an equal," she said honestly.

Tom responded with a grunt.

"An equal? Do you know how ridiculous that sounds? An equal to what, exactly – to *you*?" he snorted derisively. "Cool. Well, enjoy that. I can't fucking believe you. I've given you everything and this is how you repay me?"

Elodie had perched herself on the edge of the armchair but now she stood up. She had had enough now. She didn't want to fight with Tom; what would be the point in that? There was no reason to argue, she had made her decision and all of this just cemented her belief that she'd made the right one.

"I'm sorry, I really am. But I'm leaving, I'm going upstairs to pack my stuff and then I'm going to leave."

Tom snorted again.

"You'll be back, and I'm warning you, El, when you come crawling and begging, I'll just laugh in your face and slam the door shut. If you go, that's it. You're never coming back."

She looked at Tom, hardly able to believe how he could change so much in such a short space of time. It was as if for the first time she could see him for who he really was.

She began to make her way upstairs. She would pack her clothes in the two suitcases she owned and carry whatever else she could. She knew deep down that Tom would make getting anything she left behind almost impossible, so she resolved to take absolutely everything she could with her. He was so difficult if he didn't get his own way; she'd witnessed it before but never had had to deal with it on this scale. She rolled her eyes at herself. The fact that she'd never dealt with Tom like this spoke volumes; she'd never stood up to him, never put her foot down and never really had a say in anything that they had ever done.

Elodie pushed open the door to what had been their bedroom: the light in there suddenly seemed flat and pallid. She had to do a double-take as she saw Christie and Al asleep in her bed. Between them lay another woman, someone Elodie had never seen before. She had a sneaking suspicion that this mystery woman's name would be Tina, the woman Christie and Mimi were so intent on setting Tom up with. Elodie thought about waking them, about kicking them out and screaming at them as they left. But she knew that doing that wouldn't make her feel any better; in fact, it would probably make her feel a whole lot worse. She took a deep breath and then, as quietly as she could, began to pack her belongings.

Elodie was amazed at how little she actually owned. There was a time when her wardrobe had been fit to burst, packed with going out dresses, smart jeans and a plethora of tops for any occasion. Her wardrobe had certainly become more streamlined as she'd gotten older. She realised, as she went through her remaining clothes piece by piece, that it had actually been Tom who had encouraged her to strip back her style. He had often made her change before nights out, insisting that she was showing a bit too much flesh and justifying it by telling her it was only because he worried about her, or because he loved her, that she should change. The more Elodie thought about this, the more she realised that Tom had been an over-ruling force in her life and the more secure she felt about leaving.

Elodie had expected Tom to follow her up the stairs; maybe not straight away, he was far more likely to sulk for a bit first. But he never showed and when she went downstairs with two large suitcases and an over-filled backpack she found that he was asleep again. His mouth was partially open and emitting faint rattling snores every few seconds. She took a moment to look at him: she knew this was it. She tried to muster some sort of emotion towards Tom, knowing that if she had to force herself to feel something, that if there were no feelings there at all, then she had done the right thing. She felt satisfied that she had everything she needed to start afresh. She took out her keys and carefully slid her house key off the chain. She set it down on the tall occasional table by the door, the thud it made as she set it down sounding very final. She took one last glance around the room and had to smile to herself. Tom would finally get a taste of what it was like to be her when he had to clear up all this mess.

Just as she turned to leave something caught her eye: her pastel patchwork throw. She bolted over to it and swept it up in her arms, not able to believe she had almost left it behind. She buried her face in it and basked in its familiar comfort. She felt tears begin to prick her eyes but blinked them back: she wouldn't cry, especially not here. Steeling herself, she folded the blanket up and turned to Tom.

"Tom, this is it," she said in a small voice.

Tom lifted his head, not quite fast asleep after all, and glared at her.

"You're jacking us in because I booked us a holiday, you

know that, right? You know you'll be sorry, don't you, you spoiled princess?" he said flatly.

"And this is why this is right, it's because you think things like that. You can't see the bigger picture, Tom, and that's not your fault, it doesn't make you bad, it just makes you... you."

Elodie gave him what she hoped was a caring smile and made her way to the door. She slid the backpack over one shoulder and picked up the suitcases before turning to say goodbye. Tom was glaring at her, a nasty sneering look on his face now. Elodie wasn't surprised. He was a man running out of options and, given his previous comments, Elodie had already braced herself for a little more nastiness and a little less understanding.

"Go on then, off you fuck. Go running to your idiot friends just like you did last night when things weren't perfect for you. Bet they've told you to do this. That's it, isn't it? This is all them," he exclaimed, clearly clutching at straws. "The snob and the weirdo want you to be single. It's because that wannabe can't get a boyfriend, she's sad and lonely and wants you to be the same. She's pathetic, they both are."

Elodie didn't need to listen to this. She could take the snide comments aimed at her, but Steph and Carla had done nothing wrong. They were good people who didn't deserve to be spoken about like that. Shaking her head sadly, she turned back to the door and pulled it towards her. The fresh air swept in and Elodie revelled in how nice it was. She walked through the door and, dragging her belongings behind her, stepped into her future.

CHAPTER 6

THE WEEKEND WAS OVER FAR TOO QUICKLY FOR Elodie's liking. She was supposed to work on Sunday, but given recent events managed to trade shifts with one of the other staff members at Betty's. All in all, there were eight of them that worked there. Elodie rarely, if ever, worked with the others; Steph always seemed to work the rota to their advantage which meant that the three friends got to see a lot of each other and that work rarely seemed like work, no matter how busy they got. Despite this fact, Elodie couldn't bring herself to don a smile all day and pretend like nothing was wrong. She was feeling very up and down so falsifying her mood would definitely have been an unmanageable task, one that would have surely backfired and resulted in the customers getting a side of tears with their slice of cake. She wasn't regretting her decision, she knew she'd done the right thing but still, it was the end of an era and knowing her life was to change irrevocably filled her with an odd unsettled feeling that she couldn't quite shake. Instead, she had spent the day unpacking and making her new room her own.

Elodie was amazed at how quickly she felt at home in Carla's flat and by the following weekend felt as though she'd properly settled in. There was one, disconcerting, niggling thing that Elodie just couldn't shake. She couldn't fathom why, after over a week since their breakup, she hadn't heard from Tom. Not so much as even a text message. It wasn't that she wanted him to contact her – a clean break was what they both needed – but something just didn't feel right about it.

Elodie unpacked. She hung up her clothes and arranged

her few belongings in an effort to make her room feel homely. Elodie had arranged a couple of photos in frames on her windowsill, placed her small cream leather jewellery box on her dressing table along with her makeup collection, which she had neatly arranged. She had laid her patchwork quilt over the end of her bed, deciding that now she was master of her own destiny it would take centre stage. She had bought a giant canvas print of a painting of swirling, foaming waters. Although the subject was frenzied the colours calmed her; the teal green, periwinkle and powder white soothed her. It was the first piece of décor she'd ever bought and successfully managed to showcase. Her mind flitted back to Tom again. He would never have let her put anything like this up; if it wasn't an action film poster or something to do with cars then it wasn't going up. Elodie took a step back to admire her handiwork as well as the painting itself. She couldn't remember the last time she'd done a spot of DIY. Then it dawned on her: she never had. It had always been done for her. It felt nice to be in control of her life for once, even if that control was over something as small as hanging a picture on a wall.

Carla's flat was auspiciously well placed: it was situated on the top floor of an old Victorian building on a quiet residential street. Carla always told people she lived in Camden, but in reality, the flat was closer to the less cool and quirky, but still very lovely Finchley Road. Elodie padded from her bedroom and into the living area-cum-kitchen diner and surveyed the room. The flat was very bright and airy, open plan and had an incredibly calm ambience to it. The walls were all painted a crisp white and reflected the light that streamed in from the French doors. These led out onto a small, secluded terrace area, which enjoyed far-stretching city views. Carla had decorated the place with bright bold prints which adorned the walls; brightly coloured cushions were scattered around the place and a large zebra-stripe rug covered most of the wooden floor.

Elodie checked her phone for what seemed like the millionth time that day. She hadn't heard from Tom at all, he hadn't phoned, text or emailed: she had heard nothing. She slipped the phone back into her back pocket and decided that a cup of coffee on the terrace would be just the tonic she needed. Elodie wanted to do some serious thinking and she could think of no better place.

Elodie pulled out one of the bistro chairs and sat down. The days were getting warmer now, so much so that Elodie didn't even need a cardigan. She let her head fall back and enjoyed the sun as it beat down on her face. Elodie let out a long, contented sigh and vowed to herself that the first thing she would do, once she had a proper job sorted and some money, would be to book a holiday for herself. She knew she wouldn't be able to afford the five-star, far-flung getaway she dreamt of but that wouldn't stop her: who said you couldn't see the world on a budget? A little thrill of excitement sparked within as another realisation dawned on her. She would be able to go wherever she wanted, whenever she wanted, with whomever she chose. She wished she'd remembered to take her travel magazines with her, she hadn't even remembered one. The magazines came every single month; the subscription had been a gift from Tom's parents. Elodie thought now that maybe he'd asked them to do it by way of indirectly appeasing her. She wouldn't be able to get them now, she needed to save every penny she could and there was no way Tom, or his parents for that matter, would go as far as to redirect her mail.

Elodie's phone began to vibrate in her back pocket. She removed it and looked at the screen. Her hand froze mere inches from her face as she saw the name 'Tom' flash up on the screen. Feeling her heartbeat quicken she set the phone down on the table in front of her: it continued to buzz. Now Tom was actually calling her, she realised that she didn't need closure. She didn't actually want to speak to him, all she wanted was a fresh, clean start. Silence. The phone had stopped, she'd left it too long to answer. She knew Tom wouldn't leave a message; he would see that as failure. As if her mind had been read, his name began flashing on the screen again, accompanied by the loud, insatiable buzzing that only pressing the answer key could satisfy. She picked up the phone and stared at it for a moment, wondering if maybe Tom was really suffering; maybe he hadn't called before now because he just couldn't. Suddenly Elodie felt extremely bad about everything and knew that the only way to make herself feel better was to speak to him.

"Hello Tom," she said, surprised but somewhat comforted by the natural joviality of her tone, "are you alright?"

"You mean aside from being chucked, do you?" he replied bluntly, Elodie didn't reply, the only sound between them for a few moments was the faint static of the phone call. "Look, I didn't ring to have a go, I didn't want to ring at all, but I had to."

"I understand," Elodie said reassuringly, "I know it's tough Tom, but you'll see in the long run that it's far the best. I'll always care about you, you know that, right?"

Tom let out a cynical laugh that was more akin to a bark than to anything else.

"You think a lot of yourself, do you know *that*?" he said. "I had to ring you, the washing hasn't been done and I'm out of clean pants. Look, the machine's playing up. It says 'CL' something on the screen, what's that mean?"

Elodie rolled her eyes internally. *'So this is what closure feels like.'*

"Ha," she managed a dry chuckle. "It's the child lock, Tom, you need to turn the child lock off." She could hear the words coming out of her mouth, but they seemed distant and alien.

"OK, how do I do that?"

Elodie was amazed. What kind of person acted like this? They had broken up only days ago and here he was ringing for washing machine instructions. She didn't know whether to laugh or cry; instead, she decided on neither. All this did was strengthen her belief that Tom was a user and she was his little housewife whose only purpose in life was to make sure he was catered for, look good on his arm when he needed her to and not make a fuss. She decided then and there, that for the second time in her life, she wasn't going to let him walk all over her.

"I don't know, Tom, look in the book or something. I need to go."

"Ha! Busy, are you?" he mocked. "Got some coffee that needs pouring or cake that needs cutting? Fine, don't help me then. Not like you ever did anyway. I'll get my mum to do it."

Elodie rolled her eyes, this time outwardly.

"I'm going Tom, please don't call me again, I'm not your assistant anymore," she said, with a far more forceful tone than she had ever mustered before. She hung up the phone, her hands shaking slightly, then scrolled to Tom's name and hit 'block caller'. She didn't want a repetition of that phone call any time soon. The conversation had annoyed her, but it had also given her strength. She knew at that precise moment that she was exactly where she needed to be; she just needed to figure out *what* she wanted to be as well.

Elodie was deep in thought when she heard the door open. She could have been anywhere in the world and she still would have known it was Carla emerging into the room. She was a whirlwind of chaos sometimes. Elodie heard her drop her bag, swear, then kick off her shoes and head straight to the kitchen. A few moments later she appeared on the balcony, with two glasses of blush wine, a box of chocolates and a sincere expression on her face.

"Thought you could use some cheering up," she offered kindly, holding out a wine glass for Elodie to take.

"Ahhhh, you really shouldn't have. I'm totally fine," Elodie said. Although fine, she still held out her hand to take the inviting-looking, rose-coloured liquid from her friend. There was something about a sunny day that lent itself very well to an ice-cool alcoholic beverage.

"Well you won't need this then, will you?" Carla said jokingly and withdrew her hand, causing Elodie to reach out a little further and almost topple off her chair. Laughing, she righted herself and stuck out her hand in a mock-brattish fashion that made Carla grin from ear to ear. Carla handed the glass over, dropped the box of chocolates into Elodie's lap and plonked herself down in the spare chair opposite Elodie.

"He phoned me today," Elodie said after taking a sip of crisp cool wine. The taste filled her senses, it was delicious and so very refreshing.

"And?" Carla asked, staring at her friend.

"That's it, really. I didn't answer at first, I thought, 'This is it, we're going to have a massive talk, there'll be tears', etcetera, but no. Do you know what the git wanted? He couldn't work the washing machine. What a shit, eh?" Elodie ranted.

"He is a git, El. But do you know what? He's not your git anymore. So try not to worry."

"I am worried, though. What if I *have* made the wrong decision? We did have some great times, you know, we had fun. When I look back, it's really only the last few months or so when things have changed."

"Elodie, it's okay to look back occasionally, but the trick is to glance and not stare. This is totally normal after a breakup, but you've got to move on. I know it's easier said than done but 'fake it till you make it' and all that. Keep your head up, be strong, fake a smile and eventually you'll have moved on. You've got yourself to concentrate on now. So how about we look forward instead? Have you had any idea about what you're going to do yet?" Carla asked sincerely.

Elodie scowled; she was still completely clueless on that front. She needed more time, a lot more.

"I'm kind of going to hope that it just comes to me," she offered optimistically.

"Hope isn't a valid plan, El," Carla said combatively. "Why don't we get a pen and paper and write some stuff down? It'll seem like less of a daunting task once you've got it out of your head and in the open."

Carla stood up and disappeared back into the flat only to reappear moments later clutching a pen and notepad. She handed them over to Elodie who opened the pad up and, pen poised, began to write. After several minutes of silence, Carla leaned over to take a look at Elodie's ponderings. The paper contained several bullet points, a list of Elodie's past jobs and underneath a wish-list of dream career paths. Carla's brow furrowed: amongst her friend's best-case scenario career choices was 'millionaire, travel writer and film star'.

"I know what you're thinking," Elodie said, "I can feel it. Look, I'm not being serious, well not entirely. That bit's just a joke," she finished, gesturing to her dream job list.

"You've got to get serious, El, time's running out. Dora's rent is paid up until the end of the month, that's two weeks away. I can cover for a bit, but I'm worried for you. You won't be happy staying at Betty's forever. We all know you love it there but it's not your forever job, is it?" Carla said firmly.

"I thought you said I was an early bloomer next to J.K Rowling and Kristin Wiig?" Elodie argued glumly. She felt Carla's hand rest on her shoulder and give it a little squeeze.

"I don't want to upset you, El, far from it. I just want you to be happy and I think that long-term happiness might mean some short-term decision-making."

Elodie nodded. She knew Carla was right, but it was so easy for her. She had rich parents who helped her out a lot. She was fine part-time waitressing and part-time modelling; she didn't have to make any hard, life-changing decisions. Elodie reached for the chocolates and shoved two in her mouth, she chewed furiously, taking out what she knew was ill-felt annoyance on the caramels instead of her friend.

The two women sat in relative silence for quite some time. They sipped their wine and took it in turns taking chocolates out of the box. The only sounds breaking the stony quiet were the odd aeroplane in the sky or siren on the ground. Eventually, Carla got up from her chair. She finished the dregs of her wine and walked inside, leaving Elodie sat on the balcony. Elodie sat there for quite some time, lost in thought. She was brought to her senses by a sudden chill in the air: the sun had dipped behind a nearby building, which resulted in an almost immediate wintry feel. This made the hairs on Elodie's skin stand to attention. She rubbed her forearms and, picking up the box of chocolates and her now empty glass of wine, went inside to join Carla.

The doorbell sounded loudly; grudgingly, Elodie arose from her bed to answer it. She had spent the last hour on Carla's laptop taking careers quizzes to try and get some idea to what she'd be most suited to. Carla had been in the bathroom for almost the entire time Elodie had spent online. Elodie heard her periodically belting out whichever song happened to be running through her mind at that particular point in time: so far she'd been privy to a rendition of 'How do I live without you?', a version of 'I will always love you' and finally an enthusiastic performance of 'Un-break my heart'.

'What the hell is she trying to do to me?' Elodie mused as Carla started belting out yet another sad song. She padded her way through the living room and to the front door. Stood in the doorway with a bunch of flowers and a smile was Steph. Elodie was overjoyed to see her. She'd spent a lot of time on her own over the last few days and even though she'd needed that time to reflect and re-engage with herself, it was still more than nice to see one of her closest friends there.

"Carla texted me," Steph said as if by way of explanation. "I thought you might like these?" She extended the brightly coloured flowers and Elodie accepted them gratefully.

"She told you about Tom, then?" Elodie asked, stepping to the side to let Steph in.

"He's a dick," she offered, smiling. "Let's not dwell on him, it's you I want to talk about."

Elodie should have known. Carla didn't like playing both good cop and bad cop at the same time, she needed back-up; and who better to have by her side than Steph?

"Ugh, not you too. I don't know what I'm going to do, I've done career questionnaires online and I'm basically unqualified for everything," she said dejectedly.

"So qualify for something then. Pick something you want to do, something that interests you and work towards it. Careers don't just happen overnight, you've got to work for them."

"That's rich, coming from the woman who's been given a business on a silver platter," Elodie said, sarcasm dripping from every syllable.

Steph looked affronted for a split-second, then ran her fingers through her long, flame-red hair and sighed.

"I'm going to let that one slide because you've had a rough couple of weeks, but a rough couple of weeks doesn't give you the right to be a bitch. I only want the best for you, and you should want that too," Steph reprimanded.

Elodie, feeling rather sorry for herself, cast a downward glance, more out of embarrassment than anything else. She knew Steph was right, it was just a difficult juncture for

her and a little bit of not-so-tough love would be appreci-
ated. She was saved from having to apologise by Carla who
emerged from the bathroom in a cloud of steam, which bil-
lowed out after her in silvery wisps, making her look almost
angelic.

"Ahhhh, you made it," she said gleefully, walking past
them towards her bedroom. "I'll just be a sec, there's more
wine in the fridge if you want it?" she said, calling over her
shoulder as she closed the door behind her.

Elodie, although not a big drinker, thought that another
glass of wine might be a good idea. She felt very much as
though she needed a bit of liquid lubrication to relax her a
little.

"You sit down, I'll get it," Steph said before Elodie had a
chance to play host.

Moments later the three women were settled, Carla now
clad in a fluffy white bathrobe, which bore the words 'Drama
Queen' in beads on the back. They talked and talked; they
had known each other for such a long time now that their
conversations, if overheard, would make very little sense to
anyone else. They seemed to be able to follow one another's train of thought and regularly managed to cover more
than one topic at a time. Elodie had missed this. If her time
with Tom had taught her anything, it was that if your man
encouraged you to neglect your friendships then he wasn't
the right man for you.

It wasn't long before Carla and Steph managed to turn the
conversation back around to Elodie and her troubles. She
knew that if it were the other way around and they were in
her position that she would be doing exactly the same thing,
and as annoying and uncomfortable as it was to have to put
yourself under the microscope, Elodie also knew that it was
the only way to move onwards and upwards.

"So let's have a look at your career results, then," Carla
said, reaching over and grabbing the laptop, which had been
placed back underneath the coffee table where it belonged.
"Elodie!" she scolded when she opened the laptop and saw
that the last website Elodie had been on was a fashion outlet.

"What?" Elodie said sheepishly. "I literally have no decent
clothes!"

Steph gave her a reprimanding look and told her that there would be plenty of time for shopping when she had a job, and the money to fund extravagant shopping trips. Elodie rolled her eyes and turned to Carla for support; Steph was always so sensible. Sadly for Elodie, Carla was not on her side but added that until she could afford a whole new wardrobe of her own she could borrow whatever she liked for as long as she liked. This cheered Elodie up somewhat, she settled on the fact that this compromise was actually the best of both worlds: technically a brand-new wardrobe without a brand-new credit card.

Elodie watched as Carla opened up the website which showed the results of the careers she'd be best suited to. The careers website had offered Elodie a choice of three 'perfect' careers: hospitality manager, customer service rep or tourism advisor. Carla rolled her eyes in anticipation of Elodie's reaction.

"Let me guess, you don't want to do any of these?" she said knowingly.

Elodie nodded and took a deep drink of the wine.

"I know it sounds silly, but I want to do something that isn't serving other people. I mean, I like that, it comes naturally to me you know the whole waitressing thing but if I'm going to it I don't want to be stuck in one place. I'm young, I want to either have a job so well paid that I can take luxury holidays whenever I like." All three of them shared a look that said that they knew that probably wasn't going to happen. "Or… I want to do something that allows for a bit of travelling."

"Why don't you just go travelling, then?" Carla proposed. "You know, just pack a bag, go see all the things you're desperate to see and have no regrets about it?"

Elodie had thought of this. She would have loved to be able to go and do that. The only problem was, as it was for most people who dreamt of seeing the world, that she didn't have the money.

"Because going travelling is expensive. I already looked into it when I thought it'd be something Tom and I might do." She paused. Sadness had crept into her voice but she didn't want this evening to be ruined by the ghost of her relationship with Tom, so she pressed on. "It's incredibly expensive. It's a nice idea but that's all it'll ever be for me," Elodie finished resolutely. She cast a downward glance at her friends: both of them were looking at her sympathetically.

"OK, so maybe you need a bit more time. Maybe do a spot more research on all the different jobs out there. I could do you a spreadsheet?" Steph suggested helpfully.

Elodie smiled and thanked her friend, fearing that she would need a little more help than a spreadsheet to get her through. She groaned and rubbed her shoulder. She was already beginning to feel stressed by this. Carla leaned over and gave her friend a little squeeze.

"Until then, though, you need to let your hair down. You're too tightly wound at the moment, El, I can practically see the tension, you're tighter than my Spanx were after last year's Christmas dinner," Carla said, laughing.

"Well…" Elodie trailed off, "we could have that girls' night out, you know I'd love that. What's everyone's plans this weekend?"

"Working," both Carla and Steph replied in unison.

Elodie's face fell. She had completely forgotten; she was meant to be working, too. *'There goes that idea, then,'* she thought sadly.

"Let me see what I can do, I'll phone Mum and ask her if we can swap. That reminds me, speaking of mums…" Steph said, trailing off and fixing Elodie with a dogged expression.

Elodie knew exactly what Steph was getting at. She wanted to know if Elodie's parents knew about the break-up yet. Elodie had put off telling them, not wanting to upset them or to be upset herself by their reaction. Finally, she had talked herself into calling. They had taken the news as well as could be expected: her mum asked if she'd done the right thing, alluded to the fact that she should have stayed with Tom because of his prospects but finally had come to see that Elodie needed more than someone else's prospects to make her happy.

"I phoned her already, she took it as well as could be expected," Elodie answered.

Steph looked her up and down and, when satisfied that her friend was telling the truth, gave a small nod and smiled.

"See, I knew it wasn't worth getting worked up over. They're your parents, El, they just want what's best for you." Steph added.

"What's best for my bank balance, more like," Elodie said gloomily.

The three women shared a knowing look and Carla pretended to play a very small, very sad violin before bursting into a fit of giggles. Elodie couldn't stay forlorn for long with these two around.

"So that's settled then, parents know, we're off the hook work-wise and we're going *out* out," Carla cried happily. "I know, let's choose your outfit," she finished, jumping up from the sofa and darting into her bedroom as if she were running a race and the starting gun had just sounded. Moments later she materialised with swathes of material in hand, she must have been holding at least a dozen different outfits. She thrust them towards Elodie who took them gladly. She placed them on the seat next to her and rifled through the pile outfit by outfit.

"Don't just hold them up, go put them on," Steph encouraged.

Elodie cast a permission-seeking look in Carla's direction but she needn't have bothered. Carla was already nodding vigorously at Steph's suggestion and pointed towards Elodie's new bedroom.

"Go on then, try everything on, I want to see it all," Carla said enthusiastically as she plugged her phone into her speaker and pressed play. Music filled every corner of the flat as Elodie scooped up the clothes, gave her friends an excited look and disappeared into her bedroom, ready to debut in what seemed to be her first-ever fashion show.

Outfit by outfit came and went. Elodie was average height with an average build and an average dress sense, so some of Carla's more risqué outfits were fun to try on in the privacy of her own home but weren't something she'd ever dream of wearing in public, not unless she wanted to be slapped with a public indecency order. Her particular favourite was a pair of high waisted dark denim shorts, which Carla had teamed with a baggy white T-shirt which read 'Kanye not' on it and a pair of black, heeled gladiator sandals, whose laces reached all the way to the middle of her thighs. When she had emerged wearing that particular outfit it had been a firm no from Steph but an avid yes from Carla.

After what seemed like the one hundredth outfit change of the evening, Elodie emerged in one outfit that had both of her friends giving a sure and excited thumbs-up. It was a red, panelled dress that was less form-fitting and more figure-hugging. Normally not one to have both legs and cleavage on show, this type of dress would have been something that Elodie would have skipped straight past on the clothes rail. Surprisingly, though, she felt extremely comfortable in it. She surveyed her reflection in the full-length mirror hanging on the back of her bedroom door and thanked the heavens that Carla was so generous. Her long, chocolate-coloured hair tumbled over her shoulders. Elodie knew that with a bit of Carla's expert teasing and tousling she could really look her best. She stood on her tiptoes to try and get an idea of what it would feel like to wear this dress with a pair of heels. Elodie was excited and happily realised that part of that was down to the fact that she felt more daring and far sexier than she had felt in a very long time. She brushed the silky material of the dress downwards and admired how the luxurious fabric felt across her skin. When she had finally entered the living room, both of her friends clapped their hands to their faces in amazement. Carla thought that it so looked so good on Elodie that she insisted Elodie keep it.

"It looks so much better on you than it ever did on me, you should keep it. Consider it a welcome gift." Carla said.

Elodie accepted the dress graciously, so pleased with the gesture that she hadn't even managed to put up the pretence that she couldn't possibly accept such a generous gift. Elodie wasn't surprised to learn that the dress's only outing in life had been to meet a man for cocktails. Carla's date had ended unceremoniously after the guy who arrived to meet her was about twice the weight and three times the age of his online pictures. Carla had been unable to hide her disdain; she had told him straight that she should sue for false representation and given him a withering look before sauntering off. Other than that, Elodie's beautiful new dress had spent its entire life hanging up amongst the rest of Carla's extensive wardrobe.

With her outfit sorted for their night out, Elodie slipped off the dress and into a pair of jogging bottoms and a baggy T-shirt and went to re-join her friends who were now deciding on a film to watch. She stood in the doorway for just a moment, surveying the sight in front of her: if she had been told that this would be her life a month ago, she would have found it hard to believe it.

'It's amazing how your life can change so quickly,' she thought, realising that as horrible as the last couple of weeks had been, if she could get her professional life sorted then she was sure her personal life would just fall into place.

"*Pretty Woman* or *Dirty Dancing*?" Carla asked, pointing to the television. "We can't decide."

"I haven't seen either," Elodie confessed. The reaction of her friends was extreme, to say the least: if there had been someone on the outside looking in, they would have been forgiven for thinking that Elodie had just admitted to the crime of the century.

"I can almost forgive *Dirty Dancing*," Steph admonished, "but *Pretty Woman*! What's wrong with you?"

Elodie laughed and shrugged her shoulders, unsure how to answer that particular question without sounding like a repressed housewife.

"Tom just didn't like those sorts of films, I have however seen every Jason Statham movie and all those car ones too," she offered hopefully.

"It's taking all my will-power not to tit-punch you right now," Carla said, a little too seriously for Elodie's liking. She placed her arms over her chest protectively and looked to Steph for support.

"I'm with her, I'm afraid," Steph said in a matter-of-fact tone. "Well, that settles it, then: we're just going to have to watch both."

Steph grabbed the remote control from Carla and pressed 'play'. Elodie watched the first film, *Pretty Woman*, with great interest: everything about it captured attention. She couldn't believe she had gone her entire life without ever having witnessing Vivian and Edward's love story. The film finished far too soon for Elodie's liking and as the credits rolled she turned to her friends with a huge grin on her face.

"Now that was amazing," she gushed, rubbing her eyes sleepily. "I don't think I can stay up for another one, though. Sorry, ladies, but I need my bed." Elodie hauled herself from the sofa from where she'd been so nicely snuggled and gave each of them a hug goodnight.

"You're coming into work tomorrow, aren't you?" Steph asked before Elodie disappeared into her bedroom.

Elodie nodded. She would have to go back to reality at some point and if she were honest with herself, she'd probably already taken more days off than she actually needed. She had recovered from her ordeal with Tom enough to go back to work. The phone call she'd taken from him today had just been one more thing in a very long list of reasons as to why she had ended things.

Elodie yawned and stretched as she sank sleepily into the plump feather bedding. She drifted off to sleep almost instantly, vowing that the next person she allowed herself to be with would look after her as much as she looked after them. *'I need my very own Edward Lewis,'* she thought to herself before slipping into a deep sleep that thankfully went undisturbed for the entirety of the night.

Friday was an uneventful day for Elodie. It was just she and Betty running the café. Normally two staff members wouldn't be enough, but Elodie and Betty had their roles down to a fine art and could manage well enough without the need for an extra pair of hands. The café saw a steady flow of customers from the moment they opened until the moment the doors closed, Elodie didn't seem to have two minutes to herself, which suited her down to the ground. Despite getting a very good night's sleep she had woken up feeling a little out of sorts; she couldn't put her finger on it, there was genuinely nothing wrong. Perhaps it was the big question-mark about her future career that seemed to be following her like a threatening rain cloud. She just needed a bit more time: if she could buy herself a few more weeks, then things would all work out perfectly, she was sure of it.

"Excuse me," an unfamiliar voice beckoned, "could I get some more coffee, please?"

Elodie looked over and saw a handsome gentleman holding up his mug in anticipation. She offered him a smile and nodded, marginally mortified that she hadn't noticed him before. The end of the day drew nearer and before Elodie knew it she was wiping down tables, turning the open sign to closed and rearranging the books so that they were in their proper order. She stood back and admired her handiwork. The bookshelf looked immaculate and she knew that when Steph opened up the following morning she would be impressed. Betty had bid Elodie a fond farewell about an hour before they closed. Elodie had a great affection for Betty, who always seemed to be able to say and do exactly the right thing. She treated all the girls well, especially the two best friends of her daughter. Betty often joked that sometimes it felt as though she had three kids instead of just the one.

True to her word, Steph had managed to re-arrange their shifts over the weekend. They now had a full twenty-four hours to do exactly what they wanted. Elodie was looking forward to really letting her hair down: she couldn't remember the last night out she'd had that didn't involve putting up with people who didn't really like her. They had their weekend planned and had opted to go out on the Saturday evening. They would watch the film they'd missed on the Friday, spend the day together on Saturday, get ready, then hit the town. Carla seemed to know a lot of people and had managed to get them VIP entry to one of the most exclusive bars around. Elodie felt excitement bubble inside her as she locked up the café and headed back home to her new flat with a spring in each and every one of her steps.

Elodie called as she pushed open the flat door of 12a Fitzjohns Avenue, also known as home. There was no sign of Carla; instead, she found a note on the table, which read...

Hey little one,
    Sorry I'm not home, I got a callback. I didn't mention it before, didn't want to jinx it! Keep your fingers, toes and everything else crossed for me, gonna need all the luck I

can get. Don't know what time I'll be back so don't wait up, we'll have to do film night another time. I've phoned Steph and told her so she's not coming over now, hope that's OK – help yourself to the popcorn I bought! There's also a couple of mags on the side, help yourself bitch.

Big love, C x

Elodie smiled as she read the note, although she couldn't help but feel a bitter little sting that they wouldn't be having their film night. Elodie hoped against hope that Carla got it. Although beautiful, Carla didn't exactly fit the standard stereotype of most models: she wasn't exactly the tallest model out there and her look wasn't exactly what you would call 'industry standard'. This had never deterred her, though. She had been to as many castings as she could, visited agencies and really put herself out there. It had taken Carla over a year to get someone to sign her but eventually a small agency who represented some unique models had taken her on. Carla wasn't about to grace the front cover of *Vogue* any time soon, but Elodie was still immensely proud of her persistence and dedication nonetheless. Carla believed in herself to the nth degree and regardless of how many knock-backs she got she always picked herself up, dusted herself off and tried again. Elodie vowed to take a leaf out of Carla's book. She couldn't stay at Betty's forever, regardless of how much she loved the place. She would have to take inspiration from her friend: persistence and dedication would, from now on, be a mantra she would live by.

Elodie opened the fridge door and stared at its contents for the tenth time that evening. Sadly, nothing in there had changed. There was still the same lump of cheese, iceberg lettuce, half dozen eggs and half-drunk carton of orange juice. She closed the door and told herself that she wasn't even hungry anyway, especially since she'd eaten the entire bag of popcorn that Carla had left in one go. Once she started, she couldn't stop. She absolutely loved sweet popcorn, but Tom had always preferred salted, which meant she was rarely able to enjoy it. She'd popped the last piece in her mouth an hour previously and since then had done little but wander about the flat aimlessly, flick through the Friday night TV and open and close the fridge door over and over again. She knew popcorn wasn't exactly a balanced meal but she was young, free and single now and she'd do exactly what she wanted, when she wanted. This was a strange mentality to get used to: no longer having to check every little thing was incredibly liberating, and she revelled in being her own woman.

She lazily flicked through Carla's fashion magazines. One was awful: it was essentially an overpriced clothing cata- logue, broken up by the occasional advert for perfume. The other one wasn't too bad. It had more articles and even a piece on traditional Japanese fashion that Elodie found very interesting. It showed a factory which had been producing fine silks for over two hundred years that Elodie would have loved to visit. She carefully tore out the page; she would add it to her personalised travel guide later on.

As Friday night drew to a close, Elodie took a moment in the quiet calm of the flat to reflect on all that she had been through in the last couple of weeks. She felt as though a weight had been lifted. Without even realising it, she had been bound in a relationship that wasn't healthy; she could see that now and vowed never to settle for something like that again. She'd taken all the positives, such as financial freedom, the security of having a partner and the little buzz she got from slipping the words 'my boyfriend' into sen- tences with strangers, and used them as a mask, shielding herself from all the negatives. She had been blind, willingly blind. When others had tried to open her eyes she had just squeezed them tighter, happy to live in ignorant bliss, no matter what the long-term ramifications would be. She was just grateful that her friends hadn't given up on her. It would have been far easier for them to let her lie in the bed she had made, but no. Instead, they had been there every step of the way, offering advice when necessary and a shoul- der to cry on when needed. Elodie retired to her bedroom, determined that this would be the evening where she would get some reading done. Despite knowing that she needed to save every penny for things like rent and food, Elodie had decided that a mail redirection service was an absolute necessity and, in her opinion, money very well spent. She settled down onto her bed, a hot chocolate on her nightstand and a brand-new travel magazine in her hands. She flipped through the magazine lazily; given her new status in life, the places featured seemed even further out of reach. She sighed and closed the magazine, dropping it onto the floor next to her bed. It fell with a dull thud; the sound was accompanied by the flick of a light switch, which was followed by darkness. The evening hadn't been the festival of fun that she had imagined. A little niggle of disappointment flared as she closed her eyes. *'Here's hoping that tomorrow makes up for it,'* she thought to herself as she drifted off to sleep.

Elodie awoke the following morning bright and early and was pleased to see that not a trace of the disappointment she had felt the following evening had made it through the night. Instead, she now felt a renewed freshness and excitement – tonight was the night. She padded into the living room and was greeted by a very energetic Carla who seemed to be positively glowing; a golden radiance appeared to pulse around her.

"You're in a good mood," Elodie croaked. Her first words of the morning sounded dry and cracked.

Carla turned to her, smiled and handed her a large mug of steaming coffee, which Elodie took gratefully.

"I got the job, you're looking at the new face of, these!" Carla said, holding up a pair of trainers with a grin on her face so wide that it looked as though she'd grown half a dozen extra teeth overnight.

"That's amazing!" Elodie exclaimed, the hoarseness from her voice vanishing to make way for the utter joy that she felt for her friend. "But how are you the 'face' of trainers?"

"Well, I'm the feet of them, but that doesn't sound as good," Carla replied, laughing.

Elodie gave her friend a huge, bear-like hug and rocked her back and forth.

"Well, it sounds just as good to me. This is amazing, Carla – your first proper job. We should celebrate tonight, let's forget the cocktails and go straight for Champagne."

Carla gave Elodie a look that was impossible to mistake.

"We'll stick to cocktails, they're on offer until eleven and

I think given the fact that I haven't been paid for the job yet and you're on a saving spree we probably shouldn't go mad tonight," Carla said, doing a very good impression of Steph's 'I know best' voice.

Elodie burst into fits of giggles. Even though she knew Carla wasn't one hundred per cent serious, she couldn't escape the fact that there was an element of truth to her words.

"Wanna take them for a spin?" Carla asked, clapping the pink and black running shoes together excitedly.

"I don't have any trainers," Elodie said, realising that somewhere back at her old house there was a seldom-used gym bag, probably containing unwashed shorts, an old water bottle and some old trainers.

"You don't need any, I got you a pair too. You're a size five, right?"

Elodie nodded, then noticing the second shoebox on the kitchen counter, squealed with excitement.

"Thank you," she said, tearing into the box and admiring her own pair. Her trainers weren't pink and black like Carla's but instead were a lovely shade of dark blue and silver. "But next time, do you think you could get a job working with Richard Branson instead? I could do with a week or three on Necker Island more than these trainers."

"Cheeky bitch," Carla said, throwing one of her shoes across the room towards Elodie.

Elodie ducked and the shoe hit the wall behind her. Both women fell about laughing. Once they'd calmed down sufficiently to speak again they decided that their plan of attack would be to finish their morning drinks, get changed and go for a nice jog in the park. They had the whole day to kill. Steph was set to arrive mid-afternoon; even though she'd covered their shifts she still wanted to put in an appearance. Steph, being the straight and narrow kind of girl that she was, wouldn't want other staff members to think that she was taking liberties; that kind of thing just never sat right with her. She'd once said that "Nepotism is one of the biggest crimes of the twentieth century." Elodie smiled as she remembered whole-heartedly agreeing with her, and then when Steph had left having to look on the internet to see what 'nepotism' actually was.

Elodie was looking forward to getting out and doing some exercise; she couldn't remember the last time she'd broken into a sweat. She had, in the past, suggested to Tom that they should take up some kind of sport together. This suggestion had been met with an incredulous stare and the comment: *'And I suppose you're going to pay for this, then?'* That had been the last time Elodie had made such a suggestion.

"You ready?" Carla called into Elodie's bedroom.

Elodie called back that she was and took a second to check her reflection in the mirror. She felt like such a charity case at the moment; she was destined to spend the day in other people's clothes. Carla had lent her a pair of grey gym shorts and a navy t-shirt that was about three sizes too big, although she was going for a run in the park and not on the runway, after all.

Elodie was still unfamiliar with the area surrounding her new home so tried to take as much as possible of it in whilst they were out on their jog. Carla had decided that they would run towards Camden, enjoy a little jaunt along the canal and then head back after an hour or so. Elodie, having the physical fitness level of a heavily pregnant hippopotamus, thought that an hour's run sounded incredibly optimistic but decided that if the worst came to the worst she could always get the tube back instead. She'd never live it down, of course, but a bit of gentle ribbing from her friends was a small price to pay when the alternative was having a heart attack or, worse, being so stiff she wouldn't be able to walk in her heels that night.

They had set off at a steady pace, but as time progressed Carla had upped the ante and they were now bridging the gap somewhere between a jog and a run. Elodie's heart pounded against her chest and she felt the first beads of sweat beginning to form on her forehead.

"Come on, don't slow down, you'll find your rhythm in a bit," Carla said. She was barely out of breath and making this whole thing look far too easy for Elodie's liking.

"What if I don't want to find my rhythm?" she replied, panting.

Carla let out a small chuckle and slowed her pace a fraction.

"There we go, we'll go a bit steadier for the rest of the way, not long to go now. How are the shoes?"

Elodie decided that running and talking were just two tasks that couldn't be managed at the same time, so gave a thumbs up, then fixed her gaze on a building in the distance. She decided that all she would do would be to concentrate on that building: with each and every step it would get closer and, at the end of it, she would feel really proud of herself. She just hoped that pride was worth an early and very sweaty grave.

The doorbell sounded at four pm on the dot. Steph was, as usual, extremely punctual; Elodie was at that moment in the shower and Carla was compiling a playlist for their evening. Instead of jogging back home, the two of them decided to enjoy the Camden vibe and settled on the idea that a walk up and down the high street would still count as exercise. It had been extremely busy: packed with tourists, Londoners and Camden locals alike. Carla made Elodie take a little detour and navigated her to an out of the way but very expensive jewellers. Elodie marvelled at the array of diamonds, pearls and other fabulous jewels, all glinting invitingly in the window. Carla pointed out a pair of earrings that were positioned on a pedestal, bang in the middle.

"When I'm rich they're the first thing I'm going to buy," Carla said as she lustfully gazed at them. "I've had my eye on them for months. I know they cost a fortune but they're one of a kind, handmade on the premises. The guy that made them has done jewellery for loads of celebs."

"They're stunning," Elodie said in agreement, before wincing when she saw the one thousand pound price tag.

Eventually, when Elodie had managed to pull Carla away from the siren-like lure of the earrings, they walked across the lock. They had stopped for a while to admire the view. The waterways were almost as busy as the streets. Several narrowboats passed one another; happy holidaymakers waved and called out friendly greetings as they went. The atmosphere was electric. Elodie hadn't spent much time in this part of London before. Tom had deemed it too 'hippy,' but now she was here, she could see that it wasn't like that at all. It was an eclectic plethora of people, places and different shops selling all sorts. Above each shop front were extremely artistic and very colourful installations, so captivating that after a while Elodie found she had a very sore neck from looking at them.

Carla had suggested they go for a drink in one of the beer gardens and Elodie had gladly accepted. She had drunk more alcohol in the last two weeks than she had in the last two years, but she couldn't complain; she was really enjoying letting her hair down and revelling in her new life. Carla had sat and chatted with her for over an hour. Unsurprisingly the topic of Elodie's career path cropped up. Elodie still had no idea what she wanted to do. She had wondered ever so fleetingly if perhaps there was a job on a cruise ship she could apply for. They were bound to need people with her expertise as a waitress and at least that way she'd get to see some of the world. She'd told Carla her plan. Carla wasn't overly impressed; she had a friend who used to do the same thing and it really wasn't all that.

"She called herself a 'waitress on water', hun, it's probably not quite as glamorous as you think. Crazy long hours, terrible pay and months away from home," Carla had said to her whilst sipping on a Hendricks and tonic.

Elodie had thought about this comment whilst she showered. The warm water beat down onto her with an almost therapeutic ferocity as she massaged her scalp with her favourite coconut shampoo. She inhaled deeply and the scent immediately transported her back to the bathroom she had shared with Tom. She made a mental note to throw the shampoo away and try something new instead,

'Maybe I'll go for lavender,' she thought, deciding that 'out with the old and in with the new' summed up her life quite perfectly right now.

"Bathroom's free," Elodie called when she was done. She noticed Steph's arrival by the large overnight bag and bottle of Champagne that had been placed on the dining table. Steph appeared from Carla's room moments later, apologising and pointing to her phone.

"Sorry, sorry. Andy had a free half-hour so he rang, we haven't spoken voice to voice in over a week." She smiled a dreamy smile and then, catching Carla's raised eyebrow, added, "No more boys, though, just us girls tonight."

This seemed to satiate Carla's desire for female-focused festivities. She nodded her approval and then expertly popped the cork from the Champagne; it exploded from the bottle with a loud pop.

"Here's to the single life, fabulous jobs and a boyfriend with half an hour free," Carla said cheekily.

The three friends clinked glasses and each, in turn, drank deeply. Elodie felt the first flushes of fizz begin to sweep over her and smiled.

'This is going to be a great night,' she thought to herself excitedly.

"Come on then, let's see you." Steph's voice called from the living room. Elodie was still in her bedroom, not quite feeling brave enough to come out. Carla had done her hair and makeup and looking at her reflection now, Elodie wasn't sure if it wasn't all a bit much. She had dark eye makeup and her long eyelashes had been curled and finished with lashings of deepest black mascara. Elodie's long, burnt-umber locks had been teased into waves that had then been backcombed to attain what Carla described as 'spectacular volume'. Elodie patted the crown of her head in an effort to rein it in ever so slightly. Carla's last words to her before she set to work were: "Trust me, I'm a genius." Elodie didn't doubt Carla's makeup skills; however, it seemed as though her friend had failed to recognise that they did both have vastly different styles.

Elodie turned around and gave herself another once-over and thought that maybe she just needed a couple more drinks in order to pull it off. She did love the dress and the heels were so comfortable – well, for the moment, at least. Elodie owned just one pair of heels high enough to satisfy Carla's exacting standards of what you were allowed to wear on a night out. They were black, open-toed stilettos that up until now had only ever been out of their box on one other occasion. Elodie shuddered as she remembered the night Tom had insisted she wore them in the bedroom for him.

She hadn't wanted to but had done so anyway. He'd loved it, she hadn't. It was the story of their life, really.

"El? Are you coming or what?" Carla shouted.

Elodie thought she heard a slight slur to her words and had to smile: Carla really was, in the words of Betty, a law unto herself. Elodie pushed her bedroom door open and with trepidation, stepped into the living room.

"Give us a twirl, then," Carla said, pointing her finger and spinning it around.

Elodie obliged and, for added measure, gave them a pretty good impression of a catwalk model. She strutted down the length of the living room and when she reached the end struck a pose that she hoped came across as sexy and cool. It didn't. She stumbled and had to catch herself on the table to stop herself from crashing to the floor. She looked up sheepishly and laughed.

"Maybe I need a bit more practice in the shoes," she reasoned.

Carla and Steph were all dressed and ready to go, Steph had elected to wear a very elegant but rather conservative black dress. Her straight red hair had been tied back in a low, chic ponytail and she had accessorised the look with a selection of gold jewellery. Carla, on the other hand, occupied the opposite end of the style spectrum. Her wild hair had been pulled on top of her head in a stylish knot, which was surrounded by a very complicated-looking plait.

"Carla! Your hair looks amazing." Elodie couldn't help but blurt out appreciatively.

"Thanks. Took me forever, though," Carla replied, casually flicking her hair over her shoulder.

Elodie highly doubted that. Carla seemed to have an incredible knack for this kind of thing; complicated techniques always seemed to come easy to her. Elodie had often asked why Carla didn't do something with this skill but Carla always said she was destined to be in front of cameras, not behind them.

"Let's have a toast," Steph suggested, handing out freshly filled glasses. "To friendship, freedom and a whole lot of fun."

They cheered their agreement and clinked glasses, not

for the first time that evening. The music they had been enjoying cut out as Carla's phone began to ring: it was the taxi driver phoning out of courtesy and giving them a five-minute curtain-call.

"Right, girls, this is it," Carla said once she had hung up the phone. "Remember your ID, bankcard, lip-gloss and bail money," she finished, laughing.

Elodie downed the last of her drink and picked up her bag; she had packed it and repacked it three times that evening. She was extremely out of practice when it came to 'night out' necessities and didn't want to hold everyone up at the last minute.

"You got the keys?" Elodie asked Carla as they exited the flat. Carla held up her set of house keys and jangled them.

"Sure do," she answered. "You both ready?"

Elodie nodded and took a deep breath, feeling as though the few short steps out of the flat and into the taxi were the biggest and most important steps she had taken in a long time.

CHAPTER 7

THE BAR CARLA HAD CHOSEN WAS UNLIKE ANY
venue Elodie had ever been in before. The entrance was
hidden down a side street behind a black, foreboding, bolted
door; stood outside was a smartly dressed blonde woman
with blood-red lipstick wearing a headset and holding a
clipboard. A tall, dark-haired man who had a James Bond
kind of vibe about him and a very serious expression on
his face accompanied her. As the three friends approached,
the woman smiled curtly and asked for their names, which
Carla gave in a business-like fashion that was quite alien to
her personality. The woman moved her pen down the list in
front of her and held it still about halfway down. She pressed
a button on the side of her headset and repeated their names
and party size. There was silence for a moment and then the
woman nodded to her partner who in turn opened the heavy
black door and ushered them inside.

Elodie shared a nervous glance with Steph. Carla may
have been used to places like this but they certainly weren't.
The bar itself was an amalgamation of luxury, indulgence
and extravagance. Private booths were dotted around, some
shielded by beaded curtains and others protected by high,
intricately-carved dividers. It was dark inside with minimal
lighting, which Elodie assumed was to provide even more
secrecy for the guests. Candles had been placed around,
which cast dancing shadows across the walls and added to
the exclusive ambience of the place. Elodie looked around.
The bar wasn't exactly quiet but it was far from the over-
crowded multitude of revellers she had imagined when
they'd left the flat. There were three men at the bar, drinking and talking in hushed tones. They stopped and looked up

as Elodie passed and she caught the eye of the youngest of the three. He was a good-looking guy with dark features and a sharp, expensive-looking suit. He offered her a smile and fixed her with an admiring stare. Elodie looked away guiltily. She didn't want to encourage anyone of the opposite sex tonight; after all, this was an evening just for the girls.

They were shown to a small round table situated in a quiet corner. The hostess pulled back the beaded curtain and led them through. It seemed quieter at the table, the hum of the music deadened somewhat by their position. Elodie perched on the edge of the padded circular bench that surrounded the table and placed her order with the hostess, she ordered a Cosmopolitan, Steph requested an Aperol Spritz and Carla asked for an Old Fashioned. The hostess committed these to memory, smiled and sauntered back to the bar.

"He's hot," Carla said, as if reading Elodie's mind. She tried to feign ignorance but Carla was having none of it. "I can read you like a book, El. I see you glancing in the guy's direction every time you think we're not looking."

Elodie opened her mouth; sometimes she hated the fact that Carla knew her so well.

"I'm not at all," she answered defiantly. "OK, maybe I am a bit, but he's really handsome and I've not been allowed to look at another guy for forever."

"You don't have to justify it to us," Steph interrupted. "There's no harm in looking and, Elodie, try and remember that you're single now. You're allowed to look. Tom isn't here to kick off and Carla and I would love to see you with someone nice."

"I don't want to be with anyone right now," Elodie admitted, "and I'm not hung up on Tom anymore, I promise."

"Good," Carla said, interrupting. "The only person you should be hung up on right now is yourself."

Elodie nodded; she was in complete agreement with Carla on this. She ran her fingertips through the ends of her hair but despite her protestations that the single life was the only one she wanted, she couldn't help but notice that the man from the bar was looking at her again. Elodie shifted in her seat a little uncomfortably and turned her head slightly away from the man. Fortunately, the arrival of their drinks saved her from having to administer any other little falsities. By the time the waitress had handed their drinks over, asked them if there was anything else they needed and gone, Elodie had clean forgotten about the man at the bar. When she did eventually look up from their conversation, both he and his friends had gone.

'Pity, he was quite nice to look at,' Elodie thought as she sipped her Cosmopolitan. The bartender had created an absolute masterpiece and Elodie was enjoying each and every sip, perhaps a little too much because she finished her drink in record time. Carla still had half of her Old Fashioned left and Steph still had most of her cocktail.

"Take it steady, El," Steph said. "We've got all night and you don't exactly have a liver of steel, do you?"

"What's that supposed to mean?" Elodie asked, looking faux-affronted.

"You're a total fucking lightweight," Carla interjected, laughing and knocking back the rest of her drink in an effort to show that she wasn't a lightweight at all.

Elodie couldn't argue: she'd often been called a cheap date. Her absolute limit on a night out was four or five drinks, and that was if she'd eaten and didn't drink too quickly. She made a mental note to order something a little less delicious next time. *'Perhaps I'll even have a soft drink,"* she thought and then dismissed the idea as quickly as it had formed.

Elodie settled into her new, high-class surroundings very quickly. After an hour she no longer felt like someone who had accidentally found themselves at a party they hadn't been invited to and started to feel more comfortable. They ordered another round of drinks once Steph had finally finished hers. This time they elected for a bottle of Prosecco. Carla had desperately wanted Champagne, but when they had had a look at the drinks menu they decided that a day's wages for a bottle of fizz just wasn't worth it, so Prosecco it was.

"It tastes the same anyway," Steph said with an authoritative tone in her voice. She had been the one to put her foot down. Carla gave her a withering look and told her that it only tasted the same to idiots.

"Well I'm an idiot then, and so is Elodie because she agrees with me," Steph said calmly, returning Carla's withering look with one of triumph.

"Don't drag me into your lovers' tiff, I like both equally," Elodie said diplomatically.

This seemed to appease both of her friends because the conversation quickly turned back to normal. They chatted about anything and everything; the Prosecco slipped down easily and they became slightly more raucous. Carla's infectious laugh echoed around the room and the three friends had to rein themselves in more than once; they were, after all, in the most exclusive bar in the entire city. Elodie had never been in a place like it. She felt like a rock star.

"Ladies?" the pretty waitress who had served them earlier said as she walked over with another round of drinks. This time she carried a bottle of the bar's overly priced Champagne on an expensive-looking copper-flecked tray; the gold of the bottle reflected dazzlingly in the candlelight. The Champagne, unlike the Prosecco, was served in saucers and not flutes.

"Oh, we didn't order this," Elodie said, her words laced with panic. She definitely didn't want to be landed with the bill for this.

"I know," the waitress replied loftily. "The gentlemen in the Grosvenor Suite did."

"The Grosvenor Suite?" Elodie asked, still not quite understanding what was going on. Surely if the gentlemen in the Grosvenor Suite had ordered it then the gentlemen in the Grosvenor Suite should be the ones drinking it.

"Get there faster, Elodie," Carla said exasperatedly, helping herself to a saucer of Champagne from the tray. "They've bought this for us." She turned the golden bottle around so that the label was facing her and let out a low whistle. "Armand de Brignac. Wow!" she finished, clearly impressed with their choice. The men had sent over a bottle of the bar's most expensive Champagne.

"This stuff was almost five hundred pounds a bottle," Elodie said, gobsmacked. "It's top of the menu. Although I kinda just wish they'd given us the cash instead."

"Me too," Steph agreed, looking at the bottle as if it contained the secret to life and not Champagne.

"I don't," Carla said defiantly. "If they want to buy us this, then that's their prerogative. Come on then, girls, shall we?" Carla handed the bottle back to the waitress who expertly poured it and then set it in a nearby ice bucket before taking her leave.

Carla raised the delicately-cut saucer high in the air: "To men with more money than sense."

Steph and Elodie echoed her words and all three of them sipped the Champagne at the same time. Elodie felt as though she had gone to heaven; the crisp amber liquid was definitely not the same as Prosecco.

Strutting across the bar Elodie felt on top of the world, she felt a confidence exude from her that she hadn't felt for years, if ever. So far the evening had been perfect and, with their new friends in tow, promised to get even better. One of the Champagne-bequeathing gentlemen had sent a message to them through the waitress, inviting them to join them in their suite. Steph hadn't been keen at first, but when she found out the Grosvenor Suite was actually a private room with complimentary bar, even she couldn't argue against joining them. The waitress led the way, her blonde ponytail swishing from side to side as she walked. Elodie could barely contain her excitement; she felt as though she were about to meet royalty and, despite being quite certain that she was in no way, shape or form ready to start dating again, thought that just being in the company of an attractive man, a little bit of tipsy flirting, couldn't do any harm.

They walked across the length of the bar, the soft music drowning out the sound of their stilettos on the highly-polished parquet flooring and after what seemed like an age were presented with the door to the Grosvenor Suite. A dark wooden sign with the words embossed in gold leaf hung proudly above the heavy-looking door. Elodie felt a little chill of excitement course through her as the waitress pushed it open to reveal the sumptuous interior. The sight almost took Elodie's breath away. Never had she imagined that the room would be this vast. It stretched out for metres and had a private bathroom at one end, a bar at the other and, in the centre, an expertly crafted and extremely large circular booth made from one whole piece of highly polished copper with a high back that shielded its occupants. The Grosvenor Suite had been decorated in the bar's signature look, yet somehow this room seemed to boast even more luxury. Perhaps it was the enormous chandelier, which emitted a soft iridescent glow and boasted more glittering crystals than any Swarovski store Elodie had ever been in. She stepped inside fully and held her hand out, which was immediately held by Steph; she too was in complete awe of their surroundings.

"We don't belong here," Steph whispered to Elodie who nodded in agreement.

Carla, who had been bringing up the rear, heard Steph's comment and shot them a warning look that seemed to say: "If I say we belong here, we belong here!"

"Here we are," the blonde waitress said, turning around to them and gesturing to the room in which they now stood. "The Grosvenor is paid for in advance, everything is complimentary. This is our mixologist, Grant. He'll be here to take care of you all evening; whatever your heart desires, Grant will be happy to acquiesce. There's a private bathroom just over there, inside you'll find everything you could possibly want, including an array of sample scents and cosmetics." She gave them a warm smile and left the room. The door closed softly behind her.

"Well don't just stand gawping," Carla admonished. Brushing herself down and giving her hair a bit of a tousle, she stepped forward. She headed over to the booth with such confidence and self-assurance that Elodie couldn't help but feel slightly envious of Carla's conviction in herself. Carla flipped her hair over her shoulder one last time and disappeared around the side of the booth. Elodie and Steph shared one final 'now or never' look and headed after her in a slightly less demure but altogether more enthusiastic way.

The three men in the Grosvenor Suite happened to be the same three men that had been propping up the bar earlier. After introductions Elodie discovered that the youngest and considerably more raucous of the three men was called Adam; his broad-shouldered friend Chase looked to be about ten years his senior and Edward older still. Elodie put Chase at thirty-five and Edward at forty or so. They all seemed nice enough. Adam, although very good-looking, was a little full of himself and talked non-stop about how crazy his life was, all the places he'd visited and the people he'd met.

"So what is it you do?" Elodie had asked, more out of politeness than anything else.

"Private pilot, babe," Adam replied nonchalantly. "Well, second officer actually. It's nothing, really. I mean, it's an amazing job: the places I see, celebs I meet, money I make. It's next-level shit, just now it's so normal to me, you know?" Elodie nodded, despite not knowing at all. "Of course I'm not the best yet, that'd be Chase. He's the level I'm aiming for. I keep asking him to get me a job on his line but he likes his co-pilot a little too much, if you know what I mean."

He gave Elodie a wink and continued, listing all the amazing perks to his job and why his life was just so damn exciting. Elodie couldn't help but roll her eyes. This guy was more than a bit full of himself, he was downright arrogant; but, however boorish he was, Elodie couldn't help but find his stories fascinating and couldn't help engaging him in conversation. The fact that he had been to Australia, Thailand and Dubai was amazing; the fact that he'd visited these places *this year* alone was absolutely mind-blowing.

"Out of all the places you've been, which was your favourite?" Elodie asked eagerly, her thirst for travel drowning any irritation she felt towards his demeanour.

"Hands down, has to be Dubai: everything's so new and the shopping centres are amazing."

Elodie nodded and took a sip of her drink, trying not to feel bitter that someone who counted a shopping mall as a worthwhile exotic sight had a passport absolutely busting with stamps. She shifted her gaze to the man she now knew as Chase. He kept glancing at her disapprovingly. She'd caught his eye twice now; he looked so serious sat there, nursing a Scotch that, from the sour look on his face, Elodie could only assume was made with lemons instead of barley. He didn't seem to be having a good time or to be making the most of their lavish surroundings and Elodie just couldn't fathom why Adam and Edward hung out with him, or why he hung around with them for that matter. They were both gregarious men who had made Elodie and her friends feel immediately at ease, whereas Chase had been anything but welcoming. He'd done nothing but check his phone, sip his drink and occasionally add an uninterested comment to the conversation. Elodie looked away a little embarrassedly and returned to Adam, who was now regaling her with a story of drinking until the early hours of the morning with two supermodels and a film star on a beach in Barbados. Elodie didn't ask who the models or film star were; she probably wouldn't have known them.

"So how do you get to be a pilot?" she asked. It did sound like an amazing job and after all, she was in the market for a new one of those.

"Why? Think you'd be good at it?" Adam asked.

Elodie thought she heard a touch of sarcasm in his voice and immediately felt a little down-hearted.

"I don't know, I'm just asking," she said defensively.

"Well, babe, you need decent A-levels, a degree, then training. You need flying hours under your belt, a lot of them. Then you qualify and progress through the ranks, costs a pretty penny though. My parents funded me, I was lucky that way. I reckon nowadays a PPL, that's private pilot's licence to the likes of you, would probably set you back about fifteen grand or so." Elodie's mouth dropped open. Fifteen thousand pounds? She couldn't have heard that right.

"Sorry, fifteen thousand pounds? You mean they don't pay for you?" she asked, visibly taken aback.

"You're just so cute, of course not," he guffawed, then seeing her disdainful expression and confusing it for hurt, added, "I wouldn't worry about it, babe, you'd be wasted in the cockpit anyway. You're more of a front of house type," he said proudly and gave her shoulder a little pat.

'How am I supposed to know about that kind of stuff?' she seethed inwardly. She looked over to Carla and Steph who were sat on the far side of the booth with Edward. Elodie managed to catch Carla's eye and give her a warning look intended to deliver a message of 'Save me'. The connection the two women shared meant that messages like this were

always received loud and clear and barely a beat skipped before Carla acted.

"Steph, Elodie, bathroom break?" Carla called across the length of the table.

Elodie offered Adam an apologetic smile and excused herself. She stood up quickly, turning her back to him as she did so. She didn't want to give him even the slightest of moments to protest her departure.

"So, how're things going with hot Adam, then?" Carla teased as she touched up her lipstick in the mirror, her eyes never leaving her own reflection.

Elodie shrugged. Adam was attractive, but oh so arrogant. Elodie felt mean even thinking that; she didn't know him at all. He was probably just trying to show off and impress her but missing the mark entirely.

"Well, he's nice enough. But, other than his job he's just a bit... big-headed," Elodie said truthfully. "He reminds me a bit of, well, of Tom actually. Babe this and babe that. He just brags a lot."

"Must be trying to make up for his shortcomings else-where," Carla replied, winking. She had moved on from reapplying makeup and was now rooting through the nearby glass shelves, which housed an array of beauty products.

Elodie looked around. Even the toilets in this place were lavish. There was even a dressing area, with plush velvet stools in front of gigantic mirrors, which Carla was certainly making the most of.

"Well, he's got to be better than the boring guy. What's his name?" Steph added, gingerly plucking a small bottle of perfume from the top shelf, the lure of the freebies finally getting the better of her.

"Ugh, Chaz, Cash, Chase, isn't it. Whatever it is, it's a ridiculous name. Although I don't think he's boring, I think he's bored," Carla quipped and Elodie had to agree: "Adam may be hard work but at least he isn't rude."

"Shall we move on?" Steph asked. "This is really lovely and all, but it's not exactly what we set out for. Especially since I have a boyfriend, you don't want one and El isn't ready for one."

Elodie had to agree; their night certainly had been forced into an unexpected direction.

"Won't they be annoyed? They did buy us Champagne, after all," Elodie said in a small voice.

"Don't be mental, they bought the Champagne, they didn't buy us," Carla said decidedly. "Let's go girls, we can hit up Club Hush instead, I know the bouncer there."

Carla swept out of the bathroom, once again leaving Elodie and Steph to trail in her wake. They got back to the booth and made their excuses, Adam protested at this, more out of a dislike at being rejected than actually wanting them to stay. Edward seemed as though he would genuinely mourn their departure and Chase barely looked up from his phone.

"Let me give you my number," Edward practically begged of Carla. She smiled sweetly and opened her mouth to answer but before she had chance Edward was already pulling a silver business card holder from his pocket. He opened it with a flourish and sighed, "Shit. I gave the last one out at the conference."

"It's really OK, if it's meant to be we'll meet again," Carla said as she turned to leave.

"No, wait. Chase, chuck us one of yours," Edward pleaded.

After a moment of hesitation, Chase obliged. For the first time Elodie saw his face in full and felt her breath catch in her throat. Elodie couldn't help but stare at him and the more she tried to fight the temptation the weaker she became. He had a smooth, tanned complexion, a strong jawline, very dark hair and a few soft lines around his eyes, which suggested that he wasn't a complete stranger to laughter after all. He had rugged good looks that simply blew Adam's out of the water. She offered him a smile, which he didn't return. Instead, he deftly retrieved his wallet and took out a business card. He passed it to Edward with a fluidity that showed just how practised this action was. Elodie couldn't help but notice his muscular physique, even through his shirt, as he moved to pass the card over. Edward took it and pulled a silver pen out of his pocket, which glinted as he wrote. He scribbled down his phone number on the back of the card and pushed it towards Carla. She eyed it almost suspiciously; the card lay on the tabletop for a beat too long, because Steph, clearly impatient, reached over, snatched the card up and pushed it into Carla's palm. Steph offered all three men a warm, yet apologetic smile before bidding them good night and turning on her heel to leave, Elodie and Carla followed suit. Elodie noticed, with much surprise, that Carla didn't discard Edward's phone number but instead slipped it into the pocket of her bag. Elodie wondered if perhaps Carla had liked Edward's attentions a little more than she was willing to let on.

The rest of the night passed in a blur of cocktails, dubious dancing and lots of laughter. For someone who didn't normally drink to excess, Elodie was certainly putting in a concerted effort. She was having an incredible night and when the time came to go home at two am Elodie felt heartily disappointed that their evening was to come to an end.

"Come on, you two," Steph said in a mum-like fashion. Despite having her own fair share of alcohol, Steph didn't seem anywhere near as drunk as she should have been. "I've ordered an Uber and it'll be outside in a few minutes so come on, let's get going."

"Ahhh, but I want food," Elodie said, almost managing to get through the sentence without slurring.

"There's food back at yours," Steph said. "Come on. My feet hurt and it's late."

"There isn't drunk food at ours, though," Carla moaned, "We need pizza, don't we, El?" Elodie nodded enthusiastically and, placing her hands together in prayer, shot Steph a pleading stare.

"You'll thank me in the morning."

Even in her drunken haze, Elodie couldn't mistake that the determined note in Steph's voice now sounded less mum-like and more dictatorial. Elodie protested a little but soon found herself sat in the back of a taxi and shortly after that in the comfort of her bed, after polishing off a slice of toast and two glasses of water.

Elodie closed her eyes. It had been a long night. She felt herself slipping into the world of slumber. It welcomed her with open arms and the promise of an embrace so warm she just could not refuse. She allowed herself to fall towards it and a comforting darkness began to surround her. She was dragged back to the land of the living by a light but persistent knock on her bedroom door.

"Hello?" She called, her voice husky from the cocktail of sleep and Champagne.

There was no answer. Grudgingly, she pulled herself from her bed, her body sleepily protesting as she did so. Elodie opened the flat door, tentatively expecting to see Carla on the other side. Perhaps, unbeknownst to Elodie, Carla had felt that the party wasn't over yet. Maybe she'd be stood there, bottle in hand, desperate for Elodie to continue the night with her.

Elodie's breath caught in her throat. The door had slowly swung open to reveal not Carla, but Chase. The handsome man from earlier sauntered in the doorway. His pristine attire from earlier was now dishevelled, his tie askew and the top button undone. He held his jacket in one hand and with the other, reached out for her.

Before Elodie could protest he had taken her in his arms. She let herself melt into him. For something so alien, this felt completely natural. The musky smell of whisky lingered on his breath and Elodie felt her stomach flip; she usually hated the stuff but for some reason she didn't mind it so much now. She opened her mouth to say something, anything, but he pressed a finger to her lips and shushed her before any words could escape.

Elodie looked into his deep brown eyes; she was confused. A million questions danced around her head. How had he found her? Why was he here? But the most important question of all elbowed its way to the front of her subconscious: why had he not kissed her yet? As if reading her mind, Chase bent down. He pressed his lips to hers in a soft yet purposeful way that encouraged a soft moan to emerge from her lips.

Elodie simply could not believe this was happening. She didn't have time to dwell on the whys and wherefores, though: the gentle kiss had escalated into something far more passionate. Chase pulled her into him and in return Elodie placed a hand on his chest. She could feel the steady, unwavering beat of his heart and knew that hers would in no way echo the rhythm of his. Before she knew what was happening she had led him to her bed, she looked down at herself and was surprised to see she was wearing a satin negligee that, up until now, she had not remembered putting on. Chase pulled at the smooth material and Elodie felt herself succumb to his touch. She allowed him to undress her and the material slipped easily over her head. She watched as Chase let it slip through his fingers and onto the floor. Elodie was completely naked in front of a man that she had barely exchanged two words with and finding herself completely comfortable with it.

She reached for him hungrily; his shirt, now unbuttoned, revealed a taut, toned stomach that Elodie felt unable to resist. Chase leaned in towards her; Elodie's heart began to beat faster. Desire left her wanting more. Without regard she reached out for him, desperate to feel his muscular physique, her fingers not quite able to reach. She tried once more and, again, her fingers did nothing but brush his firm form.

Elodie opened her eyes and squinted in the darkness. Her heart was pounding and a fine layer of sweat had formed on her brow. She fumbled in the dimly-lit room, completely confused as to what had actually happened. She couldn't believe she had just had a drunken one-night stand with a man she'd never even had a proper conversation with. Was he still here? Her memory was hazy, to say the least. She tentatively reached out and, with trepidation, turned on her bedside lamp. A warm light filled the room and Elodie's breath caught in her throat as she slowly turned her gaze to the other side of the bed. She exhaled loudly, relieved to see that she was alone. She looked down and saw, to her surprise, that the negligee had been replaced with nightwear that she could actually remember putting on.

The dream had felt so real. If she closed her eyes and inhaled she could have sworn that she could still smell his aftershave mingled with whisky, and on top of that, a faint note of desire. Elodie sat in her bed for a long while; it took several lengthy moments for her heartbeat to return to its normal pace. At last, she switched off the light and closed her eyes again. Sleep was determined to evade her now. She could do little to tempt it, but eventually it succumbed and allowed her into its docile embrace.

"Good morning, sleepyhead."

Elodie looked up to see Steph hovering over her, far too bright-eyed and bushy-tailed for this time of the morning on a normal day, let alone one after a night out. Elodie opened her mouth and managed a helpless croak before burying her head in the pillow. Steph had, for the second time this month, brought her breakfast in bed. Elodie's head was pounding: it was as if some tiny, angry man were beating a drum in the deepest recess of her brain. She groaned helplessly and rubbed at her eyes as she very slowly and very gingerly dragged herself up into a sitting position. She blinked heavily against the morning sun and squinted at the plate Steph had placed on the lap.

"I don't think I can," Elodie said dejectedly, pushing the plate away.

"Yes you can, have one bit of toast and a tiny bit of orange juice, you'll feel much better once you get something inside you and besides, you've got a lot to do today," Steph said. She pushed the plate back towards Elodie before getting up and leaving the room. Elodie did as she was told, opting for the plainly buttered piece rather than the one heavily laden with marmite. She didn't think her hungover palate could handle that much excitement just yet.

"What have I got to do?" Elodie called confusedly through the now open door.

"Sort your life out!" came the joint response or both Carla and Steph.

Elodie groaned again, she feared that sorting her life out would be far easier said than done. Elodie wondered why she couldn't just continue at Betty's. It might actually be OK. Who knew, perhaps a lifetime of refilling coffee cups and chatting about the weather would be fulfilling in some way. 'So what if I'd never be able to afford a trip to the coast let alone the coast of the Maldives,' she thought, knowing deep down that if that were to be the case she'd spend her life being thoroughly miserable.

It was with that thought that something Adam had said the previous night floated into her consciousness. "You'd be better off front of house." She was sure he'd said that to her. As his words came back to her she gave them some thoughts and realised that it wasn't actually a bad idea. In fact, it was an absolutely brilliant idea. The more Elodie thought about it, the more it made sense. She loved waitressing and that was certainly a part of it; she'd get to travel the world at no cost to herself, and it was bound to pay more than Betty's did.

Elodie didn't dare get too excited too quickly, but she found that she was unable to stop the exhilaration of possibility from bubbling up inside her. She could feel an excited glowing warmth spreading, promising to burst to the surface at any moment. A smile erupted on her face; she just knew that this was the perfect solution to her predicament. Her hangover had been forced to the back of her mind; she got out of bed and headed into the living room. She felt lighter than she had done in days, as if she were floating along the floor rather than walking on it. Perhaps it was the toast or perhaps it was the promise of a better, brighter future that was having such a positive impact. Elodie couldn't help but grin when she saw her friends on the sofa watching Sunday morning telly. They barely had time to look up from the screen before she was telling them her newly formed plan.

"I'm going to be an air hostess," she said excitedly. Her subsequent words fell out in a jumble of excitement and relief. When she had finished both of them looked at her, warm smiles on their faces.

"That's a wonderful idea," Steph said, adding that Elodie already had the requisite skills and would just need the qualification to go with them now.

"Plus, you know, staff discount and free upgrades to first class," Carla added cheekily. Steph's eyes slid sideways and Carla took the hint immediately. "Er, I meant that's amazing, babe. You'd be amazing."

Elodie grinned wider, she knew that she had a fair bit of research to do and undoubtedly there would be some pretty challenging obstacles to overcome; after all, she hadn't taken an examination in years. But she'd have plenty of time to dwell on that. Right now, Elodie was determined to bask in the sunny rays that a little bit of certainty provided.

Elodie spent the rest of the day on Carla's laptop. She covered every base she could think of and by the time the sun was beginning to set she really felt as though she had gotten to grips with what she would need to do. There were only two tiny problems. Every decent course seemed to be booked up for months and all of them, decent or not, cost a lot more than Elodie could afford. Closing the laptop, she sighed. She had been so sure this was the answer and now felt even more daunted than ever.

"What's up, hun?" Carla said, not looking up from her phone.

"Everything just costs so much money, the courses are a fortune and then you'd have to pay to stay in a hotel near the venue as they're all in the middle of nowhere and even if I could afford it the best courses with the best prospects are booked up months and months in advance," Elodie sighed. "I just don't know what to do."

Carla set her phone down and without a word stood up and disappeared into her bedroom. She wasn't gone for many moments when she reappeared and made her way over to the sofa where Elodie sat. She bent down and placed her petite hand on Elodie's shoulder.

"Why didn't I get an invite?" Carla asked, a serious expression on her face.

"An invite to what?" Elodie said, wondering how Carla had managed to completely ignore her and then change the subject so quickly.

"To your pity party," Carla finished, a smile creeping onto her face. She took Elodie by the shoulders and gave her a little shake. "You, Elodie Taylor, need to leave the defeatism by the door and be positive. These are not unscalable mountains, Elodie, these are just bumps in the road and you can't see every little bump as a barrier to happiness."

Elodie looked at Carla thoughtfully. It was very easy to say that but no amount of positive thinking would put pounds in her bank account or a qualification in her hand.

"I'm not having a pity party, I'm being realistic," Elodie counteracted quietly.

"Nope, you're being defeatist. Think about what you have, or more to the point what *I* have." Carla said.

Elodie looked at her; she searched her friend's face for any sort of clue as to what she could be going on about. Carla didn't have the kind of spare cash that Elodie would need and even if she did Elodie would never take it.

"What are you going on about?" Elodie asked carefully.

"Here," Carla said and dropped a crumpled piece of paper into Elodie's lap. Elodie picked it up. It wasn't a crumpled piece of paper at all but rather the business card Edward had written his number on the night before, albeit in a less than pristine state now it had been in Carla's handbag all night. Elodie opened it up and was a little repulsed to find a used piece of chewing gum stuck to the inside of the card.

"Ewww," she said. "Carla, that's gross."

"It isn't. What's gross is chucking your gum in the street or sticking it under a table."

Elodie had to agree, although almost putting your finger in someone else's used gum was still a bit grim, no matter which how you tried to spin it.

She turned the card over in her hand. The chewing gum had been stuck to the side with Edward's number on, rendering only three of the digits still visible. Elodie knew that this was probably intentional. Carla was happy being single and, as she often reminded Elodie, she liked her encounters to be like a special attraction, one night only. Elodie flipped the card back over and stared at the other side: in embossed silver lettering it read 'Chase Ford, Private Pilot', followed by what Elodie could only assume was his personal telephone number.

"I don't think I can," she said, looking up at Carla. "I didn't speak to him all night and now I ring him and ask for a favour? Bit desperate, isn't it?"

"You *are* desperate," Carla said bluntly, bending over and picking up Elodie's phone from the arm of the sofa and handing it over expectantly. "Give him a ring. The worse thing that can happen is that he says no and the best thing is that you get exactly what you want. Oh, go on, just do it."

Elodie hesitated and then reluctantly took her phone from Carla, her hand shaking an almost imperceptible amount.

"OK, I'll do it, but not tonight. It's getting late and he's probably busy. It is still the weekend, after all."

"It's not that late, it's barely seven o'clock. You should do it, grab the bull by the horns, he'll think you're tenacious," Carla combatted.

Elodie dropped her gaze from Carla and back to the card. Maybe he would think she was tenacious, or maybe he'd think she was a complete chancer who wanted something for nothing from someone who certainly didn't owe her anything at all.

"I don't know, Carla. Isn't it a bit cheeky?" Elodie said after a lengthy pause.

"Well, put it this way, if it's cheeky now it'll be cheeky tomorrow, and the day after that and the day after that. The benefit of doing it now is that you won't be left wondering. Go on, strike while the iron's hot."

Elodie raised her eyebrow.

"I dunno, Betty always says it," Carla finished by way of explanation.

Elodie, who still held her phone tightly in her hand, nodded as she mulled over her decision. She deciding that if *'persistence and dedication'* really was going to be her mantra then she better start living by them.

"OK, well I'm not doing it in here, I need peace, I need a clear head."

Elodie picked herself up and, setting the laptop down on the coffee table, she dusted herself down and made her way into her bedroom. She closed the door and heard an ominous "Good luck" echo from the living room.

Elodie sat at her little dressing table and placed the phone and Chase's business card in front of her. She then reached into a small side drawer and pulled out a little notepad and a pen: she wanted to be prepared in case Chase did decide to help her. He was sure to be a fountain of knowledge and she wanted to write down every single word of wisdom that slipped from his lips. She picked up the phone and gingerly typed in the number from the card. Her finger hovered over the screen and lingered there for a second too long. Suddenly, an inexplicably frosty cloud had settled itself over her and she found herself unable to press the button. She suddenly felt nauseous; although Elodie hadn't even wanted this job for a full day, she felt very much like it were the right, and only, path for her. Knowing that this man, who Elodie didn't know at all, could potentially help her filled her with such a sense of apprehension and dread that she couldn't stop herself from shaking. Her heartbeat quickened and she felt cool prickles of sweat begin to form on the back of her neck. Elodie reclined in her seat, closed her eyes and took a deep, steadying breath. Then, pushing her hair back from her face, she tapped the dial button and snatched the phone up to her ear. Elodie held her breath as the call connected. The phone rang and rang, which didn't surprise her. If an unknown number called her at this time on a Sunday, she would probably let it go to voicemail too.

"Hi, this is the voicemail of Chase Ford, sorry I'm unable to take your call at present. Please leave me a short message and I will try to get back to you." Chase's voice was deep; a rich, smooth baritone that was like an aural massage.

Elodie paused. She was unprepared for this eventuality and wondered if leaving a voicemail would be the right thing to do. There was a beeping sound and the line went silent in anticipation of a message.

"Er, hi. This is Elodie, Elodie Taylor. We met…" Elodie broke off. Her phone was beeping at her: she looked at the screen and saw that the number she had just dialled was calling her back. She stammered a goodbye and with her cheeks flushing accepted the incoming call, eternally glad that Chase couldn't actually see her.

"Hello, who is this?" the smooth voice of Chase Ford asked.

Elodie felt herself blush further at his very businesslike tone, she opened her mouth to reply but found that she was lost for words.

"Hello?" Chase said again, this time with an icier edge to his voice that made Elodie feel even more nervous.

"Hello," she managed before taking a big breath. "It's Elodie, Elodie Taylor. We met last night."

"We did, did we?" Chase replied, "I meet a lot of people, Elodie, but I don't remember handing my number out to anyone, especially anyone named 'Elodie, Elodie Taylor'." He sounded a little annoyed but Elodie was sure she heard a hint of amusement mixed in there too.

"Edward took a card from you to give to my friend Carla, she was the beautiful one he was chatting to. I was the one talking to Adam," she explained.

"Lucky you," Chase quipped. "So what is it I can do for you, Elodie Taylor?" he asked. The hairs on Elodie's arms stood up at this point: there was something in the way he said her name that gave her the shivers.

"I wanted to ask you about becoming a flight attendant. I mean, I know you're not one. I know you're a pilot, the best pilot by all accounts, but I thought you might know someone I could speak to. All the courses are so expensive or all booked up and I just thought someone in your position might be able to help me?" Elodie trailed off, realising that she was rambling now and that flattery probably wasn't going to work on a man like Chase Ford.

There was a palpable silence and Elodie wished he'd just say something, anything to break it. She was beginning to seriously regret taking Carla's advice; this wasn't something Elodie would normally do and now she was out of her depth. She had no clue how to handle the situation so remained silent as well. The reticence was broken by a rustling noise in the background; Elodie strained to hear but couldn't quite put her finger on what the sound was exactly.

"Hello?" she asked again with trepidation. She didn't want to annoy Chase but equally didn't want to stay on the phone in silence. She could have kicked herself for thinking that phoning a perfect stranger, on a Sunday, for a favour was a good idea. She blamed Carla entirely for this. Carla had a great way with people and Elodie was sure that if she had been the one to call she would have found herself inundated with offers of help, *'Hell, he'd probably offer her the co-pilots job and pay her twice the going rate,'* Elodie thought glumly. She just wasn't that confident or lucky, and it showed.

"I'm here," Chase said, breaking Elodie's reverie. "OK, leave it with me. I'll see if I know anyone. Bye now."

Her mobile beeped three times and then went dead. Puzzled, Elodie looked at the phone: the picture of her, Carla and Steph in the park now looked back at her.

Elodie walked back into the living room, an odd, dumbstruck expression on her face.

"How'd it go?" Carla asked eagerly.

"I don't know," Elodie replied truthfully.

She sat herself down in the armchair in the far corner of the room and placed her head in her hands. She relayed the conversation back to Carla and when she was finished she looked up, expectant that Carla would be able to decipher exactly what had happened and would be able to enlighten her at once.

"Well, I think that's a victory. So what if he was a little standoffish? You remember what he was like at the bar. Maybe that's just how he is, maybe he wasn't being rude, maybe he was just being himself."

Elodie nodded. Perhaps Carla was right. However, she couldn't shake the feeling that what she had just done hadn't put her in a favourable light in the eyes of Chase Ford. She doubted very much that he saw the phone call as tenacious and determined and was sure he'd interpreted it as annoying and childish.

She shook her head violently: she didn't care what Chase thought of her. So what if he thought she was a touch immature? She just needed enough of his regard for him to help, no more and no less.

CHAPTER 8

ELODIE PUT HER PHONE BACK ON HER DRESSING table, screen side down, with a little more force than she had intended. She had spent the entire morning checking and re-checking her phone, like a teenager awaiting a message from her crush. She found it impossible to go a full minute without the overwhelming urge to inspect it again. She'd turned it from silent, to loud, to do not disturb and to vibrate over and over again, hoping against hope that one of these settings would result in a phone call or message from Chase. She didn't know exactly what she was expecting from him; she doubted very much that he'd pull some strings and just get her a job at the drop of a hat, but maybe he'd know someone who could get her onto a course, or better yet someone who'd be willing to waive the fee *and* get her onto a course. Elodie groaned and conceded that staring at her phone was not going to make Chase get in touch. She made a conscientious decision to leave it in her bedroom. She opened her drawer and dropped the phone inside before getting up from the dressing table, determined that she was going to enjoy at least one whole hour of phone-free time. With the decision made, she closed the bedroom door tightly behind her; however, not before nipping back and taking one last look, just to make extra sure.

"Who are you talking to?" Elodie asked Carla, who was on the phone herself. She held up a finger to signify that she'd be a minute.

Elodie waited, eager to know who was on the phone and what they had said to cause Carla to smile in such a way that you'd be forgiven for thinking that she'd just won the lottery. Elodie tapped her foot impatiently; this was turning into one very long minute. Eventually, Carla said her good-byes and pulled the phone away from her ear.

"Just been booked in officially for the footwear gig, the shoot's been organised and everything, photographer booked, the works. They're sending a car for me next week and the best bit is that my agents just told me how much I'm going to get paid. El, they're paying me eight hundred pounds, just to take pictures of my feet. Can you believe it, it's amazing, isn't it?" Carla said, beaming as she rubbed her hands together eagerly.

Elodie couldn't believe it. Eight hundred pounds seemed like an awful lot of money, especially to her. She smiled at her friend, trying her absolute best not to let the jealousy she was feeling show on her face; she didn't want to taint this moment and was determined not to let her own situation tarnish Carla's.

"It is amazing," Elodie agreed, adding that she knew that this was only the beginning for Carla and wrapping her in a huge, warm hug that did nothing to thaw the frostiness she felt inside.

"Shouldn't you be getting to work?" Carla asked, once Elodie had released her.

Elodie snapped her head around to look at the clock hanging by the door. Carla was absolutely right. She really should be getting to work, Elodie kicked herself for spending the morning staring at her phone instead of sorting herself out. Her apron was crumpled in a pile on the floor, unwashed from the last time she wore it. It wasn't the only thing in need of some soap and water: Elodie hadn't even been in the shower herself. 'No time for that now,' she thought as she darted back into her bedroom. She pulled on a pair of dark blue jeans, an old Fleetwood Mac T-shirt Betty had given her and scraped her long brown hair into a high ponytail. She grabbed her apron from the floor and shook it out, deciding that other than being a little creased it really wasn't all that bad after all.

"What time do you call this?" Betty reprimanded, "you were meant to be here at midday. I've had to manage with just Sara during the lunchtime rush."

Elodie looked over at Sara, one of the other waitresses with whom she rarely worked. Sara was looking both shame-faced and a little put out by Betty's tone and cleared one of the tables with a more than miserable look on her face.

"I'm sorry," Elodie said genuinely, "I was waiting on a call about a…" She trailed off. Elodie didn't want to tell Betty she was looking for another job, especially when it was as an excuse for being late. "I was just waiting for a call," she finished lamely.

Betty looked her up and down and rubbed her temples in exasperation, clearly unimpressed with the flimsy excuse. To make matters worse, Betty then caught sight of what Elodie held in her hand: a bundled up, very creased, clearly unclean apron. Betty's eyes narrowed and her brow knitted together and she sighed.

"There's a clean apron in the back. Go and put it on, and be quick about it. Sara should have left half an hour ago, poor thing's dead on her feet. Oh, and while you're there, bring me one of my headache tablets, I can feel another bad head coming on."

Elodie nodded as she scurried past Betty and into the back. She found the apron hung up and hurriedly tied it around her waist, not wanting to spend a second longer than she needed to flouting Betty's lenient nature.

After a hectic afternoon, Betty reached up and turned the open sign to closed with one hand and bolted the door shut with the other. Elodie, who was putting the last of the chairs up, was glad that the day was almost over. As well as feeling physically tired from a long afternoon of work, she felt men-tally drained too. She couldn't stop her imagination from running away with her and had split her thoughts between ideas of travelling the world as an air hostess and the loom-ing, far more real, possibility of Chase being unable to help her.

This last shift had been somewhat of a turning point for Elodie. She had always been very certain that she loved her job at Betty's and that she could happily do it for the rest of her life. However, with this new possibility within her reach, the idea of remaining a coffee shop waitress seemed to suffocate her.

"Come on then," Betty said, "you've been wiping the same table for a full five minutes now. What's on your mind? You've not been yourself all day, love. I can see something's up, so why don't you do yourself a favour and get it off your chest? Come sit with me for a minute or two and tell me what's wrong." Betty lowered herself into a nearby armchair, letting out an exhausted sigh as she did so.

"It's nothing," Elodie said resolutely as she slumped down in the chair opposite.

The last thing she wanted to do was upset Betty. Telling her that she didn't want to work for her anymore wasn't something Elodie was looking forward to at all, so had decided to put the moment off for as long as she could. Betty was having none of it. Her no-nonsense nature, which was so beautifully reflected in Steph, rose to the surface in a burst of shrewdness.

"Let's not dance around it Elodie, just tell me. You'll feel so much better and besides. I think I've got a pretty good idea what's on your mind. You're missing Tom, aren't you?" Betty said, dropping her voice in what she hoped was a sympathetic tone.

Betty had been fiercely single since Steph's father had left more than twenty years ago. Elodie couldn't help it; a little giggle erupted from her lips, which grew from a small chuckle to a full-on laugh the more she thought about the idea of missing Tom. She probably should have felt guilty about reacting in such a way, but the idea seemed too funny to stifle. Betty pulled back and cocked her head, unable to understand what was so funny.

"Sorry," Elodie said, catching her breath and wiping a tear from the corner of her eye. "You're so off the mark. It's not Tom at all."

"Well, what is it, then? You're not pregnant, are you?" Betty asked, looking half-perplexed, half-incredulous. She had an air of motherly concern and was clearly under the impression that if it wasn't boy trouble, it must be something far worse. After all, what exactly could a recently-single, twenty-something-year-old have to worry about? "You've been out of sorts all day. You know you can tell me anything, don't you?"

Elodie decided that it was now or never and that she would be best off grabbing the bull by the horns before the bull jumped to another wrong conclusion.

"OK, I'll tell you, but please don't hate me," Elodie said, a sombre tone creeping its way into her voice without a trace of the joviality of only a few moments ago.

Betty was like a dog with a bone sometimes and deep down Elodie knew that honesty would be the best policy. Betty put her warm hand on Elodie's shoulder and told her that no matter what it was, no matter how bad Elodie thought the situation would be that she, Betty, could never hate her. This made things all the worse. Elodie would have found it much easier to break this sort of news had she been met with cold hostility rather than warmth and understanding.

"Come on, it can't be that bad, surely?" Betty said, looking a little concerned now. Her brow furrowed and she crossed her arms over her chest. Elodie sighed: it really was now or never.

"OK, well you know the other night when we all went out?" Betty nodded but didn't say anything, not wanting to interrupt Elodie's flow now she was finally opening up. "We met some men, some pilots to be exact. No, nothing like that!" she exclaimed, seeing Betty's raised eyebrows. "Nothing happened in that way, it's just that one of them, Adam, his name was, told me all about his job, the places he gets to see and the things he gets to experience and it all sounded amazing."

She paused for breath. Betty still looked a little confused and chose to remain quiet and let Elodie continue, which she did with increasing haste. "Anyway, to cut a long story short, I could never be a pilot, but I could be a flight attendant. I'd get to enjoy the same perks and I'd learn so many new things and get to do something that I'm good at. It's kind of like being here but several thousand feet in the air," Elodie finished.

Betty said nothing but instead chewed on her bottom lip.

"Well, it sounds like a wonderful idea. Of course, I'll be sad to see you go, no one will be able to replace you, you know, but I can't keep you here forever and you'll come and visit us, won't you?" Betty said, that warm motherly tone returning.

"I'm not doing it. Well, truth be told I can't do it. It's way too expensive. I haven't got savings. Oh, Betty, I've been so stupid. It's not a case of you keeping me here, it's more that I've trapped myself. I can't afford the training course, not even by half. I'm so irresponsible; I can't think what I've frittered all my money on. I mean, Tom paid for pretty much everything and I've basically spent every penny on meaningless shit!"

Elodie buried her face in her hands. She felt hopeless and utterly exasperated with herself. If she couldn't save the money beforehand, when she'd had pretty much a free ride, then how the hell was she going to manage it now that she had rent and bills to pay?

The two women sat in silence for a few moments, staring ahead. Elodie twisted her fingers together in an awkward way, which after some time caused Betty to place her hand over Elodie's in order to stop her from doing it anymore.

"How much is this course?" Betty said, not looking up from her own hand, which was still placed gently over Elodie's.

"Too much," Elodie replied bluntly. She brushed Betty's hand away and stood up, tightened her ponytail, untied her borrowed apron from around her waist and handed it back to Betty. "It doesn't matter, I'll figure it out. I can always sell my liver or something," she managed a wry smile, "although after all the booze I've had recently it's probably not worth much now."

"Maybe I could sort you out an extra shift here and there?" Betty offered kindly.

"Thanks, but I think it'll take more than that. I need hundreds of pounds for the course and then there's the hotel stay I'd need, food and travel money. Ugh, it's just too much. Plus the deadline for the application is looming and it'd take me months of extra shifts to save that kind of money. I could always get a second job, I suppose," she mused.

However, Elodie knew deep down that even a second job wouldn't help matters, there just wasn't enough time. She'd just have to save and wait. So what if she had to put her dream off for a year or two? It's like Steph always said, *'Nothing worth having comes easily.'* Which was rich, considering Steph had basically inherited a successful business without lifting a finger. Elodie shook her head in an attempt to dislodge the thought; it wasn't Steph's fault Elodie was in the mess. Elodie vowed not to let jealousy rear its ugly head again, especially when it came to her friends.

"Well if you want to take me up on those shifts you'll have to let me know," Betty said as she switched the café lights off, "I'm going to go up now, love, I'm shattered. I'll sort the takings out tomorrow, can't remember the last time a normal working day took it out of me like this. I'm going to have a soak and get an early night. Lock up on your way out, would you?"

Betty stifled a yawn and gave Elodie a little wave before she disappeared through the doorway and into the back. Elodie heard the old staircase creak as Betty ascended. She stood there in the empty café and looked around: this had been her life, her second home and her hub for such a long time now, was she really ready to throw it away for a pipe dream? Elodie let out an exasperated sigh as she grabbed her bag from behind the counter. She'd managed to achieve absolutely nothing and felt well and truly fed up. If only there were a way she could make some quick cash. *'Maybe I could get into stripping?'* she thought to herself glumly. Even if that were something she'd be up for, she doubted very much that anyone would be willing to pay to watch her take off her clothes. She let herself out of the back door; her arms were weary and the door felt much heavier as she pushed against it. It closed behind her with a thud of finality. She took the keys from her bag and sighed: that was it, the day was done, and so were her dreams. Snuffed out before they had even had a chance of being realised, like a candle blown out by a cold breeze just as it had been lit.

Elodie squinted at the clock on her bedside table, it hadn't even gone seven am and already her phone was ringing. A small sense of panic grew inside her: was she supposed to be at work? Elodie knew she had the next two days off but that she was working three full shifts in a row to cover the weekend.

"Steph? Everything OK?" Elodie asked after seeing her friend's picture flash up on the screen and rapidly pressing the answer button. The phone was barely up to her face before the words tumbled out of her mouth.

"Did you lock up last night?" Steph asked, her voice strangely tense and high-pitched. Elodie sat up, she didn't like Steph's tone one bit.

"Yes. Your mum wasn't feeling great, she said she had a headache so she went up early. Why?" she replied cautiously, the sleepy tone slipping from her voice.

"Locked the door and everything? Because when I came down this morning the alarm wasn't on, the door wasn't locked and money has been taken from the till. No one cashed up, did they? The till hasn't been zeroed, I've just done a read and almost a thousand pounds has gone," Steph finished, her voice strained, as if the weight of what she was faced with had begun to press down on her.

Elodie clapped her hand across her mouth. She had been so distracted she hadn't set the alarm, that much she knew. But she could have sworn she had locked the door, she remembered having her keys out, but did she actually use them?

"I, I..." she stammered, "I'm so sorry."

"El! We're not insured, if there was no alarm, no lock and more money than we're allowed..." Steph trailed off, the panic in her tone beginning to rise. "I need to ask you something," she added before going silent; the only sound audible was the faint buzzing of static.

"Go on," Elodie replied. She didn't like the blunt way Steph had said this.

"Is there anything else you need to tell me, about this? Anything at all?"

"No..." Elodie trailed off, she didn't know anything about it and told Steph as much.

"So it's purely coincidence that the amount of money taken is near as dammit the exact amount you need for your course? If you tell me honestly what happened then we won't say another word about it. I get it. People sometimes do crazy things when they're under pressure. I know you've had a really rough time of it, I just need you to tell me the truth, El, before I call the police," Steph finished with a deep sigh.

Despite the kind tone her words had taken, Elodie felt as though they'd been laced with poison.

"I don't know anything about it at all," she said in defence, "nothing, honestly. I would never steal from you, from Betty, from the café… never."

Elodie was shaking now. Never in a million years would she imagine having this conversation. Elodie recoiled as if Steph's suggestion had been made from a fist that had reached through the phone and hit her hard in the face.

"I need to speak to my mum," Steph said bluntly. "Figure out how we're going to deal with this mess."

"You haven't told her already?" Elodie asked.

"Of course not, I wanted to get the facts first before worrying her. You said it yourself, she's not been well and the last thing I want to do is stress her out even more." The phone went dead.

Elodie sat there for several long moments wondering what she should do. Her head was spinning as a cocktail of anger, resentment, hurt and sadness bubbled within her. Elodie couldn't help it. Warm, salty tears began to erupt from the corners of her eyes; they streaked their way down her pale cheeks and fell in fat droplets onto her crisp white duvet.

There was a knock at the door and Carla appeared, a look of concern etched on her face. Before she could draw breath to pose the question of what was wrong, Elodie had begun to tell her everything, the words coming almost as quickly as her tears. When she eventually paused for breath Carla interjected.

"You must have got it wrong somehow, babe. Steph knows you'd never steal, Christ! You were antsy about trying to use that out of date free cinema ticket, remember when we went to see *Magic Mike* and you almost cried when I made you risk it." Elodie managed a meek smile and nodded, Carla was right. Steph should know her better than that, and it was that fact that hurt her the most.

The morning passed in a blur. Having been woken up

much earlier than she had anticipated, Elodie found herself with the gift of time and being unsure what to do with it. Annoyingly, it was a phrase Steph used all the time that kept echoing in her subconscious: *'life admin,'* which, no matter how much she tried to ignore it, did make a lot of sense. It was because of this she found herself, for the first time in her adult life, on top of her washing, ironing, cleaning, odd jobs and correspondence. Between all of this, she checked her phone religiously. She had tried phoning Steph but the phone just rang and rang, she didn't want to trouble Betty so had opted for an apologetic text and she had left the landline of the café well alone knowing that the café would certainly be shut for the day whilst the police were called. Elodie wracked her brain: she was so sure she had locked that door. After the one-millionth time of checking her phone, only to find it worryingly void of any form of communication, Elodie switched it off and hid it in her bedside drawer again. Occasionally she opened Carla's laptop and searched for other courses, hoping that at some point since her last search a new one had been added that required far less from its applicants. The idea of becoming a flight attendant now seemed to be more of a pipe dream than ever and Elodie was annoyed at herself for being so certain, so decided that it was the right path for her.

After closing her laptop down and, in an annoyed haze, shoving it under her bed, she decided that getting out of the flat would be a good idea. The weather was pleasant and a nice long walk might just shake her out of this mood. She readied herself, choosing a pair of old jeans and a faded jumper to dress herself in and headed for the door. Carla emerged with a look on her face that Elodie found hard to read: somewhere between wild abandon and smugness, she thought.

"You have to get to the café now, El. Both Steph and Betty have been trying to call you. Steph says your phone goes straight to voicemail," Carla said carefully.

"I turned it off. To be honest, I'd forgotten about it, was actually just about to head out without it. Well, she can save her apology. I take it the police found something. CCTV of the real robber? Fingerprints? What? Because I know that the only thing I'm guilty of is complacency and a dash of stupidity." Elodie seethed, her placid nature seemingly steamrollered out of the way by a new, more aggressive one.

"El, just go to the café, hear her out at least," Carla said, her eyes pleading with Elodie.

Elodie looked at her friend and couldn't help but notice the smallest of smiles forming on her lips. Did Carla think this was funny? It most certainly wasn't. Elodie was being accused of a crime that she wouldn't commit against her worst enemy, let alone her best friend. She stood there resolutely for a moment before the steamroller of aggression and contempt began to idle.

"Ugh, alright then. I was just going for a nice calming walk but I know I need to go. Betty should hear my side," Elodie said, resigning herself to the fact that no matter how much she protested, she would, eventually, back down anyway so she may as well get it over with sooner rather than later.

Betty looked up as she heard the bell above the café's door tinkle. She had sat herself and Steph down on one side of the table that sat in the centre of the café and positioned an empty chair for Elodie on the other.

"Will you please tell me what's going on," Steph said, turning in her chair to face Betty, a look of determination on her drawn face. Betty didn't reply at first but instead stared fixedly straight ahead as if something on the wall happened to be the most interesting thing she had ever seen. Steph huffed; she was so angry, so hurt by Elodie. It was the dishonesty of it all, the fact that she'd played dumb and denied knowing anything at all despite conveniently forgetting the alarm, the door and knowing that all the day's takings were in the till. Never in a million years would Steph had thought Elodie capable of such a thing, but it seemed that the old adage, 'Desperate times called for desperate measures' was true. After what seemed like an age Elodie crossed the cafe looking nowhere near as sorry as Steph would have liked.

"Sit down love, we need to talk," Betty said, motioning to the chair opposite her, but before she had time even to retract her hand a torrent of apologetic words erupted from Elodie's lips.

Steph sat there the entire time, stony-faced and unable to look her friend directly in the eye. She was going to do exactly as her mum had said earlier that morning and take a backseat.

"I genuinely have no idea what happened to the money, I don't, really I don't," Elodie finished sadly, looking wildly from Betty to Steph and back again.

The barefacedness of it all made Steph's blood boil. She couldn't fathom why her mum was being so calm about it all; she hadn't even called the police yet and it had been hours since the burglary. Steph decided then and there that it was time to take matters into her own hands, despite Betty's stark warning not to. She opened her mouth to draw breath, she was going to let Elodie have it.

"Elodie, we know…" she started, but before she could finish Betty had put a hand up to silence her.

"I know you don't know where the money is, Elodie, and I know you had nothing to do with the robbery. That's because, putting it plainly, there wasn't one," Betty said. "The money was taken from the till last night, that much is true, but I was the one that took it."

Both Steph and Elodie stared at her in disbelief, their eyes widening further when Betty, after a moment of rummaging in her apron pocket produced a white envelope with Elodie's name written across it in black pen. She placed the envelope on the table and with one fluid movement slid it across the table and towards Elodie. All three women looked at the envelope before Elodie tentatively picked it up and peered inside.

"I don't understand," she whispered, her eyes not leaving the envelope even for the briefest of moments.

"I'll explain, then," Betty replied in a matter-of-fact tone. "Last night, after I went upstairs to bed I couldn't drop off, despite feeling awful and being dead on my feet. Something was bothering me, niggling away in the back of my mind, like. Anyway, I tossed and turned for hours, even thought about taking a sleeping pill. Then it hit me: I couldn't sleep because I was worried about you, you daft thing. So I came down here, took the money and put it in this envelope ready to give to you today. Only thing is, by the time I'd done all this it was the early hours meaning I ended up sleeping right through my alarm. Steph here opened up for me and saw the missing money, put two and two together and came up with five. Sorry, love, I should have told you," Betty finished.

Elodie stared at her, agog.

"You're giving me this? All this money?" she asked unbelievingly.

"Well, I'm lending it to you. Pay me back when you can. You've been a brilliant employee, a fabulous friend to me and an even better one to Steph, which reminds me. Don't you have something to say, darling?" Betty said, turning to her daughter with an accusatory glance.

"I, I... I'm sorry. I knew you wouldn't do something like that. I was just manic this morning and with the alarm and the door, well, I didn't know what to think. I'm so sorry, El," Steph said lamely.

Elodie looked at her. She did look genuinely sorry. Elodie accepted her apology, though she was still sore from how quickly Steph had been able to jump to the wrong conclusion. Elodie knew it would take some time before their friendship was back to normal.

"But what about the door? I'm so sure I locked it," Elodie asked.

"Oh, you did. When I came downstairs I still felt a bit out of sorts so I opened it for a bit of fresh air. I must have not closed it properly. I was really, very tired. Now, I want you to head off home. Stop in at the bank on your way and pay this in, then book yourself onto the best course you can find. You want to have the best chance at getting the best job once you're qualified, don't you?" Betty smiled. "Oh, and one more thing..."

Elodie looked up from the envelope of money; for some reason, it seemed very hard to keep her eyes from it.

"You're sacked, love, in the nicest possible way, of course. Now go on before I get emotional." Betty wiped a fictional tear from her cheek and stood up. Leaning over the table to give Elodie a hug, she whispered "Good luck!" in her ear and released her. Elodie stood up; she felt as though she were floating. Things seemed to be going in the right direction for once. She gave Betty a thankful smile, which faltered slightly as her gaze travelled from Betty and to Steph.

"See you then, I guess," Elodie said, before adding, "Thank you, Betty. You've no idea what this means to me."

"Sure I do, love, that's why I did it," Betty replied before waving Elodie out of the door. Once the door had closed behind her she turned to Steph.

"Looks like you've got a lot of making up to do, darling," Betty said.

"She'll come around," Steph said. "Elodie's incapable of holding a grudge, she won't stay mad for long, it's just not in her nature."

Betty gave her daughter a disapproving glance before making her way to the door, where she promptly turned the closed sign to open.

"Well, we're a woman down now. Looks like it's an all-hands-on-deck situation for a while. I'll ring round the girls and get Elodie's shifts covered. You'll be OK to hold the fort for a while, won't you?" Betty instructed as she made her way into the back so she could make her phone calls in relative peace and quiet.

CHAPTER 9

"LADIES AND GENTS, COULD YOU PLEASE TAKE your seats we're about to start," said a small, portly man at front of the room. He ran his hands through his thinning hair, which had been shaved short – probably to give the illusion of 'bald by choice'. Elodie looked around nervously; she hadn't spoken to a single person other than one of the cleaning guys who she'd got in the way of earlier, as he'd moved around her. She caught a sensual, musky scent that took her by surprise – she did not expect that from someone who emptied bins for a living. As the other students began pairing off together and sitting at the tables, all of which were facing the front of the room, Elodie began to panic. This was just like school all over again: she knew instantly that it would be she who was left on her own. Out of the corner of her eye, she saw a very attractive woman with long blonde hair and immaculately applied makeup waving at someone behind her. Not wanting to be in yet another person's way Elodie moved to the side and, more out of habit than anything, issued an apology. No one moved past her. Elodie turned around and saw that there was no one behind her at all. She looked over at the waving woman again, who was now laughing. She mouthed the words *'Sit here...'* at Elodie and patted the seat of the empty chair next to her. Elodie felt herself blush.

'Why am I such a dumbass?' she thought to herself as she hesitantly negotiated her way through the throng of new students.

"I'm Jessica, Jessica Kellah but everyone calls me Jess for short," the woman said once Elodie was seated. Elodie offered her new companion a small smile. The blonde woman, who Elodie thought must be in her mid-twenties, had been attractive from across the room, but now Elodie was mere inches away from her she could see that her new friend wasn't just attractive, she was downright beautiful. She had flawless, sun-kissed skin and the brightest of blue eyes, which were framed by long, dark eyelashes.

"Elodie Taylor," Elodie replied, holding out her hand in a business-like fashion and regretting the action immediately. Jess seemed not to notice Elodie's awkwardness; she flipped her long blonde hair over her shoulder and took Elodie's hand, shaking it in a soft yet business-like fashion.

"People, please," the man at the front of the room issued loudly. "Can we have some quiet? Otherwise you'll never get your wings."

The general hubbub fell to a soft whisper and finally descended into silence. Elodie looked around the room eagerly. She couldn't believe how much had changed in a couple of weeks. She had managed to get herself a place on one of the best courses in the country. It was a fair distance from her flat so a hotel stay was required, but with Betty's generous loan she could more than afford the extra expense. She'd been lucky: a previous student had fallen ill. Their loss was Elodie's gain, for now she sat here among her soon-to-be colleagues on a course that saw over seventy per cent of its graduates find their dream job. Anticipation coursed through her veins; she could hardly believe she could be so lucky and that Chase had put in a good word for her.

She returned her attention to the speaker, who had just announced himself as Gareth Townsend. He had been an air steward for over a decade and, as well as working for a swanky private airline, managed to find time to run one of the most sought-after, and expensive, courses in the country.

"So that's me, folks," he said, a pleasant northern lilt to his voice. He finished off his introduction with a lavish hand gesture and a small bow. "Now let's do that awful, cringe-worthy thing they do on company retreats and get to know one another. If you could stand up one by one, introduce yourself and give us a fun fact, that'd be fab."

The class obliged and as instructed stood up one by one, said their names and a little something about themselves.

Elodie met Louise Davies, a Glaswegian woman who had run several marathons and loved to ski; Natalie Thompson, who was first cousins with a very famous film star; Nick Pickett, who had once swum for Britain's under-eighteens team; and finally Lisa Jean, or 'LJ' as she liked to be called, who had once appeared in an episode of *Holby City* as an extra and could eat an entire Terry's Chocolate Orange in one go without feeling sick.

"Okay, who's next, then?" Gareth asked as he surveyed the room. Elodie looked around and, realising that she would be last if she didn't go now cleared her throat and stood up, she couldn't think of anything that made her sound even half as interesting as the people that had gone before her.

"Hi, I'm Elodie Taylor and I, well I'm honestly not that interesting," she said, a tone of weary resignation in her voice.

She glanced around the room; no one said a word. Her new course mates merely looked at her, some with a mixture of curiosity, others with a distinct air of indifference, or was that disdain? Elodie let out a small cough and decided that now was not the time to be self-deprecating she opened her mouth to speak but again, no words came. How was it that she couldn't think of one single, tiny thing that made her stand out?

"Oh come now, you came to me highly recommended so there must be something that sets you apart from the rest?" Gareth replied.

Elodie's mind raced, she hardly dared to believe it but Chase had come through for her after all. She must have made a really good impression for him to recommend her and highly as well.

"Well," Elodie thought hard. She must have one discernible talent, and then it struck her. "I guess, well there is this one thing. I can do this…" Elodie proceeded to stick out her tongue, curl it up and touch her nose with its very tip.

Elodie's special skill was met with an unappreciative silence, which caused Elodie to flush pink and sit down quickly. *'Ugh, that was so lame!'* she fumed at herself. Elodie glanced over towards Jess, feeling very much as though their fledgeling friendship may be over before it had started.

To her surprise, Jess was smiling; she bought her hand to her face as if she were going to whisper some big secret then proceeded to replicate Elodie's special skill superbly. Elodie broke into a relieved grin and felt instantly at ease. She was extremely grateful that Jess had taken pity on her. Elodie knew that she was going to like Jess. She had already shown herself to be fun and Elodie found herself looking forward to getting to know her better.

The course lasted for two weeks. In that time they were expected to learn absolutely everything about what it took to be a member of the cabin crew. Elodie was amazed at how much went into it; she marvelled as delivery of top-notch service gave way to health and safety, first aid, emergency landings and perhaps the strangest of all, how to talk properly. Apparently, according to Gareth, an overly strong accent was an absolute no-no. This information caused Louise Davies, the Scottish runner, to utter an explosion of expletives under her breath. Evidently, as it turned out, Louise hadn't been quite as subtle as she had thought, as the following day there was nothing but an empty chair where she had previously sat.

Elodie had forgotten what it was like to be a student but she took to it like a duck to water and had wished whole-heartedly that she'd been this diligent during her earlier years. Every morning she carried in her brightly coloured notepad and took thorough notes, determined that not only would she pass this course, but she would do so with flying colours. Jess, as it turned out, was every inch the perfect human being Elodie had thought. She wasn't the strongest student but always tried and wasn't afraid to ask for help and always seemed to have a constant air of sunniness emitting from her. Elodie wasn't jealous of Jess; maybe a previous version of herself would have been, but as it stood now, this new and improved Elodie was in absolute awe.

Elodie had rung Carla from her hotel room one night. She wanted to check in and after a few days thought it was best that she made contact. She hadn't had time to reply to anyone's messages. She had spent every waking minute either studying or socialising with her classmates as several of them had booked into the same hotel, including Jessica whose room was a few doors down from Elodie's. Carla hadn't sounded impressed with Jessica and had issued a stark warning about people like her.

"El, I'm telling you, no one is that perfect. She could be a psycho murderer, with bodies in her freezer for all you know," Carla had said, only half-joking.

Elodie had laughed and quickly changed the subject, getting the distinct feeling that Carla was more than a little jealous. Instead, Elodie concentrated on what had been happening at home. Carla's mood had lifted when she got onto the subject of her own work. A big modelling job she had really wanted had come off and she had been booked for the same day as Elodie was to take her final exam. Elodie was so excited for Carla and momentarily forgot about her looming examination; instead, she focused on how great it would be to graduate from her course the same day Carla got her dream job. The excitement Elodie felt was almost palpable, the idea of her and Carla achieving their dreams in unison delighted her. She didn't know what was more exciting, the idea of that, or the prospect of the celebration they would have afterwards.

It was the evening of the penultimate day. A few of the students were going out for 'last night drinks' but Elodie had elected to get an early night instead. She ran herself a bath, put on some chilled music and disrobed. Looking at herself in the mirror she admired her reflection, and for the first time in a long while was happy with what she saw. It was amazing what a fortnight forgoing cake as a substitute for a proper meal had done to her body. She was no size zero, but her figure was definitely more streamlined. She felt healthier, fitter and more in control of herself than she had done before. Elodie lowered herself into the hotel bath and took in a sharp intake of breath as the water burned and prickled her pale skin. She shot out a hand and instinctively turned the cold tap on full blast. Cold water cascaded into the bath and after a few moments the temperature was far more bearable and she was able to lower herself in fully. She let out a low, contented sigh as she reclined but immediately regretted not bringing her magazine in with her. The course had proved to have a few extra perks that Elodie hadn't banked on, including a seemingly endless supply of travel magazines littered about, ripe for the taking. She had made the most of this and had gathered several of them up for a little extra-curricular reading. Right now, in the bath, would have been the perfect time for that reading, if only she hadn't left them on the bed. Elodie weighed up her options and decided that a bubble bath this good wasn't to be wasted by just lying in it so she got out and with water dripping onto the plush carpet padded back into the bedroom. She snatched up the closest magazine and darted back to the tub. As she lowered herself back into the bath she heard the familiar buzz of her mobile. She'd plugged it in to charge and left it on the bedside table. Elodie knew that it would be Carla, calling to wish her luck. Elodie gave herself a mental nudge; the following day wasn't just a big deal for her it was also the day of Carla's first big modelling job.

'I'll message her before I go to bed,' Elodie compromised, determined to let Carla know that she was thinking of her. The idea of getting back out of the bath again didn't even flit across her mind; she tuned out the vibrations of the phone still buzzing away noisily and opened her magazine, immediately getting lost in the pages before her. She closed her eyes momentarily and pretended that the warmth of the water around her was actually the hot sun beating down on her skin and the sound of it moving when she did was actually the waves breaking on the beach. Elodie managed to spend a record-breaking amount of time in the bath and only hauled herself out when her skin was puckered and the water had gone cold. Once she had dried off with the hotel's oversized fluffy white towels, she slipped into her pyjamas – an oversized T-shirt and shorts combo – and settled down for the night. Finding herself beginning to doze Elodie reached out for her mobile and set the alarm, she noticed with perplexity that the call she had missed earlier was from a number she didn't know. A mild sort of panic began to settle over her. The only thing she could think was that tomorrow's examination had changed somehow: maybe the time, or possibly the place? Was it too late to call the number back? She decided that she had little choice on the matter,

as the alternative was to potentially miss her exam and fail her entire course. She couldn't possibly go back home, with no qualification, no job and her tail firmly between her legs, having wasted Betty's money.

"Hi, Elodie," the unfamiliar voice said down the line. Elodie pulled the phone away from her ear and checked the number again but she knew neither number nor voice. "Hello?" the arcane voice questioned.

"Errr, hi. Sorry, I don't have this number saved…" she trailed off, not wanting to ask outright who it was she had called. It somehow seemed impertinent, especially considering it was she who had made the call.

There was a noise not unlike a sigh, and then the voice spoke again.

"Elodie, it's Chase Ford. I just wanted to wish you well for tomorrow. Gareth says you've taken to the course like a duck to water, I'm glad it seems to be working out for you."

Elodie's heart beat faster: his voice was so smooth and she found herself wishing that he were saying these words in person instead of down a phone line. She wrestled with herself, tearing her thoughts away from how good his words sounded and instead tried to focus on what they meant.

"Oh, thanks," was all she could muster before adding, against her better judgement, "Sorry, why are you ringing?"

"Just to wish you well. That's all. I don't often put myself out for other people, Elodie; this is what you'd call a first for me. I want to make sure you do well."

Elodie was unsure how she should react to these words. Calling to wish her well was a kind gesture, but she couldn't help but feel that this benevolence came with a dash of selfishness. Letting out a small cough she thanked him. There was silence down the line for a moment.

"Is there anything else?" Elodie asked somewhat awkwardly, partly in an effort to fill the silence and partly to try and find out exactly what this was about.

"That was all I wanted. Goodnight." Chase hung up with these final words, the point of the conversation still unclear.

She pulled the phone away from her ear and stared at it.

"Well, that was surreal," she said aloud, questioning what on earth that had actually been about. Shuddering, she wondered why it was she suddenly felt even more pressure bearing down on her? Sure, Chase had pulled some strings, but really, how far out of his way had he actually gone? Elodie thought not far enough to warrant a call like that. *"I want to make sure you do well."* Had they been words of encouragement, or a well-veiled threat?

Elodie didn't have time to dwell; the hour was late and she needed to get plenty of rest in order to be at her best for the following day. Putting her phone back down she settled into bed and drew the covers around her tightly before turning off the light and rolling over. Tomorrow was going to be a big day and she was going to need all the sleep she could get, especially now.

CHAPTER 10

ELODIE'S HANDS WERE SHAKING EVEN MORE NOW than they had been when she had sat the exam. Against her better judgement, she tore the large brown envelope open but found herself unable to go any further.

"Go on then," urged Carla. The two friends looked at one another, Elodie's eyes meeting Carla's.

"Hey, Hey! No, don't!" Elodie shouted as Carla ripped the envelope from her hands and took out the letter within.

Elodie's protests fell silent as she watched Carla's eyes scan the document in front of her. Carla folded the letter in half and put it on the table next to them, Elodie felt her spirit dip as she saw the look on her friend's face.

"I knew it," Elodie said, a stony tone to her voice. "It took me three attempts to pass my bloody driving test, in an automatic! Well, I'll just have to try again. I'll ask Betty for my job back, I'll work every hour, I'll save and I'll just have to take it again. I really want this, Carla, and I'm not going to let one measly failure stop me."

Carla nodded before turning away from her friend. She opened the fridge and took out a giant bottle of Champagne and turned to Elodie, unable to suppress her smile for a moment longer.

"Are you kidding me?" Elodie said, not knowing whether she should fling her arms around Carla or slap her. She instead opted to snatch up the piece of paper lying on the table and read it for herself. "I got a distinction!" she said, her voice trailing off in amazement. Elodie couldn't believe it: the result that lay there in black and white, mere inches from her face, was something she had never expected, not even in her wildest dreams.

Suddenly, and without warning images of an older man flooded her mind. She thought about their bodies writhing together, about being lifted from bed to dresser in an effortless movement that made her feel as light as air. She couldn't seem to escape these thoughts of Chase; she had managed to push them to the back of her mind whilst she concentrated on passing her course, but now that was behind her it seemed that now he was only ever absent from her mind momentarily, concealed by a thin veil of self-control.

"Earth to El," Carla said, her voice bulldozing into Elodie's consciousness.

Elodie looked up and saw Carla's face smiling and holding out a glass of Champagne, which Elodie took without question, despite it being eleven in the morning.

Steph joined them a few hours later. Things had been frosty between her and Elodie since Steph had all but accused her of robbing the café. Elodie still couldn't quite believe that one of her oldest and dearest friends could jump to that conclusion so easily. Carla agreed, it hadn't looked good, but Steph should have known instantly that Elodie would never, and could never, do anything like that.

"Congratulations," Steph said, holding up another bottle of fizz and smiling at Elodie wanly.

Elodie returned the smile, took the bottle from Steph's hands and without looking into her eyes stepped aside to let her in. Carla was in the bathroom and as such meant that the two women didn't have their mediator to navigate them through the tricky rivers of best friends that have fallen out.

"So, how are you?" Elodie asked as she placed the bottle of Champagne in the fridge. She was trying so hard to be friendly, but somehow she was only just managing to be civil. There was an awkward silence that filled the room and Elodie internally begged for Carla's speedy return.

"I'm not good, El," Steph began. "I feel so bad about what happened at the café. I don't know why I said the things I did. I was just, oh I don't know, being a bit of a bitch, I guess. I felt like shit for ages about it, still do. I didn't want to talk to you while you were on your course. Not over the phone or text and certainly not while you needed to concentrate. I thought I'd leave it till you were done; you know,

154

damage limitation and all that. I'd have felt terrible if you'd failed."

"Yes. I'd hate for *you* to feel bad," Elodie said sarcastically, then seeing the crestfallen expression on Steph's face decided that accepting her apology would be the right thing to do. She obviously felt bad and Elodie couldn't stand the idea of making her feel worse; and after all, what real harm had been done? Elodie was no good at holding a grudge, she never had been. Ill-feeling had always made her feel just that, ill.

"I'm really sorry, El, please can we go back to normal? Please?"

"Of course," Elodie said after a pause, wrapping her arms around her friend and drawing her in for a hug. She was almost certain she had heard a stifled sob from Steph but, given Steph's no-nonsense and steadfast demeanour, thought it best not to highlight it. Instead, she released her friend and turned quickly to the cupboard to retrieve a glass for her.

"Thanks," Steph said taking the glass from Elodie and raising it in the air. "Cheers, here's to you, passing your course and all the exciting possibilities that lay ahead of you."

They clinked glasses just as Carla appeared from the bathroom; she broke out into a grin when she saw the scene in front of her.

"Jesus, it took you guys long enough. I'm glad the claws are away and we're all being a little more Katie Holmes and a little less Katie Hopkins now! You didn't see me throwing my toys out of the pram when Elodie forgot to say good luck for my first ever, oh so important, best thing in my life, modelling job, did you?" she said, convivially giving Elodie a wink.

Elodie's mind flew back to that night: it had been that call from Chase that had done it. She had had every intention of wishing Carla the best, but once she'd got off the phone to Chase everything other than him had been flung from her mind. Carla had been annoyed, Elodie could tell, but she was so easy-going she didn't make a thing of it and instead taunted Elodie by insisting that she took her out for a slap-up meal by way of apology.

"Hello… earth to Elodie, come in Elodie," Carla said, waving her hand in front of Elodie's face. "Ah, there you are. Now, can we please drink ourselves into oblivion and order a god damn pizza?!"

Elodie laughed: trust Carla to have her mind on food. She had never been able to work out how Carla managed to keep her figure; the odd run definitely did not cancel out all the booze and takeaways she consumed. Elodie made a mental note to rein in her own dietary extravagances, Gareth had issued words of caution about staying in shape, which now echoed in her mind. She didn't want to give potential employers any reason not to take her on. She shuddered slightly as the realisation set in that the course had only been the first step. Now all the hard work would really start. Getting qualified was one thing, but finding a job was quite another.

The evening passed by quickly. Carla had been sent a few of the raw shots from her shoot and, even though only her feet were in the pictures she proceeded to show them off proudly. Elodie and Steph made 'oohing' and 'ahhing' noises as each picture appeared, and after a while, Carla seemed to be satisfied because she slammed her laptop shut and exclaimed that she had had a fabulous idea that consisted of Elodie showing them what she had learnt on her course.

"Oh go on El," Steph said coaxingly, "let's see what my mum's money paid for."

Was that bitterness Elodie thought she could hear in Steph's voice? She looked at her friend, expecting to see her tone reflected in her expression, but all that was there was mild curiosity and a half-smile. Elodie scolded herself for thinking badly of her friend and stood up.

"OK then, passengers, if I can have your attention," she said in an authoritative tone that made both Steph and Carla sit up straight and give Elodie their full consideration. "Welcome! We're excited to have you aboard this 'Elodie Airlines' flight and we appreciate your attention as we demonstrate the safety features of this aircraft," Elodie went on. She delivered a perfectly rehearsed speech and mimed her way through it in expert fashion. When she was done she gave a small bow to the applause of her friends, who both raised their glasses and with the last dregs of their Champagne toasted her performance.

"Bravo, bravo," Carla said, sidling up next to Elodie and placing a slender arm around her.

Elodie returned the gesture, noticing that although Steph's reaction had been one of warmth and pride, she did not get up from the sofa and join her and Carla in a celebratory hug.

"I need to get to bed," Carla said through a yawn. "I've got three castings tomorrow and a date afterwards. I figured, why waste a face full of makeup on auditions only?"

"Three?" Elodie asked in disbelief. "Wow, that's amazing, why didn't you say anything?"

"I didn't want to steal your thunder," Carla replied. "Besides, they're only casting calls, I probably won't get any of them."

"Not with that attitude you won't," quipped Steph as she zipped up her bag and slung it over her shoulder in a very final way. "I'm going to get a cab back, girls. I fancy waking up in my own bed in the morning."

"Sure thing, Grandma," Carla said, giving Steph a kiss on the cheek and opening the door for her. "Let us know when you're back home safe."

"I will," Steph promised, although all three of them knew that she wouldn't. As the door closed behind her Carla turned to Elodie with a stern sort of look that seemed alien across her features.

"I need to talk to you, El. I don't want to sound like a nag and I'm not having a go, but I don't know if you remember when you moved in and we talked about you taking over Dora's rent when it ran out?"

Elodie nodded, she knew this had been coming. She'd shoved her money worries to the back of her mind; she knew that she should have earmarked some of Betty's money for rent, but there just hadn't been enough for that and the course. "Well, Dora's rent runs out really soon and I don't want to put pressure on you but I really can't afford to cover both lots, even with ol' Papa helping out. I don't mind holding out for a little bit, say another week? I can put it on my credit card, but after that..." she trailed off. Carla really wasn't good at this sort of thing.

Elodie nodded morosely. She couldn't expect a free ride from Carla anymore; she'd been lucky so far and she knew it. Feeling like she had only herself to blame, she decided that her number-one priority really had to be to find a job; the pressure to start earning was starting to loom further forward. She'd worked really hard to get qualified and she was damned if she was going to do anything other than chase her dream. The world was hers now and all she had to do was take it.

As it would happen, taking the world for her own was far easier said than done. Elodie applied for job after job and for her efforts received rejection after rejection. She had aimed her bow high, to begin with: she had a strong desire to work with only the best, and despite her lack of actual experience she still applied. Living with Carla had begun to have an effect on Elodie; she no longer felt quite so useless and felt a fire, a longing within, that, up until recently, had been a completely alien feeling to her. Elodie found these new desires unnerving and empowering in equal measure and each fresh rejection letter only made her more determined.

"Why don't you just call that guy again?" Carla asked after Elodie slammed her laptop shut following one particularly blunt rejection email.

"Because," Elodie argued, "I am not relying on him to babysit every step of my career. I've done the relying on a guy, remember? It doesn't work out so well. Besides, I don't actually know him and I can't keep begging favours from someone I don't know."

"But you want to know him, don't you?" Carla asked slyly as she sidled up next to Elodie who up until that moment had been happily sat on the sofa by herself.

Carla took the laptop from Elodie's lap and placed it on the coffee table.

"Look, I know you like him. You do this thing whenever he comes up in conversation," Carla fanned herself in a mock 'hot under the collar' kind of way and gave Elodie a coy, swooning grin.

"Is that supposed to be me?" Elodie asked incredulously.

"It isn't *supposed* to be you, it *is* you!" Carla exclaimed.

"Come off it, you know you do it. You go all gooey-eyed every time he's brought up."

Elodie retorted by rolling her eyes, snatching the laptop back up and getting back to work.

"I do not," she said resolutely and just a touch haughtily. "Look, he did me a favour because he could and for that I'm grateful, but nothing else. I don't want or need anything else from him! Now, if you don't mind, I need to get back on the hunt."

Carla chose not to respond to this, she knew Elodie was kidding herself. It was obvious that she fancied the guy and her protestations only fanned the flames of Carla's suspicion.

"Okay then, suit yourself. I'm just saying that if you've got the option, why not use it. It's not against the law to ask for favours from men, or does that offend your delicate, feminist sensibilities?" Carla laughed and ducked as Elodie threw a cushion at her.

"Don't you have an audition to get to?" Elodie asked, more out of hope than any real inkling.

"No, actually I've got a job to get to and I'm late. Sorry, I don't have any more time to try and beat some sense into you about this," Carla said as she slipped on a silky-looking sports jacket and headed for the door. She was part-way through when she stopped and turned to Elodie. "El, don't feel guilty about liking someone, of course I'd prefer it if you stayed single with me forever! But, you know, you've got to put yourself first sometimes. Just think about it, OK?"

"I don't, I don't." Elodie protested, pretty sure it was obvious that the only person she was trying to convince was herself. "He's way too old for me."

She knew that even if she was interested in him in a romantic sense he wouldn't be interested in her: she was young enough to be his, well, not his daughter – the idea of that was just too inappropriate. She shook the thought of Chase from her mind. The thought of the rent, however, seemed to be lodged there. It was due in less than a week and although Carla had bought her some time with the promise of putting half on her credit card, Elodie knew that she would have to step up sooner rather than later if she didn't want to find herself homeless.

A week later and with her rent now overdue Elodie opened Carla's laptop and logged into her email account. She had been invited for several interviews and was awaiting the results. She didn't hold out much hope; her confidence seemed to have taken a bashing. One of the women that had interviewed her had been more a little standoffish and Elodie hadn't felt great vibes from her, and the others had been, at best, OK. But she was trying to stay positive and told herself that something great would be just around the corner. She just needed patience and a positive mental attitude.

She scanned her inbox. There was the usual junk mail, fifteen per cent off her favourite clothing website and a whole host of stuff that she wasn't interested in. There were also two rejection letters. Elodie sighed and thought that maybe she needed help with her interview technique. She scrolled down and about halfway down was an email from an address she didn't recognise. Her pulse quickened as she double-clicked, before doing a double-take. She skimmed the email twice, and then a third time just to make doubly sure she had read it properly.

Dear Miss Taylor,

We are delighted to inform you that your application with 'Zip Air' has been successful and that we would like to invite you to join our team. An introduction day has been arranged for Thursday 1st June commencing at 9 am. Please phone the above number to book your place, cite your uniform requirements and your unique employee code as listed. We look forward to seeing you then.

Warmest regards,
Vanessa Jane Priestly
Cabin Manager.

Her hands shook slightly. The moment she'd been waiting for was finally here: the start of her career. All the rejection, the failed interviews and the feelings of being not quite good enough melted away as she re-read the email once more. She wished more than anything that Carla or Steph were here to share her news. A text message would have to suffice; she got out her phone, took a picture of the screen and sent it to her friends. Elodie waited, staring at the group chat, expecting any moment to see excited replies from her friends, but nothing came. The message had been delivered, and read, yet still, there was nothing. No words of congratulations, nothing at all. There wasn't so much as even a thumbs-up emoji, which would have been insulting at first but now would be rather gratefully received.

Elodie looked at her watch. She knew that both of them were at the café. Carla, although doing well with her modelling, wasn't about to give up the comforting stability of a regular pay packet just yet. This was something Elodie had regretted doing up until this moment in time. Now, throwing caution to the wind, packing it all in and chasing her dreams seemed like the best decision in the entire world. She smiled to herself: she had an overwhelming urge to hang out of the balcony and scream at the top of her lungs that she had done it, but propriety forced her hand so instead she did a little fist bump as the word "Yes!" escaped her lips. She looked at her phone again, still nothing from the girls. *'They're probably busy, rushed off their feet or something,'* she thought to herself as she got up and poured herself a small glass of rosé wine. She leant over the kitchen counter and took a sip. She had done it, and not even being ignored by her friends could take that away from her.

Elodie suddenly remembered Jessica, the woman she had befriended on her course and wondered how she was getting on. They had been firm friends during the course's duration. Elodie had helped her out whenever she could. Jessica had struggled with the workload. Elodie had been so happy to have a friend that she had been delighted to lend a helping hand. She fired off a quick message to Jessica, not sure whether or not she genuinely wanted to see how she was doing or whether she just wanted someone to share her news with. The phone vibrated in her hand moments later: Jessica had replied in rapid fashion and with way more than just a thumbs-up emoji. She congratulated Elodie over and over again and insisted that they meet up that night to celebrate. Elodie drafted out a response: she couldn't think of anything better than putting her glad rags on and celebrating in style, especially with someone that had gone through the same thing.

"Well, until tonight it looks like I'm celebrating on my own," she said aloud. Her voice echoed around the empty room and suddenly Elodie didn't feel like celebrating very much at all, in spite of Jessica's positive reaction. She couldn't help but feel saddened by Carla and Steph's lack of interest. Why hadn't either of her best friends called, texted or made contact in any way? She knew they had seen the message, the tell-tale blue ticks told her so, but still she heard nothing.

Mid-afternoon, Elodie started to get ready for her evening. She really went to town with the pampering, believing that she well and truly deserved it. Before long she was sat amidst a sea of bubbles in a lovely hot bath with a face mask on and her wine in hand. It had been several hours since she had received the news of her job offer and the giddy bliss in which she had been so wrapped in was beginning to relinquish its grip. She hadn't heard from Steph at all and Carla had managed a 'well done' and invited her to come for a coffee at the café after hours. Elodie hadn't replied yet; she was still feeling sour that they hadn't made more of a fuss. She knew they were both busy and tried not to feel annoyed so washed the ill-feeling back with some wine. She had even seen that Carla had posted a very arty picture of some cakes to Betty's social media feed, which made her even more annoyed, so she had done her old trick of putting her phone in her dressing table drawer. Removing the temptation seemed to have had the desired effect because now she felt happy, calm and contented in her bath.

She took another sip of wine and closed her eyes, allowing the water to wash over her. She still couldn't believe she was going to start work, and so soon as well. She would take the next week to really enjoy herself, she decided that she might even treat herself to a little shopping trip and couldn't see why not. After all, she would have a decent salary coming in soon enough and with everything she'd achieved, surely she deserved a little extravagance?

Elodie was just drifting off into a daydream, which consisted of white sandy beaches, hidden coves and beautiful waterfalls when she heard the unmistakable sound of the front door creak; she opened her eyes and sat up sharply.

"Hello?" she called aloud, uncertainty creeping into her voice. The café still had a couple of hours until it closed so she knew it was far too early for Carla to be back yet. There was no reply so with her heart beating fast Elodie reached for her towel and climbed out of the tub. She placed a near-trembling hand on the doorknob and was about to turn it and confront the intruder when common sense took hold of her. She removed her hand and instead slid the bolt across as quietly as she could manage. What on earth had she been thinking, what was her plan? To confront the stranger in nothing but a towel, with sopping wet hair and her face caked in a bright pink clay mask?

"Hello?" she called again, louder this time and with as much confidence and bravado as she could muster. If someone was out there she didn't want them to know she was frightened. She could have kicked herself for leaving her phone in that drawer. *'Of all the stupid things to do,'* she thought angrily.

"El, are you in the bathroom?" Carla's voice sounded. Elodie felt relief wash over her, although she thought she detected a note of panic in Carla's voice. Perhaps she too had assumed someone who shouldn't be was in the flat.

"For God's sake!" Elodie exhaled. "You almost gave me a heart attack. I thought you were someone trying to rob the place!"

"Nope, just me. I forgot something so had to nip back, you are coming to the café later, aren't you?"

"I am for a bit but I've said I'll meet a friend later. You know, Jessica from my course?" Elodie said, a little hurt that Carla hadn't offered any congratulations in person.

"Jessica eh? Should I be jealous?" Carla said laughing. "Just come to the café for seven, OK? Oh and wear something nice; we might go out for dinner or something."

Elodie opened her mouth to reply. Hadn't Carla been listening? She was going out afterwards! But before any sound could escape her lips, the front door had creaked once again and Elodie knew that Carla was no longer there. Elodie bristled: Carla had dragged her out of the bath, scared her half to death and then done a runner without even a word of well done.

Elodie scrubbed the face mask from her skin a little too pugnaciously, as when she looked up at her reflection her complexion was almost as pink as the mask had been. She left the bathroom in favour of the bedroom; water fell in fat droplets onto the living room floor as she crossed it. Determined not to let Carla's apparent disinterest mar her evening, she closed her eyes and took in three deep, calming breaths that, Elodie was pleased to note, had an instant effect on her mood. She vowed not to turn into a diva about this and reminded herself that both Carla and Steph had been with her through thick and thin. Steph had always been a source of support and advice and Carla always knew how to cheer her up. Elodie sat down at her dressing table and rubbed her damp hair with a towel. She pulled her hair into a loose ponytail and began to ready herself. She applied her makeup carefully and with effort, wanting the first evening of properly having her shit together to be reflected in her appearance. She opted for an understated smoky eye, a pale pink blush and a slick of peach-coloured lip-gloss, which finished off her pretty yet professional look perfectly.

Elodie accidentally spent a little too much time on her makeup so that she now barely had any time to do her hair. She pulled the hair-tie away from her and let her chestnut hair fall around her face; it was still damp. Elodie checked the time: she needed to be leaving soon. She blasted the hairdryer on it for a few moments, tipping her head upside down as she did so. After a minute or two she decided that enough was enough and righted herself, she brushed her hair quickly and, once satisfied that it looked OK, pulled on a pair of black skinny jeans, grey vest top and black jacket that was, in all honesty, the smartest thing Elodie seemed to own. She had time for one last look in the mirror before heading out the door and was rather pleased with her reflection. She slipped on a pair of mid-heels and bolted for the door.

"Shit!" she exclaimed, "when will I ever learn? Phone!"

Elodie darted back through the living room and into her bedroom, pulled the drawer of her dressing table open and

164

grabbed her phone, noticing with a grim hesitation that she would soon have to switch it to low power mode if it were to last the night.

As she marched down the road towards Betty's Book Café, Elodie checked her watch. It was a ten to seven: she would have just enough time to manage a quick coffee with the girls before heading out to meet Jessica. A spark of resentment flared as she walked and Elodie found herself being annoyed once again that they hadn't made more of a fuss. She shook her head dramatically as if to dislodge those thoughts; her usual sunny disposition being momentarily overshadowed left her feeling at odds with herself. She vowed not to be so petty and powered on. After all, they had been at work all day and it would be nice to have a celebratory coffee with them.

Catching her reflection in the window of Creaseys, the estate agents, she couldn't help but smile to herself and found herself administering a little pat on the back. She was proud and excited at the thought of her new job and also impressed that all her pampering had had the desired effect. For once she liked the way she looked; maybe it had something to do with the fact that she had taken complete control over her life that filled her with a new-found confidence, or maybe it was the new contouring kit she'd borrowed from Carla. The stark contrast in their skin tones meant that Carla had plenty of what she called 'pale waste' left. *'Not too shabby, Taylor,'* she thought to herself as she felt a little spark of certainty flare within. Everything was falling into place for her. The few short weeks in which she had found herself without a home to call her own, newly single and in need of a job had been a trying time, although made immensely less stressful by her friends, who offered their support and help and asked for nothing in return – except rent, which she could of course now pay for with her new job. As she rounded the corner and saw the familiar frontage of Betty's looming ever closer, she quickened her pace, the desire to see Steph and Carla doubling with each step.

The café was in semi-darkness and the front door had been left ajar, which Elodie found most odd. She pushed it open and the familiar jingle sounded from above. The last chime had barely ceased when the café was thrown into a blaze of light.

"Surprise!" many voices declared from all around her.

Elodie glanced around, completely dumbstruck. She broke out into a wide smile: there, in Betty's Book Café, were all of her friends. Cute bunting hung from the ceiling, which read 'Congratulations Elodie!' and balloons of all colours had been placed as far as the eye could see. The table closest to the window was laden with party nibbles and a huge cake in the shape of an aeroplane, which Betty must have spent all afternoon on. Someone thrust a glass of something sparkling into Elodie's hand and the group raised their glasses to Elodie and her new job. Happiness swelled and Elodie was taken over by a distinct sense of belonging and love, something she hadn't felt so strongly in such a long time.

"Jessica!?" Elodie exclaimed, now the shock had worn off and she was able to take in who was actually in attendance. "What are you doing here? Were you in on this?"

"Not at all. I got a text message, from your phone telling me about the plan." She nodded towards Carla who was pouring out glasses of fizz and laughing wildly at something that she obviously found very funny.

Elodie was confused, she remembered all too well Carla coming back into the flat but her phone had been hidden away; how would she have known where it was? Carla, having seen the two women talking, made her way towards them, a warm smile on her lips and an almost smug spring in her step.

"Congratulations El," she said, leaning in and giving Elodie a kiss on the cheek. "Sorry if you thought we were ignoring you, we were in overdrive trying to sort this out last minute."

Elodie thanked her for all the effort they had gone to and took a sip of Champagne. The crisp amber liquid slipped down her throat easily and she felt a warming sensation in her chest.

"I don't understand, you were in and out in minutes. How did you know to text Jessica? Hell, how did you know where my phone even was?" Elodie asked, nonplussed.

"Honest answer, I didn't. I was looking for something else

and just opened your drawer and there it was. Jessica had sent you a message so I replied and filled her in on what was going off. I didn't want her to get stood up, after all!"

Elodie nodded: that made sense. But did it?

"What were you looking for?" she probed, not quite satisfied with Carla's explanation. Before Carla had a chance to reply, the tinkle of the doorbell sounded again and Elodie, more out of habit than anything else, looked around. Standing there in an impeccable outfit of dark denim jeans and black roll-neck, which showcased his broad physique, was Chase Ford. He gave a stiff smile as he entered and Elodie thought for a moment that she saw his suave self-confidence waver. She must have been mistaken, though, because he greeted everyone as if they were old friends. His eyes met hers and she found a smile begin to play around the corners of her mouth.

"Congratulations young lady," he said as he took a glass of Champagne from a nearby table. "Gareth tells me you passed with flying colours, if you'll pardon the pun." Elodie nodded, unable to find any words. "And now I hear you've got a new job to boot," he gave her a pat on the shoulder and Elodie found that she was disappointed that his touch was of a professional, perhaps bordering on friendly, disposition.

"Thanks," she stammered, taking a sip of Champagne herself, more out of discomfiture than any real desire for a drink. "I... Sorry, I... I don't understand how you're here?" she finished uneasily.

Chase laughed. It wasn't a cruel laugh so much, but the sound made Elodie feel small.

"Ah, the man of the hour managed to make it," Carla said happily. "Hope you don't mind, El, but that's what I was in your room for."

Elodie looked at her, still not completely sure Carla meant.

"I don't understand..." Elodie began.

"The card? You know, the one that Edward wrote his number on the back of. Well, I remembered that it was Chase's card, wasn't it? I thought it was only fair to invite him, he was the one who put all of this in motion, after all."

Chase seemed to swell with pride and Elodie felt a twinge of annoyance. Sure, Chase had helped her get on the course but she was the one who had done all the work. He hadn't helped her pass the exam, or aided her job hunt. He hadn't been the one filling out application form after application form and he certainly hadn't been the one fighting back the tears as he read his umpteenth rejection letter. It seemed very much like he was the one getting all the credit when it had been she who had done all the work. She figured that this was how a racehorse must feel when it sees its rider lifting the winning trophy.

"I'm afraid I can't take all the credit," Chase said, as if reading her mind. "Gareth tells me you excelled in all areas, you really put the others to shame. Well apart from one girl who, from what I hear did almost as well as you."

As if knowing he was talking about her, Jessica appeared by Elodie's side. She had teased her long blonde hair into loose curls and had draped it elegantly over one shoulder. She flipped it back and extended a hand towards Chase with such confidence that it made Elodie feel envious. She shrugged the feeling off and continued to play spectator as the two conversed.

"Almost as well. I beat you to getting a job, though. I started at Argent Private Air the week after we completed the course. One-nil to me," she laughed and gave Elodie a playful tap on the arm and ran her fingers through her hair.

Elodie couldn't help it, a wave of dislike for Jessica washed over her and she found herself wishing that Carla hadn't invited her at all. Chase and Jessica fell into easy conversation that flowed as easily as a river does running downhill. She felt very much like a third wheel and more than once tried to make a break for it. Jessica seemed to sense that something was wrong and kept drawing her back in. Elodie knew this was an act of friendship but it felt more and more that Jessica was just doing it out of pity and she was cast out of the conversation almost as quickly as she had been drawn back in. Elodie felt well and truly trapped. She glanced around and caught Steph's eye. Steph raised a knowing eyebrow and beckoned her over. Elodie felt a great wave of gratitude rush towards her friend and, making her excuses, managed to back away from Chase and Jessica. Jessica didn't seem to notice Elodie leave this time. She was still chatting animatedly, flicking her hair over her shoulder repeatedly and flashing Chase a perfectly polished smile that would have any Hollywood A-lister jealous of her dentistry. Elodie sensed more than saw, Chase's eyes follow her as she retreated towards Steph and felt embarrassment begin to bubble inside her.

'*He must think I'm such a dork,*' she thought to herself, before shaking her head and deciding quite honestly that she didn't actually care what he thought.

As the evening drew to a close Elodie reflected on the day. She felt really quite tired now, which could have a fair amount to do with the fact that she had drunk more than her fair share of Champagne and eaten more than her fair share of cake.

"Not keeping you up, are we?" Chase's voice said from behind her as she stifled a yawn. She wheeled round and shook her head.

"No, no not at all," she said apologetically. "It's been an eventful day, that's all."

"You wait. The life of a flight attendant is a busy one: you won't know tired until you've done back-to-back shifts, been through three different time zones and travelled thousands of miles all in one week." He offered her a smile and then leant over and gave her a kiss on the cheek. He pulled away and Elodie's hand shot to the place where his lips had been. "Seriously, though, Elodie, well done." With that closing statement, he turned on his heel and in the blink of an eye had disappeared out of the door and into the cool night air.

Elodie stood there for a few long moments, her fingertips still pressed against her cheek. She had felt something in his kiss: electricity. It had been such a small gesture but something so big at the same time. She didn't know whether he had felt anything; his demeanour and tone certainly hadn't given anything away. She was probably reading too much into it, the alcohol clearly playing tricks on her mind. She cast her thoughts back to the rest of the evening: Chase and Jessica wrapped up in deep conversation, exclusive to the two of them.

CHAPTER 11

ELODIE HAD BEEN WORKING FOR ZIP AIR FOR TWO weeks. They operated from City Airport, which was a bit of a nightmare to get to but Elodie wasn't about to start complaining about her commute just yet. She had made friends with her colleagues and although the workload was challenging in parts Elodie had, thus far, found it a bit of a letdown. Zip Air flew all over Europe, and while that wasn't exactly the far-flung destination line Elodie had hoped to work for, she had fathomed that you couldn't have everything you wanted all at once. You needed to work your way to your goal. Nothing happened overnight and it was a certainty that no one was going to hand her dream job on a platter. Life just didn't work that way.

She was looking forward to the weekend; she had booked the time off to cover for Carla. The idea of being able to slip back into her old life, even just for the weekend, was a comforting one to her. Carla had wanted the weekend as her own in order to visit her dad, a wealthy, briefcase-carrying businessman, as it was Father's Day. Since mothers, fathers, grandparents, cousins or any other day invented by the greetings card industry had never been important in Elodie's family, she had told Carla that she would cover her shift. Betty had been thrilled at this news, which made Elodie's decision all the sweeter.

She apologised as she bumped into one of the cleaners. He was a young guy, Elodie thought perhaps mid-twenties, maybe a little older. He wore what every cleaner here wore: black overalls with a grey top on underneath and a grey cap with the airport's logo embroidered across the front. She'd seen him around before but hadn't had a real chance to speak to him, or any of the cleaners, properly. Most of the cleaning staff worked for an agency and there appeared to be some sort unwritten rule of 'them' and 'us.' Elodie smiled at him as he squeezed past her. Her heart skipped a beat. His smell was something so familiar to her; she couldn't place it but found that her breath had caught in her throat. Her eyes must have lingered on his for a second too long because instead of carrying about his business he turned to her and stopped.

"Do I know you?" he asked. His voice was deep and possessed a softness that was akin to song. Elodie shook her head, she definitely didn't know him; but this sense of familiarity still remained, it was almost palpable.

"No I don't think so, but…" she trailed off, not wanting to add that he seemed familiar to her for fear of it sounding tawdry.

"I'm sure I've seen you before," the man added. Clearly, the appearance of tawdriness was of no concern to him. He paused for a moment. His large hand stroked his chin as he looked to be in deep thought. "I do know you. You did the Triple C at Langley, didn't you?"

"Triple C?" Elodie echoed, not understanding his meaning.

"Cabin Crew Course," he explained. "You did, you always sat next to that blonde lady, the tall one." He looked at Elodie as if hoping to communicate the memory somehow.

Elodie didn't need her memory jogging, she vaguely remembered him. Any fleeting fancy flew from her as she realised that he could only be talking about Jessica. At this rate, Jess would have to literally beat off her admirers, and she'd need way more than just a stick to do it with.

"Oh yeah, you mean Jess. She's stunning, isn't she?" Elodie asked, not knowing why on earth that question had slipped from her lips.

"Not my type, I'm afraid," he said, shaking his head. "I'm Aaron. I'm agency staff, work here sometimes, and other places others," he finished, holding up a bottle of cleaning spray in a cowboy-like manner and, after spinning it expertly around his finger, re-holstered it in his cleaning belt, which made Elodie laugh.

"I'm Elodie, but my friends call me El for short." She answered holding out her hand, he took it and administered a soft kiss on its back. She pulled it away awkwardly, causing him to smile. He wasn't conventionally good-looking, but there was definitely something about him.

"Well, lil' lady," he said in a bad southern American accent, "I best be getting, don't you know I got places to go, toilets to clean? You take care of yo'self now." He pushed the peak of his faded baseball cap up slightly as if it were a Stetson and gave her a small nod. There was that smile again, that infectious smile that meant that Elodie couldn't help but smile back.

She said goodbye and turned back to her locker feeling a little too much like a schoolgirl who'd just realised her crush knew her name. She took her bag from the locker and breathed out a sigh of relief; the job wasn't bad, she supposed. The people weren't bad… well, she had her suspicions that her manager Vanessa was secretly an evil overlord. But maybe that was mainly her fault. She had, after all, started her career at Zip Air a little hungover. The party Steph and Carla had thrown for her the night before had been a lovely, but terrible, idea. Turning up looking a little worse for wear on your first day was not only unprofessional but made learning the ropes so much harder. Vanessa had clocked it almost at once and had given her a stern talking to at the end of the day. Since then she had definitely had to go the extra mile to prove herself – but apart from that, everyone else was really nice. It was the lack of one thing that was getting her down, the one thing she had craved since starting this entire journey. She had wanted to travel, to see some amazing sights and visit some beautiful places, and to be frank, the only things she really saw at Zip Air were the inside of airports. The most exciting thing to happen to her was when a reality TV star had boarded one of her flights. Of course, Elodie had had no idea who she was but the rest of the crew were awestruck and Elodie had joined in, not wanting to be the odd one out. Sure, she was technically going all over. She'd officially been to country after country: in fact, she'd set foot in Germany, France, Sweden and Iceland in the last week alone. But she didn't get to actually see anything. It was a budget airline, which there was nothing wrong with, but it wasn't what she had imagined and certainly not what she had dreamed of.

"Elodie, a word please?" Elodie turned around to see Vanessa who was stood a little too closely behind her. Elodie opened her mouth to answer but Vanessa ploughed on regardless. "I'm afraid there's been a change to the scheduling this weekend, unforeseen staffing issues you see. Which means, I'm sorry to say, that I'm going to need you to work. I realise you had requested the weekend off but it's just not going to be possible. Your flights are timetabled on the crew calendar as usual. I'll see you tomorrow, sorry again."

Vanessa didn't look sorry at all and gave Elodie no time to protest because as soon as the last word was out of her mouth she had spun round and marched off, her heels clacking on the tiled floor as she went. Elodie stood there agog for a few moments. Her happy thoughts of returning to Betty's were long gone now and all that was left was a bad taste and an even greater dislike for her job. Elodie simply wasn't used to working for someone who was just plain mean. This feeling of contempt weighed heavily; she felt trapped between a rock and a hard place. She had taken money, much-needed money from Betty to do this and now, well, what if it wasn't what she wanted, after all? How would she tell her friends and family that it had all been one huge mistake? The bottom line was that she wouldn't, she couldn't do that to them, to herself. No, Elodie decided that she would give it more of a go, she just needed to be a little more enthusiastic and a little less expectant. Elodie reasoned that it was more than likely the upheaval and change in lifestyle that she just needed to get used to. After all, it was a very full-on job.

Her bag, which had up until now been held redundantly in her hands, was unceremoniously thrown over her shoulder as she stalked through the busy staff area and towards the shuttle bus that would take her back home. The more she thought about what had happened, the more annoyed she became. Realising, in horror that she needed to tell Carla, she typed out an apologetic message, deleted it, typed out another and then deleted that one. No, this was the type of thing that you needed to do face to face.

"What do you mean you can't cover?" an altogether more unpleasant tone had replaced Carla's usual jovial one and she spat the words out as though they tasted of something repulsive.

"I'm so sorry. Vanessa's making me work and I can't get out of it. I tried," she added untruthfully. In reality, she had stood there dumbstruck, allowed Vanessa to dump the bad news all over her like rubbish at the tip and said absolutely nothing, but Carla didn't need to know that.

"Ugh, El! This is really shit, you know. Why didn't you check and double-check and then check again that it was OK? What am I going to tell my dad now?"

"You could invite him here?" Elodie suggested meekly. She had never suffered a dressing-down from Carla before and knew straight away that she never wanted to again.

"Oh yeah, he's going to love that, isn't he! 'Sorry Dad, I know you're really busy and hate coming to the city but my dumbass friend can't manage to sort herself out and has really dropped me in it so now I have to inconvenience you?' Um, that'd go down really well." Carla said sarcastically. Although he loved his daughter Carla's dad was a bit of a stickler for the rules, he liked things done a certain way and, from what Carla had said of him, in the past was constantly disapproving of her lifestyle. Which is why whenever family visits were arranged, Carla always journeyed to see him.

Elodie retired to her room feeling terrible. She hated letting people down, especially when the person in question was one of her best friends. She tossed and turned for most of the night, her mind at a crossroads. She couldn't quit, wouldn't quit, but something was nagging her, needling her like a sharpened stick in the furthest recesses of her thoughts. She knew deep down that this wasn't what she wanted and she knew that at some point this job would get the better of her and that she would leave. She decided to talk to Steph about it; out of everyone she knew, Steph was the one with the most level of heads. She slumped down on her bed and clutched the phone to her ear awaiting Steph's answer, which as it turned out would be on the third ring. For someone who didn't 'believe' in mobile phones, Steph seemed to always be able to answer hers at the drop of a hat. Elodie explained what had happened and once the floodgates had been opened found them extremely difficult to close; she rambled on and on, with Steph listening on the other end patiently. Once she had finished, Steph had only one piece of advice.

"El, if you're desperately unhappy then quit and find something else. My mum gave you the money so you could do something that makes you happy and if you're not doing that then it really is a waste," Steph had said.

Elodie hadn't thought of it like that, she hadn't thought about it rationally at all. She had been swept up in a panic, worried that she'd upset those she loved or ruin anything her future may hold by leaving her first-ever full-time job after only a couple of weeks – it hardly screamed that she was 'serious' about her career. After talking it through some more, Elodie decided to give things at Zip Air more of a go, and that she'd be more positive about it all and, as a sort of compromise with herself she would keep her eyes open for other opportunities in the interim, just in case her dream job arose.

To Elodie, it seemed as though any and every menial job was assigned to her. She didn't complain, though, she was determined to put her best foot forward and make the most out of whatever time she had left there. Vanessa appeared to delight in lording her station over Elodie and took every opportunity to make her life on shift difficult. This upset and confused Elodie to an identical extent: as far as she could tell, she had done absolutely nothing to this woman and yet Vanessa acted as if Elodie had wronged her in some way. If there were a less than agreeable chore to be undertaken, Elodie could almost guarantee it would be tasked to her. The fact that Elodie did all of this with a smile on her face only seemed to exacerbate Vanessa's condescension towards her, something that had not gone unnoticed by the other members of the crew.

"Why does she hate you so much?" one of her colleagues Shaun had whispered in her ear halfway through her return flight on Sunday. "You know she could have let you have the weekend off, don't you? Gary's not in and Becky hasn't

worked since Thursday. She's just being, well you know…
Vanessa."

Elodie hadn't taken this news well. She hadn't even thought about the other members of staff. She had just taken Vanessa's word for it and trusted that she was needed and that there was just no other way to make it work. Elodie felt rage roil within her and kicked herself for not being more on the ball. This was just another brick in the wall of dislike she had for Zip Air, which was steadily growing taller and taller with each passing day.

"You OK, hun?" Carla asked, looking up from her magazine as Elodie slumped down onto the sofa sighing.

"I'm alright. I'm just, you know… tired, I've worked back to back pretty much all weekend." Elodie answered tonelessly.

Her hand reached for the television remote control and moments after pressing the on button the TV blared into life. She scrolled through the channels aimlessly, flicking past cookery shows, chat shows and soaps. Her finger hovered when a smiling blonde lady appeared: she was walking down a sun-soaked street festooned with market stalls, brightly coloured tarpaulins hung over the small stands, which were populated by industrious locals selling their various wares. The presenter was talking about the market's history, dazzling the viewer with her incredible knowledge about the place all the while smiling that huge Hollywood beam. Elodie sighed and hit the off button. *'That's as close to travelling as I'm going to get,'* she mused dolefully.

Carla had disappeared from the living room. Elodie hadn't even noticed her leave; she felt very restless. There was a niggling feeling in the pit of her stomach that she couldn't seem to shake. She could hear Carla in her bedroom talking to someone on the phone. Her voice rose in waves, at one point she sounded almost feverish. This spiked Elodie's attention: her ears pricked as she tried to listen more closely, but it was no good, Carla had shut the door so everything she said was muffled. Elodie didn't have to wait long to find out what all the fuss was about as less than five minutes later Carla re-emerged from her bedroom which a gigantic grin on her face, which would give the Cheshire Cat a run for his money.

"Oh my God, guess what?" she said, the words tumbling out of her mouth so quickly that it sounded like one single word. Elodie opened her mouth to reply but was cut off before she could say anything. "I'm only going to be modelling for Maxx Hair!" Carla squealed. "Their usual model has the flu and someone who's working on this campaign was on the shoe job I did and put me forward. I guess it really is all about who you know."

"That's great news," Elodie beamed. The weariness she had felt only moments before seemed to wash away instantly. Things seemed to really be taking off for Carla: she had been to loads of castings for various things and had a few call-backs and now it seemed that slowly and steadily she was starting to book jobs and really forge a career for herself. "So tell me everything then, when is it? Where is it? And do you get to take a friend?" Elodie joked.

Carla filled her in on everything she knew. It was short notice but that didn't matter.

"It's not like I have anything better to do," Carla explained.

"Don't let Betty hear you say that," Elodie quipped before asking if Carla would get any freebies this time around too. Carla shook her head, but said that if she did Elodie could have it all: Carla wouldn't need any freebies with the one thousand pound pay packet she stood to collect. Elodie's mouth dropped open at this revelation; she couldn't believe her ears. Surely that sum of money was reserved for top models only. Carla just shrugged and explained that there really wasn't a rulebook when it came to this kind of thing.

"It all just depends how much is in the campaign's budget," Carla said. Elodie nodded her understanding without really understanding at all.

The following day Elodie waved Carla off bright and early, five am to be exact. She hadn't planned on getting up at the crack of dawn but Carla, being in such an excitable mood, hadn't been able to contain herself and Elodie found herself waking up to the sound of her friend belting out a rendition of 'I'm every woman' and the smell of overdone toast. Once she was roused, Elodie, despite still being shattered, found that she just couldn't get back to sleep so instead chose to join Carla and see if she needed help with anything. She didn't, so instead Elodie ate Carla's discarded burnt toast and watched her ready herself for the day ahead. Elodie couldn't help but feel a pang of jealousy, which she swiftly washed away with a mug of sweet, milky coffee. She wished more than anything she could get this excited about her own job.

"All set?" she asked Carla, who was practically electric with excitement.

Carla nodded, flung an arm around Elodie and planted a kiss on her cheek. Elodie laughed and pushed her away. "Have fun and be safe. Text me when you get there OK?"

"I will," Carla said as she pulled a cap over her unruly hair and headed out the door. "I don't know how long I'll be, so don't wait up."

The door closed behind her and Elodie stole a glance at the clock on the wall. *'Don't wait up? God, it's five in the morning. How long do these things actually take?'* Elodie wondered. The flat was now a place of calm tranquillity. The dewy morning light washed in through the full-length windows and made the whole place feel incredibly peaceful and warm. She pulled out Carla's laptop, vowing that when she was earning good money she would buy herself one of her own. She had a quick look on a couple of job sites she knew advertised cabin crew work, but there was just more of the same thing. Maybe her dream job didn't exist; maybe she'd been led by naivety. She shut the laptop, tucked it away and reclined on the sofa. Elodie closed her eyes. She had the next two days off, just forty-eight hours to do all her life admin, relax, recuperate and prepare for the rest of her very hectic schedule.

Carla walked back through the front door at a little after six pm, with an expression on her face akin to absolute glee.

"Went well then, did it?" Elodie asked as she poured Carla a large glass of wine and handed it to her. Carla nodded enthusiastically before taking a drink. She set the glass down on the countertop and fixed Elodie with a dogged stare.

"It was honestly the best day of my life. I loved every

single second of it. Don't get me wrong; I'm knackered now, but a good kind of knackered. I can't wait to see the pictures. They're going in all the magazines; I met some other models too. Everyone was really nice and," she trailed off and did a twirl that would have scored her top marks on *Strictly*, "look at what they did to me!"

Carla whipped the baseball cap off the top of her head and to Elodie's surprise a long sheet of dark coffee-coloured hair fell down, past her shoulders and to the small of her back. Elodie's mouth hung open; she stared at Carla, completely agog. They had stripped her hair back to its natural colour, straightened it and then, judging by the length and thickness, added in a decent amount of luxurious extensions.

"Oh my God, that looks incredible." Elodie managed, still completely taken aback by Carla's new look.

"I love it! Martin, the hair guy, said he'd take them out for me for free in a few weeks when they're past their best but until then I'm giving Naomi Campbell a run for her money," Carla laughed and took another sip of wine. "How come you're not having one?" she asked Elodie pointedly.

Elodie shrugged and explained that she didn't want to risk it. She had too much to do and far less time to do it in than she had banked on. Carla said nothing and instead walked over to the cupboard, took out a glass and poured Elodie a generous measure.

"You're having one. There's nothing sadder than celebrating a day gone good by drinking alone, so please... save me from social suicide and have a damn drink."

This was more instruction than question so, without too much protest, Elodie took the glass and joined Carla. They chatted for the next hour, finished off the rest of the bottle and proceeded to start on a second. It took Carla an entire hour before she told Elodie something that, if Elodie hadn't heard it directly from her friend's own lips, she wouldn't have believed.

"I've met a guy," Carla announced.

"You've met someone?" Elodie asked incredulously. "When?"

"Today actually, but when you know you know, I'm completely in love!" Carla replied, a serious expression on her face. Elodie stared at her wide-eyed. "I'm kidding! His name's Chris and he was one of the male models on the shoot and he has a face you would *never* get tired of sitting on!"

"Carla!" Elodie exclaimed, bursting into a fit of giggles.

"Seriously though, he's just a really nice guy. We spent pretty much the whole day chatting. Nothing really flirty, it was just friendly. But, just as I was about to head off, he asked if he could take me out. I played it cool, obviously but I let him take my number. He texted me there and then, said he wanted to make sure I hadn't given him a fake one, which this time, I hadn't. He is insanely hot, absolutely next-level kind of shit, imagine the love child of Channing Tatum and Ryan Reynolds, that kind of hot! The best thing about it is he doesn't know even really know it. Funny, handsome and modest – what's not to like?" Carla finished.

Elodie smiled. She had quite literally, in all her years of knowing Carla, never heard her utter those words.

"So when are you meeting up?" she asked, a sly smile on her face.

"Dunno, I'm not texting him till tomorrow. I don't want to look too keen, do I? Besides, what happens if he mugs me off? I'll look like a right knob." Somehow, Elodie didn't think that this Chris would be mugging Carla off; he wasn't the only one who didn't appreciate how good-looking he was.

Elodie finished the last of her wine, rinsed the glass and set it on the drying rack. She gave Carla a squeeze, told her how happy she was for her and then retired to her bedroom to sort out her washing. She closed the bedroom door behind her and was surprised to feel the threat of tears. She swallowed hard and told herself not to be quite so ridiculous. She needed to stop comparing herself to other people: Carla's success was not a mark of her failure. She knew this, yet she still felt the keen sting of disappointment. Instead of allowing it to take over, she decided that she would use it to do something about her own situation.

"What is this?" Vanessa demanded in a pitchy voice that sounded half-angry, half-wounded. She had both arms crossed tightly in front of her chest and protruding from one hand a slip of paper Elodie recognised as being her letter of resignation. Elodie looked around wildly: there were still other cabin crew members milling around and now more than one of them were staring in her direction.

"It's errr…" She hadn't banked on Vanessa outing her in front of other people. Elodie looked around wildly for some way to escape but came up with nothing. "I'm sorry, Vanessa, it's my…"

"It was a rhetorical question. I know perfectly well what it is!" Vanessa snapped, not giving Elodie even a second to defend herself. Not that she needed to explain herself; people resigned every single day and in far worse ways than this.

"I'm sorry Vanessa, this just isn't working for me. I've really tried, honestly I have. I've given it a good go, but I'm just not happy and I'm not doing a good enough job because of it."

"Well, you're right on that count," Vanessa replied sullenly. She looked like a puppy that had just had a telling off for peeing on the carpet. Elodie marvelled at how quickly Vanessa managed to go from enraged, to bitchy, to hurt and back round again all in a matter of moments.

The two women stared at each other, Elodie finding courage from the fact that she knew that she had done nothing wrong. She had given it a try and it wasn't for her. There was nothing more she could do and Vanessa certainly wasn't going to make her rethink her decision by acting the way she was. "Is this about your weekend off?" Vanessa asked finally.

"Yes and no," Elodie decided that a truthful answer was the only way forward. "The way the company operates just isn't ideal and I need to be able to have a life outside of work." Elodie thought about adding, "especially if the work in question is boring, repetitive and stifling," but thought better of it. She didn't need to add insult to injury, especially when it seemed to work for so many of her colleagues.

"Well, there's nothing more to say, then. You're still in your probation period so technically you can go, but ideally, you'd stay until the end of the month. Do you think you can do that?"

Elodie nodded slowly. The end of the month was just two

days away and she wondered what the point was in making her work them.

'*Oh well, at least that's a bit of extra money I suppose,*' she thought to herself, trying to be positive although it seemed more like an aluminium lining, rather than a silver one. She slung her bag over her shoulder and made to leave the airport. It had been a busy day and Elodie was exhausted: each step seemed to take more effort than the last and by the time she reached the exit, she was about ready to keel over.

"Excuse me, missy?" a smooth-voiced American man asked from behind her. She automatically apologised and stepped to the side to let him pass. "Elodie, it's me, remember? We met by the lockers?" Aaron laughed and waved a hand in front of her face. Elodie flushed with embarrassment. He was doing his 'bit' and Elodie had been too preoccupied with how tired she was to notice.

"Of course I remember," Elodie said, perhaps a little too keenly because for a second she thought she saw Aaron's smile falter. "How are you?" she pressed on.

"Can't complain, work's work. It pays the bills and keeps me in gear," he answered, gesturing to his cleaning cart.

"Gear?" Elodie asked, trying not to sound too judgemental but judging all the same. '*No wonder he's always so cheerful,*' she thought.

"No! Not *gear* gear, Jeez! I'm talking about camera gear," Aaron said, looking both bewildered and panicked at the same time. "I'm a photographer in my spare time. As in I take pictures. I don't have anything fancy; camera kit's so expensive. But it's like my dad always said, '*You don't need top of the range equipment to take top of the range pictures,*' you know?"

"Well if you ever need a model, my best friend's one. You should book her quick, though: I reckon she'll be out of your price bracket in the not so distant future, she's doing so well for herself." Elodie said proudly.

"Well, unless she currently charges no money at all then she's already out of my price bracket. And besides, I'm not interested in people, I'm into landscapes."

Elodie smiled wanly and stifled a yawn, which provoked a hurt expression from Aaron. She instantly felt bad. She really did want to hear about his photography; it was just that she was well and truly shattered.

"Sorry, I am interested, I promise. I'm just really tired too." Elodie could hear how lame the excuse sounded, but it didn't stop her from making it all the same.

"No worries, look, here's my number." He scribbled out a number on a piece of paper he'd plucked from the depths of his pocket. "If you ever feel like listening to me drone on about photography – believe it or not, emptying bins is not my main passion in life – then give me a call, and if not, I guess I'll just see you around."

He gave her a nonchalant smile and headed back, dragging his cart behind him. Elodie opened her mouth to tell him that there probably wasn't going to be an 'around' seeing as she only had two more days left, but he had disappeared before the words could leave her lips. She held the piece of paper out in front of her: the number had been written in a hand that she found surprising. Bold slanted writing showed eleven digits that Elodie now knew to be his mobile number; she realised that this would probably be the only way to contact Aaron ever again and somehow that made this piece of paper extra special to her. She folded it in two and tucked it neatly into her back pocket for safekeeping. Elodie knew she didn't want to date, at least not yet anyway, but there was no harm in hanging on to it, and besides it felt nice to have the attentions of a good-looking man for once.

Elodie worked her last two days, and hated every minute of it. It was as though Vanessa was determined to make her remaining time as miserable as possible. Vanessa's ill-temper and frosty demeanour seemed to have spread to the rest of the crew as on her last day she barely managed to extract a single goodbye or good wish from anyone. As Elodie emptied her locker she felt a sense of exaltation: it was over. So what if her first steps into her new career had been more of a stumble? *'Onwards and upwards,'* she told herself resolutely. The Elodie of old would have felt beaten by this, and there was still a part of her that hung on to that negativity, but she knew she couldn't let herself fall at the first hurdle. This was a lesson and she was damn sure that she would indeed learn from it.

Elodie once again found herself jobless. Betty had offered her a few shifts here and there which she had taken, partially from desperation and partially because stepping back into her old life was comforting when everything else seemed pretty bleak. The extra two days' worth of money that she had from Zip Air did little to stem the flow of impending financial doom. She had managed to pay Carla her share of the rent, but that was last month; she now had this month's to worry about. Elodie kicked herself for being so impulsive. Were things at Zip really that bad? She wasn't so sure now. She doubted very much that Vanessa would welcome her back with open arms.

'No,' she thought. *'I've got to move forward, something will turn up.'*

Elodie spent her days either looking for work or feeling sorry for herself. Carla had begun dating Chris, the handsome male model she'd met on her hair shoot and Steph's boyfriend Andy was back from tour. They were wrapped up in each other and probably would be until he had to leave again. Elodie felt purposeless: no boyfriend, no job and no money. Still, she had her health and her friends so that was at least something. She had resigned herself to the role of housekeeper. Carla was becoming increasingly busier by the day. She had booked a few more modelling jobs, nothing as glamorous or high end as her hair shoot but still, they paid a lot more than a shift at Betty's did.

Carla's hair was practically back to normal; the colour, now a fabulous combination of dark roots that faded to icy silver tips, suited her far better. In her new role as housekeeper, Elodie felt that she was at least contributing to the running of their home in some way. She was so grateful to Carla for all she had done and wanted to show her, at least in some way, that she was thankful. She did all the washing and ironing and continually marvelled at just how many clothes Carla managed to get through each week. She cooked, cleaned and paid for things as and when she could.

Elodie was midway through loading the washing machine when a thought suddenly hit her: Carla was basically the new Tom and she was the old Elodie. She didn't know whether to laugh or cry. It was barely a few weeks ago that she thought that she had come so far, and now she had fallen right back to where she had started. She shoved the clothes in angrily and shut the door with so much gusto that it bounced back open and a pair of her jeans flopped out. She shoved them back in but not before noticing a slip of paper protruding from one of the pockets. She retrieved the note and set the washer going. Opening the folded piece of paper made her heart skip a beat. How could she have forgotten? Aaron's number, written in his distinctive, slanted handwriting, was right in front of her. Maybe she would give him a call. OK, maybe not a call – no one did that nowadays. She would drop him a text.

'*He might be the perfect distraction,*' Elodie thought, '*and, more to the point, he might know some inside scoop about one of the airlines hiring.*'

She paced up and down the length of the living room, her eyes flitting between her phone and the note Aaron had given her. So far she had managed to type nothing, absolutely nothing. Why was she getting so wound up about this? He was a nice guy, a simple, uncomplicated guy; Jeez, he was an airport cleaner, he was hardly going to judge her badly for where she was right now. She typed a brief message: 'Hi Aaron, it's Elodie. Would be good to catch up if you're free? No worries if not, x.' She had felt that the last part had been essential. She didn't want to look too eager or give him the wrong impression, so left it with one kiss on the end; two looked weird and three far too many. She pressed send. That was it now. She would just have to wait and see if he replied.

He did, seconds later, by calling her! His number, which she hadn't yet saved, flashed up on her screen as the phone pulsated in her hand. Staring at the phone as if it were something from outer space, Elodie sat down, then stood up and began to pace. She wasn't about to answer his call, that wasn't the way you did things. Everyone knows you message for a bit first, then meet up. You don't jump straight to phone calls, Christ. Carla had once said to her that "*Talking on the phone is more intimate than sex.*" At the time, Elodie was sure she was joking, but now she wasn't so certain. Aaron had hung up, or given up and Elodie breathed a sigh

185

of relief; that was, until her phone buzzed in her hand signifying that a message had come through.

Call screening eh? Pick up this time? Aaron x

How did he know? Well, that was pretty obvious: she had messaged him only seconds before. The phone rang again, and against her better judgement, she answered.

"Hi," she said a little self-consciously. "Sorry, I was just in the middle of something," she finished lamely.

"Yeh, screening my call," Aaron said without a hint of annoyance. If anything, he sounded as though he had found it amusing.

Elodie decided not to protest: what would be the point? The two chatted amiably and when Elodie glanced at her watch she was amazed to see that time had flown. Just when the conversation seemed to be drawing to a natural conclusion Aaron asked her a question she had not been expecting.

"So I was thinking, why don't you let me take you out for coffee some time?"

"Oh I don't know, I'm…" she trailed off, she had been about to say "not ready to date", but even Elodie couldn't deny that she liked Aaron. Even though they had spent little time in one another's company, she had warmed to him instantly; his easy-going personality and the fact that he didn't take himself too seriously were worlds away from anything she'd experienced with Tom and made a refreshing change.

"Oh Jesus, you're married aren't you? Or taken? Or just plain old not interested? It's alright, I'm a big boy, I can take it," Aaron said jokingly. "But surely you've got room in your life for another friend?"

Elodie laughed. She had to hand it to him, he did bring up a good point.

"OK, yeah, coffee sounds nice," she replied.

"Yikes, 'nice'. That's like an arrow to my heart," he said.

Elodie imagined him clutching his chest, which made her laugh even louder. "OK, well I'm pretty free all this week. You tell me when you're free and I'll find us somewhere good, how's that sound?"

Elodie said that it sounded good and, not wanting to let on that she was currently jobless and completely available, pretended to check her diary for a free time in which to meet.

"Ummm, how about next Wednesday?" she suggested, flicking the pages of one of her travel magazines and hoping it sounded like a diary.

"I can't do Wednesday I've got a thing, are you free Tuesday instead?" he replied.

"I can be," Elodie said, trying to give the impression that she may have something she'd need to move around in order to accommodate him. He didn't need to know that Tuesday for her would largely consist of cleaning the bathroom, watching daytime telly and maybe, if she felt like it, changing into something other than pyjamas.

"OK, great," Aaron said enthusiastically. "I'll text you the details when I've figured it out. Gotta go now, see you soon."

Elodie said goodbye and Aaron hung up. The phone went dead and she went back to the washing with a smile on her face. For some reason, these menial tasks seemed far more enjoyable now.

Elodie had told Carla about the date the second she saw her. Carla seemed really pleased that Elodie was beginning to put herself out there and in the days that followed promised to help her look her best.

"OK, let's do your hair first," Carla said when the day of the date arrived.

"I'm going to a coffee shop, not the opera," Elodie said. "Besides, I don't want to go all glammed up, he's only ever seen me after work when I'm all sweaty and tired, he won't recognise me."

"Don't be ridiculous. If you don't make any effort he'll think you're not interested," Carla admonished, ignoring Elodie's protestation as she rummaged in her dressing table drawer.

"Well, to be honest, I'm not sure I am. I'm not ready..."

"To start dating yet, blah, blah, blah. You're totally ready, you're just nervous," Carla said, producing a curling wand, firm hold hairspray and a backcombing brush. She brandished them at Elodie as if they were items of great value.

"Don't be so dramatic, it's a date El. You're not marrying the guy."

"Okay fine, but nothing too OTT. Like you said, I'm not getting married. Just nice and relaxed," Elodie instructed as she let Carla loose on her locks.

Carla twisted Elodie's hair around the curling wand and backcombed the roots for a bit of extra lift. She then ran her fingers through the lengths and brought it forward over one shoulder.

"*Voilà*! I have officially worked my magic again, I've pulled a phoenix out of these ashes, Elodie," she said triumphantly. "Look: beautiful, natural, relaxed waves."

Elodie thanked Carla and made to stand; she had only twenty minutes to put on some makeup and choose an outfit. She hadn't done this in such a long time and marvelled at how much effort it took to achieve the 'natural' look. She quickly applied some makeup and dressed herself in black jeans, a pair of heeled boots and a white top. She felt exhausted after all the preening and the date hadn't even started yet.

Elodie arrived at the coffee shop a few minutes late. The tube had been suffering from minor delays and, despite Aaron texting her very specific instructions as to how to find the place they were meeting at, Elodie had still managed to get lost. She pushed the door of the café open and immediately felt at home. The warm atmosphere, welcoming smells and tinkle of the bell above the door all reminded her of Betty's. She glanced around: no sign of Aaron yet. She pulled out her phone and checked for messages. Still nothing. Deciding to settle herself, she picked out a small table in the corner of the room. The lighting was dimmer over there and she'd read something about low lighting making you appear more attractive. Not that she wanted to appear attractive; she kept telling herself over and over again that she wasn't going to rush into anything. She didn't even really know if she wanted to start dating at all. A little voice inside her piped up, telling her that it was a touch late for that, seeing as she was already on a date, or at least she would be when Aaron eventually turned up. She checked the time again: he was fifteen minutes late.

One of the waiting staff sidled up next to her and asked what she would like to drink. Elodie wasn't sure whether she should order now or wait for Aaron. She decided to wait and told the waitress she was waiting for someone. The waitress nodded, spun around, her ponytail swishing, and began clearing some mugs from a nearby table. Elodie hadn't brought a book, or any form of entertainment; she honestly didn't think she would need it.

Aaron arrived almost half an hour late, at this point Elodie was getting ready to leave. He sat down blinking heavily at her.

"You're early," he said, checking his watch.

"No, you're late," she said frostily. If this was what the world of dating was nowadays, then she wasn't interested.

"I am?" Aaron said, looking puzzled and pulling out his phone. "No, I'm not, see...? It's not even half past yet."

"You said three pm. Myro's Coffeehouse, three pm, thirty High Street." Elodie said with hesitation, a little confused herself now.

"No, I said Myro's Coffeehouse 3:30 pm, on the High street."

Elodie pulled out her phone to prove him wrong, loaded his message and then stopped in her tracks. He was right. No wonder she'd gotten so lost. She felt foolish and despite her best efforts couldn't help but blush furiously. Aaron simply chuckled and flagged down the waitress.

"I take it you know what you want?" he asked jovially. "After all, you've had plenty of time to check the menu."

Elodie felt herself turn a deeper shade of pink and mumbled her order. Aaron said that he would have the same and added a piece of cake to their order. "With two forks," he added, gesturing to Elodie.

The pair of them chatted warmly whilst they waited for their drinks. Aaron was sincere, welcoming and really quite sweet. Elodie found herself confiding in him. She told him about the demise of her career with Zip Air and in return, he confided his own life. It soon transpired that neither of them were where they wanted to be career-wise just yet. Aaron had such a positive take on life and Elodie found it hard to have any negative thoughts whilst she was in his company.

They ordered a second round of coffee and when their fingers accidentally brushed over the same packet of sugar Elodie felt a pang of desire grab hold of her so strong that she had to catch herself. She pulled her hand away from his as if it had burnt her; she ran those same fingers through the ends of her hair and wondered if Aaron had noticed her imprudent reaction.

"So do you want to move on to the second part of this afternoon's delights?" Aaron asked, raising one eyebrow and stroking his chin in a comical, question-master-type manner.

"Second part?" Elodie probed. She thought that this *was* their date. It was a coffee date; they'd had coffee, so therefore hadn't they had their date?

'Damn,' she thought, *'I'm so rusty at this.'*

"OK, so you know how I told you that I'm into photography? Well, there's a little exhibition on just down the road, I thought we might check it out? That's if you think you'll like it? We don't have to, but it is meant to be really good."

Elodie checked her watch. They'd been chatting over coffee for well over an hour. She thought that maybe she should leave now and end things on a high note. However, what she thought and what she did were completely at odds: before she knew it she had agreed to go and was walking happily alongside Aaron, down the high street and towards the gallery.

They walked through the reception area and into the lofty bright space that Elodie now knew as the Eason Art Space. Several well-lit corridors led to individual spaces housing different works from a number of artists. The heels of Elodie's boots clacked against the wooden floor and she found herself altering her gait in an effort to muffle the sound.

"So what I want to show you is down this way, I think," Aaron said, beckoning her to follow him down one of the many hallways. They walked almost the entire length of the corridor and just when Elodie thought that they'd never reach the end they rounded a corner. The room that had opened up before them was a vast, expansive and almost silent space. Classical music played very quietly in the background and Elodie found that she couldn't raise her voice above the smallest of whispers. Beautiful images of landscapes hung from the ceiling; they were suspended by sturdy-looking cords and arranged in a maze-like display.

"What is this?" she asked, leaning in towards Aaron so that he could hear her properly. She caught his scent and felt her stomach tighten: did he always smell this good? Elodie couldn't put her finger on it; it wasn't cologne as such, it was an earthy, musky scent that she seemed to notice at the most inopportune of times. She was meant to be concentrating on the art and now all she could think about was how good it might be to kiss him.

"It's an exhibition by one of my favourite photographers. See those red dots by the pieces? That means they're sold. There's not one single piece up for grabs, not that I could afford one, even if there were. One day I hope to follow in her footsteps, all the greats display their work here. Show-casing mine at the Eason is sort of a dream of mine." He blushed slightly and Elodie thought that perhaps he hadn't meant to share that particular fact about himself. "She's showing here this week only. She's amazing; her eye, her skill and not to mention the lengths she goes to capture an image. Honestly, her work is just incredible, look…"

He pointed to one of the photographs suspended from the ceiling. It stood at well over a metre tall and probably close to two in width. Elodie took a step back so that she could take it all in. It was a dramatic, moody scene depicting a scorched forest. The photo had been taken at sunset; the shadows of the remaining blackened trees stretched along the floor and disappeared into the charred and barren ground. The photograph certainly was breathtakingly beautiful, but it made Elodie feel loss and sadness. She felt Aaron's strong hand clasp around hers and found that she did not pull away this time. She loosened her fist and allowed him to entwine his fingers within hers; he held her with a gentle pressure that felt both comforting and secure.

"So what do you make of it?" Aaron asked.

"It's beautiful," Elodie replied quietly. "It's making me think of someone grieving, I get a real sadness from it, do you know what I mean?" Elodie wasn't sure if she sounded silly or not, she was certainly no art critic.

"I know exactly what you mean," Aaron said, squeezing her hand.

Elodie felt the warmth of his palm against hers and the feelings of sorrow melted away. It was in that moment that Elodie decided that she liked art galleries very much.

They paced the rest of the exhibition slowly, Aaron talked animatedly about each photograph and Elodie listened intently. His passion and enthusiasm made him seem more attractive.

They left the gallery hand in hand. Elodie's heart still fluttered whenever he gave it a little squeeze. She was surprised to find that dusk was upon them; the tawny July sun had almost dipped out of the sky completely and there was very little natural light left to see by.

"Are you getting the tube back?" Aaron asked innocently.

Elodie nodded and Aaron said that he would walk her back to the station. She made to protest but he just laughed and asked her if she never let anyone do anything nice for her, or whether it was just him.

"It's not that…" Elodie began but trailed off. Maybe it was that. Maybe she had become so used to it with Tom that, now, the mere idea of someone going out of their way for her felt wrong.

"Elodie, I'm not your ex," Aaron said softly, seeming to hear her thoughts. "Come on, I know a nice walk." He took her by the hand and Elodie felt a jolt electricity spark between them.

He took her past a cosy-looking bar called The Cocktail Club that he reliably informed her did the best Whisky Sours in town and after a short while arrived at a pair of tall, wrought iron gates that guarded the entrance to a concealed park.

"We can't go in there," Elodie said pointing to a sign that read 'RESIDENTS ONLY' in bold red letters.

"Don't be daft, no one's around, and besides, it's so beautiful in there. Come on, I really want you to see it," Aaron said as he pushed one side of the gate back and pulled the other forward, creating a small gap for them to squeeze through.

Elodie was surprised by the very existence of the park: it

was barely a stone's throw from her house and she'd never even known it was there. The streetlights above illuminated the winding path in front of them, which was lined by with old-fashioned-looking benches. It was tranquil: the sounds of the city seemed to be miles away, silenced by dense trees that lined the perimeter, protecting them from the intrusion of the outside world. At that moment in time, Elodie felt like they were the only two people on the planet: a feeling that she rather enjoyed.

"Elodie?" Aaron asked gently.

She turned to him. His eyes were wide in the dimly-lit park. He leaned in toward her and placed his strong hands around her waist. Under their attention, she felt so small. He pulled her nearer to him and without warning or caution she found that his lips had met hers. Elodie soared: the kiss was so soft, yet so powerful and she felt herself melt into him, completely defenceless and more than willing. He parted her lips with the tip of his tongue, searching for the wetness within. Elodie felt herself fall deeper, their tongues gently probing one another's, eager to explore more. Elodie understood in that moment that every other kiss she had ever had before now had been wrong. What was happening now was so much more: it felt like the beginning of something, something wonderful. After a long moment where the world seemed to stop and time stood still, they parted.

"I've wanted to do that since the moment I first saw you," Aaron said huskily.

Elodie could manage no words, her lips still burned with the residue of him. He raised his hand to her face and gently tucked a stray piece of hair behind her ear.

"Come on," he said, taking her by the hand, "let's get you home."

CHAPTER 12

"STILL NOTHING?" CARLA ASKED AS ELODIE stalked into the living room. Elodie's hair was dishevelled and she wore the remnants of yesterday's makeup under her eyes in dark circles that reminded Carla of a zombie film she'd once watched.

"I just don't understand it, we had such a good time. Why wouldn't he text? It's been two days. Do you think I should text him? I've messaged him a couple of times already, though…"

Carla shook her head vehemently and took a sip of coffee. She placed the mug down on the kitchen table and walked over to her friend.

"Do not text him again, Elodie. Are you listening to me?" Carla said fiercely. Elodie *was* listening, but she was also thinking.

"What if he's working? He might be doing something really important. Or, what if something terrible has happened? He could be ill, or worse…" Elodie rambled hopefully.

"Unless he's dead, there's no excuse. It takes thirty seconds to send a text," Carla said stonily. "Chris texts me every day and if he's on a shoot or busy or whatever then he texts me to say that. I don't ask him to, it's just common courtesy, isn't it?"

Elodie's mood nosedived. Carla and Chris had become somewhat of an item; they weren't official yet by any means but they may as well have been. Elodie had never seen Carla into a guy before; it was definitely a bit strange – but in a nice way.

"I suppose you're right. Maybe he just was acting like he

had a good time. Maybe I'm just crap at dating?" Elodie let out an exasperated moan and got up to pour herself some coffee. She drank it in one. It was barely lukewarm; the pot had been stood on the side for a while now and the addition of plenty of milk hadn't helped matters.

"Why don't you come out with me and Steph tonight? We're going to that new place in town, you know, The Clifton? That'll cheer you up."

Elodie was puzzled; Just Carla and Steph? She wondered why hadn't they mentioned this before.

"Just you and Steph?" she asked, a note of suspicion in her voice.

"Well… and Chris and Andy, but it's more of a group thing anyway." Elodie definitely did not want to play third, or in this case fifth wheel, but what else was she going to do? Sit at home and mope?

"I'm not sure, it sounds a lot like a double date to me," Elodie said uncertainly.

"Don't be a dick, you're coming. Our treat and it'll give you a chance to get to know Chris properly. You're gonna love him! Right, what are you doing today?"

"Nothing. Job hunting, I guess," Elodie answered.

"You can take a day off from that, let's go out. I'm free all day and it's so nice outside, let's do lunch." Carla checked the time and saw that it was barely ten in the morning. "OK, brunch then. Go get a shower, you definitely need it." Carla said, drawing imaginary circles around her eyes with the tip of her finger.

Elodie got up, handed her used mug to Carla who put it in the sink, and headed into the bathroom, understanding at once what Carla had meant the second she saw her reflection in the bathroom mirror.

The day passed in a bit of a blur, peppered with moments of disappointment each and every time Elodie checked her phone. She had heard from Aaron only once since their date: to his credit, he had thanked her for a lovely evening and asked if she had gotten home OK. Elodie had replied with words to much the same effect, but since then had heard nothing back.

"What's his surname?" Carla asked as they took a break from window-shopping.

"It's…" Elodie racked her brain for his surname. "Do you know, I've got no idea."

"OK, not a problem, so we know his name's Aaron, he's based here and he's a wannabe photographer, but not just any photography, nature and landscapes only, right?" Elodie nodded, "OK, give me five minutes." Carla pulled out her phone and began tapping away furiously.

"What are you doing?" Elodie asked, panic rising in her voice. "Carla, please don't message him or anything!"

"Message him? What do you take me for? I'm just doing a bit of social stalking. Nothing wrong with that El." Carla cast her friend a rebellious look. "Jesus, unclench Elodie, there's nothing wrong with that, everyone does it."

As it transpired, Carla didn't need her five-minute deadline because after just a few moments she had found him. "*Voilà*, Aaron Ber*nard*," she said, adding extra emphasis to the last syllable. "Travel photographer and landscape artist."

Carla turned her phone around to show Elodie the screen: she had discovered a website where he had uploaded some of his pictures and from that had found his Instagram account. "Doesn't take a genius to know that if you're into photography, you're into Insta. His account's only open to his followers though, so, I've followed. Well, that was quick: he's accepted me, look!"

Elodie clicked on the most recent picture: it was a photograph of a sprawling field, uploaded yesterday. It was a snapshot really, definitely not professional work. She looked closer and felt her heart sink. Aaron's shadow was visible in the bottom left-hand corner; unfortunately, so was someone else's, someone leaning against him, their shadows entwining, becoming one.

"I'm sorry, El, he's a dog," Carla said, shoving the phone into her back pocket and wrapping an arm around Elodie. Elodie shrugged her off.

"He's not a dog, dogs are nice," she mumbled. "I'm fine. It was only one date. It's just annoying that it was my first date since Tom and I really liked him. Ugh, and what's worse is that I actually thought he liked me too."

Carla didn't say anything. The two women sat across from one another in complete silence for several long moments. Eventually, with the afternoon closing in on them, they headed for home, the mood considerably more sombre than it had been at the start of the day.

The last thing that Elodie felt like doing that evening was getting dolled up and heading out for a fancy meal at The Clifton with two loved-up couples, but the alternative was to pig out on the sofa and sulk, which Carla had absolutely denied her the privilege of. She had grudgingly extricated herself from the living room and gotten ready, selecting a simple black dress from her wardrobe and pinning her hair up in a messy bun that took all of two minutes to achieve. Joining Carla, Steph and their other halves in the living room, she felt more than a little self-conscious. It was the first time she had properly met Chris, and Carla was right, he did seem lovely. He was extremely tall, almost impossibly good-looking with a chiselled jaw that looked like it had been sculpted by the gods. Together, Carla and Chris sure made one attractive couple.

The conversation flowed easily throughout dinner; well, it did for everyone aside from Elodie. She felt very much an outsider, despite everyone's best efforts to include her, and even though everyone was more than friendly towards her she still felt as though she was gate-crashing. More than once Chris had retracted his arm hastily from around Carla's shoulders when Elodie had glanced their way or Steph had changed the angle of her head at the last minute in order to give Andy a peck on the cheek rather than a kiss on the lips. Elodie didn't like the modification of behaviour; it didn't make her feel better, it made her feel worse.

She took out her mobile from her handbag, which she had strategically placed over the back of her chair: still nothing from Aaron. The three drinks that had been paired with her meal were beginning to take effect, and seemed to be all she needed for that little extra bit of confidence. Typing out a message to him she felt a sudden burst of anger; she was done with playing nice. It wasn't alright at all, taking someone out, treating them like the most important person ever and then dropping off the face of the planet. If anything it was bad manners, and even if he didn't reply at least she would have gotten things off her chest. She typed out the message quickly, keeping her face as neutral as possible to avoid questions. This was hard work, especially since she felt a raging inferno begin to flare inside her.

"Everything alright, El?" Steph asked from across the table. Elodie stuffed her phone back into her bag and nodded; she even managed a smile that could have passed for genuine.

"Come on, toilet time," Steph said as she folded up her serviette neatly and placed it on the table in front of her.

Carla got up too and Elodie, although not in need of the toilet, grabbed her bag and followed suit.

The toilets at The Clifton were almost as spectacular as the dining room itself. Elodie didn't know if she'd ever been in anything quite so extravagant – almost unnecessarily so. Suspended from the ceiling were several large, ornate and extremely dazzling light fittings, which cast a very glitzy light about the place.

"So are you going to tell us what's wrong?" Carla asked as she applied a new layer of pink stain to her lips.

"Nothing's wrong," Elodie replied shortly, rummaging in her bag so that she didn't have to make eye contact.

"Fine," Carla replied. "I know you're lying, though; you're a terrible liar."

Elodie recoiled at this accusation. She wasn't lying, she just didn't feel the need to whine about it, especially when all it would do would be to cause tension between them. Elodie didn't want to create a sour atmosphere because she was feeling a bit down.

"El, just tell us. You'll feel better after a rant. You've been really quiet all evening, it's just not like you."

"Sorry if I've made things awkward," Elodie said, a little self-pityingly.

"We've tried to include you," Steph combatted, "but you seem determined to have a bad time."

That was it: there was something in Steph's tone, Carla's look and her heart that pushed her close to the edge. Elodie felt tears prick at the corners of her eyes and turned around so that Carla and Steph couldn't see.

"I'm just not feeling very sociable right now," she managed, her voice cracking.

Carla snaked an arm around her waist and Steph put a hand on her shoulder. Well, if she had been close to the edge before she was well and truly over it now. Elodie burst into tears; silvery droplets rolled down her cheeks and suddenly she felt very silly.

"I'm sorry," Elodie mumbled, once she had succeeded in regaining her composure. She dabbed under her eyes with some tissue that Steph had handed to her. "It's everything really, work or my lack of it, mainly. There is literally nothing out there, well nothing that I want anyway. Plus, Aaron's pissed me off… I know I hardly know him and we only went on one date, but it's still hurt my feelings. And now, being here with you guys, all loved-up, just makes me feel a bit crap about myself. Then I feel crap about feeling crap, because it's just really selfish and shitty of me when I should be feeling happy for you," she sighed.

"You should feel exactly how you feel," Carla said, giving Elodie another squeeze. "You can't help it and beating yourself up about it is definitely not good for your mental health."

Steph nodded her agreement and Elodie sniffled again, grateful that her friends were being so understanding.

"OK, so I think we ought to call it a night. It's getting late anyway and I've got an early start with the café tomorrow," Steph said, looking at her watch. Carla nodded and Elodie felt a surge of gratitude towards them. "I'll phone a cab, Elodie why don't you wait outside, we'll settle up and meet you there."

Elodie nodded, thankful for this small mercy. At least this way she wouldn't have to walk back through the restaurant with a blotchy face and puffy eyes.

Elodie had been waiting outside for almost ten minutes. The warm July evening had dropped cool and she wished very much that she'd opted to wear a jacket with her dress. Elodie was rubbing her arms to try and create some heat when she spotted a familiar-looking and impeccably-dressed man walking along the opposite side of the road.

"Chase?" Elodie called out before she was really certain

whether the man she could see was Chase or not. The man turned around and squinted at her. Several long seconds went by before a look of recognition stole across his face and he held up a hand. He seemed to falter slightly, as if he wasn't entirely sure whether the small hand gesture would do and he could carry on with his journey. He decided against it and crossed the road towards her.

"I trust you're well?" Chase asked, almost abruptly once he had stopped beside her. She gave him a small nod and glanced at him nervously. He always managed to make her feel anxious.

"How are you?" Elodie asked.

Chase grunted a response. They stood in relative silence for a few moments; the only sounds were the dim clamour from the restaurant behind them and the occasional black cab driving past.

"Are you up to anything fun tonight?" Elodie eventually asked when the silence had become too much. She couldn't figure out why Chase was still there. If he had nothing to say to her, surely he would just leave?

"I'm meeting a friend in Casa, the gin bar a little further down. I'd invite you along but..." he trailed off.

"Ah, I've had a pity invite once this evening already. I'm good for another."

"Pity invite?" Chase asked, turning to her and fixing her with an in-depth stare that caused Elodie to look away.

"Errr, yeh. I had a bad date and my friends felt bad for me so now I'm third-wheeling with them and their boyfriends."

"Well, all I can say is that the guy's an idiot. Anyone I know? Want me to rough him up?" Chase said, offering her as much of a smile as Elodie thought Chase capable of. *'Is he joking?'* Elodie thought.

"You might know him: Aaron? He works at loads of airports. Well, he ignored me afterwards and it looks like he's got a girlfriend. You don't know him, do you?" Elodie asked, suddenly wondering if maybe Chase could be the one to shed some light on things.

"Oh yes. Aaron. I know him alright. I'm not one to get involved in petty gossip but I don't think he has *a girlfriend* if you catch my meaning, I think *girlfriends* is probably more accurate."

"Oh," was all Elodie could manage as in that moment Carla, Steph, Chris and Andy emerged from The Clifton in a raucous fashion.

"Have a pleasant evening, Elodie," Chase said, his eyes darting to her approaching friends.

He bid Elodie a swift farewell and made his way back across the road. Elodie glanced over her shoulder at her friends and then back towards Chase: he was now no more than a shadow in the distance.

'*He's such an oddball, he has literally no people skills,*' she thought to herself as she watched the shadow disappear to nothingness.

"Was that who I think it was?" Carla asked, flipping her sleek hair over her shoulder.

"Yeh, he's just off to meet a friend at Casa," Elodie said without enthusiasm. The news about Aaron had hit her hard. Up until now, she had hoped that maybe she'd got it all wrong. Elodie elected not to tell her friends until later. She didn't fancy being the centre of attention for yet another poor life-choice.

"Oooh, let's go and spy!" Carla said excitedly. "Come on, it'll be fun. It'll help take your mind off things." She nudged Elodie in the ribs, Elodie shrank away from this unwanted attention and shook her head.

"I don't want to spy on him, I want to go home," she answered decidedly.

"Well let's go get a cab, but walk past there first," Carla suggested. "Maybe his friend's hot?"

Elodie reluctantly agreed and off they went. The bar was little more than a few minutes' walk away and before Elodie knew it they were outside.

"Shall we go in?" Carla asked mischievously.

"Absolutely not," came Elodie's reply. She hadn't wanted to walk past it in the first place. It was childish of them and she was surprised that it was only she who seemed to realise this.

"He's there," Steph said in a whisper, pointing through

the window of the busy bar. "Look, he's sat on his own. No friends in sight."

"Tragic," Carla said pityingly.

"Why don't you like this guy? He looks alright to me," Chris asked.

"It's not that we don't like him, he's just a bit of a stiff. We met him on a night out and he was really up himself," Carla replied.

Elodie watched Chase intently. Her feelings of discomfort had waned and now she surveyed him with interest. He was indeed sat by himself; he sipped his drink gingerly, swirling the contents of the short, crystal-cut glass and examining them before taking a sip. He had no form of entertainment, which was odd considering that most people, when faced with spending time in their own company, chose to stare at a screen instead. *'You're never alone with a phone,'* she thought to herself.

Just then, a very leggy blonde woman, wearing an off-the-shoulder, figure-hugging dress, appeared. She bent down and draped an arm around Chase's shoulder, planting a soft kiss on his cheek as she did so. She gracefully slid into the seat beside him and beckoned a waiter over. Elodie saw her place an order and wave the waiter away, which she thought was really quite rude. Chase seemed not to notice; Elodie saw him look at the woman, his expression unreadable. He looked, perhaps nervous – Elodie couldn't tell.

"Let's go," Elodie said abruptly, suddenly feeling as though they had intruded on a very private moment and feeling bad about it. "This feels really weird."

A more sombre mood fell over the group now, and feeling slightly ashamed and more than a little immature, they left the frontage of Casa, hailed a cab and set off for home.

The following day Elodie felt strangely disconcerted. Her encounter with Chase played at the forefront of her mind. He could have easily given her a wave and carried on walking, but he chose to cross the street and talk to her, if that's what you could call what they had done. The conversation had been awkward, to say the least. He had claimed that he was meeting a friend and had been on the verge of inviting her. But when they had seen him he hadn't been meeting a friend at all, he had been on a date. Why would he ask her along to a date? At best it was bizarre and worst it was just plain cruel.

Over the next few days, Elodie split her time between Betty's Book Café, scouring the internet for decent jobs, and moping around the flat feeling rather sorry for herself. Carla had been a constant source of positive energy, which had been fine to start with, really helping Elodie to keep looking on the bright side. Still, she couldn't help but feel as though her life was spiralling downwards in contrast to her friend. Elodie knew she shouldn't compare herself to Carla, and for the most part she didn't. But she had to admit that it felt a little as though they were on a seesaw: as Carla's luck went up, hers seemed to go down.

"I can't believe how many jobs I'm booking, I know they're only little ones but it's really great for my portfolio. At the beginning of the year, I had nothing, and now I've got tonnes of great shots," Carla had said. Elodie had nodded and quickly picked up her coffee cup and sipped at the contents within. They were stone cold now, which made Elodie wince; but feigning needing a drink was far better than actually having to talk to Carla and hear all about how amazing her life was.

Carla hadn't mentioned the end of the month, and the fact that their rent was looming, but it was like an ever-present issue hanging over her. Barely an hour went by when she didn't feel a shudder of dread at paying it.

Elodie pressed refresh on her emails. This seemed to be completely second nature to her now, and she watched the laptop's little wheel spin as it scanned for incoming mail. As usual, nothing landed in her inbox. Elodie had been about to close the laptop when she let out a little squeal: her heart leapt as she saw an email invitation for an interview at 'Wing Star'. As quickly as her heart had soared it dropped, plummeting to the very pit of her stomach. It was another budget airline.

'Oh well, beggars can't be choosers,' she reasoned, determined to look on the bright side. The interview was on the last day of the month, Elodie was fairly confident she'd get the job. She would just need to think of a decent explanation

as to why she had jumped ship on one budget airline but wouldn't do the same to another. *'Family issues, good old family issues,'* she decided. No one would pry, especially if she could pull off a solemn enough expression.

"OK, I'm off now, how do I look?" Elodie said. Nerves had begun to creep into her voice and it wavered slightly.

"You look great, now go and knock 'em dead, you sexy bitch," Carla replied.

Elodie smiled. Maybe Carla's positivity wasn't all that bad, after all. Elodie got the train and then the bus to her interview. It was being held at some offices in town, which was fine by her because she could celebrate with a well-earned drink at a bar afterwards. Elodie walked in feeling really confident and, her ponytail swishing behind her, she walked into the room and took a seat opposite the panel conducting the interview. All of them looked stern and none of them smiled at her. Elodie found that her confidence disappeared, like a cloud of smoke in a strong breeze.

Elodie walked back through the door at a quarter to nine that evening.

"Sooooo how was your day? You're a lot later than I thought you'd be," Carla said the second Elodie had sat down. Steph was sat on the sofa, smiling uncertainly and brandishing a ginormous pizza box in Elodie's direction.

"Thought we could have a pizza and wine celebration, or commiseration depending on how you're feeling?" Steph offered.

Elodie smiled, her friends really were great. But as it happened, she didn't need cheering up all that much. She had news.

"You got the job?" Carla exclaimed, "I knew it! Well done, El!"

"Well not exactly," Elodie answered. "I didn't get *the* job, but I got *a* job."

"What on earth do you mean?" Steph asked confusedly as she bit off the end of a slice of margarita pizza.

"Well, the job I interviewed for I didn't get. It was almost as if they'd asked me to the interview just to haul me over the coals about why I left Zip Air, I tried saying personal

204

reasons but it just sounded lame. They saw through me before the words were even out of my mouth. Anyway, the reason I'm a little later than I thought is because I went to drown my sorrows after, but before I could I bumped into Gareth. You know, the examiner from the course?"

Carla and Steph said nothing but nodded. How could they forget about Gareth? Elodie's incredibly camp, incredibly funny and incredibly scathing examiner. Elodie had once described him as "Alan Carr on speed." This had made them all laugh, Steph so much so that she had snorted wine from her nose, which was very un Steph-like indeed.

"So anyway, I was walking along in a foul mood, wishing that we'd never gone out that night, never gone to the Grosvenor Suite and never, I repeat never, met Chase, when I bumped into Gareth. We got chatting and it was pretty stale to start with, you know the usual 'Hi, how are you?' back and forth kind of thing. But then, he asked me how I was, and I just kind of broke. I told him about the interview, about how badly it had gone and all about leaving Zip. For some strange reason I just blurted everything out, it was like once I started I couldn't stop. I quite literally chewed his ear off, told him the whole thing from start to finish." Elodie stopped for breath. Again, neither Carla nor Steph spoke.

They both just sat there, nursing their glasses and waited for Elodie to carry on with her story.

"OK, so once I'd finished he sort of just looked at me for a minute or two, like he was deciding on something, and then he sort of offered me a job, well a trial, on a private jet!" Elodie inhaled sharply. "He isn't just an examiner, he only does that one course every few months. He works for some fancy-pants airline as well, which is bloody lucky for me. Apparently there's a long probationary period but, still, it sounds amazing. Gareth says they're really picky and hardly anyone works out, so it's not even a definite, but according to Gareth it's one of the most prestigious private airlines around. Guys, I can't wait, I've got a really good feeling about this!"

Elodie paused for dramatic effect. Carla clapped her hand over her mouth in awe and Steph raised an eyebrow apprehensively.

"So he'd just offered you a job out of nowhere and he barely knows you? Hasn't asked for references or anything like that and just happens to think you'll be a perfect fit even though the success rate is absolute crap? Which brings me on to my next question… Fit for what? What exactly is this job and where is it? Is it safe? Is it legal? You've got no idea what it is he wants you to do? You could end up a drugs donkey, for all you know."

Carla snorted and immediately began to choke. Steph rolled her eyes; Carla always did have a flair for dramatics.

"I won't end up a drugs mule, Steph, and if you'd let me finish you'd already know that the position is for cabin crew, for Alpha Whiskey Airways owned by some guy called Alex Walker…"

"Alex Walker?" Carla asked incredulously. "*The* Alex Walker, owner of *En Mode* magazine? El, that's insane!" Carla immediately took out her phone and began typing furiously. "Yeh, it says it right here, Alex Walker, CEO at *En Mode*, photographer to the stars, owner of AW stock images, Alpha Whiskey Air and several charities, plus he's a huge philanthropist. Wow, Elodie, this is incredible."

"Philanthropist? Why would they list that as an achievement?" Elodie asked with incredulity. "I don't think being a misogynistic creep is worthy of a mention," she continued, a bad feeling creeping over her. Maybe the reason that hardly anyone worked out was because the boss was a sex pest. She looked up to see both that both Carla and Steph, instead of nodding in agreement, were shaking with laughter.

"OK, so you know misogynistic but not philanthropist? Do you want to tell her or should I?" Carla asked Steph.

"A philanthropist isn't a womaniser, El, that's a philanderer! A philanthropist is someone who does good deeds, you know, for the world. Like gives to charity and raises awareness for things, like Bono or Oprah," Steph said once she had managed to get a hold of herself.

Elodie felt her cheeks flush; thank God she had made that mistake here and now and not in front of Gareth or worse, Alex Walker himself.

"God, I'm such an idiot!" Elodie exclaimed exasperatedly. She couldn't stay annoyed at herself for too long. Carla and Steph had dissolved back into fits of giggles and Elodie couldn't help but join them. "Anyway... As I was saying, it's a private jet company, run by a *very nice* man. There's just three aircraft, all of them Boeing Business Jets, AKA 'The flying hotel' and they need a new staff member. One of the girls apparently over-stepped the mark with one of the pilots and, well, it didn't work out well for her. So I need to watch my step but.... It's a door, and my foot is firmly in it!" Elodie finished proudly. She took a deep drink of wine and, giving Steph and Carla a confident look held her glass out for them to cheers.

Carla, being ever the optimist, clinked her glass with Elodie's at once. Steph's good mood had apparently evaporated now and she was a little less enthusiastic, although after a pretty glaring sideways glance from Carla offered her glass and the three women chinked them together in celebration.

After a couple of glasses of wine and several slices of pizza, they decided to call it a night. The evening had flown by, with lots of giggles and fast-flowing conversation. They had put a film on in the background, a period drama starring Jenna Broderick, a film Elodie had probably seen a thousand times. She was far from an expert when it came to the world of celebrity but she never missed a film starring her favourite actress. Steph was staying the night; Carla had offered up her bedroom but Steph was insistent that she would sleep on the sofa.

"I want to give Andy a quick call before bed. We've barely spoken all week and I just want to hear his voice. It's the only chance I'll get to speak to him before my birthday," Steph said.

Carla and Elodie reacted in opposite ways, of course: Elodie thought that it was rather sweet, whereas Carla mimed vomiting.

"That reminds me, what do you want to do for your birthday? And don't say nothing, like you usually do," Carla said through a stifled yawn.

"Actually there's a new dim sum place opening on the same day and I'd love it if we all could go," Steph replied.

"Consider it done. We'll sort it, won't we, El?" said Carla.

Elodie nodded fervently as she went to get Steph some

bedding. It was a rare occasion that Steph would let you make a fuss of her, even on her birthday.

"Here you go," Elodie said, handing Steph a couple of pillows and her cosy patchwork blanket before bidding her goodnight and retiring to her room.

Elodie slipped into her nightclothes and clambered into bed. She put her phone on charge and as it lit up saw that she had a message. Her stomach flipped as she read the name: it was from Aaron. She could only see the first line of his message, which Elodie saw didn't contain the word sorry. She was instantly annoyed: she didn't need to open the message to know it would just be a host of excuses. She had decided that she didn't need this kind of negativity in her life so, without so much as opening the message up, deleted it, and instantly felt as though she'd done the right thing. She wanted to end today on a high; it had been a good day, after all, and she intended to keep it that way. Elodie rolled over and soon felt herself drifting off to sleep as the familiar feeling of fatigue gave way to slumber. Elodie's last conscious thoughts were those of happiness, anticipation and ever so slight apprehension. This new job promised to be everything she had hoped for: it offered excitement, variety and, most importantly, a chance for new experiences and to see the world. Elodie just knew that this was the opportunity she'd been waiting for and that it was really going to open her eyes.

CHAPTER 13

"I'VE GOT THREE HOURS UNTIL I NEED TO LEAVE," Elodie sputtered as she dashed back into her bedroom wearing nothing but a towel; droplets from her badly towel-dried hair fell onto the floor as she went.

"If you've got three hours then why the hell are you rushing about like Usain Bolt on speed?" Carla asked as she got up from the sofa and followed Elodie.

"I need this induction to go perfectly," Elodie answered, sitting herself down at her dressing table and applying a thin layer of moisturiser to her face. "Gareth said that hardly anyone works out. It's too good an opportunity to mess things up so I need to be completely on the ball, and look fantastic. I don't want to give them one single reason not to hire me. Now are you going to help me, or what?"

"Your wish is my command," Carla said as she took a low, sarcastic bow towards Elodie.

"Okay, so can you pick something for me to wear, nothing too edgy. I want to be smart, sophisticated and maybe just a touch sexy?"

"What does it matter if you're sexy? It's not like Gareth's going to give you the job because you look hot. You're on totally different buses, if you catch my drift."

"I'm not thinking about Gareth, I'm thinking about Alex. If he owns the company he'll probably have a say and before you get all judgemental, I'm not doing anything wrong, I'm just…"

"Working with what your mamma gave ya? As if I'd judge you for that. Hellooooo, I'm a model, for God's sake, using my looks is what I do!" Carla said, batting her eyelashes and giving Elodie a little twirl. "Now, let's get you sorted. Dry your hair, I'll do clothes and we can decide on your makeup together."

Elodie gave Carla a grateful smile and did as she was told. Elodie was so excited: if she played this exactly right then by the end of the day she would have everything she had wanted.

Elodie's phone rang a little before ten am. It was a very stern-sounding man named Mr Bosford, her new driver, informing her that he would be waiting outside Cockfosters tube station in exactly one hour ready to drive her to Langley private airfield. Elodie was incredibly impressed: she had envisioned getting the tube, then perhaps a bus or maybe a taxi to Langley. Never in her wildest dreams did she expect to have a driver and her own private car to take her there. She stole a glance at the clock and with a heady mix of exhilaration and apprehension made her way towards the tube station. She wore an outfit that Carla had hailed a 'Monochrome masterpiece', consisting of simple black fitted trousers, a loose-fitting black top and off-white jacket. Her hair had been teased into relaxed waves and pinned up in a chic style that Elodie liked very much. She walked briskly; the heels of her court shoes clicked against the pavement and a few stray pieces of hair danced on the warm breeze.

As she descended the escalators into the tube station Elodie's confidence began to erode, like the plain of a cliff face when met by a tempestuous tide. *"One step at a time, Elodie, you've got this,"* she repeated to herself as she boarded the train. Her hands had begun to shake and palms to sweat as time slipped by, pushing her ever closer to the precipice that was her future. She pulled out a magazine from her bag in an attempt to distract her mind from what lay ahead. She flipped to the middle page: the centre pages were always the best and this article certainly didn't disappoint. It was entitled 'Untamed Madagascar' and was packed with loads of things to do and see if you were to visit there. The article included several beautiful photographs of wild animals and the breath-taking views of the Masoala National Park, Nosy Be and countless other attractions. Elodie felt a little pang in her chest as her eyes roamed over the photographs accompanying the article; they were eerily similar to some in the exhibition she had seen on her date with Aaron. She shook her head, thinking that she most certainly did not need to be thinking about Aaron at a time like this. She needed a clear head and to make sure there was nothing that could scupper her chances. Elodie closed the magazine, folded it over and placed it on the back of the bench behind her. *'Someone else can enjoy that, I've had my fill,'* she thought soberly.

The train reached the end of the line and Elodie disembarked. Now all she had to do was find Mr Bosford and allow herself to be whisked away.

Finding Mr Bosford was easier said than done. He had called her from a private number so she couldn't call him back and when she emerged from the underground she was dismayed to see that there were several cars all waiting for their passengers. She glanced around, hoping against hope that maybe there would be some sort of logo, separating her car from the others, but there wasn't. Sighing, she began going down the line of vehicles, opening one door at a time and asking the same question over and over again, "Are you waiting for Elodie Taylor?" She was met with the same answer time and time again, "No." Eventually, after more tries than she cared to remember, she found Mr Bosford, whose appearance was completely at odds with his voice. Over the phone, his tone had been forthright and he had a rich resonant quality which had commanded Elodie's attention. She had imagined him as some sort of army general, with a no-nonsense attitude and a buzz-cut. However, in the flesh, he was nothing of the sort. He wound the window down as she approached the car and welcomed her with a warm smile and a cheery nod.

"Miss Taylor?" he asked. Elodie nodded and got into the car, a brand-new black Audi which was extremely comfortable inside. Mr Bosford was in his mid-fifties, he had mousy blond hair, which was greying at the temples, and extremely blue eyes, which twinkled kindly when he spoke. The journey took less time than Elodie had expected; either they had been closer than she had thought or Mr Bosford's amiable conversation had made the time pass more quickly. As they drew up into the small car park, Elodie felt her nerves begin to flair again. Mr Bosford pulled the car to a standstill and turned round in his seat.

"Elodie, you seem like a lovely girl so I'm going to give you some advice. Keep a cool head when you're on the job and act completely professional at all times. I've heard that Mr Walker is a stickler for propriety and considering the types that use his jets, it's no wonder why. Just keep things, you know, collected. I'd hate to be driving you back for the last time any time soon."

Elodie nodded. She had no intention of being anything other than a complete pro at all times, especially since Gareth had already given her the heads up about why they were looking for a replacement in the first place.

"Thank you Mr Bosford," Elodie said genuinely. He really did seem like such a nice man.

"Don't mention it, and good luck. Remember what I said and you'll do fine. Now, see that big door over there, you'll need to go through there and down a short corridor to the lounge. Someone will meet you there."

Elodie nodded and thanked him once more before getting out of the car. She stared ahead. The private airfield was upon first glance completely unremarkable. She hadn't been quite sure what to expect; she knew that there would be no red carpet, paparazzi or A-list celebs just hanging out, but she expected something a little more than this. There was a short-paved area leading up to a largely glass building with enormous cardinal coloured letters that spelt the word 'Langley' hanging over an imposing white door.

Elodie made her way towards the terminal and braced herself for the challenge that lay ahead. The large doors swung open as she approached and upon entering found that her breath had been taken from her. Elodie discovered that she was in an immaculately appointed, extremely luxurious reception area, which seemed to gleam from every angle. The floor was white polished marble that glinted as she walked along it. The room was furnished with two large white sofas, several copper tables and lots of fresh-cut flowers in large glass vases. In front of her was a modern reception desk and behind that sat a very smartly dressed woman with dark hair tied so tightly back that it almost looked painful.

"Name, please?" the woman asked before Elodie had a chance to speak. She picked up a black clipboard glanced at it momentarily then returned her gaze to Elodie.

"Elodie Taylor, I'm here to see…"

"Mr Townsend will be out shortly. Take a seat and I'll let him know you've arrived. Have your passport and relevant documents ready, please."

Elodie nodded, perched herself on the edge of the closest sofa and rummaged in her bag for all the things she'd been told she would need to bring. Mr Bosford's words echoed in her head: *'Keep it professional at all times.'* As the receptionist had predicted, Gareth wasn't long; he rounded the corner and without hesitation beckoned her over. Elodie obliged and wondered when professionalism meant impoliteness.

"Thanks so much for this, Gareth. I'm really am so grateful to you. This place is fantastic," she said as she quickened her pace in order to keep up with him. He walked her past the reception desk and down a well-lit corridor, her heels clacking against the marble floor as she went. Soon enough they came to a crossroads of sorts: two imposing and identical doors stood on opposite sides of the hall, between them a substantial water feature, which provided a trickling soundtrack that Elodie found quite relaxing.

"Don't mention it, if you work out you'll be the one doing me the favour. Finding people who are the right fit for Alpha Whiskey is a bit of a hard job. Right, a quick tour and then down to business, OK?" Gareth said.

Elodie nodded enthusiastically and braced herself for a barrage of information. "Through that door over there is Argent Air. Langley has only two companies operating from it. It's small, but perfectly formed. You'll never need to go through there, so don't worry yourself about Argent. They pretty much keep themselves to themselves and that's the way we like it.

Elodie tried to peer and get a glimpse of the competition but to no avail. She felt as though she'd heard of Argent Air before; it felt familiar, but she couldn't for the life of her figure out why.

"Now through here," Gareth gestured to the door closest to them, "is Alpha Whiskey. The waiting room is basically a lounge-type bar where our clients can wait in comfort. Alpha Whiskey prides itself on taking better than first-class care of its patrons. First, though, you need to go through passport control, I'm afraid there's just some things that money can't buy and that's a free pass out of the country and back in again." Elodie handed over her passport, which was checked and handed back to her. There was a small red light above the door, which turned to green; Gareth's hand was reaching for the doorknob when a thought struck her.

"What about security?" she asked Gareth, almost alarmed.

"You've already been through it," Gareth said smugly. "We have discreet full-body scanners and a team of security professionals analysing them behind the scenes. If you were carrying anything so much as a pair of tweezers you'd have been stopped, searched and had them confiscated. If you had been a passenger, then you would have relieved of your bags, which would have gone through security separately, loaded on to the plane and put back into your care upon landing at whatever location the plane has been chartered to go to."

"Wow, that's amazing, I mean it's crazy but absolutely brilliant. They should have them all over." Gareth nodded his agreement and pushed the door open: Elodie was in. If she had been impressed with the reception area then she was quite frankly gobsmacked by the lounge. It looked like something out of a film: the floor was now a plush cream carpet, which felt positively heavenly underfoot and the lighting, almost overly bright in the reception and hall, was now much softer and far more welcoming. The décor adhered to the same theme: the colours white and copper had been accessorised with hints of boysenberry, which enhanced the opulence even further. At the far end was a heavily-set wooden bar; behind it stood an array of expensive-looking bottles, crystal-cut glassware and, hung on the wall behind it all, an enormous mercury flecked mirror that served to make the room appear to double in size. Elodie positively loved it. She had never been anywhere quite so lavish; even the extravagance of the Grosvenor Suite paled in comparison to this. She let out a low whistle and tried to take it all in.

"I know, right," Gareth said, clearly pleased with how impressed Elodie was. "OK, so we're quiet today as we're grounded on Thursdays, unless something, or someone extra special, comes up. It gives us a chance to stay on top of everything. You'd be amazed at how much paperwork I have to do, it's not all glitz and glamour for me."

Elodie smiled. It was good to see the Gareth she knew starting to surface; she didn't much care for the prim and proper one she'd been met with at reception.

"So what's first?" Elodie asked eagerly. Gareth paced over to a small clerk's desk in the back corner of the room; up until that moment, Elodie hadn't even noticed it was there. "So you'll be stationed here while the plane is grounded, your duties are both on and off the plane; everything you did in your previous job, plus a few added extras in terms of making sure our clientele have every wish catered for. We've had some pretty outrageous demands over the years; obviously, everything that happens inside these walls stays inside these walls."

"What's the craziest thing that's happened?" Elodie asked, in spite of herself and Mr Bosford's warning.

"I couldn't possibly name names, Elodie, but let's just say that a certain pop star threw every single toy out of his pram when we said no to his pet leopard travelling in the cabin with him. The idiot even demanded it sleep on his bed. We said no, of course. But usually, whatever they want, they get. They pay megabucks and expect the very best," Gareth replied. He handed Elodie a wad of paper, which she was dismayed to see were questionnaire-type forms. "Fill these in and then give me a shout when you're done. I'm on channel seven," he said, handing her a small walkie-talkie and setting off through a door on the far side of the room.

Elodie sat there for what seemed like hours filling in the forms. They really did leave no stone unturned. When she was done, Gareth showed her around the rest of the building. She saw that through the door Gareth had disappeared through were the boarding gates, three of them. There were also toilets, where the extravagance continued, and a compact treatment room, complete with beauty therapist, should any of the guests wish for some pampering. Gareth had told her that up the stairs lay the staffroom, a changing area and also a kitchen where Michelin-starred food was prepared and sent down for the guests. "Everything comes down through a dumb waiter behind the bar, all you need to do is remember who ordered what." Elodie smiled; she could do that in her sleep. 'This is going to be a piece of cake,' she thought to herself confidently, until a thought struck her: she'd never worked behind a bar before and she had absolutely no idea how to make the fancy cocktails she was certain the high flying clients of Alpha Whiskey Air would want.

"I've never worked behind a bar before," she said, her confidence waning.

"You don't need to worry about that, we have professional and qualified mixologists to do the drinks. Don't worry, we won't stretch you *that* far." Gareth said. "So I think that about wraps it up on the ground, now for the main attraction. Let's have a look inside the jet, shall we? They're all the same, so I'm afraid it's a case of once you've seen one you've seen them all."

Gareth led Elodie through gate number one; she stared out of the window at the three business jets on the tarmac beneath. The cleaning team were leaving the farthest plane, their luminous tabards shining brightly in the summer sun. Gareth extended an arm, indicating that she should go first. Elodie obliged and led the way down an external covered walkway and onto the plane.

"Jesus," Elodie said, unable to help herself. This wasn't a plane at all, more like a hotel suite with wings. There was everything anyone could possibly want on board, and more besides. Elodie was utterly gobsmacked. She had seen the planes through the boarding gate windows; from the outside, they looked like regular jets but on the inside, they were a completely different world.

"Here we are, one thousand square feet of pure, unadulterated luxury," Gareth said, extending a hand as if he were showcasing the star prize on a game show "We have secure seating just here." He pointed to six comfy-looking armchair-type chairs that were the closest thing on the aircraft to what you would usually find on a plane. "We also have a dining area, two bedrooms, a lounge area and of course, a bathroom with walk-in shower and his 'n' hers sinks. Well, that's everything for the passengers, for us there's a small room at the back for a little rest and recuperation and of course a kitchenette for preparing meals. There's an extensive menu for both food and drink, but don't worry, everything is pre-made or mixed, all we have to do is serve."

Elodie could barely take it in. She had searched for private jets online and had seen some pretty spectacular sights, but nothing compared to this.

"It's just, incredible," she said, awestruck. "I can't believe there are people who can afford this… It must cost an absolute fortune."

"It most certainly does, our guests are extremely lucky. But then again, so are we. There are definitely perks to the job. Paid-for accommodation on layovers in the best hotels, round the globe travel – and the luckiest of us get tickets to the Autumn Gala, courtesy of Mr Walker, but I wouldn't hold out much hope. He reserves that honour for only one or two staff. I'm yet to get an invite, but I just know that this is my year," Gareth said hopefully. "Now, let's get you acquainted with the team."

He turned on his heel and Elodie followed in hot pursuit back towards the terminal. She was excited to meet her colleagues and hear their stories. Gareth took Elodie to the staff room, a small area at the back of the building. The room was a stark contrast in comparison to the rest of the airport. It was far simpler in design and, other than a small office-type kitchen, a couple of tables and a smattering of chairs, there really wasn't much to write home about. Sat at the table, amiably chatting and enjoying steaming mugs of coffee, were two women. They stood up when she and Gareth walked through the door. Elodie was surprised and a little proud to see that one of the women wore pilot's wings on the breast panel of her deep-purple coloured blazer.

"Elodie, this is Amelia Coleman." Gareth gestured to the woman with the winged badge attached to her lapel. Amelia stuck out her hand and shook Elodie's in a firm, yet friendly fashion.

"Pleasure to have you joining us," she smiled warmly. "I trust Gareth's given you the guided tour?"

Elodie nodded, unable to find any words. Amelia was a tall, almost Amazonian woman with dark skin and deep, penetrating eyes framed by long eyelashes. Elodie liked her at once; she exuded a warmth that reminded Elodie of Betty, although the two women couldn't be at further ends of the spectrum when it came to appearances. Elodie's attention was directed to her other colleague now, and she turned to her with her hand outstretched. After an uncomfortable pause, the woman took Elodie's hand and rang it just once.

"Grace Stone. Happy to have you with us," she said, although her tone seemed anything but happy. "I'm cabin crew too."

"Brilliant, just like me," Elodie said trying to thaw Grace's icy exterior with her enthusiasm.

"Not quite," Grace interjected. Elodie felt her heart sink.

Grace was to be working directly with her. She was far less pleasant than Amelia and, as Elodie had been reminded of Betty earlier, she was now reminded of Vanessa.

"Err, well I'm Elodie," she replied, then with not much more to offer added, "I'm very excited about working here, it's going to be so much fun."

"It's going to be work. Now, if you'll excuse me I have a few jobs to do." Grace set her coffee cup down on the table behind her and gave the room a small nod before striding out, the door shut behind her and Elodie felt the first flush of embarrassment caress her cheeks.

"Don't worry about Grace," Amelia said. "She's lovely when you get to know her, and she's got a lot on her plate at the moment. Gareth, can I go through a couple of things with you before tomorrow?" Amelia pulled a small notepad from her breast pocket and flipped it open.

"Elodie, why don't you go back through to the lounge? It's far more comfortable in there. I'll be through in a minute." Gareth smiled at Elodie, who was savvy enough to know when private business was afoot, so left them to it.

"It was nice to meet you," she called to Amelia as she made her way back to the lounge.

Elodie struggled at first to remember where to go. There wasn't an awful lot of signage; it would seem that the richer you were the less you had to rely on getting from A to B on your own. Eventually, she found her way back to the lounge. She pushed the door open and stopped dead in her tracks; the door swung back and almost hit her square in the face.

"Chase?" she stammered. "What, what are you doing here?"

Chase whirled round, he had been stood at the bar with his back facing her, but she had known instantly that it was him, from the way he stood, to the way he swirled the contents of his glass before raising it to his lips.

"Elodie," he said. "I was wondering when I was going to bump into you."

"You knew I'd be here?" she asked with a disconcerted edge to her voice.

"Of course, Gareth told me. Wait, you mean you didn't know I would be here?" Chase asked slowly, taking another sip of his nectar-coloured drink that Elodie was now almost certain was whisky.

Their eyes met and Elodie saw that he surveyed her with a look of mild amusement, as though she were a curio he had just stumbled upon. He placed his glass down and walked over to her, slowly. Elodie felt as though an eternity had passed before he finally drew up to her. She felt her heartbeat quicken, he was almost too close to her. She could smell the intense aroma of his aftershave: a heady mix of musk and masculinity that seemed to engulf her senses.

"How are you finding it so far?" he asked.

Elodie gave herself a little mental shake: what on earth was she doing? Whatever it was, it certainly wasn't professional. Her thoughts had wandered back to the recesses of her mind, where the memory of her dream had been kept. It had been so real, so visceral that for a second Elodie felt as if it were happening all over again.

"It's good, thanks," she said, casting her eyes to the bar where Chase had first been stood.

"Are you drinking whisky?" she asked. It was

mid-afternoon and despite the airline being grounded for the day didn't deter from the fact that as far as boozing went, it was still pretty early.

"Want one?" Chase asked, making his way back over to the bar.

"No thanks, it's a bit early for me," Elodie said, feeling awkward.

'So much for professionalism being Alpha Whiskey's modus operandi,' she thought. Chase responded by dropping two cubes of ice into a glass, which tinkled as they hit the base and then poured a small measure of whisky from a small decanter. He handed the glass to her and against her better judgement she took it. Elodie was not a big spirits drinker; in fact, she couldn't remember ever having had whisky before. She took a sip; surely if Chase, the pilot, said it was OK then it would be fine. Elodie coughed and sputtered, amazed: how could something so cold taste like fire?

"You OK?" Chase said, barely able to hide his amusement. "Not a fan?" Elodie shook her head and handed the glass back to him.

"I think I'll stick to wine," she said, handing the glass back to Chase and wiping the corner of her mouth with the back of her sleeve. "Whisky is officially gross." Chase laughed and set her glass down on the bar.

"I like it, there's something far more satisfying about enjoying something you have to take your time over."

"Is that why you had it the other night?" Elodie asked, the words out of her mouth before she had the chance to stop them. Chase raised an eyebrow, "I, erm, we walked past you guys on our way home, I saw you," she finished, casting her eyes downwards in order to avoid his gaze.

"I see," Chase said measuredly. Elodie couldn't help herself, she suddenly needed to know why he had almost invited her to join him. It had been playing on her mind and now felt like a good time to find out the truth.

"When you spoke to me outside The Clifton, you seemed as though you were going to ask me to go with you, but you were on a date, and I..." she trailed off.

Chase had turned to her and fixed her with a look so intense it drew the breath from Elodie's mouth.

"I wasn't on a date, Elodie, I was actually going there on my own. I wasn't meeting a friend. I just said that, I don't know why. I guess I didn't want to look like a sad old man. The woman is just someone I know, who happened to be there. She's very strong-willed and I didn't have the heart, or the capacity, to turn her away."

Elodie stood there stunned. She hadn't expected such a blunt answer from Chase; his honesty was as refreshing as it was unusual.

"Oh," she managed, "I, errr, I didn't mean to overstep the mark."

There was a pause in the conversation, a moment of reflection. Chase turned away from her and ran a hand through his dark hair.

"So what do you think to it all so far?" he asked, turning back round to Elodie as though the last few minutes had never happened.

Elodie swallowed hard, and with trepidation began to tell him what she thought of the place. It didn't take long for her to warm back to him. She told him that so far she loved it, that she was excited to travel, that the prospect of working for such an airline was utterly incredible and that she felt extremely lucky to have bumped into Gareth after her unsuccessful interview with Wing Star. Chase listened intently and when she was finished gave a kind smile. It was the sort of smile that Elodie had never seen on his face before. It softened him, made him seem more human, somehow, more attractive.

"Well, I hope it's everything you're hoping for."

It was Elodie's turn to smile now.

"Me too," she agreed, "although I think getting Grace onside might be easier said than done, she's not very welcoming, is she?"

"Grace? Ah, don't worry about her; she's an absolute kitten when you get to know her. She's probably just in a bit of a mood. She's been having a few guy problems recently, last I heard. I dunno, it's all just gossip to me. But that may be why she doesn't like you. I wouldn't pay it any attention, just give her a wide berth."

"Yeh, I think I'm going to have to," Elodie said in a matter-of-fact way.

"Atta girl," Chase said encouragingly. "You'll be fine. Now I'd love to stand around and chat all day, but I've got to get off."

He gave Elodie a playful look, again something Elodie had never seen from Chase. He seemed different somehow, as though being in his own environment had encouraged him out of his shell. He was far more likeable inside the walls of Alpha Whiskey. Chase gave her shoulder a little squeeze, his broad fingers resting there for just a second too long. He drew his hand back sharply as if surprised by this bold action and looked almost awkward. He mumbled something that Elodie didn't quite catch and before she knew it, he had left the lounge, replaced by Gareth as the two passed each other in the doorway. Gareth held a tape measure in one hand and a tablet in the other.

"Right, let's get you measured for your uniform," he said happily.

"Uniform? So I've got the job?" Gareth laughed at her,

"Of course you've got the job, you're exactly what we need. Young, keen and eager." Elodie grinned: this was turning out to be a very good day indeed.

After being weighed and measured, prodded and poked, Elodie was all done. Gareth informed her that they each were given two sets of uniforms and it was up to them to ensure they were spotless, pressed and most of all that they fitted. Elodie nodded her understanding; she realised at that point that she didn't actually know what the uniforms looked like. Grace had not been wearing hers and she would bet her life savings, non-existent as they were, that her uniform would not be the same as the pilot's one that Amelia had worn.

When everything was done and dusted, contracts signed and hands shaken, Elodie made to leave. Gareth had told her that her schedule would be emailed to her every Friday at seven am. She had been given her own pass now, which got her through the majority of doors. She pushed open the door and walked through the corridor, but before she could round the corner to the exit, she heard a voice she recognised. Aaron was talking to someone.

Elodie stopped dead in her tracks, hardly able to believe her bad luck. She heard a woman's laugh and couldn't help herself from peering around the corner to get a better look. She saw Aaron immediately, dressed in dark denim jeans and a grey top, his luminous yellow cleaner's tabard held loosely in one hand. Elodie's heart skipped a beat. Aaron looked great. She leaned out further to catch a glimpse of the woman he was with: it was Grace. Elodie hadn't recognised her voice for two reasons. Firstly, she had only just met her, and secondly, she had never heard her sound happy. Grace was smiling and had her hand placed delicately on Aaron's shoulder. She threw her head back and laughed; obviously, Elodie had caught them in the midst of a private joke. Grace leaned forward, gave Aaron a kiss on the cheek and strode off, giving him a wave over her shoulder as she went. The truth hit Elodie like a tonne of bricks: Aaron and Grace were an item. He was the one she had been having 'guy problems' with and it was Elodie who had been, unbeknownst to her, the one causing the trouble.

Elodie felt sick: no wonder Grace had been so frosty. Aaron must have told her, probably on the day he had uploaded that romantic picture of their shadows. Aaron began to turn and Elodie shot back and out of sight, well aware that she had only moments before Aaron rounded the corner and she came face to face with him. She racked her brain for something to do, somewhere to go, but the hallways of Langley private airport provided no obvious solution so, instead, she took out her phone and stared at the blank screen. Aaron came around the corner; he too was looking at his phone and didn't look up from it as he strode past. Elodie, her heart beating fast, breathed a sigh of relief.

'That was close,' she thought to herself as she left the building.

Mr Bosford, true to his word, was waiting for her in the same spot that he had dropped her off.

"So, how was your first day?" he asked in a fatherly tone. Elodie regaled him with a blow-by-blow account and when she had finished he congratulated her and asked her how she planned on celebrating.

"Well, I think I'm going to treat my friends to a meal. They've been amazing to me over the last few months and I've been a right pain, not to mention pretty skint. But now, well, let's just say that this job pays a lot more than my last one so I can afford to show them how grateful I am."

"That's a lovely idea," he said as he popped his indicator on and pulled up to the tube station.

"Here already?" Elodie asked, a little taken aback that the journey was over so soon.

"Afraid so," Mr Bosford answered. "Now, I take it you're starting Monday?" Elodie nodded; she had the rest of the week to herself.

"Thanks, Mr Bosford," she said, getting out of the car and giving him a grateful little wave as she disappeared into the tube station.

Elodie could hardly contain her excitement all the way home; she kept wanting to tell the other passengers her news, to run up and down the carriage shouting about how everything was slotting into place. She didn't, though, and instead she had to be satisfied with holding it all in until she got home.

Elodie practically fell through the door, a tangle of arms and legs. Carla looked up; she was sat on the sofa with a face mask on, painting her nails.

"I got it!" Elodie exclaimed. Carla looked up and smiled, her face mask cracking around the corners of her mouth.

"That's brilliant," she said a little stiffly, obviously trying not to move her lips too much and damage the pink clay mask any further.

"I could do with a drink, though. You'll never guess who I saw," Elodie went on to say.

"Someone famous?" Carla said again in that stiff voice that was almost inaudible. Elodie just stared at her with a blank look on her face. "Was it someone famous?" Carla asked again, her question louder but no clearer the second time around.

"I genuinely have no idea what you're trying to say," Elodie laughed as she poured herself a glass of cold rosé wine. Carla held up a finger, shot up and bounded to the bathroom. Elodie heard the running water and moments later Carla reappeared, sans face mask.

"That's better," she said clearly. "I said, was it anyone famous?"

"Oh no, nothing like that, the airline's grounded on Thursdays, so I only met some of the staff, speaking of which…" she trailed off.

"Oh my God, Chase. Shit, it's Chase, isn't it? He's the pilot! El, this is fate, you know: it's got to be," Carla said.

Elodie laughed, she had literally never in her life heard Carla talk about fate when it came to men. Dating Chris really had had an effect on her.

"Well if it is, then fate certainly has a twisted sense of humour. Aaron was there too."

"Oh, big conundrum, who to go for, the fabulously handsome, no doubt rich, manly pilot or the cheating cleaner? Hmmm, let me think." Her voice dripped with sarcasm.

"I'm not going for anyone," Elodie replied bluntly. "Aaron's dating one of the other flight attendants, Grace, who now hates me because I think he took me out while they were seeing each other; and Chase… Well come on, he's too old, there's too much of an age gap and besides, even if I didn't care about his age, I just don't like him like that, he's too… standoffish."

"You don't like him like that? He's good-looking, successful and makes you smile like that," Carla said, pointing at Elodie who, despite her words, had a silly half-smile on her face. "It doesn't matter about the age gap, it matters about the page gap. Are you both on the same page? Anyway, methinks the lady doth protest too much," Carla finished dramatically.

"Well methinks the lady protests just the right amount," Elodie said, giving Carla a look that told her to leave it there.

The truth was that Elodie didn't know how she felt about Chase – or rather, she didn't know how he felt about her. He was hot one minute and cold the next. Sometimes he seemed sweet and vulnerable and others, just plain intolerable.

"Okay well deny it all you want, but I can tell, you know. You can lie to yourself but you can't lie to me," Carla said, tapping the side of her nose in a secretive fashion that Elodie found annoying.

"Carla, drop it. It's getting old now," Elodie said, beginning to lose her temper.

"A bit like Chase? Ha, sorry, OK, OK I'll stop now," Carla said, throwing up her hands in exasperation. "Enough about boys, tell me about the job. Is it as glamorous as I imagine?"

"More so," Elodie confirmed. "The planes are like luxury hotels, the best you've ever seen, honestly they're out of this world. They put me up in places all over, pay for everything and when you've been there a while, you get to go to this gala thing that the owner puts on."

"Gala thing?" Carla said in shock. "Elodie, that gala thing is practically bigger than the Oscars! Anyone who's anyone goes. You've got to get me in, please. If I could just meet one person from *En Mode* it could change my whole career, my whole life. Please, I'll do anything you want, I'll clean your room for an entire year!" Carla said desperately.

"I can't. I would if I could, you know it but I don't just get to go. Gareth's never even been. You get chosen for it, and I'm the new girl so I don't stand a chance."

Carla looked very glum at this; Elodie didn't want the shine to be taken off her day just yet, so quickly changed the subject.

"Shall we get dinner?" Elodie asked. "My treat."

"I really don't fancy going out, let's order a pizza," Carla replied, her forlorn expression dissolving into one of excitement. It was truly amazing what some bread with cheese on could do for the spirit.

"Pizza again? Haven't we had enough recently?" Elodie asked, her stomach positively roiling at the idea.

"I'll pretend you didn't say that," Carla said, before picking up her phone and calling Pizza Rova, who were so accustomed to her calls that they practically had her order prepared and ready to go. "Pizzas will be here in forty minutes," she said once she'd finished on the phone.

"OK, well I suppose I should celebrate the job, but after this I'm on a health kick, I need to fit into my uniform. Gareth measured me earlier and I kind of lied a bit."

"How can you lie about your size if someone is measuring you?" Carla asked.

"Well, if someone comes at you with a tape measure you breathe in," Elodie replied laughing, "It'll be fine, I just need to watch myself this weekend. Shall we put a film on?"

"You choose. I'm going to drop Steph a message and see if she wants in," Carla grabbed the remote and threw it to Elodie before picking up her phone to text Steph.

"She's going to say no," Elodie said knowingly. "She's with Andy this weekend and I'm betting they won't leave the bedroom."

"Don't!" Carla cried, burying her face in one of the sofa cushions. "I just can't think of Steph like that, she's too straight-laced."

As it turned out, Elodie was right. Steph turned them down in favour of spending the evening with Andy; the couple had plans for a romantic meal out followed by a cosy night in.

Through the slit of one cracked eye Elodie could just about make out the time, four forty-five am. She groaned: her dream job had interrupted her dreams. This one had been fraught; she couldn't remember exactly what had happened but she woke up feeling anxious.

'These early mornings are going to take some getting used to,' she thought to herself as she dragged herself out of bed and padded into the bathroom, taking care to be extra quiet so as to leave Carla undisturbed. Elodie packed her overnight bag. She knew that her first flight was to New York and that there would be a two-day layover, during which time she could do whatever she wanted. Elodie found that there were definitely perks to being up and about at such an early hour. The walk to the tube station was far more peaceful and the tube itself practically empty. She reached Cockfosters in good time and, as she had expected, Mr Bosford was there to drive her the rest of the journey. They passed the time by making small talk; Elodie was keen to keep her mind on the job and if she were being honest with herself, her nerves were in such a state that she didn't think she'd be able to hold down a proper conversation even if she tried.

"Okay, here we are," Mr Bosford said, switching the engine off and turning to face her just like he had done the last time. "I can tell you're nervous but don't be. Just take your time and if in doubt, just ask."

Elodie nodded, thanked him, got out and then thanked him again. Walking to the front doors, she felt as though every single move was an effort. Her shoes seemed to get heavier with each step. Eventually, she was there, with nowhere to hide and nothing to do but venture inside.

"Morning briefing please, everyone," Gareth called over the swell of the room. Elodie looked around: there were more people here than she had met previously. She gave herself a little kick. Of course more than four people worked here. She smiled at one of the other crew members, who gave her a blank stare, and returned her attention to the front of the room where Gareth was stood, clipboard in hand. He went through the run-down of the day, including personal assignments, names of prestigious passengers, special requests or 'riders' as he called them and who would be needed where and to do what. Elodie listened intently but there seemed to be so much to take in that no sooner had one piece of information gone in one ear, it seemed to come out the other. Gareth called the meeting to an end and the small crowd dispersed.

"Elodie," Gareth called to her. She went over to him and opened her mouth to speak but was cut off before she could say anything, "I know that's a lot to take in so I've arranged for you to shadow Grace for your first flight."

Elodie's heart sank a little but was lifted when Gareth presented her with a large, dark purple box with the airline's insignia embossed on its top.

"What's this?" Elodie asked with trepidation, unsure as to whether she was allowed to open the box or whether she was merely supposed to take it somewhere.

"That's your uniform, love – well, uniforms. You have two of everything in there. You have your own locker, you're in number…" he studied his clipboard for a second, "twelve. Now, off you go, get ready and find Grace up there, she'll see you through your next few days."

Elodie nodded, as a small wave of excitement washed

228

over her. She still had no idea what she would be wearing and being given free clothes, uniform or not, was very novel.

Elodie made her way to the changing area. She located her locker and set the box down on the bench to the side of it. Lifting the lid, Elodie let out a low, impressed whistle. Inside was a beautifully-made cream pencil dress; it had a boysenberry-coloured belt around the waist, matching flight hat, neckerchief and heels. Elodie sighed: the dress was going to be a squeeze, to say the least.

She glanced around and saw that the other members of the crew were fixing their hair and makeup, with most of them looking as though they were about to embark on a night out, not a flight. Elodie glanced in the mirror: she had applied a little makeup this morning and twisted her hair into a messy top knot, but she looked nowhere near as well turned out as the rest of the crew. She opened her locker, which was actually far more similar to a wardrobe. Inside were padded coat hangers, all of which were covered in sumptuous purple and gold. Elodie stepped out of her civilian clothes and into her uniform: it fit like a glove, a pretty tight glove but a glove nonetheless. She tied the chiffon necktie around her neck. The heels fit remarkably well, probably down to the fact that they were made from buttery-soft leather that seemed to mould around her feet the instant she slipped them on. The inside of her locker housed a full-length mirror, in which she surveyed her reflection. Elodie was in love with her uniform. It was stylish, sophisticated and ever so elegant: the ensemble was a far cry from the garish orange polyester shirts of Zip Air. In this outfit she felt womanly and as though she could take on the world.

'So this is power dressing eh? Feels pretty good,' Elodie thought to herself as she closed the locker's door and repacked her travel case. She picked it up and looked around for Grace, whom she spotted almost at once. Grace was undoubtedly beautiful, if not a little stony-looking. Elodie noticed that she wore slight creases around the corners of her prominent eyes, which made Elodie think that, despite the evidence, she must like to laugh. Grace boasted a strong brow and smooth dark skin; there was no denying it she was definitely very striking and Elodie could see what

Aaron must see in her. She felt a little pang: she was still hurt by Aaron's actions and couldn't understand how their date could have seemed so wonderful when it was all so false. Aaron had struck her as an honest person, but this just shone a spotlight on how little she really knew him. Elodie decided that when the time was right she would speak to Grace about it and apologise if she needed to. She wouldn't let one man's foolish act mar a good working relationship.

"Grace, hi. I don't know if you remember me but I'm..."

"I know who you are," Grace cut across, her tone not unpleasant but far from friendly, "You're my shadow this week, right?" she asked. Elodie nodded enthusiastically, "OK, well we're on Alpha Whiskey three, direct flight to New York with four passengers. Has Gareth briefed you on this?"

"Not really, I've just had the email..."

"OK, well let's walk and talk and I'll fill you in," Grace said, sounding exasperated at this prospect but proceeded nonetheless. "We'll be hosting Jenna and Sven Broderick and their two adorable rug rats."

Elodie stopped in her tracks and Grace turned around and stared at her.

"Jenna Broderick? As in *the* Jenna Broderick?" Elodie managed, her voice barely a whisper.

"How many Jenna Brodericks do you know? Yes, of course, *the* Jenna Broderick. Now come on, we've a lot to do before they arrive."

Elodie stood there gaping; she simply could not believe she was about to meet the award-winning actress Jenna Broderick. A woman who had starred in pretty much all of Elodie's favourite films, who ran her own fashion line and makeup range and who regularly graced the front covers of magazines. Elodie didn't usually care for the world of celebrity but in the words of Carla, *"This was some next-level shit."*

"I, errr, just didn't realise that I'd meet someone so famous, straightaway," Elodie said lamely.

"Oh, I'm sorry, would you like me to lock her in the toilet until you feel more comfortable?" Grace quipped.

Elodie said nothing, Grace was right, what did she think was going to happen? Grace explained the ins and out of what the flight would entail and Elodie realised that it was all pretty usual, other than the A-list passengers and luxurious surroundings, this was a standard flight. The same health and safety checks had to be done, the same security procedures, the same border control, the same everything. Elodie entered the plane feeling pretty confident; she knew she could do this job. The only thing that would make the whole experience more enjoyable would be having Grace onside.

It seemed as though time were no more than sand slipping through her fingers, because before she knew it Elodie was stood, feet away from the entrance, welcoming Jenna Broderick and her family on board. She found it far easier than she had expected, it was as though someone else had taken the wheel and Elodie was on autopilot. She fetched the drinks, entertained the children and waited on them hand and foot. The flight went smoothly and they touched down in New York precisely seven hours and five minutes after taking off. Elodie had done extremely well to avoid the cockpit. Grace had liaised with the pilots: it seemed that Elodie wasn't quite trusted to be a part of that particular procedure just yet.

The Brodericks disembarked and were met by a team of security on the tarmac. Elodie watched in awe as they were bundled into a Range Rover with blacked-out windows and driven off, leaving behind only a handful of staff to collect their luggage and personal effects from the plane. Elodie breathed a sigh of relief: her first flight was over and it had gone well. Even Grace had seemed pleased with her, which, when you considered what a disadvantage Elodie had, was really quite remarkable.

"So what happens now?" Elodie asked once the plane had been cleared and they had readied themselves to leave.

"Well, we go through security and customs as you usually would, and then you do what you like. You have the address of the hotel?" Elodie nodded. They had an expenses card for travel costs and a daily subsistence allowance, anything else they wanted to do was on them.

"So we just go?" Elodie asked, seeking clarification. She didn't want to put a foot wrong and risk losing this job.

"Yes Elodie, we just go. Ground crew clear up, obviously. Dear God, are you always this dim or are you putting on a special show just for me?"

Grace gave Elodie a frosty stare that seemed to undo all of the hard work Elodie had put in over the course of the flight. In one swift movement Grace had swept past her and Elodie found herself alone. She stared in her wake and watched as Grace navigated the jet bridge with precision and purpose and before Elodie could blink she had rounded the corner and was gone. Elodie couldn't explain it but she didn't want to leave the jet.

She wanted to experience more. She was still so new to this and she felt that if she could just spend a little more time on board the plane then she'd be better equipped to handle anything the job could throw at her. She walked the length of the cabin, letting her fingers run over any surface that they could find. The Brodericks had left behind a half-drunk bottle of Champagne; Elodie picked it up and rotated it to read the label. It was the same make that she had drunk with Steph and Carla that night in the Grosvenor Suite. Elodie set it down; it wouldn't be long before the cleaning team descended and she didn't want to be caught red-handed handling the celebrities' cast-offs. Elodie's mind wandered: this world that she had been thrust into was something most people could only dream of. She imagined herself sat on of the plush sofas, sipping expensive Champagne whilst adorned in only the finest garments money could buy. She wondered just how much you had to be worth in order to make something like this affordable and if the people here were any happier than her?

"Penny for them," a man's voice said from behind her, breaking her out of her reverie. Elodie spun around and wasn't disappointed to see that it was Chase.

"I was just, errr, taking in my surroundings, I guess," Elodie said, taking a step backwards and accidentally bumping into one of the chairs.

"How are you finding it?" Chase said, taking a step closer. "Enjoying it, I hope?" Elodie nodded.

Chase was almost uncomfortably close to her now. She could smell the hazy aroma of him; she detected no aftershave, just a hint of raw masculinity that seemed to penetrate her very being. She tried to ignore it, but there was something in the way he looked at her, something dangerously enticing.

"Everything's fine," she managed after a protracted pause, realising that an uncomfortable silence had begun to build between them.

"Are you going to the hotel first? We could share a taxi?" Chase said, turning to face Elodie. He fixed her with a stare that bordered on uncomfortable and waited for her answer.

Elodie wasn't sure what to say; Chase made her feel on edge. To say he was intense was an understatement and Elodie found his presence a difficult pill to swallow. He never seemed to be able to relax. Even when she had seen him 'enjoying himself', he appeared stiff, maybe even stressed. Elodie didn't really know what his deal was; all she knew was that it made her feel disconcerted. Still, she didn't want to seem rude, especially to someone who had, when it came down to it, helped her out for no reason other than he could.

"That'd be great," she replied, offering him a sweet smile, which he did not return.

"I'll call down and sort a car. I just need to take care of something first, I'll meet you at the exit. You know where to go and what to do, right?"

Elodie nodded. This was all part and parcel of the job now, and it didn't matter whether you flew economy, first-class or sat on the captain's lap, everyone had to go through passport control and have their bags checked. You just got to do it a whole lot faster if you were crew.

Elodie walked out of the airport and waited. She couldn't quite believe she was here, in New York, with an entire weekend to do what she pleased. The passengers on her return flight were to be American property tycoons off to visit London. Elodie wasn't looking forward to that flight as much as she had been with her first one: when pitched head to head, millionaire property tycoons definitely came second to superstar celebrities.

'Now there's a sentence I never thought I'd say,' Elodie thought to herself as she took out her phone She should

really let everyone back home know how her first flight had gone. After sending out the relevant messages Elodie stuffed her phone back into her bag and glanced around. The airport was busy and a far cry from Langley.

After traversing the bustling concourse, Elodie made her way to the taxi rank. She looked around, hoping to see Chase so that they could share a taxi as he had offered, but he was nowhere to be seen. Elodie was getting hot and bothered as the New York sun beat down on her heavily. She took a few steps to her right and took shelter in a covered area; the shade came as an instant relief.

Elodie was still in her uniform and, after a long flight, wanted nothing more than to shower and change into something a little less restrictive. She checked her watch and saw that it had been almost twenty minutes since she had left the plane. Elodie decided to give him another ten. If he hadn't made an appearance in that time, she would make her way to the hotel on her own. She bristled with annoyance.

'Why on earth am I waiting for him?" she wondered. The grace period in which she had gifted Chase came and went; each time Elodie looked at her watch she decided to give him just a few more minutes.

"Elodie?" Chase said questioningly when he eventually appeared. "I didn't think you'd wait this long."

Elodie started to say that it was OK, to accept his apology but she stopped short of herself when she realised that none had been offered.

"I didn't want to leave, I thought you might…" she trailed off, "not know where I am."

"I would have assumed you'd left."

Elodie bristled: not only had he not apologised, he was making out as though she had been stupid for waiting. Elodie flushed, feeling like a reprimanded schoolgirl. Chase stuck out his hand and flagged down a car.

"Here we are," he said, gesturing towards the cab as it crawled to a stop beside them.

Chase leaned forward and opened the door. Elodie hung back, fully expecting him to get in first. He didn't; instead, he stepped aside and allowed Elodie to go ahead. She thanked him and climbed in, vaguely aware that his eyes followed her a little too closely as she went. The journey to the hotel was a pleasant one, the cab driver chatted amiably to start with, asking which part of England they were from and, jokingly, if they'd ever met the Queen.

"Oh yeh, all the time. I have her to tea at least once a year," Elodie had said, giving Chase a mischievous smile. It was at this point Chase did something Elodie had not expected... he laughed. It was a gentle sound, full of good humour and incredibly contagious, Elodie felt her stomach dip and she realised that, maybe, Chase wasn't that bad.

As the drive progressed they chatted affably. Chase retained his unyielding nature but began to soften a little as time went on. Elodie liked the fact that she seemed to be able to see him thaw before her very eyes and continued to chat animatedly to him about everything and anything.

"So, that's about it, really. I went from housewife, to girl about town, to career woman," she finished.

"You don't regret anything? Lots of women wouldn't have done that, you know," Chase said.

"They would have if they weren't happy, and the bottom line is that I wasn't happy. I guess if it's just one area of your life that isn't perfect you can just put up with it, but when it seems to be all areas, then you're kind of forced into action. It was hard at the time, I'm not going to lie, but looking around now it was definitely worth it."

Chase nodded his understanding. He shifted in his seat and Elodie looked down with a start: he had placed his hand right next to hers. Their fingers were barely an inch apart. Elodie felt the breath catch in her throat as she stole a glance at Chase.

He hadn't seemed to notice and was nonchalantly gazing out of the window. Elodie glanced back down, his hand had crept closer: their fingertips were almost touching now. She froze, her hand lay there motionless. She waited, wanting to see if he would move even closer, if their fingertips would brush. The idea of it sparked electricity within her and Elodie realised, like a bolt out of the blue, that she wanted it to happen. Elodie felt a desperate desire to feel his skin on hers. She shook her head and yanked her hand away, suddenly causing Chase to turn his head and look at her quizzically,

"*What on earth am I doing, he's practically your boss,'* she reprimanded herself for her slip in professionalism, *'and besides, he's too old and one hundred per cent not interested, plus you'd be trying to compete with girls like that blonde leggy one at Casa.'* Elodie gave herself a little shake and vowed not to get caught up in the whirlwind that was Chase.

CHAPTER 14

THE FOLLOWING MORNING ELODIE AWOKE BRIGHT and early. The time difference meant that she was up and out of bed before the bedside clock could show seven am. She had planned to head over to a little bakery that sold the 'world's best' half-doughnut half-croissant first, and after that she would take the subway and check out some sights. She showered, her second one since she'd checked in. The hot water beat down against her skin and Elodie took a deep, contented breath. She was still getting used to the fact that this was now her life. Once dried and dressed, she packed her small backpack with a bottle of water from the hotel mini-bar, her mobile phone, the visitors' guide given to her by the hotel check-in clerk and a small tube of factor thirty sun cream. She glanced around her hotel room and sighed: she had spent one night there and it was already a mess. Deciding that she had far more pressing matters to tend to than keeping her room orderly, she headed to the door and made to leave.

"Chase?" Elodie said, startled to find him pacing up and down right in front of her door. For a split-second, Elodie hadn't been able to place him, as he was wearing a T-shirt and shorts, which were a far cry from his usually smart attire.

"Breakfast," Chase said. He seemed to jump, as if he weren't expecting her to appear from her own hotel bedroom door. Elodie said nothing. Was this meant to be a question? Did he want to know where to go?

'He shouldn't have turned his nose up at the guide,' Elodie thought to herself, remembering how he'd waved it away when the desk clerk had offered him one during check-in.

"Do you want to get breakfast with me?" Chase said slowly, this time the question clear.

"Oh right," Elodie replied as she shifted her weight from one foot to the other. She hadn't banked on having company. She wasn't exactly against the idea in theory, it was just that she had been looking forward to exploring the city and had a very set idea as to what that would entail. "I was just heading out, actually, sightseeing."

"Well, you'll need sustenance for that," Chase said, any trace of awkwardness vanishing from his voice entirely. "I know a great place, my treat."

Elodie didn't know what to say. It was kind of Chase to look out for her. He knew it was her first job and her first time in New York, but what he didn't know was that she had been looking forward to exploring it by herself. Still, Elodie found herself agreeing to breakfast; she reasoned that she still had two more mornings in which to get her croissant-cum-doughnut.

Chase led Elodie through the streets of New York; they were dense with commuters and even at such an early hour were alive with energy. Elodie marvelled as they passed yellow taxicabs, street food vendors, newspaper stalls and department stores she'd only ever seen in films. She glimpsed Chase out of the corner of her eye who was smiling a curious sort of smile at her.

"What?" she asked defensively, suddenly feeling self-conscious.

"You look like a kid at Christmas," Chase said, his tone strangely flat despite the jovial look on his face. Elodie couldn't decide if he were remonstrating or teasing her. Either way, she felt her cheeks begin to colour and hoped that he would put it down to the already warm weather rather than embarrassment.

"I've just never been anywhere like this before," she vacillated lamely. She was beginning to regret changing her plans to accommodate him.

"I didn't mean anything negative by it, it's nice," Chase said, not seeming to notice the change in atmosphere at all. "Right then, here we are," he said proudly as he came to a standstill outside of a place that looked very much to Elodie like somewhere you would go for a fancy meal on payday and not somewhere you would just nip for breakfast whilst out sightseeing.

She glanced at the menu hung on the wall outside and practically reeled when she saw the prices. *'Thank God Chase is paying,'* she thought. Elodie scolded herself internally: *'I'm on a really decent wage now, I should pay my own way.'* Chase held the door open for her and she walked in, feeling once again as though all eyes were on her. The restaurant Chase had chosen, The Rodney, was impeccably decorated and emanating from the kitchen were the most deliciously inviting smells Elodie had ever experienced. They were seated on a small two-person table in the far corner and waited on by a smartly dressed man whose name tag told Elodie that he was called Paul. Elodie scanned the menu looking for a single word that she recognised. *'Where's just plain old scrambled eggs on toast?'* she thought to herself as her eyes scanned dishes such as 'Dauphinoise with Hashed Serrano' and 'Ballotine of dejeuner meats'. She looked to Chase who was completely engrossed in his menu; he didn't seem to be having any issue with it at all and when Paul reappeared with their drinks Chase ordered his food, Elodie took a breath to order hers but was interrupted.

"And she'll have the same," Chase said, taking Elodie aback. "So what do you think?" He asked her after a moment of silence. Elodie looked at him, trying to figure out exactly what this was. He seemed so relaxed, so nonchalant, so confident. She still wasn't sure of him, of what he was about. "Earth to Elodie…" he said, waving a broad hand in front of her face. "Come in, Elodie? Everything alright?"

"Yes, sorry, everything's fine. I'm just curious, I guess…" Elodie trailed off. Was she going to come across as immature if she said what she was about to? Chase raised an eyebrow and, seeing his eyes narrow slightly, changed her line of questioning. "Curious about what the food will be like." An air of relief seemed to wash over Chase, and Elodie thanked her quick thinking.

'As if I was about to ask him what this was, it's obviously him being nice. Lucky escape, you idiot, just be cool… think like Carla!' Elodie smiled to herself, the thought of Carla

provoked such a strong, warm feeling that she just couldn't help it. She made a mental note to give her a ring later; they were due a catch-up and, besides, she wanted to see what her friends thought about the whole Chase thing, if it even was a thing.

Once Paul had brought out their meals the conversation quickly turned to Alpha Whiskey and work. Elodie wanted to know everything: she asked question after question, which Chase answered without hesitation. If Elodie was annoying him, he didn't let it show. In return, he probed further into her life. He stepped carefully at first, only asking neutral questions that wouldn't cause offence, but familiarity brings about a certain sense of confidence and as Chase became more comfortable with Elodie and Elodie with Chase, the topics of conversation transformed from the pleasant and polite to something a little more personal. Chase offered a few of his own stories and it transpired that he too had been through a breakup. His fiancée had run off with her boss and left Chase to pick up the pieces.

"She's totally ruined me. Relationships just don't interest me now. They're just not worth it, you know?"

Elodie nodded in a way that she hoped conveyed sympathy. It was obvious that he found it hard to trust in people and didn't give his time to just anyone. Elodie felt a little bubble of pride float within: he must think she was worth his time.

Once their plates were clean and the bill paid, they took their leave.

"So what are your plans for the rest of the day?" Chase asked as they walked out of The Rodney and into the street.

"Just tourist stuff," she answered, half-hoping that he would have more things planned for them. "What about you?"

"I'm meeting a friend this afternoon. Going to head back to the hotel now to freshen up. You can tag along if you want?" he said.

Elodie would have liked to have spent more time with Chase. Breakfast had piqued her attention; she enjoyed his company and the more she got to know him the more attractive he was to her. She politely declined his offer, not wanting to appear too keen; and besides, tagging along was never a good look. They shared a look and Chase bent down and administered a soft kiss on her cheek. He pulled away and brushed a stray piece of hair from her face; Elodie felt the back of his strong fingers brush against her skin and a spark of desire ignited deep inside her.

"This has been really, really nice, Elodie,' he said, smiling. "We should do it again sometime."

"I'd like that," Elodie said, rather meekly. She suddenly felt self-conscious again. Why was it he was able to make her feel like this at the drop of a hat?

Chase gave her a warm smile, a wave and turned on his heel to leave. Elodie watched him go and wondered if he too felt her eyes on him just as she had felt his on her.

After a morning of sightseeing, Elodie made her way to Carnegie Deli and picked up one of their hefty Reuben sandwiches before heading over to Central Park. She had planned a one-woman picnic for lunch and was determined to stick to her schedule as much as possible. She couldn't quite believe she was strolling through New York City: it just all seemed so incredible and so far away from her old life that she had to pinch her arm to convince herself she wasn't dreaming. The weather was positively glorious; the sun beat down on Elodie's skin and felt heavenly as she settled herself in a secluded spot within the park. She sat there, legs crossed, and ate her sandwich. It was absolutely delicious and most certainly enough for two people. She wished that Chase hadn't left her. Despite her initial reservations, she had had a great time with him and by the time he had gone she had completely warmed to the idea of spending more time with him. She pulled out her phone, plugged in her headphones and tapped play. Maybe it was the jet lag, or perhaps it was the fact that if she closed her eyes she could still smell Chase... Either way, she found herself drifting into a sun-soaked sleep; her last thought before she drifted off was just how perfect the day had been.

"Ow!" Elodie exclaimed. "What the fu…"

"Sorry!" A young-looking American guy came running over to her; Elodie found him strangely familiar. The frisbee he and his friends had been throwing had gone somewhat awry and had struck Elodie clean in the face. Since she had had her eyes closed this had come as a complete and utter shock. The guy, whom Elodie placed at around twenty-one, was apologetic, to say the least. Elodie shrugged it off, despite the hot feeling she felt beginning to kiss her brow. She just knew that she would have one pretty hefty bruise to deal with later.

"It's alright," Elodie said, wishing the ground would swallow her up. Trust her to be the only person in this massive park to get hit in the face with a frisbee.

"Ahhh, you're British, you live here?" the guy said, smiling. Elodie nodded; he hadn't been the first to clock her accent. It was almost as if an accent here was a golden pass to conversation.

"I am indeed, but I don't live here though. I'm staying in The Washington Hotel. Just for a few days," she answered, rubbing her forehead with the back of her hand. She looked the guy up and down. He was young, good-looking and had the kind of casual air about him that made her feel instantly at ease.

"I'm Trent," he said, sticking out his hand in a rather business-like fashion. Elodie shook it, knowing full well that he had only done this because he was under the impression that this was the adult thing to do.

"Elodie," she replied coquettishly, taking his hand and wringing it once.

"Pretty," Trent said confidently. His blue eyes glinted in the sunlight. "The name and you."

Elodie's mouth fell open. People didn't talk like this in real life, did they?

"Ha, thanks," she replied, completely caught off-guard. *'Maybe it's different over here,'* she thought to herself.

Trent continued to kneel next to her, he had a relaxed manner about him, a confidence that could only come with youth. Regardless of this, it was a confidence that was definitely attractive. Trent seemed to understand that the appropriate amount of time to invade a stranger's space had come to an end and stood up to leave, picking up the frisbee and spinning it in his hands as he went.

"Sorry again," he said genuinely before setting off to

rejoin his friends. Before he had made too much headway, he turned around and added, "You don't feel like coming for a drink tonight, do you?"

Elodie found herself caught off-guard for the second time in as many minutes.

"I err..." she stammered.

"... Have a boyfriend?" he surmised, nodding his head. "I figured as much."

"No, no, nothing like that. It's just that we only just met and we kind of started out with assault, and I don't know you, so..." Elodie shifted her weight and chewed the edge of her thumbnail. Who was this guy? Was he some kind of hybrid, super-confident breed of male that you could only find in America?

"It's alright, thought it was a long shot," Trent said. He gave her a carefree, cheeky smile and turned once more to leave.

"I'd love to," Elodie blurted out, not knowing where the words had come from.

Trent turned back around and was grinning, as if he had expected this from her the entire time. Digging in his pocket, he pulled out his phone and took her details.

"I'll pick you up at eight tonight," he said.

Elodie had to admit, Trent's confidence had piqued her interest but she couldn't shake the idea that perhaps she was being a little irresponsible. The feeling of uncertainty seemed strangely liberating. Elodie had always done everything by the book; maybe it was time to start living on the edge a little. She had literally never done something like this before, so perhaps it was only natural to be apprehensive. She had well and truly rounded the corner from Tom and she felt extremely happy about it. Aaron had been a welcome distraction; Chase an unobtainable fleeting fancy, and this guy, a proper date. The best thing about it was that it was basically practice for the real thing; no one need ever know about her evening with a younger man. Nothing serious could happen between her and an overgrown teenager who lived on the other side of the world.

Elodie picked up the phone on her hotel bedside table and

answered it; the voice down the line told her that there was a gentleman waiting in reception for her. Elodie thanked the receptionist and in a voice as smooth as butter said that she would be down momentarily, before hanging up. *'Thank God that was a phone call and not Facetime,'* she thought as she pulled the towel from the top of her head, letting her damp hair hang messily around her face. Elodie had fallen asleep once she had arrived back to the hotel and hadn't woken up until thirty minutes before she had arranged for Trent to pick her up. The bruise she had feared had never actually materialised; she was, however, sporting a nice red mark, although it was nothing that a bit of concealer and a touch of bronzer wouldn't fix. She readied herself as quickly as she could. The dress she had chosen to wear was a little black number that she had borrowed from Carla; it was low cut and backless. She pulled it on and hoped that it was under-stated and sexy and not over the top and slutty. She really could have done with Carla's expert style advice. First date outfits were not something she had lots of experience with. For some Dutch courage, Elodie knocked back one of the miniatures from the hotel's mini-bar and, with one last look in the mirror, said goodbye to her room for the evening.

Elodie rounded the corner and tumbled into the reception area almost twenty minutes late, which wasn't bad going when you considered the state of undress a little while before.

"Thought you'd changed your mind," Trent said jokingly.

Elodie shook her head and made a vague excuse about jetlag. He was dressed smartly in a button-down shirt and tan trousers. He looked somehow younger now; maybe it was that he no longer wore sports gear and that his adult clothes only served to highlight his youthful features. "You look positively splendid, ma'am," Trent said in a bad British accent and gave her an overly dramatic bow.

Elodie managed a smile but not a laugh. It had suddenly struck her that he reminded her of Aaron, only in reverse. She couldn't believe she hadn't seen it until now. She had thought he was familiar but what with being so far away from home and him so far out of context she hadn't been able to place the resemblance. This realisation made her take a step back, as though it had been some kind of force able to affect her balance.

"Woah! Are we all right here? Have you been at the mini-bar already?" Trent said, laughing. Elodie couldn't see the funny side. She suddenly didn't feel like going out and couldn't for the life of her work out why she'd agreed to it.

"I'm fine. It's just like I said, I'm a little jetlagged," Elodie explained.

Trent took her hand and, looking her square in the eyes, told her that what she needed was one good meal and a few good drinks. Elodie nodded and thought that maybe this evening wouldn't be a waste after all.

They were just leaving the hotel when Elodie heard a voice she had been hoping to avoid. Chase was on the phone, strolling through the reception area. Elodie looked around for a place to conceal herself but found none.

"I'll call you back," Elodie heard him say as his footsteps grew closer. "What's this, then?" he asked nonchalantly, a casual tone in his manner. Elodie opened her mouth to answer but only managed to say his name before Trent cut her off.

"Name's Trent, and you are?" he asked smiling broadly, raising one eyebrow in a quizzical fashion and holding out his hand in the same business-like manner Elodie had witnessed earlier.

"Pleasure," Chase answered, coolly ignoring the question completely. He glanced down at Trent's outstretched palm and after a long pause shook it briefly. Elodie didn't know where to look, unlike Chase who seemed unable to take his eyes off her.

"We're just..." she began.

"On a date," Chase surmised. "I can see that." He moved his gaze now and Elodie felt the blood drain from her face as he inspected Trent. She felt like a schoolkid caught doing something she shouldn't behind the bike sheds.

"Is there a problem?" Trent asked, ignoring Chase entirely and turning to Elodie. His lips remained upturned but the smile had gone from his eyes. Elodie shook her head; she stole a glance at Chase who was looking almost puzzled, as though he couldn't quite believe what was in front of him.

"Not at all," Chase said, once again leaving a little too much time between question and answer. "Have fun… kids."

It was Elodie's turn to wince now; she gave Chase an awkward smile and followed Trent out of the door, feeling completely mortified by what had just occurred.

"Jeez, what was that guy's deal?" Trent asked, snorting with disgust as they climbed inside the cab. "What an absolute douchebag." Elodie didn't respond, she had only half-heard him. Her thoughts had been left behind, back in the reception area, back with Chase.

Trent took Elodie to a bar across town. He had ordered a cab from the hotel reception and when it arrived he'd opened the door for her, like a proper gent. They soon forgot the awkward start their date had gotten off to and within minutes were chatting amiably. Elodie was fascinated by Trent; she had never hung out with someone from America before and found all of his little nuances completely charming. She still couldn't shake the occasional feeling that he was a little too much like Aaron, though. Trent wouldn't let her pay for a drink all night and insisted on going to the bar himself for every single round.

"Want to try some of my whisky and ginger?" he asked once he had re-seated himself opposite her. He held the glass out to her and swirled its contents invitingly. Elodie wrinkled her nose and shook her head vehemently.

"No thanks," she answered, pushing the glass way. "I hate the stuff."

This was only partly accurate. It was true that she didn't care for whisky, but the real, more predominant reason was that she was already pretty inebriated without the addition of hard liquor. Elodie put it down to the change in time zone and the fact that she was still pretty tired because normally a few drinks would have had her tipsy but nowhere near this drunk.

"Suit yourself," he said, taking a deep drink. "So, go on then, the guy at the hotel. Ex-boyfriend, right, or should I say 'man-friend'? That guy was old!"

Elodie began to explain but Trent waved her words away. "I'm kidding, I'm not worried about a relic like that. Want another?"

Trent got up to head to the bar but Elodie shook her head. She had had enough already and, if she were honest with herself she wasn't exactly having the best time. Trent was nice enough but he was basically a child. He had been asked for his ID when they had first arrived at the bar and had made such a fuss that Elodie had felt embarrassed to be seen with him. This, coupled with the fact that he really didn't understand the idea of pacing yourself, made Elodie feel a little on edge. What Elodie had thought to be confidence earlier on was actually just arrogance in disguise. She suddenly realised that she was in an alien city, with someone she hardly knew and she was pretty drunk. She glanced up at the bar and saw the bartender pouring Trent a straight Ginger ale, not a drop of whisky in sight; she then saw Trent point to the gin and hold up two fingers. Elodie watched as the barman poured two healthy measures of gin into a glass before topping it up with tonic.

'*That's not right, I said I didn't want one,*' Elodie thought to herself. She stole another glance at the bar. Trent was handing his card over to pay. She grabbed his glass from across the table and downed the dregs. It was watered down from the leftover ice but there was no mistaking it. Trent had been drinking nothing but ginger ale all night.

'*No wonder he can hold his drinks,*' Elodie thought angrily. She didn't want to jump to conclusions but the evidence was right there in front of her. Her head was swimming now, why was he plying her with so much alcohol and not drinking himself? Maybe he had a health problem and didn't want to confide in her, or perhaps he was a real lightweight and wanted to save face? Elodie wasn't sure what the reason was; all she knew was that she didn't feel comfortable anymore, and what was it Carla used to say? "*If it doesn't feel one hundred per cent right, then it's one hundred per cent wrong.*" Granted, Carla had been speaking about things being right emotionally, but Elodie figured that the sentiment extended itself to the safety aspect of dating too. Trent was now making his way back to their table and Elodie felt a sudden wave of panic settle over her. She had no idea what to do. What if he turned out to be a serial killer? Elodie smiled a wry smile to herself: she had gone from feeling absolute panic to absolutely stupid in one flat minute. This wasn't a soap opera, this was more than likely just a young guy trying to impress a girl he'd only just met.

"I know you said you didn't want one and you don't have to drink it but I thought I'd get you one just in case."

Elodie thanked him and took a sip.

"Tastes strong," she said, wanting to give Trent the opportunity to confess. "Is it a double?"

"'Course not, darling. It's just good ol' USA measures for ya right there." Trent smiled. "Now come on, drink up."

Elodie studied him for a moment: Trent's smile never wavered. He picked up his glass, drank deeply and pulled a face.

"Ugh, shouldn't have ordered myself a double, though, now that's a strong drink." Suddenly his eyes seemed to take on a whole other nature. Elodie could have sworn they were electric blue in colour before, but now they seemed cold and grey.

"Excuse me for a moment, would you? Ladies' room," Elodie said, getting up from her chair, the room swayed slightly and she gripped the table for balance. Trent glanced down at her delicate fingers. Her knuckles began to turn pale as her grip tightened, which for some reason caused Trent to smile. She let go and began to walk off, careful to place one foot firmly in front of the other to avoid stumbling over. She breathed a sigh of relief as she put some distance between herself and Trent and cursed herself for being so reckless with her own safety. How many times had she and Steph remonstrated Carla for the very same behaviour? Suddenly she felt a hand on her shoulder.

"The bathroom's this way, darling," Trent whispered in her ear and with one effortless movement turned her a complete one-eighty and began walking her back across the bar to the far corner where Elodie could just about make out a sign for the ladies' bathroom.

"Of course," Elodie said, hoping her voice came off far more relaxed than she felt.

Trent walked her all the way to the bathroom and pushed the door open for her. She walked in and felt his eyes on the back of her. His gaze didn't provoke the same feelings she felt when Chase looked at her: this didn't feel nice at all. She felt the hairs on the back of her neck stand to attention and heard the door close behind her. Elodie let out a small, shallow breath and in that moment knew that she needed to get back to the hotel. Uneasiness settled over her: she didn't want to annoy him, and couldn't for the life of her see how she was going to give him the slip.

Elodie steadied her breath: was she being ridiculous? She thought about what she would say to Carla or Steph if there were in her shoes and she knew in that instant that ridiculous or not, it was far better to err on the side of caution. She would simply tell Trent she'd had a few too many and leave. He couldn't stop her, and to top it off they were in a bar in one of the busiest cities in the world: there were plenty of people about if she needed help.

Elodie emerged from the bathroom and was pleased to see that Trent was no longer outside the door. She let out a low sigh of relief. He was back at their table and furiously tapping the screen of his phone. Pushing her shoulders back and taking a deep, calming breath she ventured forward, hoping that this was all in her head and Trent wouldn't make a scene.

"Hey Trent, I'm not feeling great," she started. Trent looked up from his phone, a large smile on his thin face.

"How about we head back to mine then? Got the place to myself. We can chill there until you're feeling better?" Trent said without a hint of suggestion in his voice. Elodie was quite sure that this wasn't a question, it was a command.

"I don't think so, maybe another time." She glanced at the door, and in that moment Trent had risen from his seat and was by her side. Once again his hand was placed on her shoulder: this no longer felt protective and comforting and now seemed predatory and creepy.

"You can't go yet," he said, squeezing her shoulder slightly. Elodie resisted and tried to escape his grasp. The smile on his face faltered and Elodie saw a look she really didn't like replace it: he was no longer good-looking, and instead of the warmth he had shown earlier a cold, menacing expression now seemed to dance behind his eyes. Elodie drew herself up to her full height and didn't argue or protest.

"I said, no thank you. The gentlemanly thing to do would be to accept that."

Confrontation was not Elodie's forte and she wasn't surprised when her voice wavered and cheeks began to flush. She didn't give him a chance to answer back and before she knew it was tumbling out into the street, which was considerably quieter than she would have liked. Trent followed her. She expected this; he was proving to be a tenacious little bastard.

"I'd really appreciate it if you'd just leave me alone," Elodie said, spinning on her heel and turning to face him. Her previous uncertainty had begun to give way to anger, he was practically harassing her now and she didn't care for it one bit.

"And I'd really appreciate a little co-operation. I thought we were having a nice time?" His tone softened. "Look, I'm sorry. Just come back inside, let's start over?" He gave her a look akin to a puppy that had just been kicked and for a moment Elodie felt pity. Maybe she had got it all wrong and was over-reacting. She hadn't even given him a chance to explain himself. "Come on Elodie, let's finish our drinks at least, you owe me that much."

"I owe you?" Elodie asked. "I don't owe you anything. You bought the drinks, you didn't buy me," she said, channelling Carla now. "I saw you get me a double and I know you're not drinking whisky. Why would you do that?"

"Well, excuse me for trying to get you to loosen up a little," Trent said indignantly. "You British chicks are so frigging uptight. I knew you'd be a challenge, but this is just ridiculous. Come on..."

He reached out for Elodie who managed to step back just in time. She absolutely wasn't going anywhere with him. He fixed her with a look of pure disdain, his lip curled in a silent snarl. Taking another step backwards Elodie wheeled round, she had bumped into someone and was awash with relief. The presence of another person seemed to shrink Trent, especially when Elodie realised just who that person was.

"Are you alright?" Chase said, his voice thin. Elodie met his gaze and saw a stony resolution there, which somehow instantly made her feel safe. She nodded, finding herself unable to speak, the words seemingly stolen from her.

"You're welcome to her, I'm out." Trent stalked off, offering them a cursory look before he rounded the corner.

Elodie hadn't realised that up until that point she had been holding her breath, she gasped as she watched him disappear out of sight and for some inexplicable reason found that she was fighting back tears. Chase placed his hand on her shoulder: the gesture, although practically identical, was worlds away from how she had felt when Trent had done the same.

"Are you OK?" Chase asked concernedly. "I knew I shouldn't have let you go with him. He was too, too arrogant."

"I'm fine," Elodie replied after some time, feeling silly now. "How did you know?"

"I asked the front desk where you had ordered a taxi to, said I was meeting you there and had lost the name of the bar."

"I meant how did you know that, well that I needed...?" she trailed off. The how didn't matter.

"I know men like him. He certainly wasn't good enough for you."

She stared at him, taken aback and wondering if she had just heard him right.

Elodie had no idea that it was possible for something to happen so quickly, yet in slow motion. Chase took one step forward and held both of Elodie's hands in his before pulling her towards him. She allowed herself to dissolve into him as everything around her seemed to fade, she was vaguely aware of his hands, now on the small of her back pulling her in closer, She moved her hands upwards and she felt his muscular form beneath his shirt. Her stomach flipped. Chase bent lower, their faces now barely an inch apart. Elodie closed her eyes, his masculine scent invaded her senses and she found herself overcome by the irresistible desire to be taken. Finally, his lips were on hers and they shared a kiss, which Elodie would later find herself describing as otherworldly. Chase's warmth enveloped her and it was in that moment in which she felt herself falling for him. He had been her knight in shining armour: Elodie could now see that every little thing that had happened between them had been building up to this very instant, and she realised that, try as she might to fight it, she was powerless to resist. Elodie parted her lips a little, allowing him to kiss her more deeply. He accepted her invitation with pleasure and his tongue probed hers, tentatively at first but intensifying with every beat of her heart. When they broke apart Elodie was almost breathless. The kiss had come from nowhere and had taken her by complete surprise, she opened her mouth to speak and then closed it again: it would seem that Chase had temporarily stolen her words, as well as her heart.

They had caught a cab back to the hotel and with purpose journeyed straight up to Chase's suite. He had offered her a drink, which she refused, thinking that she had had quite enough for one evening already. Chase didn't press her and instead poured himself a drink before they settled themselves in the living area of his chambers. Elodie kicked off her heels and placed them on the floor next to a black leather case with silver detailing and Chase's initials embossed on the top. *'Fancy luggage,'* she thought to herself as she rubbed the sole of one foot with one hand.

"Let me," Chase said, undoing the top button of his shirt and kneeling on the floor in front of her. Elodie pulled her foot away, feeling self-conscious, but Chase took it in his hands anyway and began to massage its sole. Elodie glanced down and found that his eyes were already locked onto her: he appeared to be looking into her, searching her expression for some hidden meaning. Whatever it was he was searching for, he seemed to find it. He raised her foot to his mouth and kissed it, never letting his gaze slip from hers. He leaned in closer and kissed the inside of her calf. Elodie slid forward in her seat and allowed her head to fall backwards. Lengths of her walnut-coloured hair fell down the back of the chair as her head came to rest. Chase was gliding up her leg, administering soft butterfly kisses intermittently. Elodie revelled at the feeling of his lips on her skin and basked in the attention that he lavished upon her. She was broken from her abstraction only when he paused. She looked down at him, her lips slightly parted, short soft breaths escaping from them.

"Are you sure this is what you want?" Chase asked.

Elodie nodded: at that moment in time she couldn't think of anything she wanted more. His broad hands were on her in seconds: they scooped her up as though she were no more than a wisp of cloud. The drink she had only sipped half of fell to the floor; the glass landed onto the plush carpet with a dull thud that Elodie was only marginally aware of. He carried her to the bed and set her down. Elodie's heart was beating so strongly she was sure he'd be able to hear it. Her breath caught in her throat as she sat up to meet him. He reached forward, and taking the waistline of her dress pulled it up and over her head in one swift movement. He pulled back, drinking in the sight of her. A look of pure, unrestrained desire filled his eyes.

"You're beautiful," he murmured as he climbed onto the bed.

He knelt before her and unbuttoned his shirt fully. Elodie reached out for him and slid the cool cotton material down past his shoulders. She allowed her fingers to trace his bare skin and felt a shiver of anticipation wash over her. Chase wore his masculinity like a badge of honour. He was svelte with a body befitting an athlete; his smooth, tanned skin felt utterly delicious beneath her fingertips. Chase undid his belt and freed himself. Elodie gasped. Beneath the white cotton of his briefs, she could make out a generous bulge. She felt a deep longing for him and reached out, he gently pushed her back down, and after hooking a finger on each side of her underwear pulled them down. She raised her hips from the bed and, finding herself completely naked, allowed him to part her thighs with his strong hands. He nestled between her legs and inhaled, the smell of her seemed to spur him on and before she knew it he was running his warm, wet tongue over the essence of her femininity. She gasped as he moved in delectable circles, each time homing in on her most sensitive spot. A moan escaped her lips as Chase took one finger and ran it over her delicate folds. He was teasing her, bringing her to the peak of pleasure and then withdrawing before she could fully let herself go. She lifted her hips to him, begging with her body for more, but each time he pushed her back down. He was going to do this on his terms, and this prospect filled Elodie with excitement. She settled back down and gave herself to him: she was at his mercy and knew that there was nothing to be done that could change this. Elodie cried out huskily as he repeatedly brought her to the edge of absolute gratification, she ached for her release and at the point where she thought that she could take no more was rewarded. Chase slipped two fingers inside her; his digits entered her easily and, with expert precision, located her internal sweet spot effortlessly. Elodie was powerless to resist: a hedonistic swell burned within as she felt herself convulse under his attentions. In that moment nothing else mattered. Elodie clutched at the bedsheets, the cool material a stark contrast to the all-consuming sensation she felt building between her legs. As she reached the apex of unbridled pleasure, Elodie reached for Chase: her fingers brushed his skin and immediately gripped him as tightly as she could, anchoring herself to him in an effort not to be swept away in the sea of satisfaction that she now found herself in. Her climax hit her hard and Elodie felt a release akin to nothing she had felt before.

She lay there, her breath laboured, her skin glistening and her body quaking. Chase came up to join her; her essence still visible on his flushed lips, which were parted in a small, but very satisfied smile. Chase was eager for his own release now. He removed his underwear and Elodie couldn't help but stare greedily at his impressive manhood. Chase pinned her hands above her head and Elodie heard the rustle of a packet of protection.

"Tell me you want me," he instructed huskily.

Elodie obliged and without another word he guided himself into her. She felt the head of his swollen shaft part the entrance to her sex and felt so alive she wondered just how much more she could take. He slid into her slowly; she was wet and inviting and Chase wanted to make the most of every single moment. Elodie could feel him mustering every modicum of control that he had, and that made her feel incredibly sexy. He moved inside her with ease, pausing every now and then to watch her as she lay beneath him, enraptured by the journey of desire she was on. Chase was the master of pleasure suspension; he wanted to make her wait. It was as though her desperation turned him on more than anything else. Elodie knew that the longer she was made to wait the more powerful her climax would be. She was right; the orgasm hit her like a freight train and shook her to her very core. She moaned throatily, crying out in adulation and shaking from tip to toe. This sight was too much for Chase and he joined her, his body tensed and she felt him spasm inside her.

Elodie lost count of the number of times she climaxed that night. They lay awake for hours, trading lazy conversation for indulgent lovemaking, peppered with sensual moments that made Elodie quiver. She had never felt sexier, more wanted, or more fulfilled in her entire life.

CHAPTER 15

THE TIME ELODIE SPENT IN NEW YORK POSITIVELY flew by and the long weekend slipped by in the blink of an eye. Elodie's tightly packed schedule had fallen into disarray since she had fallen for Chase. He had told her that they needed to keep this between them and that if anyone at work found out it would be curtains for both of them. Elodie understood the rules when it came to inter-staff dating; still, she couldn't help but confide in Carla and Steph upon her return. Both of them were completely shocked but for very different reasons.

"But he's basically your boss," Steph said in a tone of disbelief. Elodie had explained that Chase wasn't her boss; sure, he was her senior, but boss was a bit far-fetched. Carla, on the other hand, was ecstatic with her news and had said that it was high time she got over Tom by getting under someone else.

"So, have you spoken to him since?" Carla asked excitedly as she positioned herself on the sofa next to Elodie. Elodie shook her head.

"He's got an absolutely packed schedule and I don't want to look too keen, especially since..." She trailed off as her cheeks began to colour.

"Go on," Steph probed.

Elodie looked at her friends and stammered something that neither could decipher. Steph fixed Elodie with a stare that Elodie knew meant that she wouldn't rest until she heard the truth from her.

"You're going to think I'm mad, or desperate, or maybe both. But," she took a deep breath, "I, well I think I'm falling for him."

"Pffft," Carla made a dismissive noise and waved Elodie's words away. "You are not. You barely know him and, besides, it was only ten minutes ago you were all gaga over Aaron. What you're feeling, my dear, is pure, unadulterated lust."

Elodie sighed and sat down, feeling a little wounded at Carla's words. It wasn't just lust; Carla hadn't felt the connection between them, the inexplicable way he knew her and knew her body. It was like nothing she'd felt before, more powerful and more consuming than anything she'd had with Tom. He was a dominating force and she was happy to be dominated.

'No,' thought Elodie to herself. 'Carla doesn't know what she's talking about because she's never felt what I have.'

"Well, it sure feels like it," Elodie said in defence, irritated beyond belief that she had to justify her feelings to her best friend, "but I'm not going to say anything because, like I said, he's too busy for a girlfriend. His schedule's absolutely packed and after what happened with his ex, is it any wonder he's cautious?"

"You've got to take what you want in this life, El," Carla said, switching tack. "Look, if you want him, tell him. Honestly, he'd be mad to turn you down and he must like you too otherwise, he wouldn't have, you know…" She made a circle with her finger and thumb on one hand and pushed her outstretched finger from the other hand through it several times.

"That's enough," Steph said, looking around as if they were in a public place and may have offended someone.

Carla rolled her eyes but said nothing as she let her hands fall back down.

"So with Aaron well and truly out of the picture, when are you going to ask Chase out properly?" Carla asked.

Elodie hadn't thought of this. She'd never asked someone out before and wasn't entirely sure she wouldn't make an absolute fool of herself.

"I'll just wait for him. I've told you, he's busy and I'll just look like a stalker or something."

"Don't be daft, you'll look fabulous because you are fabulous and if you want to see him again then you better make it known, but not in an obvious way. You need to be yourself, but not completely; you still need some mystery. But don't come on too keen: you should just flirt, but only a little; not too much, but just enough. Oh and you need to leave his messages a bit before you answer them and never ever text him first, to play the game, you know?" Carla advised sagely.

Elodie's head spun. That was way too much information to take in all in one go.

"Well, I've got to say that's the worst dating advice ever. Don't listen to 'Miss One Night Wonder' over here. Just be honest with him. Acting cool, playing games, making him wait... all code for immaturity. Game-playing isn't attractive and just comes across as juvenile, and you don't want that, especially as you're already worried about the age gap between you." Steph added, "But, and I've got to say this, I think it was wrong of you to have ignored Aaron without finding out some cold hard facts first. He was very nice to you and you should have at least given him a chance."

Elodie happened to agree with Steph on the latter point, Aaron *had* seemed pretty perfect. He was relaxed, funny and had made such an effort on their date. But he had gone cold, been photographed with another woman and had barely tried to contact her since. If this showed anything, it was that *he* was the game player, not her. Elodie decided to sleep on it for a night or two.

'Who knows?' she thought to herself. *'Chase might come to me first.'*

Two days passed. Elodie had an extremely brief but busy couple of shifts where she flew to Copenhagen and back in one day. Chase hadn't piloted either flight; instead, it had been Amelia and a co-pilot Elodie hadn't worked with before. Grace had been marginally less unpleasant towards her, which had been nice, and Gareth had been his usual flamboyant self, which certainly helped to pass the time.

Upon landing, Elodie went through the usual checks and as she walked through the terminal, her heels clicking against the marble floor, she pulled out her phone to message her driver Mr Bosford to let him know that she had arrived. Out of nowhere, she had collided with a fellow traveller; the phone flew from her hand and clattered to the floor.

"Woah, you wanna watch where you're going," a familiar voice said.

Elodie looked up and saw Aaron's face smiling down at her, "You alright? Didn't hurt you, did I?" Elodie shook her head and felt her stomach lurch. She had successfully put off seeing Aaron for weeks and hadn't expected to quite literally bump into him. "I haven't heard from you much, well at all really," Aaron added, his smile faltering a little.

"I've been really busy," Elodie mumbled.

Aaron bent down to retrieve her phone and as he handed it back to her. As he did so the screen lit up, displaying a message from Chase. Elodie's eyes flew to Aaron's; she wasn't exactly sure why she wanted this message to go unnoticed, she just did. Her heart sank as she saw Aaron's eyes flit from the phone's screen to the floor. A crestfallen look darted across his face. It was never nice to make someone feel sad; however, Elodie couldn't feel too bad about it as Aaron was the one with an 'other half' and she was the one who was single and free to get messages from whomever she liked. She snatched the phone from Aaron, mumbled a thank you and slinked past him, feeling very much as though this interchange had already gone on too long.

"Hey, hold up," Aaron called after her. Elodie paused and turned on her heel to face him. The concourse was busy and several people had stopped to look when Aaron had called out to her. "Are you doing anything later?" he asked. "Maybe we could have that second date?

"I can't," Elodie replied, making her way past him again and averting her eyes to avoid his.

"If you don't like me enough Elodie, just say. It's kind of embarrassing for you to ignore my messages and then pie me off in person too, just be honest with me. I'm a big boy, I promise I can take it." He gave her a heartfelt look that almost had Elodie finding herself feeling sorry for him – almost.

"Are you kidding?" she asked hotly. To keep a relationship a secret was one thing but to outright deny it was another. "I know about Grace, I'm not angry, I'm just… done."

"Grace?" Aaron repeated, puzzled. "What about her?" Elodie raised one eyebrow in reply. "I don't get how you know?' Aaron said eventually. "Did she tell you?"

"I saw a picture on your Instagram. I've seen you two together and, besides, it's common knowledge."

"It's common knowledge? What is?" Aaron asked, his puzzled look giving way to one of indignation and finally one of realisation. "Elodie, look, it's not what you think. The thing with Grace is…"

"No, *you* look," she said sharply, cutting across him midsentence. "I've been embarrassed enough. I told literally everyone how nice you were, what a great date we had, how bloody wonderful the whole thing was and all the time you had a girlfriend. Who I now have to work alongside and who absolutely can't stand me. So, thanks for that."

Elodie gave him a disdainful look and stalked off, anger bubbling with each step; some men were solid gold dickheads. Aaron called after her; she could hear desperation in his voice but she carried on regardless. *'You've had a lucky escape there,'* Elodie thought as she rounded the corner and made her way to Mr Bosford who would be, as always, waiting patiently for her in the collection bay.

Her journey back to the tube station was fraught. No matter how many times she repeated the mantra that it was only one date, that it didn't matter and that she was moving on now, she couldn't help but feel hurt and agitated by Aaron in equal measure. It was more the fact that she had felt something, really felt something that evening. She had been tricked into feeling a connection and it was that which hurt her the most. She would just have to keep her eyes firmly fixed on the future from now on, and who knew what that held?

"Are you alright?" Mr Bosford asked. Elodie saw his eyes flick to hers from the rear-view mirror.

"Boy trouble," she said expressionlessly.

"Is there any other kind?" Mr Bosford asked kindly. "Want to tell me about it? We've still got another twenty minutes or so and it might help to bend my impartial ear."

Elodie was at a crossroads; she felt as though talking about it merely extended the pain and that by burying everything resignedly she would be far better off. Reluctantly, and after some encouragement, she eventually told the entire story, leaving out a few choice details. No matter how kind Mr Bosford was, he didn't need to hear about the more intricate intimacies of her love life.

"Well, for what it's worth I think you shouldn't throw the baby out with the bathwater. You don't *know* anything for certain, you didn't let the lad finish, and as for the pilot, do you not think you might be a bit young?"

Elodie bristled. She knew there was an age difference, but it was like Carla said: *"It's not about the age gap, it's about the page gap."*

"Age is just a number, we get on, and besides at least he's single," Elodie quipped.

"Alright, well if you're sure. You should be happy, you know, and at the minute you look anything but. Why not speak to a friend and get a second opinion?"

Elodie thanked him. Maybe getting an outsider's opinion wouldn't be such a bad idea. She took out her phone and texted the only person she could think of who would be totally impartial.

"I feel like I haven't seen you in ages!" Jess exclaimed, wrapping Elodie in a big bear hug. Elodie had messaged her and suggested they meet on her way home. Jess had replied almost instantly saying she'd love to and the two had met up at a cocktail bar in town not long afterwards. "So what's up? How are you getting on with work, tell me everything."

Elodie and Jess chatted non-stop for the next hour; they talked so much that they barely touched their drinks.

"So tell me, are you seeing anyone yet?" Jess asked. Whilst on the course Elodie had told Jess all about Tom and their breakup, she had told Elodie that to get over someone you needed to get under someone else, a notion that Carla had echoed as well.

"Actually, yes. I went on a date with an absolute dickhead first, but then I met someone else and, well, we've had a few dates really and I think it's going really well," Elodie replied coyly.

"Good for you, well you're doing better than me. I was seeing someone but he was too hot and cold. Kept messing me about. He was a bit weird, really. It all got super-intense and I ended up leaving my job. I just couldn't handle seeing him. Anyway, that's over now, unless he calls me, and then of course I'll go running back. I can't seem to stop myself." Jess rolled her eyes at herself and took a sip of her cocktail. "Men, eh?"

"You were seeing someone at your work?" Elodie asked. She knew exactly what it was like to be trapped in 'male jail'; it was one of the reasons she'd stayed with Tom for so long. She took a sip of her own drink and felt thankful that she'd figured out what Aaron was like before she'd become too involved and that Chase was a nice guy who, so far, had treated her well.

"Kind of, well not anymore. To be honest, I don't really want to go into it: mixing business with pleasure just doesn't work," Jess said, taking a long sip of her drink.

Elodie wanted to ask her advice on Chase, but judging by Jess's deflated demeanour at her own lacklustre love life, hearing about Elodie's new man probably wouldn't go down well. Instead, Elodie decided to try and cheer her up by telling her about her disastrous date with Aaron.

After their drink, Jess had to go. She was on a mid-morning flight the following day and as she no longer worked at the fancy airline she had been with when she first passed the course she needed to get to bed at a reasonable hour as her new work had a much tighter schedule with very quick turnarounds.

"Let's not leave it so long next time," she said as she climbed into the back of a cab and waved goodbye to her friend. Elodie watched the taxi disappear down the street before making her way towards the nearest tube station.

A week had passed and Elodie had spoken to Chase properly just once, which was fine. They had bumped into each other a couple of times, but Chase was always on his way to a flight or on a quick turnaround. Elodie didn't mind, though: she had every intention of playing it just as cool.

She had just finished a shift. She was utterly exhausted and needed to rally herself around. It was Steph's birthday meal in a few hours and, as it stood she would be falling asleep before they'd ordered their first course. She decided to grab a quick coffee from the staff room: the machine in their produced the most powerful coffee known to mankind. Elodie hated it but thought she could manage one cup if she viewed it as medicine. She pushed the door open and was dismayed to see Grace leaning against one of the tables in conversation with Chase.

"Excuse me," Elodie muttered, averting her eyes and making her way across the room. She stood there, watching the dark liquid trickle into her paper cup. Their voices were barely above a whisper now and, try as she might, Elodie couldn't make out what it was they were saying. Suddenly she felt a hand run the length of her side, she turned and saw that Chase had leant against the counter, his body precariously close to hers. Elodie snapped her head around, knowing that Grace was still in the room. She was staring down at a clipboard, her brows furrowed.

"Grace?" he said.

Grace turned round and gave him a withering look.

"Yes?" she answered coolly.

Chase proceeded to ask her if she would be able to re-stock one of the planes. This had not gone down well; she had told him that re-stocking wasn't in her job description and that she was incredibly busy at that moment. Grace had given Elodie a purposeful look as if to communicate that it was alright for some, swanning off to attend a birthday party.

"Well, can you spare Elodie for a while?" Chase asked.

"I can always spare Elodie," Grace retorted snidely before heading out the door. Elodie, baffled and a little offended, turned to Chase.

"I don't have time," Elodie said, starting to explain that she needed to leave sooner rather than later. Chase gave her a sneaky sort of look, raised one eyebrow and beckoned her to follow him.

Elodie stepped onto the plane and did a double-take. Even with the last passengers' wares still lying about, the lavishness was still utterly breath-taking and Elodie found that she was still not yet used to the sheer opulence in which she worked.

"Take a seat," Chase said, pulling the door closed behind him. He gestured to one of the plush armchairs. Elodie looked at him with uncertainty: this wasn't his personal plane and she wasn't a passenger. As if reading her thoughts he placed a strong hand on her shoulder and gently, but persuasively, coerced her into the chair.

"Chase, what's going...?" She trailed off as he took a step towards her. Elodie felt a tingle as she saw the expression on his face.

"I've missed this," he said, taking her hand in his.

Elodie suddenly realised that this had been his intention all along, to get her on her own. This sent thrills through her veins and she suddenly found herself feeling flushed. Chase stood in front of her, drinking her in; a heady look of lust graced his features. Without breaking his stare he pulled off his tie and unbuttoned his shirt, letting the cool white material brush over his smooth, olive skin and fall to the floor. Elodie's gaze followed it and when she looked up again she saw that Chase had abandoned the rest of his uniform and stood there in just his underwear.

"I..." she began, but no other words came, her breath purloined by desire.

Her eyes ran over his body appreciatively, just the sight of his smooth muscular chest and strong arms made her shiver. He reached out for her and, in one effortless movement lifted her from the chair up towards him. She wrapped her legs around his torso instinctively and let her heels slip from her feet; they fell to the floor with a dull thud, but Elodie barely noticed. Their lips met and she felt her heartbeat quicken as everything else seemed to slow. She could barely breathe as she was overcome by a wash of longing. Pulling her in closer, the tentative kiss became more urgent, as though being together was their sole purpose in life and the two became completely entwined in one another.

Reaching behind her Chase began to unzip her dress; he did this slowly as if to savour every single second. Elodie opened her legs slightly and slid back down to the floor, Chase eased her dress down the very second the tip of her toe reached the soft carpet and she stepped out of it. She stood there before him; he took a step back and looked her

264

up and down admiringly, devouring the sight before him. Elodie noticed a hungry look in his eyes and suddenly felt a little like his prey. The feeling was fleeting, as before Elodie had a chance to react, Chase was upon her. He sank to his knees and joined her in a lustful embrace, never once breaking away from one another. Chase slipped the strap of Elodie's bra down, freeing her breasts, and inhaled deeply.

"You are absolutely gorgeous, you know," he said before taking one of the pink buds in his mouth.

It stiffened under his attention. Once satisfied, he transferred his attention to the other and gently sucked on the soft, pink mound. Elodie's head fell back and a soft moan escaped her lips. He pulled away from her and traced soft butterfly kisses down her midriff. She gasped as his lips brushed her skin, the feeling as soft as silk. He trailed the kisses lower and lower until he had made his way to her most sensitive parts. Elodie's breath caught in her throat as he removed her underwear; she parted her thighs ever so slightly to allow for his eager fingers, which had found their way there without direction. Chase parted her soft folds, gently stroking her most intimate area and leaned towards her. She felt his breath on her neck and reached out for him. Running the tips of her fingers through his dark hair, Elodie let out a gasp of pleasure as Chase pushed his fingers further into her sanctum. He curved them upwards and stroked, beckoning the climax from her. Elodie felt herself ache for him, she wanted more than anything to feel him inside her and she yearned for their bodies to move as one. Seeming to sense her need Chase withdrew his fingers and, kneeling between her legs grasped her thighs firmly. He eased them apart further, his eyes transfixed on her glistening wetness. Elodie's heartbeat quickened, she could feel a pulsing in her deepest recesses, a hunger akin to no other. She lay there, on the plush carpet, bathed in soft sunlight and completely naked, with a man that up until recently she could only dream of. The idea that someone could stumble upon them at any moment only made things more exciting and she felt a jolt of anticipation as he moved in closer. The tip of his shaft began to penetrate her; he paused, and Elodie stole a furtive glance at him. Chase was looking at her intently; she looked away, but he reached out and pulled her face back towards him. As he leant into her, Elodie could smell his raw, masculine scent. It invaded her senses; it was an animalistic smell that rendered her powerless to resist.

Chase kissed her. It was not the tentative kiss of before, it was different. Overwhelmingly and commandingly he bore down on her. She responded passionately and felt his hips thrust towards her. She broke away, unable to keep herself from crying out as he drove himself inside of her. His imposing erection filled her entirely and momentarily quenched her thirst for him; however, it seemed like the more she was given, the more she wanted. Greed took over and Elodie raised her hips to allow him to enter her more deeply. He obliged and pushed in further, a guttural moan escaping his lips. The two writhed in ecstasy; each and every second that passed journeyed them closer to the peak of their pleasure. Elodie felt herself flushing: she was so close to climax but wanted to delay her gratification., knowing that the sweet release was yet to come. Elodie's efforts to resist were futile as Chase bucked inside her; his own movements were becoming wilder now and she understood that he was close too. She felt the pending waves of climax begin to break over her body as she went into spasm and lost all control. In the wake of such intense pleasure she was feeble and was barely aware of Chase reaching his summit too. She cried out as fresh jolts of ecstasy pulsed within and grabbed onto Chase's shoulders in an effort to brace herself. She felt him jerk inside her and buck hard. His hair fell over his face and a bead of sweat trickled down his torso. He cried out one last time and held himself above her. After a few moments he withdrew and lay next to her, his body warm against hers.

"That, was, incredible," he murmured as he lazily stroked up and down her arm. Elodie nodded not yet able to find her voice. "Well, we should probably make a move, think you're probably on the verge of pushing it."

Elodie sat up, her hair wild and skin clammy. Chase was right: she really should make a move. Her career would be completely over if she were caught here, a fact that up until that very moment had conveniently seemed to escape her. Suddenly the recklessness of her actions seemed monumental and Elodie wondered exactly what it was she had been thinking.

"Do you think it'd be OK if I used the bathroom?" she asked hopefully.

"If we can fuck in the living room, I think we can use the bathroom," Chase laughed, "In for a penny and all that."

Elodie giggled and, scooping up her clothes, made her way to the bathroom where after a few minutes she re-emerged looking as though nothing had ever happened – well, almost.

"You're gorgeous, you know," Chase said, echoing his earlier sentiment. He slung his tie around his neck and pulled her in for a kiss. The two broke apart just as the door to the aircraft was heaved open. The cleaning team had arrived, preparing to ready the plane for the next passengers. Elodie averted her eyes as an all-too-familiar cleaner in a yellow tabard backed onto the plane.

She wanted the ground to open up and swallow her whole: it was Aaron. *'Of all people,'* she thought to herself. Aaron turned around, wheeling in a small cleaning cart and, upon clapping eyes on them both, stopped in his tracks.

"So after you've stocked this fridge you can carry on as before..." Chase said commandingly, giving Elodie a sideways look.

Elodie looked from Chase to Aaron and back again before muttering something not quite comprehensible. Chase sidled past Aaron as if he didn't exist, leaving and Elodie and Aaron alone together. Elodie had never felt more transparent in her entire life: there was no escaping what they had been doing, but she felt that it wouldn't hurt Aaron to know that she had upgraded. She'd gone from economy to business and if that hurt his feelings a little, then who cared? It was no less than he deserved.

"Stocking the fridge, eh? Never heard it called that before," Aaron said, a little dolefully.

"I don't know what you mean," Elodie replied, smoothing down her dress and bending down to look into the drinks fridge.

"Oh come on, he hadn't even done his shirt back up properly. Be careful Elodie, I've heard about him..."

"Oh, you have, have you?" Elodie said, wheeling around to face Aaron, her eyes flashing. "Well, he *knows* what you're like and I don't need to explain myself, especially to you."

"No, but I think I need to explain *myself* to you." Aaron began, but Elodie had had enough. Aaron had had his chance and he blew it. Elodie didn't know what was worse, that or the fact that now he was trying to come between her and Chase. The sheer nerve of the guy made her blood boil.

She made to leave but he caught her by the wrist. She turned to look at him, their faces only inches apart. Elodie felt heat radiating between them. "Let me explain." Her eyes fell to his fingers, which were still wrapped around her wrist. She gazed at them for a moment; confusion swelled inside her and she looked at him. "Please," he repeated.

"I've got to go," Elodie said hotly and pulled her arm from his grasp. She moved past him and averted her eyes; she couldn't bear to be in his presence for a moment longer. Her foot had barely left the first step when a horrible dawning sensation swept over her. A shudder ran across her body as she realised that she had probably missed all of Steph's birthday meal by now. Guilt began to weigh on her as she wondered just what she was going to say to excuse her tardiness.

Elodie crept into the flat, her mind all over the place. *'How could I have been so stupid?'* she scolded herself. Carla and Steph were sat on the sofa, watching a film. Elodie did a double-take: she hadn't been expecting them to be there.

"The wanderer returns," Carla said. "Fancy enlightening us on where you've been? We've waited and waited, called and called and nothing."

"I got caught up with work," Elodie began apologetically.

"You're a terrible liar," Steph said bluntly. "How could you? I never ask for anything, ever, and you couldn't even be bothered to send me so much as a text."

Elodie rubbed her arm nervously. They knew her so well, they knew she wasn't being truthful but would they understand if she told them the truth? Elodie decided that the only thing to do was to try her luck, she'd already upset Steph enough today, she didn't need to add insult to injury.

Once Elodie had finished relaying her near-miss story to Steph and Carla they stared at her with wide eyes of disbelief. Steph could not believe Elodie had been so reckless and Carla couldn't believe Aaron had almost caught them at it.

"I'm so disappointed in you, El, I never thought you'd be the type to put a guy before your friends," Steph said sadly.

Elodie said nothing; she feared another word from her lips would push Steph over the edge. She really hadn't meant to upset her, she'd just got so caught up in things with Chase. There was a silence between them that was so palpable Elodie felt as though she could have reached out and touched it.

"I'm sorry," Elodie said truthfully, "Steph…"

Steph said nothing, her gaze fell to the floor, she looked beaten. An uncomfortable silence pressed down on them, Elodie could feel its weight on her shoulders. She looked to Carla pleadingly.

"Jesus, El, that's a near miss and a half," Carla said in an effort to break the tension. Carla exhaled loudly and rubbed her temples with the tips of her fingers. "Well, Aaron would really have seen what he was missing if he'd been a few minutes earlier."

Steph said nothing for a moment or two, but instead offered Elodie an appraising look that Elodie couldn't work out.

"Well, I think you should see this as a lesson to be learnt," Steph said eventually. "You know what happened to your predecessor and here you are making all the same mistakes. You're not a teenager, Elodie, you need to exercise some control at least. I don't mean to be harsh, but what would you have done if that had been Gareth, or worse, Grace?" Steph said, unimpressed. "And what about me? Did I just get pushed out of your mind the minute Chase put his tongue down your throat?"

Elodie stared at the floor. She had apologised already and didn't know what else she could do.

"Just imagine if you'd been caught, you'd have lost your job on the spot," Carla said knowingly.

"It wouldn't such a bad thing if Grace did know," Elodie

said slowly. "At least it would get her off my back about Aaron."

"And that's another thing, are you sure all this isn't to get back at him? You said it so many times that you didn't like Chase like that…" Steph said.

"I didn't but people can change their minds, you know?" Elodie said defensively, feeling her mood begin to spike.

"OK, ladies," Carla interrupted, raising her hands in the air loftily, as Steph took a deep breath, presumably to keep on battling. "I think that's enough. Let's put this behind us shall we, or at least try? We can safely say that we know where you're coming from, Steph. Elodie, you shouldn't have missed her birthday. But we've all been caught up in the moment before, so can we try and forget it?" Carla said in an attempt to mediate the situation.

Elodie looked from Carla, who always seemed to be on her side, to Steph who recently always seemed to be against it, maybe this time with good reason.

The three women watched the rest of the film in near-silence: fortunately, it was a comedy and a good one at that, and by the time the credits rolled the majority of the bad atmosphere had dissipated.

"Oh, I almost forgot, I was going to announce this at my meal but…" Steph said coyly.

"I knew it, you're pregnant!" Carla exclaimed.

"No, I'm not. I am however going to lay off the cake for a bit though," she said, running her hand over her stomach in a mock 'with child' sort of way. "No. As you guys know, Mum's taking early retirement in a few weeks. Well, she wants to do a sort of unofficial handing over of the baton-type thing, before everything gets too crazy with the move and stuff. So she's proposed the fourteenth of next month, if that works with you guys?"

Carla and Elodie said they weren't sure but, upon seeing Steph's face fall, quickly altered their answer.

"Yeh, of course!" they replied in unison.

"So what do you reckon, another film?" Elodie asked, glad that with the change in subject had come a change in atmosphere.

"What about this?" Carla said, scrolling to a thriller starring none other than Jenna Broderick.

"I've met her!" Elodie exclaimed proudly. She loved it when her work and private life collided, it gave her a sense of pride and fulfilment.

"Oh, really? You never mentioned it…" Carla said sarcastically, giving Elodie a grin. For the entire week succeeding that flight, it was all Elodie had been able to talk about. Elodie blushed slightly but took the jibe with the good humour that it was intended.

"Let's just watch anything, I just want to forget about today," Elodie said, unable to stop the words from coming from her mouth. "Just the bit with Chase and Aaron, not that it's your birthday, I mean."

"So what are you and Chase then? Boyfriend and girlfriend? Just friends? Or, friends with benefits? Or something else entirely?" Carla asked slyly.

"We're… I don't know. More than friends, definitely, I think anyway. He did say that he missed me, after all, and I'm not seeing anyone else, and he's not. It's complicated…"

"It isn't. I can tell you want more," Steph chimed in. "You want to know what you are."

Elodie had tried not to think about this. She wasn't a casual sort of girl when it came to relationships. In her mind, people usually knew what they wanted and if it wasn't the other person, then what was the point? Chase had said he wasn't ready for a relationship, but Elodie could tell that he liked her and that given time he'd change his mind about the whole relationship thing.

"We're definitely dating; we just don't want to rush things, that's all," Elodie said with the certainty of someone who knew this for a fact. The truth was that she and Chase hadn't yet discussed anything remotely close to 'what they were'. Elodie was fearful that sailing too close to that particular wind would result in something that she wouldn't like. No, it was far better to let things develop naturally instead of forcing things with awkward conversations. Chase was relaxed about the whole thing, so she needed to be as well.

The weekend came soon enough. Elodie had both the days

off, which came as a great relief. Carla's questions about her and Chase had been playing on her mind. She wasn't about to go proposing to him just yet, but the more she thought about it, the more she felt like maybe knowing his bottom line wouldn't be the worst thing in the world. Well, unless his bottom line was that he really didn't want to be in a relationship.

Elodie spent the day on her own, with nothing but her own thoughts, which were rapidly spiralling out of control. She kept taking her phone out of its drawer and checking it, hoping that she would hear from Chase. Each time she checked she was disappointed with the result. It was like paying top dollar to hear your favourite band play and then them not singing any of your favourite songs. She sighed, a long, low sigh that she usually reserved for cold callers, delayed tubes and people that didn't say thank you when you opened the door for them. *'Why can't he just ask me out, then everything would be so simple,'* she thought to herself as she loaded the dishwasher. Nowadays both she and Carla were busy with work and the flat had taken on an altogether more dishevelled feel. The weather was wonderful and she planned on missing as little of it as she could.

Elodie was mid-daydream when a clattering noise came from her dressing table drawer: she had a message. Moving faster than what should have been physically possible, she leapt to retrieve it. The message was not from Chase, it was from Aaron. *'Jeez, when will he get the message?'* Elodie thought, annoyance beginning to stem. Against her better judgement, she read his text. She had thought about just blocking his number but felt that maybe that was a little too dramatic and, after all, as Steph had rightly pointed out, she wasn't a teenager any more.

> Hi Elodie, it's Aaron. Can we talk, but not over text. Please give me a chance to explain? A x

Elodie let out a small derisive laugh; she really couldn't understand what this guy's deal was. Why was he so desperate to pump her full of lies just so they could be on decent terms? It just didn't make sense, did it? Aaron came across as a really genuine guy, but looks can be deceiving. Elodie tried to approach the situation from his perspective and fathomed that maybe, if she felt that she hadn't done anything wrong and someone thought badly of her, then she maybe would try and right that wrong. But that couldn't be it. Aaron had kissed her, made her feel so special and organised a really wonderful and intimate date. He'd shared his dreams with her, and she'd confided in him. No, if you boiled it all down he was a 'have your cake and eat it too' kind of guy who was only sorry because he got caught out.

As August drew to a close Elodie really felt that she'd hit her stride at Alpha Whiskey. Things with Grace were frosty still, but the scathing remarks and catty put-downs had given way to complete indifference, which in Elodie's eyes was a win. Elodie tried hard with her every day, under the supposition that, eventually, Grace would warm to her. She wished she could confess to her what was happening with Chase: perhaps then Grace would see that she wasn't a threat at all. Carla and Steph were always keen to find out the latest news when it came to Chase; sadly, though, Elodie didn't have a great deal to tell them. Work for him was extremely busy and at the moment it seemed like every flight Chase piloted went unassigned to Elodie. Because their tryst was to be kept secret she couldn't even talk to him properly when their feet were on the ground. She had messaged him asking to meet up a few times but his responses were always the same – he would love to, but he was busy. Every time Elodie thought that Chase was losing interest he would do something to quell those thoughts. A secret kiss when no one was looking, a sneaky pat of her bum as she walked by or a knowing look from across the room in plain sight of everyone. Despite all of this, Elodie was on the precipice of giving up. She wasn't used to the pursuit of romance and felt that you could only get knocked back so many times before it just didn't seem worth it.

Other than that, work was great, and luckily she had only bumped into Aaron once. She had decided to do the grown-up thing and be amiable. They had exchanged pleasant-ries for a few moments; however, Aaron quickly managed to steer the conversation into uncomfortable territory, so Elodie had made her excuses and left. She really had to take her heart in her hands with Aaron: he did a fantastic impression of a wounded puppy and played the innocent so well. Plus there was, as hard as Elodie tried to ignore it, a little bit of tension between them that had nothing to do with him having led her on. She wasn't a 'the more the merrier' type when it came to dating. She knew that she really needed to keep Aaron at arm's length, to protect both herself and her fledgeling romance with Chase. She checked her phone again, knowing full well that there wouldn't be a message but unable to help herself all the same. She had been right: there was nothing. Checking the time, Elodie decided that she needed to get out of the house, perhaps she'd give Chase a call, just to see if, on the off-chance that he was free, he'd like to do something.

"Hello?" Chase's voice said down the line. He sounded groggy, as though he had only just woken up.

"Sorry did I wake you? I thought you'd be up by now," Elodie asked, double-checking the time to make sure she hadn't got it wrong.

"I'm in LA, it's early here," came Chase's reply. "Is it important?"

Elodie suddenly felt really stupid. He had told her he was busy working and here she was pestering him, acting exactly as she had been advised not to and waking him up at God knows what time.

"I, I just wondered if you were free to meet up Sorry, I didn't realise you were away. I'll let you get back to sleep."

"You're alright," Chase said, his voice a little clearer now. "Once I'm up, I'm up. I'll get to the gym or something."

Elodie felt terrible now. Being a pilot was incredibly taxing and she had robbed him of precious sleep; she could have kicked herself.

"How long are you away for?" she asked.

"I'm not sure," Chase said distractedly. Elodie could tell he was doing something and that she didn't have his full attention.

"OK, well let me know if you want to do something when you're home," she said sheepishly, not being able to help herself. She couldn't play it cool; she wanted to see him again.

"Will do. Take care, Elodie," and with that he was gone.

Elodie pulled the phone away from her ear and looked at it. If it were possible to die from embarrassment, then she would have been struck down then and there. She cursed herself. Dating Chase was going to be really challenging and she would need to be super-chilled if she didn't want to scare him off. She took a few deep breaths and decided to head out. A walk around the park followed by a trip to Betty's Café, especially on a day like today, would be just what she needed. She decided that she would bring home with her two pieces of cake and a bottle of something sparkling for Carla; she had been enjoying a lot of success with her modelling and Elodie thought she deserved a little 'well done' gift. Carla, unlike most models, wouldn't shy away from a giant piece of her favourite Mississippi mud pie cake and she certainly wouldn't say no to washing it down with a glass or two of fizz.

Carla came through the door that evening just as Elodie had expected, only not with whom she had expected. Imagining that Carla would be arriving home solo, Elodie had bought two pieces of cake and one bottle of fizz, certainly not enough to go around for three people, especially when Chris was the third wheel: man, that boy could eat for England. Elodie remembered their meal out when he had put away enough food for two people and still had room for dessert.

"Sorry, I didn't know you were coming," Elodie said lamely, looking down at the pitiful spread she had put on.

"I'm not staying," Chris said, leaning down and giving Elodie a friendly kiss on the cheek, "just making sure this one got back home safely."

Elodie smiled, he really was a sweet guy. Chris gave Carla a hug and Elodie thought she detected a hint of awkwardness, as though he was hoping for an invitation to stay or something. Carla simply gave him a big smile and kissed him goodbye. She shut the door behind him, turned to Elodie and mouthed the words, "Oh my God" at her. They stood there in silence for a full minute before Carla descended into a fit of giggles.

"I can't take it anymore," she wailed. "He's too nice. Always walking me home, ringing to see if I got somewhere safely, leaving little notes, it's just too much."

Elodie was gobsmacked. Chris seemed like the perfect gentleman, plus he was absolutely gorgeous. She couldn't believe what she was hearing.

"But I thought you really liked him?" she said in disbelief, pouring Clara a glass of Prosecco.

"I did, I mean I do, he's sweet. He's not got a bad bone in his body and I feel terrible for even thinking this, let alone saying it but… he's just not that bright. It's like having an incredible pair of shoes that you just can't walk in. Great to look at, but not much use for anything else."

Carla clapped a hand to her head and grabbed the glass of fizz Elodie had just poured and knocked it back in one. Elodie knew Carla well enough to know that she had made up her mind about this. Carla had a very small tolerance for the ick factor. Once she felt it, that was it.

"Well you'll just have to tell him, I guess," Elodie said, thoughtfully picking up the remaining glass from the side and filling it to the brim. "Tell him it's not him, it's you."

"But it *is* him," Carla said.

"I know that, you know that, but do you really want him to know that?"

Carla grabbed the glass straight from Elodie's hands and drank deeply. She handed it back with about an inch left in the bottom.

"Thanks," Elodie said sarcastically. Carla took out her phone from her back pocket and began to scroll. "You're not texting him are you?"

"God, no. I'm going to leave a message, he'll be on the tube now so it'll be safe to call. You watch, it'll go straight to voicemail."

Elodie marvelled at Carla's practised hand. Chris wasn't the first bloke Carla had kicked to the kerb and she doubted very much that he would be the last.

Chris had left Carla's flat feeling on top of the world; he had intended on going straight home but on his way to the tube station he passed a lovely little flower shop. He popped in, just to have a look and ended up buying an extravagant and expensive bunch of flowers, which he decided to drop off to her straightaway and, flowers in hand, strolled back the way he came and towards Carla's flat. His phone rang in his pocket; switching the flowers to his other hand, he delved into his pocket and retrieved his phone. Carla's name and a picture of her sleeping that she didn't know had been taken, flashed up on his screen. Chris smiled; evidently she was as smitten with him as he was with her. He struggled to set the flowers down and in his laboured attempt to relieve himself of them left it too long to answer the call. He tried phoning back but it was engaged. *'She must be leaving me a voicemail,'* he mused, excited to listen to it. Sure enough, a notification popped up: one new voicemail. He listened, his face contorting as each second ticked by. Chris had heard these lines before: "It's not you, it's me," "You're a great guy," "Anyone would be lucky to have you." He hung up and looked from his phone to the flowers and back again.

"Here you go mate, for the special lady in your life," Chris pushed the flowers into the hands of an unsuspecting passerby. The guy looked at Chris then the flowers and finally back up again, but it was too late. Chris had spun on his heel and marched off in the opposite direction, his tail firmly between his legs.

Carla let out a long groan and ran her fingers through her unruly hair.

"I need a drink," she said in a matter-of-fact way.

Elodie went to pour her another glass of bubbles.

"No, a proper drink, a cocktail or something. Somewhere different, though, I don't want to see a single person I know. Oh, come on… let's go and put the 'sin' in 'single' for the night."

Elodie wanted to correct her, to tell her that she wasn't exactly single but thought better of it. Elodie scratched head her head for a moment, trying to think of the perfect place to take her.

"I know just the place." She said confidently. Aaron had shown her a gorgeous-looking cocktail bar on their date, it wasn't too far and considering Elodie had had no idea that it existed until Aaron pointed it out thought the chances of bumping into someone Carla knew to be very remote.

"OK, let's go," Elodie said, handing Carla her cake. "Sustenance for the journey," she added jokingly.

Aaron had decided that he was in desperate need of a drink. He couldn't fathom what had gone wrong between him and Elodie; he was mad about her and despite his best efforts to make amends she still wasn't giving him the time of day. Usually, when he was at odds with the world he took himself off to take pictures, he had tried this tactic today but to no avail. Every image he shot was either out of focus, over-exposed or just plain boring. No, he had decided that for some problems in life only hard liquor would do.

He turned the corner towards his favourite bar and quickened his pace as in front of him stood an angry-looking guy, well over six feet in height and extremely well built. The only thing that softened his appearance was the presence of a giant bunch of flowers, which judging by the way he was looking at them had wronged him in some way. Aaron lowered his gaze and tried to make his way past without making eye contact. Before he knew it the guy had mumbled something about a special lady and had pushed the flowers at him. Aaron had been so shocked he hadn't reacted straight away and when he did finally gather his wits the guy had gone, leaving Aaron with a massive bunch of flowers that he'd got no clue what to do with. He decided not to waste them: after all, he did have one special lady in his life who would love a bouquet like this one. She would have to wait until the next day, though. Aaron smiled as he looked at the flowers: she was going to love them.

"El, this place is great. How come we've never been here before?" Carla asked as they stepped into The Cocktail Club. It was a relaxed sort of bar, lots of soft furnishings, ambient lighting and comfy seating. They found a small, private booth at the back of the bar and sat down. The waiter signalled to them that he would be over in a minute.

"Oooh, what to have? Everything looks so good." Elodie cooed as she opened the menu. She remembered Aaron telling her that one specific cocktail was the best in town but couldn't for the life of her remember which cocktail it was.

"I'm having an Old Fashioned," Carla said decisively. The waiter came over and took their order as Elodie found herself a little overwhelmed by all the cocktails, so she opted for a Pinot Grigio Blush. She thought she saw a side-eye of judgement from the waiter so changed her order to a Cosmopolitan instead. She didn't want to come across as ignorant to the ways of the very exclusive cocktail club.

The two friends sat there for a while, sipping their drinks and entertaining one another with tales of their failed relationships. They laughed a lot, so much so that Elodie didn't notice that a familiar face had slipped in through the front door. They drank drink after drink and before long Elodie found herself to be quite tipsy and in need of the toilet. She excused herself and made her way to the bathroom. The moment before Elodie put her hand on the door to the ladies' room she noticed him, sat at the bar alone with an utterly huge bouquet of flowers. He was obviously waiting for someone. She felt herself physically stammer: she was trapped. She dived into the ladies' room with such a clamour that she made a woman towelling off her hands jump. Elodie apologised with a weak smile and locked herself in the nearest cubicle, her heart racing. Within a few moments, she had gone from panicked little girl to angry grown woman. Aaron was clearly on a date and all of this *'Please hear me out'* bullshit was just that… bullshit. Elodie's stomach roiled as the realisation that Grace would be joining him any moment and that she, Elodie, would have to navigate the gauntlet that was the bar, in order to get past them. The thought of that made her palms sweat. What would Grace think? That she had followed Aaron here? Or worse, that he had met her beforehand? At least she had Carla for backup. Elodie washed her hands and gave herself a good long look in the mirror. Steeling herself for battle, she took a deep breath and went back to join Carla.

"Why do you look like that? Someone push you out of the way of the hand drier?" Carla giggled. She had ordered another round of drinks and slid Elodie's towards her. "Here, get this down you, it should cheer you up a bit."

Elodie pushed the glass back and pointed over her

shoulder. Carla peered behind her and, with a puzzled expression mouthed *'What?'* at her.

"That right there is Aaron, you see the guy with the massive bunch of flowers. He's clearly on a date, probably with Grace and if we don't make a move now it'll be so horrible. Please, can we just go? I'll pay you back for the drinks."

"You won't need to. Come on, down in one for a bit of courage," said Carla.

Elodie looked at Carla and shook her head. "I don't need courage, I need to get home."

They collected their belongings in the most inconspicuous way that two tipsy people can and made their way to leave, Carla in front and Elodie bringing up the rear. They had just passed the halfway point when Elodie felt her phone go off. She paused, unable to resist the pull of an unanswered message. In that split-second, as if Aaron could sense she was behind him, he turned around. Their eyes met and Elodie felt like right now would be the perfect time for the ground to open up and swallow her whole.

"Elodie?" Aaron said, looking around. "What are you doing here?"

Elodie couldn't look at him; her gaze was fixed on the flowers. She needed to leave and she needed to leave now.

"I'm sorry..." was all she could manage, although quite what she was sorry for she couldn't say.

"Have a drink with me?" Aaron asked. Elodie looked at him unsure as to whether this was a joke or not.

"What? So I can get into even more trouble with Grace, or one of the other girls you've been seeing behind her back?" she said, suddenly finding that any air of apology had gone from her voice.

"You're so stubborn and hot-headed," Aaron said, sighing and sitting back down. "I'm not with Grace, never have been. I don't know about any other girls. I'm as single as you can get and I thought you were too."

"I *was* single," Elodie replied haughtily. "It's not my fault someone else showed an interest after you messed me about." She had no idea how, but for some reason Aaron was managing to turn this all back on her.

"Why won't you listen to me? I'm not with anyone! Hell,

up until you I hadn't been interested in a girl for years. You're special, Elodie. I don't know where you've got all this from, but it's simply not true. Please, even if it's too late for us, you've got to believe me. I know you felt it too… that night in the park… that was something else."

Elodie looked at him. *'Oh, he's good,'* she thought to herself.

"I've been told by someone who knows you, who knows both of you, I don't understand why you just can't admit it. We had one date, one mediocre date." The lie hurt her a little but not enough to feel bad about it even when she saw the look of dismay on Aaron's face. He ran his fingers through his sandy coloured hair and let out a low sigh.

"Who?" he asked bluntly, "If I'm going to be painted as a cheat then I want to know who's holding the brush."

"Chase," Elodie said curtly. "He told me, said it was not so much of a *girlfriend* situation, more like *girlfriends*." Aaron looked at her blankly.

"Chase?" he sputtered. "I… honestly, I genuinely don't know the guy. We've never even spoken. That's not to say I don't know who he is, or what he is, for that matter. Look, Elodie you've got it all wrong…"

Elodie had heard enough. Chase seemed to be a good guy who had been nothing but nice to her. He'd made time for her even when his schedule was busy, he'd missed her when he hadn't been able to see her and, more than anything, Elodie had a gut feeling that told her he was a good guy; maybe a little damaged, but a good guy nonetheless.

"Everything alright?" Carla said, reappearing from outside. Elodie nodded. For some reason, she felt hot tears threaten to spill and wanted to get out as quickly as she could. She gave Aaron a hurt, crestfallen look and allowed Carla to take her by the arm and escort her gently out.

"He's such a liar," Elodie managed when they were out on the street. Carla gave her an understanding nod.

"Don't worry, El, he's not worth it. Come on, let's go home, unless you want to go somewhere else?" Elodie shook her head, the idea of carrying on their evening in high spirits seemed impossible now. All she wanted to do was to go.

When she arrived home Steph was on the doorstep. Carla had clearly called for backup.

"Are you alright?" Steph asked, as Carla opened the door to let them in.

Elodie nodded then relayed the entire story again. Carla, who had sat through the actual event and then listened to a blow-by-blow account in the taxi on the way home, could do nothing but sit through the saga again. Steph listened intently and then, when Elodie was finished, said something that Elodie did not expect.

"Are you sure you don't like him? You seem to get so wound up by him, yet you can't just forget about it. Maybe you like him more than you'll allow yourself to believe?"

Elodie protested: she most certainly did not like Aaron. He was a lying, two-timing scumbag who, if Elodie had her own way, would leave her alone for good now. Elodie managed to divert the conversation momentarily by opening up a bottle of wine in an effort to tempt Carla and Steph away from asking awkward questions about Chase. Each and every time anything the subject came back up, Elodie would take a drink and by the end of the night, as she put herself to bed, she realised that she was really rather drunk.

Elodie lifted one heavy-lidded eye and peered towards her phone. Thank God it was a Sunday and thank God she didn't need to go to work. She had never been much of a drinker, but somehow the single life went hand in hand with a glass of wine, or four. Elodie had managed to put away a fair amount of booze the previous evening, so much so that she had almost forgotten her exchange with Aaron... almost.

"Ugh," she groaned as a drink-induced headache thudded behind her eyes. Elodie was eternally grateful not to have downed that last drink. She reached for her phone, which she had forgotten to put on charge. She had less than three per cent battery left, two missed calls and one text message, all from Chase. In spite of her fragile state, her heart soared: she'd known all along that it wouldn't be long before he was back in touch. He hadn't left her a voicemail and his text message simply read.

Absentmindedly chewing a piece of buttered toast and staring at her phone screen, her thumb hovered above the call button as her mind wandered, wondering exactly what it was that Chase would say to her. She had a good feeling about this, but she wanted to make sure she had all her faculties in order before she phoned him back. After several long minutes and a little pep talk to herself, she pressed call and brought the phone up to her ear.

"Elodie, what's going on?" he said, answering on the fourth ring. His voice seemed tense.

"Nothing, just returning your call," she replied.

"You rang me in the dead of night four times and left an incoherent voice message. I thought something had happened," Chase said, annoyance creeping into his voice.

It was at that precise moment that Elodie remembered, well kind of. She had a vague recollection of dialling his number, several times. She didn't remember leaving a voicemail, but she must have done. She felt foolish but also strangely happy, Chase had called her back, and more to the point had been worried. That had to mean something.

"I'm so sorry," Elodie managed. "I hope I didn't worry you."

"It's fine, as long as you're alright."

Elodie told him that she was and that she had been out with Carla, she didn't know why but she found that she was relaying the story of what had happened with Aaron. Chase didn't say an awful lot. *'He's such a great listener,'* Elodie thought to herself.

"So, when can I see you again?" Elodie asked in what she hoped was a nonchalant voice.

"Ahh, I'm sorry babe, my schedule's packed. I've only got Saturday evening free and I said I'd meet some friends for dinner."

"I'm free, I could come with you? It'd be nice to meet your friends," Elodie said, the words slipping from her lips as though she had no control over them.

She was met with silence. Chase breathed heavily down the phone before finally adding:

"Sure, that'd be good. We're meeting at Noho. The table's booked for eight pm." Once the conversation was over. She hung up feeling pretty good about herself; thinking that maybe on the odd occasion drunk-dialling was a good thing. Not only had they got a date fixed in the diary, she was being introduced to his friends too. To say she was excited would be an understatement.

CHAPTER 16

ELODIE'S PHONE BUZZED, AND A MESSAGE POPPED up telling her that her car was only a few minutes away. She had wanted to arrive in style, so had booked one of the cars through work. She studied her reflection in the mirror. She had gone for an understated look for Chase's friends, hoping that it exuded maturity beyond her years. She wore a loose-fitting dress, low-slung heels and her hair in a relaxed ponytail. She knew that they were older than her and she didn't want to come across as immature for him, so it was important to get everything right, even down to what she wore. Fingers shaking slightly, she zipped up her overnight bag; she figured that if she were important enough to meet his friends, she'd almost certainly be asked to stay the night. She didn't want to be ill-prepared for that eventuality.

Elodie was happy to see that it was Mr Bosford who was behind the wheel of the black Mercedes waiting outside the flat.

"I didn't expect to see you," Elodie said questioningly, giving him a warm smile.

"Well, when they put the call out how could I refuse?" he replied.

Elodie got in and fastened her seatbelt.

"Thanks," she replied gratefully.

"So you and the pilot, then: a proper thing?" Mr Bosford said, with fatherly concern.

Elodie looked at him, a little stunned. She didn't know if she really wanted to have this conversation with Mr Bosford, of all people.

"Errr… I guess so," Elodie began. "I mean, yeah, I'm meeting his friends tonight."

"Excited?" he asked, not taking his eyes from the road ahead.

"Anxious more like, I want them to like me," she replied, twisting a lock of hair around her finger nervously.

"Course they will, you're a lovely lass. Just be yourself and relax. You can't do more than that now, can you?"

Elodie nodded. He was right, of course, but somehow she thought that just being herself wasn't going to do it.

The car pulled to a standstill and a valet in a very smart black and gold uniform opened the door. Elodie's heart sank a little as she saw other diners entering the building. To say she was underdressed was an understatement. The restaurant was on the top floor of a very tall building and boasted spectacular views of the city. Elodie took a deep breath. It was too late to do anything about her outfit now, she was just going to have to wow them with her personality instead. Putting one foot in front of the other with as much confidence as she could muster, she walked inside. The splendour inside rivalled that of the private jet and everything was done to the highest of standards. The restaurant was more like a hotel: it had a waiting area, a reception desk and front of house staff to relieve you of your coats and show you to your table.

"Reservation name?" Noho's receptionist asked politely, eyeing Elodie up and giving her a slightly bemused look.

"I think it'll be under Chase Ford," Elodie said, standing on her tiptoes and peering over the desk. She hoped that the table hadn't been booked under another name. The receptionist looked down at the screen of her tablet and furrowed her brow.

"One moment please," she said, picking up a telephone receiver hidden behind her desk. She turned away from Elodie and in hushed tones gave some instruction to the person on the other end of the line. Turning back to face Elodie, she extended her hand towards the modern-looking sofa behind her and told her to wait for a moment. Elodie did as she was told and sat down. She crossed her legs, uncrossed them and then crossed them again as she shifted in her seat. The sofa was beautiful, but it sure wasn't comfortable.

'What's taking so long?' she thought to herself. The more time that passed, the more anxious she became. Eventually, a staff member came to her, apologised for the wait and escorted her to an ornately-decorated round table, where Chase and four other people sat. Elodie took her seat next to Chase and was introduced to each of Chase's friends in turn: Jules and Ian, a very good-looking couple who lived in France; and Sissy and David. Sissy was incredibly well-spoken, elegantly turned out and seemed very forthright. David, on the other hand, was exceptionally quiet and reserved. Elodie smiled at everyone as she sat and said a rather timid hello. Chase's friends were polite, but not overly welcoming. Elodie wondered if perhaps they were being protective of him, seeing as he had such a bad run of luck with women in the past, and decided to try and not take it personally.

"It's a bit of a squeeze," Elodie said in an effort to break the ice.

"Well it wouldn't have been if they hadn't had to lay an extra setting," Sissy said coolly as she gave Chase a look. "No matter, though, you're here now."

Chase gave Elodie an apologetic glance and suddenly it all made sense. The reason she had been kept waiting was so they could juggle the seating arrangement. Her cheeks flushed slightly; she didn't know what to say. She'd never felt like more of an imposition in her life.

"Drink?" Chase suggested.

Elodie nodded. She couldn't think of anything she wanted more right now. The waiter came and took her order. Sissy pointed out that she was simply starving due to being made to wait and although no names were mentioned Elodie knew this comment was aimed at her. She ordered a large glass of rosé wine, which was delivered to her promptly.

"Oh rosé, I don't think I've had that, well ever," Sissy giggled and Elodie felt herself blush a similar shade to that of her wine.

As the evening progressed Elodie felt more and more out of her depth. The conversation was very mature; they talked about things that she had little experience of and because of this she found it quite difficult to get involved. They discussed, in depth, the state of world politics, the property crisis in France and debates about religion in the workplace. Elodie tried to join in when she could, but each and every time she volunteered an opinion it was met with polite disregard. Elodie sipped on her wine and hoped that instead of looking bored she was exuding quiet contemplation.

Chase squeezed her knee under the table and Elodie glanced at him; he offered her a smile as his hand ventured a little higher. Elodie felt herself stiffen. Was he really doing this right now? She glanced around to see if anyone had noticed. They hadn't. Chase eased Elodie's thighs wider and trailed softly further and further up the inside of her leg, his touch as smooth as silk. He paused at the very top, his fingers stopping just short of her most sensitive spot. Elodie stared at her plate and took another sip of wine. She couldn't bring herself to look up, she knew that if she made eye contact with anyone then they'd see right through her. Chase didn't move, he gripped her harder and then, without warning, released his hand.

"If you'll excuse me for a moment, I need to make a call."

He got up and upon leaving gave Elodie's shoulder a little squeeze. She turned to look at him as he walked away. He looked back over his shoulder and motioned to Elodie to follow him as he rounded a corner. A wave of excitement rolled over her; she waited for a moment and then, with a sweet smile, excused herself in favour of the ladies' room. No one seemed to notice her departure. She quickened her pace as she walked across the dining room, following in Chase's wake. She rounded the same corner he had and in an instant he was on her. Chase pinned Elodie up against the wall, one hand gripping her waist, the other cupping her cheek. Their mouths became one as Chase pressed himself firmly against her.

"This way," he said, pulling away from her.

Chase led her down the corridor, trying various doors as he went. The third door offered them their haven. A small storeroom filled with table linens. Chase closed the door behind her; the moment the lock had clicked shut they were entwined in one another once more. Chase held her against the door, pinning her hands over her head. Elodie panted as he lifted the hem of her dress and felt wet desire begin to pool between her thighs. Chase pulled her underwear to the side and pushed one finger, followed by another, inside her. She gasped as he slid into her effortlessly and curved his fingers in a delicious way that made every fibre of her want to cry out. He put his free hand over her mouth and in hushed tones whispered that she needed to be quiet. She nodded her understanding and reached for him hungrily, she undid his belt and trousers in such a way that told him that she was desperate for him. He withdrew his fingers and held them up rotating them and watching as they glistened with her essence. He held them to her mouth. Elodie moved her head backwards and looked at him, not entirely sure what he wanted. Silently he pushed them further towards her; he parted her mouth with his outstretched index finger. Elodie now understood: she opened her mouth to obey him and he watched lustfully as she tentatively sucked on them.

"Good girl," he said, his voice low to keep them from being discovered. When he was satisfied with her he pushed his trousers and underwear down in unison. His manhood throbbed before her; she reached out and took it in one hand, stroking deftly up and down. Chase let out a throaty moan and, without warning, picked her up. Elodie was overtaken by fathomless lust: she felt as though she were being swept downstream and, try as she might, she could not resist. She was helpless, engulfed in the very idea of him and completely at his mercy. Elodie leant heavily on the door as Chase lowered her onto his bulging erection. He thrust into her, his muscular arms holding her tightly; she gripped his shoulders and bit her bottom lip. She wanted to scream, to cry out with pleasure but she knew that she would have to remain quiet if they were to go undetected. Elodie knew she was close, how could she not be? Chase seemed to know exactly what she needed, what she wanted and every thrust of his hips brought her closer to the edge. He felt her body tense and her grip tighten and knew it would be a matter of moments before he felt her climax. The orgasm devastated Elodie: she bit down onto Chase's shoulder to keep herself quiet and shook uncontrollably as she came. Chase wasn't far behind. It was as though her climax had brought his own on. The two clung to each other for several long moments as their breath gradually settled.

"You better go first," Chase said, pulling his trousers back up and fastening his belt. He opened the door and Elodie slipped out. She made her way to the toilets, convinced that everyone she passed knew exactly what she had been doing.

When Elodie sat back down at the table she did so without a hair out of place. However, she needn't have bothered, as not one of Chase's friends looked up. She finished her wine wondering why Chase was friends with these people: they weren't exactly welcoming, and if Elodie were to take a leaf from Carla's book and call a spade a spade she would say that they were both snobby and rude. Chase returned to the table a few minutes after Elodie, expertly pocketing his phone as he sat down to give the impression that he'd just finished with his call.

The meal passed in much the same way it had started and with each new course Elodie felt less and less as though she should be there. She kicked herself for having suggested it in the first place and started to wish that Chase had just said no. Aside from the odd glance her way, he barely spoke to her for the rest of the meal. Once their main course had been cleared the waiter sashayed back over to them in such a way that made him look like as though he were floating.

"Any desserts at all, or have we had our fill?"

Elodie could have sworn his eyes flicked from his notepad to her at these words. She opened her mouth to reply. She had absolutely every intention of ordering a pudding: after all, it wasn't every day you got to eat in a place like this.

"The bill please," Chase said, cutting across her. "You don't want more, do you?"

He turned to Elodie. She looked around to gauge the rest of the table's reaction: they were all staring at her, looking as though never in their lives had they witnessed someone order a dessert before.

"Oh, no. I was, I'd just like a glass of water, if that's OK?" she asked.

"Still or sparkling?" the waited asked second-naturedly.

"Tap will be fine," Elodie said.

"Table water it is," the waiter said, looking down his nose

at her. He floated off and seconds later appeared with a single glass of water atop an ornate silver tray. Elodie sipped at it under the watchful eye of Sissy, who had raised one eyebrow in a perplexed sort of way. Feeling self-conscious, she reached out for Chase under the table, who upon feeling her fingers brush his leg moved it out of reach abruptly. Elodie knew that she'd done something wrong. She wasn't used to places like this. Everyone acted so differently and practically spoke a different language; it was totally at odds with how she usually was. Still, she knew that in order to impress Chase she would have to pull her finger out and learn the ropes quickly; she didn't want to embarrass him again.

When the bill came, Chase insisted on paying. There were lots of cries of protest but in the end he won, taking out his platinum credit card and waving it at the waiter. Everyone rose from the table, administered air-kisses left, right and centre and then went their separate ways.

"Well that was an experience," Elodie overheard Sissy mutter to Jules. "How old is this one? I swear they get younger by the day."

The two sniggered to themselves and Elodie pretended to be busy rummaging in her bag. She wished she'd worn her hair down; perhaps then they wouldn't have been able to see her furiously reddening cheeks.

"Of course they liked you," Chase reassured her once they had said their goodbyes and were now alone on the street outside. "They're just a tough crowd to please – that's all."

Elodie gave Chase a sideways glance. They hadn't had reason to like or dislike her as she'd gone largely unnoticed all evening.

"They didn't even give me a chance," she sighed.

Sissy's words played on her mind: *"They get younger by the day."* Elodie wanted to know what she had meant but daren't ask Chase. She didn't want to look bitchy. Still, the words rang in her head like a gong. Chase wrapped an arm around her and pulled her into him.

"You're worrying about nothing. Besides, it doesn't matter if they don't like you, I like you enough for all of them."

Elodie smiled; he always seemed to know just what to say.

Chase gave her a kiss on the top of the head before flagging down a cab. "You'll be good from here, won't you?"

Elodie looked at him confusedly.

"I thought I might come back to yours?" she said. Normally she would have just accepted the situation, but a bit of wine, combined with some mind-blowing secret sex, had given her an air of confidence that she just couldn't shake.

"I'd love that, but I've got an early start. Another time, maybe?" Chase said as he checked his watch and gave her a peck on the cheek.

Elodie couldn't lie: she was disappointed. She had wanted more than anything to spend the night with him. They had been seeing each other for weeks now and so far had been kept at arm's reach when it came to his personal life. Chase leaned in and gave Elodie a somewhat awkward hug. She felt his phone, still in his breast pocket, buzz. He released her and checked his messages. A frown fell across his face and his brow crinkled, which made him look much older than his years.

"Actually Elodie, yes. Yes, you should stay with me tonight," he added, pocketing his phone and wrapping an arm around her.

"Really?" she asked, thinking that maybe she was right to go down the path of gentle persuasion. Perhaps a bit of encouragement was all he needed.

Less than half an hour later Elodie found herself standing in the middle of Chase's flat in a complex called Millennium Square. It was a huge industrial-looking space with highly-polished concrete floors, giant stone-coloured rugs and a lot of sophisticated brushed chrome touches. His living room was about the size of her entire flat and had impressive views of the city. As they walked in, an alarm started beeping a shrill warning. Chase leaned over her and flipped down a steel panel to reveal a keypad. Elodie tried to avert her eyes in time but couldn't help noticing him type the numbers six, nine, six. Thankfully she didn't catch the last number and Chase didn't notice that she'd seen the first three. The last thing she wanted was for him to think her rude, or that she was casing the joint for a cat burglary later on.

"Come on then, or are you going to wait in the hallway all night?" Chase asked.

Elodie stepped into his apartment. Everything looked so expensive. He even had a giant modern art piece: the sculpture towered over her and she found herself strangely drawn to it.

"You like it?" Chase asked when he saw her staring. "Got it last week, cost an absolute fortune." She nodded, even though she wasn't entirely sure exactly what it was meant to be.

She bent down and gingerly removed her shoes. She was surprised to see that for the second time that evening her fingers were shaking. Despite the unrestrained setting she found herself in, she couldn't help but notice that there were no personal touches. Chase didn't have a single photograph on display; instead, he had lots of large, very expensive-looking prints hanging on the walls. In his hallway hung so much art that she was reminded of the Eason Art Space, and she surveyed the pieces in front of her now with much the same interest as she did on her date with Aaron.

'Aaron.' Her mind echoed his name. Something about how they had left things hadn't been right, He seemed so desperate for her to believe him, and what had she done? Branded him a liar and tried to put everything to do with him to the back of her mind. But still, one thing just didn't add up: if Chase knew Aaron so well as to know that he was a two-timing cheat, then why hadn't he even acknowledged him when they'd bumped into each other on the plane? Elodie had been so wrapped up in almost getting caught that at the time it had barely entered her consciousness. However, now she looked back on it, she couldn't remember seeing even the faintest flash of recognition on Chase's face.

"Chase? Do you remember that guy Aaron I told you about?" Chase looked puzzled and shook his head. "The one I dated briefly, the guy with the girlfriend?"

"Oh yes, of course, why do you ask?"

"How well do you know him? Are you friends?" Elodie probed.

"I know him well enough to know that you're too good

for him. Now enough with the questions, or I might start to think you've got a thing for this guy," he teased.

"I don't, I swear," Elodie said, a slight note of panic in her voice. She definitely didn't want Chase to think she still had feelings for Aaron.

Chase gave her shoulder a squeeze and told her that he believed her before manoeuvring her into the large, open space that was his living room.

"Drink?" Chase asked as he gestured to a table next to him. On top of it sat a slate tray and on top of that a bottle of expensive-looking whisky and two square tumblers. "You like Dalmore, right? It's an eighteen-year-old single malt."

Elodie wrinkled her nose and shook her head. Eighteen years or not, all whisky tasted the same: gross.

"Go on," Chase persuaded, leaning forward and pouring a half-inch measure in the bottom of one of the tumblers. He handed it to Elodie and, looking her square in the eyes, knocked back the drink he had poured for himself. She hesitated, the glass wavering near her lips before she followed suit. The amber liquid burned the back of her throat: its taste was so strong that she had to actively stop herself from spluttering.

"It's good," she said, trying not to choke. The whisky warmed her and she felt a heat settle in her chest, which she found a welcome relief in the otherwise cool space.

Chase relieved her of her glass and set it down. He stepped towards her: without her shoes, Chase towered over Elodie even more than usual. He gazed down at her a curious look in his eye. She stood in complete silence; he said and did nothing. Elodie felt the hairs on the back of her neck stand to attention and prickle as he seemed to undress her with his eyes. Elodie could feel something building between them as he looked at her, as though she were the only woman in the world.

"Take off your dress," Chase instructed out of nowhere.

"Here?" Elodie stammered, "but what…?"

"Take off your dress," he repeated calmly.

Elodie's eyes fell from his face to his lap. She saw the beginnings of a bulge forming and knew that what he wanted was for her to obey. She lowered her gaze further and slipped the fabric of the dress down over one shoulder.

"Look at me," Chase instructed.

Elodie slowly submitted and lifted her head up to meet his stare. He was completely calm and just watching, his eyes narrow and focussed. Elodie slipped the other shoulder down and let the dress fall to her waist. She pushed it lower and stepped out of it, looking to Chase for further instruction, which he wasn't slow in giving.

"And your underwear," he said, his voice taking on a gruff tone as he lowered himself into one of the large leather armchairs. He sat forward, interlacing his fingers together. Elodie did as she was told, unhooking her bra from behind and letting it fall to the floor where it lay with her dress. Her nipples were already hardening thanks to the chill in the living room; her rose-pink buds stood to attention, forcing Chase to switch focus. He stared at her breasts greedily yet he did not move. Next Elodie hooked her thumbs into the waistband of her pants and pushed them down, the lace material brushing her skin as they traversed her thighs. She stepped out of them one foot at a time and stood there, completely naked in Chase's living room.

"Lay down and show me," Chase muttered; his voice had taken on an animalistic, guttural edge, "show me how you like to be touched."

Elodie's arms hung limply by her sides. She had never been asked, no, told to do this before, ever, and she wasn't entirely sure she knew what he meant.

"I…" she started, but Chase brought his hand up to silence her.

"I want to see you pleasure yourself, lie down on the ground and show me how you like it."

Elodie did as she was told. She sank to her knees slowly, then lowered herself onto her back. She looked up and was shocked to see that the lofty ceiling was actually a highly polished steel surface that reflected the room below perfectly. She could see herself, lying naked at the foot of Chase, who was now reclining in the large armchair. He wore a satisfied look on his features as he fixed her with a stare of intent. The rug that she lay on was soft and sumptuous against her skin, offering a welcome respite to the chill she felt settling across her skin. She started by slowly tracing circles across her chest and mid-section with one hand, pausing sporadically to gently tease her nipples. Gradually her fingers travelled lower until they were at the precipice of her flushing lips. She opened her legs slightly.

"Wider," Chase instructed.

Elodie obliged and moved her legs further apart. She closed her eyes and stroked herself up and down, bathing in the absolute bliss that each caress provided. Her fingers paused momentarily before deftly encircling her sensitive nub. This sent shock waves through her body; she was becoming impatient now, desperate almost. Her clitoris was now a swollen nub, begging for attention and crying out for her touch. This time it was her own body making demands of her and she willingly obliged. The second her fingertips made contact she gasped, she was growing wetter and knew that it was only a matter of time before she would want, no, need, Chase to be inside her. She softly took her clitoris between her thumb and forefinger and applied a delicate pressure: she rolled it between her fingers and allowed the blissful sensations to flood her senses. She was vaguely aware of movement now. She opened her eyes but continued to play with herself, wishing only to please. The sight of herself in the mirrored ceiling above almost stopped her in her tracks: she had never seen herself in this way before. Glancing over, she saw that Chase, now naked, had opened a drawer in a chest that, up until now, Elodie hadn't noticed. He turned around and from the reflection above she could see him carrying a black, leather-bound box with a silver handle and matching hinges.

"Don't stop," Chase urged as he settled himself beside her. His voice sounded muffled; she turned her head and saw that the tie that he had worn earlier was now held in his hands. "That's it, show me exactly what you like."

Elodie willingly obliged. He gestured for her to open wide; she did not protest. He pushed the mid-section of the tie into her mouth and, pulling it taut, tied it in a knot at the back of her head. He then turned his attention away from her and focused on the box that he had carried over and set down beside her. He lifted the lid and emptied the contents next to her. Elodie's eyes grew wide: out onto the floor fell a plethora of sexual paraphernalia. He held up a pair of utilitarian-looking cuffs and leaned over her. Chase shackled her wrists high above her head, attaching them to the metal leg of the sofa. Elodie had never felt more alive: sparks of excitement flew within as she watched Chase masterfully render her completely helpless. He took his time, mulling over each toy as if it were a costly purchase not to be made with a light heart.

After long moments of anticipation, Elodie saw him select a heavy-looking, silver rod. It was several inches long with a deliciously inviting curved body. Chase pressed the tip of it against her skin. She winced: it was cold and her natural reaction was to shy away. He watched her lustily, sliding the silver toy down her stomach and back up, all the while watching her intently. She let out a muffled groan. The anticipation was becoming too much: she felt a warm wetness begin to flow down the inside of her thighs. She squirmed, hoping against hope that Chase would offer her some much-needed relief quickly, and he did. He held the toy at the mouth of her sex, pausing to watch her wetness pulse with desire. Slowly he penetrated her; inch by inch the toy invaded. She squirmed under its attention but Chase placed a strong hand below her navel which halted her protests. He pressed down firmly: she could feel the toy rubbing against her internal hotspot, still cold and still delicious. She writhed under his touch, which only seemed to spur Chase on: he moved the toy inside her more frantically. Never once did he pause or take his eyes from her. Elodie felt herself slipping, she couldn't help herself – it was all too much.

"Not yet," Chase said suddenly. He slid the toy out from between her legs and examined it. It was thick with her essence; he extended his tongue and tasted her, closing his eyes to savour the moment. He reached down and grabbed something from the floor that Elodie could not see, all the while stroking his hard shaft up and down with his free hand. He re-positioned himself at the juncture of her thighs, savouring the sight of her. Without uttering a solitary word he buried his face between her legs and Elodie bit down hard on the material between her lips. He flattened his tongue and circled her swollen pearl expertly, never once relenting. Elodie twisted under the delectable sensations and tried to yank free of the cuffs but to no avail, they bit into her wrists, inflicting a sharp yet strange pleasure that Elodie revelled in. Chase pulled away from her and edged up her body, stopping every now and then to pinch some of her skin between his teeth. He bit down on one of her nipples and Elodie lurched: a bolt seemed to shoot through her body, although at that precise moment she couldn't tell whether it was pleasure or pain. Finally, with their faces only inches apart Chase entered her, she spread her legs wide and linked her ankles behind his waist. She could do nothing as he pushed into her, slowly at first, but building pace each time. Elodie stared up at the ceiling and watched as his buttocks contracted with each thrust, his muscular back constricting in such a way that made Elodie soar. With one hand he produced a pair of clamps, connected by a gold chain. With one hand he deftly pinched them at their base and released them around each nipple in turn. Elodie wanted to cry out loud; her eyes widened as her head flew back. She struggled against them, but only for a moment. Her nipples ached, but in a good way, in a way that she could definitely get used to. Chase bowed his head and took the chain between his teeth, he continued to drive himself in and out of her, pressing firmly against her external hot spots with each inward thrust. Elodie could take no more as she finally succumbed to climax. As her body jerked spasmodically, Chase lifted his head: the chain tightened and pulled her stiff buds skyward. Elodie let out an animalistic cry that the gag did little to muffle. Chase pulled the chain from her mouth and pressed his lips firmly against hers as he embraced his own release.

After a little while, Chase pulled from her. He gave her a kiss on the forehead and stood up. He walked to the dresser from which he had produced the black box. Elodie was still cuffed and unable to move. She strained her head but couldn't quite see what he was doing.

"Chase?" she said uncertainly. Moments later, Elodie heard a familiar click and whirr: her head shot up and she saw that he was standing only feet away from her with an old Polaroid camera.

"Errr, What are you doing?" she asked, uncertainty creeping into her voice.

"Relax, little one, it's just a keepsake for posterity. You look too gorgeous not to capture the moment. Don't worry, it's just for me."

Elodie didn't know what to say, so she didn't say anything at all. Chase took the photo from the camera, shook it in the air a few times then threw it in the black box along with the toys that he had used on her. He bent down and undid her handcuffs; she pulled her arms free and rubbed her reddened wrists. Chase crouched next to Elodie. Now adorned in a grey robe, he held her clothes out to her, which she took from him. The material of her dress brushed past her nipples as she put it on. She stifled a gasp and winced: they were still sensitive from Chase's attentions. He leaned in and gave her a quick kiss.

"OK, let's get you home," he said casually.

Elodie was shocked, to say the least. She had been under the impression that she would stay the night. Had she known she'd be brought back only to be turned away again, she might never have come at all.

"Home?" she asked.

Chase nodded and repeated his mantra about being busy and needing to be up early.

"Don't be like that," Chase said, pulling her in for a hug, "I'd love for you to stay, but you never said anything about staying over, did you? Do you really want to be woken at silly am and then have to do the walk of shame?"

Elodie could see his point, but still – walk of shame? She wouldn't be ashamed. She opened her mouth to protest, but Chase was already calling for a cab, and Elodie found herself hoping that it wouldn't be Mr Bosford that came to take her home. Chase walked Elodie to the door, although it felt as though it was more to make sure she left rather than any real sense of chivalry.

"Can I ask you something?" Elodie asked as she stood in the doorway.

"Let's talk tomorrow, I'm exhausted right now, babe,"

Chase replied. "Taxi's outside, be safe." He gave her a warm smile and closed the door.

Elodie stood there for a moment, hardly able to believe the turn of events. Had that really just happened? She felt dirty, like a used rag that had been discarded.

'Am I being crazy?' she asked herself. Chase had said from the start he needed to be up early; and he was right, she had just said she wanted to go back to his, she'd never said anything about staying the night. Was it her? Maybe she was sending out mixed messages? She made her way to the cab making a promise to herself that she wouldn't be quite so vague next time.

Two weeks passed and Elodie still felt funny about how things had been the last time she had seen Chase. She had spoken to both Steph and Carla about it over coffee and cake at Betty's; she hadn't painted them an entirely accurate picture, but she had said that he'd taken a photograph of her after sex without her say-so. They had both agreed that it was out of order and really quite odd behaviour and weren't backwards at coming forwards about how they now felt about Chase. This put Elodie on edge. She didn't know why, but she felt as though criticising Chase was uncalled for, especially since they didn't know him like she did. All Elodie wanted was some reassurance, not for them to pick him apart right in front of her.

"If you ask me, he's too old and he's clearly into some weird stuff," Steph had said. To Elodie's surprise, Carla had agreed.

"Steph's right, El. The more you tell me about him, the more I think he's just not right for you. I know I've always said to get over someone get under someone else, but I didn't mean fall under their spell."

Elodie felt herself flush. She wasn't under anyone's spell.

"It'd be good for you to be on your own for a bit, you know, figure out what it is you want, for yourself," Steph had concluded.

"I can't believe I'm hearing this," Elodie said, aghast. "I thought you two would have my back at least." Carla and Steph both looked at each other. "And don't do that. Judge me with your sideways looks. I won't tell you things in future if this is how you're going to react."

"Elodie, I don't know where this is coming from but we..." Steph began.

"I know what you're doing, you want me to be single again because you are," she pointed to Carla, "and you can't stand anyone to be in a better relationship than your own," she turned her finger to Steph.

"El, that's just not true. We're just concerned," Carla said, her temper beginning to flare.

"Yes, it is. You think just because I'm younger than him and not as experienced that I'm not good enough. Well, you can take your concern and shove it up your arse," Elodie said. She stood up and stalked out of the room.

Elodie was so angry, and things only got worse over the passing days. She couldn't put her finger on why she felt so uneasy about it all, but she did. Thankfully, work was so busy she couldn't dwell on the state of her relationship with her friends for too long. Chase was being true to his word and working hard; or he was being suspiciously elusive and avoiding her. She was obviously sending out some kind of vibe, as both Carla and Steph had asked her on separate occasions what was wrong. Elodie couldn't tell them, though; she didn't think she could bear to hear their thoughts on the matter. She had an uneasy feeling in the pit of her stomach and, no matter how hard she tried to shake it, it just wouldn't go. She didn't like the feeling of being overlooked, and there were only so many times he could avoid her.

Elodie sat in the staff room, completely alone, sipping a cup of coffee and mulling over her dilemma. She felt as though she deserved better, and that maybe Chase wasn't the greatest thing since sliced bread after all. She shook her head in an attempt to dislodge these thoughts that refused to leave her alone. She snatched up a discarded copy of En Mode magazine that someone had left and leafed through. She flicked past fashion pages, interest pieces and celebrity gossip, and was pleased to see that she had worked on flights with more than one famous face gracing the pages.

"Do you mind if I sit?"

Elodie looked up. Grace was standing above her, a cup of tea in one hand and a chocolate biscuit in the other. Elodie moved the magazine over slightly and nodded. Why would Grace want to sit with her? There were plenty of other tables free after all. Unless she'd found out about the other night at the bar; maybe she'd seen Elodie leaving as she had ventured in to meet Aaron?

Grace sat down and staring intently at it, broke her biscuit in half and offered one piece to Elodie.

"You want some?" she asked.

Elodie looked at her and raised an eyebrow. Hesitantly she took the offering, wondering if somehow Grace had managed to poison her half. She gave the biscuit a half-hearted sniff and then popped it into her mouth. Grace picked up the magazine that Elodie had been reading and began to peruse it herself.

"It's a small place this, nothing is ever secret for long, you know." She said this without looking up from the magazine. Elodie felt her blood run cold: she knew exactly what Grace was getting at. But how could she know? They had been so careful.

"I don't know what you mean," Elodie said, trying her hardest to keep her tone casual.

"Hasn't it ever crossed your mind why he'd want you to keep it a secret?" Grace pressed, putting the magazine down now and looking Elodie square in the face.

"I, errr," Elodie stammered.

"It's OK. I don't expect you to say anything, least of all to me. I'm just saying, maybe it wouldn't hurt to think about it. I'm sure there's a brain rattling around in that pretty head of yours."

With that Grace stood up and left, leaving Elodie's alone with her racing thoughts. She felt as though she'd never been more transparent in her entire life. Would Grace tell anyone? Would Chase be mad? Would she be fired? Would he? All these questions, and dozens more, raced around her head. She needed to speak to Chase, whether he was busy or not. She stood up, shoved the half-read copy of *En Mode* into her bag and sped off to find him.

Elodie found Chase in mid-conversation with Gareth; she

hovered near them for a few minutes, not wanting to be rude, but the urgency she had felt only intensified as she waited.

"Chase, sorry. I need a word about... something," she said lamely. Gareth gave her a questioning look but said nothing. Instead, he took his cue to leave, telling Chase that he would have to have a think about it, whatever 'it' was.

"Elodie, that was a bit..." Chase began.

"Grace knows we're together. I'm sure of it, she just gave me a biscuit and was really cryptic with me," Elodie cut in.

Chase raised an eyebrow.

"Not a biscuit?" he said dismissively.

Elodie felt a bubble of frustration burst inside her. Why wasn't Chase taking this seriously? After all, hadn't it been he who was so adamant that no one at work could find out, that it must remain 'their secret'?

"Chase, you've got to listen. She hates me for kissing Aaron. I wouldn't put it past her to tell, and then you could end up losing your job." Elodie said.

Chase snorted and put a hand to his head.

"Elodie, I don't want to be cruel, but firstly we're not together. I told you, I don't do relationships. And secondly, don't you think you're overreacting, just a bit? I know you're young but let's not be dramatic."

Elodie opened her mouth to speak but Chase ploughed ahead.

"Look, it's been great, it really has. But this," he gestured up and down at Elodie, "this is too much. Wanting to stay over, gate-crashing a dinner with my friends, trying to make me jealous with this Aaron guy. It's drama that I'm just not interested in. I think it's time we called it a day."

Elodie took a step back, as if his words had taken a physical form and had tried to strike.

"I don't understand," she said weakly, "I'm just trying to warn you about Grace..."

"I can handle Grace," he replied quickly.

Elodie stared at him agog, wondering how had this conversation gone so badly so quickly. She couldn't believe that an act of what she felt was concern had been blown out of proportion, and now Chase was ending things. It just didn't make sense.

Chase gave Elodie a pitying smile and strode off. Elodie stared after him hoping that he would turn around and tell her it was all a mistake, he didn't. Elodie watched as he disappeared off in the distance and felt as though she'd been kicked as an awful feeling of sadness began to settle in the pit of her stomach.

Elodie arrived home late that evening, feeling numb. Carla was already in her pyjamas, sat on the sofa with a hot chocolate in hand. Elodie was still angry with her for how she had behaved during their spat but now, more than anything, she was angry at herself for ever allowing a guy to come between them. She wanted to tell Carla what had happened, she really did. But she had sacrificed so much for him and despite Chase's words she knew that it wasn't over between them, it couldn't be. No, she decided that there was nothing to be gained from telling Carla, and besides, she didn't think she could handle hearing *"I told you so."*

Elodie knew the day would come where she would have to work with Chase again, she had just hoped that that day wouldn't come so soon. Less than one week later she was sat in the back of Mr Bosford's car on her way to a flight to Mexico, knowing full well that Chase was piloting the plane. She was dreading it and every time she thought about bumping into him her blood ran cold. She couldn't help but hope that maybe if he saw her again he'd realise what he'd lost.

"Everything alright? You seem out of sorts," Mr Bosford asked Elodie partway through the journey.

"I'm fine," Elodie replied, forcing a smile.

"Boy trouble again?" he asked.

Elodie felt her jolt in her chest. He couldn't know, could he? She had found herself becoming suspicious of everyone lately. Every time someone asked how she was, gave a smile or a certain type of look, her heart would sink and stomach would lurch. She felt terrible for not confiding in any of her friends, but they had warned her about him, and until she knew for certain that things were over, she didn't want to say anything.

"Nope, everything's fine," she said, mustering a jovial tone. Mr Bosford gave a smile that Elodie thought bordered on pity but said nothing more.

Elodie passed through security easily as always and made her way to the changing rooms. She wanted to redo her makeup and make sure she looked her best; after all, there's no better revenge than looking incredible. She rounded the corner and almost ran straight into Aaron.

"Sorry, excuse me," she mumbled as she moved past him. Aaron said nothing; he gave her a smile, so similar to the one Mr Bosford had given only moments before and Elodie felt a swell of annoyance. *'Why is everyone looking at me like that?'* she thought exasperatedly. *'Like I'm some charity case?'*

"No worries, have a good day," Aaron said agreeably before heading off on his way.

Elodie was shocked: never had Aaron just wished her a nice day. He always wanted to talk, needed to explain things or was trying to spend time with her in some way; never before had he simply left. Elodie didn't like how that felt and realised in that moment that maybe she had secretly enjoyed Aaron's attentions; maybe Steph had been right all along. She shook this thought from her head: she didn't have time for the intricacies of Aaron.

CHAPTER 17

IT WAS DAYS UNTIL ELODIE BEGAN TO FEEL A little more like herself again, and even though she had barely exchanged two words with Carla and Steph since their falling-out, all ill-feeling slipped from her head entirely when she found herself welcoming on board none other than Alex Walker, owner of Alpha Whiskey and founder of *En Mode* magazine. She still couldn't believe just how sour things had become. The notion that she should apologise reared its head several times a day, but she just couldn't seem to find the right time or the right words to say. Not for them to tear Chase apart for no real reason. They had never been supportive of her boyfriends. They'd never given Tom a chance, and look how that had panned out; and now they were doing the same thing to Chase. However, given her new circumstances, their fight had been pushed to the back of her mind.

Mr Walker was an older man in his late fifties with salt and pepper hair and a closely cropped beard to match. Elodie liked him at once; he had kind eyes that seemed to smile, even when his mouth didn't. He asked her how she was finding Alpha Whiskey and she told him, not untruthfully, that she was enjoying it very much. He asked her if the staff had been welcoming, if she was settling in well and if there was anything she ever needed all she needed to do was ask.

The flight went swimmingly. Mr Walker was journeying to Mexico with some friends and all in all there were six of them on the flight. This was one of the first flights Elodie had been on where it really hadn't felt like work. She found Alex Walker fascinating: he was really charismatic and had an air about him that made her feel instantly comfortable. Mr Bosford had once told her that he was a 'stickler for the rules', which had made Elodie nervous about meeting him, but now he was here in the flesh she felt far more relaxed. He talked about his work, the magazine and all the passion projects close to his heart at length, and Elodie found it very difficult not to admire the man for all that he had done for others. He genuinely seemed like a lovely man. The twelve-hour flight flew by, although not long enough to stop Elodie's feet from hurting. The heels she wore as part of her uniform did pinch after a while. She stood behind the bar and slipped them off, just for a moment of respite.

"I couldn't trouble you for another, could I?" Mr Walker said to Elodie as he approached the bar. Elodie slipped her shoes back on effortlessly and took the glass. Mr Walker had been exclusively drinking soda water and lime, aside from one glass of Champagne, which he had used to toast one of his guests' latest ventures. Elodie poured his drink and handed the glass back to him. He took a sip and thanked her.

"Is there anything you'd change?" he asked out of the blue.

Elodie's first thought was that at that particular moment there were a lot of things she'd change, but she didn't think he was speaking about her personal life.

"I'm sorry?" she asked politely.

"About Alpha Whiskey. I'm always keen for suggestions. After all, it's you guys that make the company what it is," he said warmly.

Elodie thought hard. She hadn't been there that long and certainly wasn't in a position to criticise the company. Maybe Mr Walker wanted reassurance about his company in the same way she had wanted it about her relationship.

"I don't think so, all the staff get on well, the passengers are always happy and on a personal note I'm extremely grateful for all the incredible experiences offered to me here," she replied.

"The experiences are amazing, aren't they?" Mr Walker echoed. Elodie nodded; of that there was no denying. "Well, how about if I offer you one more?"

Elodie raised her eyebrow, not entirely sure what he was

getting at but hoping beyond hope that it wasn't anything dodgy.

"I'm not sure what you mean," she said truthfully.

Mr Walker was quiet for a moment and then, to Elodie's amazement, produced an envelope from his breast pocket.

"I keep a few on me. You never know who you might meet in my line of work." He opened the envelope and several crisp white tickets with gold leaf writing on peeked out. He plucked out one ticket and handed it to Elodie.

"Here you go, keep this safe. It's a top-tier ticket. That means VIP admission, Champagne, goody bags and access to every part of the show. They don't come better than that, so look after it and don't go showing it off; otherwise, everyone will want one." He smiled warmly when he saw that she was lost for words.

"I can't believe it, I thought you only gave these out as rewards or something?"

"I give them out to people who I think could use it. No offence, but despite the top-notch service and Hollywood smile, I think you look a little sad. Hopefully, this will go some way to cheering you up."

He raised his glass at Elodie and turned to rejoin his companions. Elodie honestly felt as though she could cry. She opened the drawer behind the bar and vowed to keep it safe, hardly daring to believe her luck. She felt so undeserving, but extremely grateful.

They landed a little while later. Elodie had stowed the prized ticket in a drawer behind the bar for safekeeping, not wanting to leave lying about and risk it getting dog-eared. Both she and Gareth waved the guests off the plane before readying themselves for departure. They had just one night in Mexico before they returned home. Elodie was halfway down the steps when she realised that she'd forgotten the ticket that Mr Walker had given her on board. She made an excuse to Gareth and turned on her heel to retrieve it. She had been the last to leave, so the plane was deserted and eerily quiet. She walked to the bar area, opened the drawer where she had hidden the ticket and accidentally dropped it to the floor. She bent down to pick it up and suddenly heard a voice, small at first but growing louder. Elodie wasn't sure why, but she stayed crouched down behind the bar, in an effort to go unnoticed.

"I'm here for one night and one night only." She heard the unmistakable tones of Chase echoing around the plane. "Oh come on, I've missed you. Look, let me send a car for you, where are you staying?" He paused as the person, Elodie assumed a woman, replied. "You want to go for a drink first? Jeez, I'd love to but I'm really tied up with work at the moment, it'll probably be late when I get in. But you're the first person I thought of, the only person. Tara, babe, I've missed you. I need to be honest with you, I know I played things terribly but, honestly, it's you that I want. Things were just so much better when you were by my side. Look, don't say no, just think about it."

Chase finished his conversation and Elodie felt him moving closer towards the bar, towards her. She braced herself, preparing to be discovered at any moment. She heard him lean against the bar; she could almost feel him hovering over her and then he spoke again.

"Did I wake you?" he said softly. Elodie was confused, had he seen her? Did he think she was taking a quick nap or something? "I've been thinking, I think you need to give me another shot. I can't stop thinking about you. Come on, I'll be home tomorrow. Let me take you out, treat you like the princess you are."

Elodie realised he was on the phone again, to someone else this time. Someone back home by the sounds of it.

"Come on, I screwed up, I admit it, but it's you that I want, Jess, please. I've got the next fortnight off work and I want to spoil you. I've been thinking and things were just so much better with you by my side, it's you I want. Look, I've got a new car and I'd love to take you for a spin. Come on Jess, baby, please. Let me send a cab for you." There was another pause. "That's my good girl."

He wrapped up the call and Elodie heard the sound of ice dropping into a glass. Elodie chanced it and glanced upwards; she saw his arm reach out above her and grab a bottle of whisky from a nearby shelf. She heard the glug of the liquid being poured and could do nothing but listen as he knocked one back and then another. Elodie could feel the backs of her legs beginning to burn under the strain of the uncomfortable position she found herself in. Heart pounding, she let out a near-silent sigh.

'*Tara and Jess?*' she thought. She hadn't a clue who Tara was – clearly, someone else caught in the whirlwind of Chase – but Jess, she knew who Jess was. Chase must have been whom she was talking to that night they met up for a drink. The guy who was a bit weird, who was messing her about. Elodie was surprised to feel, not hurt, but anger. How dare he treat women like this? Elodie could have kicked herself there and then. How had she not seen him for what he was? She knew why, of course: she had chosen not to. She had seen what she wanted to. She'd seen success, his good looks, his charm and, more than anything, she'd been swayed by how he made her feel: wanted, desired and incredibly sexy.

'*Oh God,*' she thought, '*he's played me. Carla and Steph were right.*'

She had the fleeting sensation that she needed to have it out with him, to spit him a few home truths and let him know what she now thought of him. Angry tears burnt her eyes; she rubbed them, determined not to shed one here on his account. But the more she thought about it, the more she felt differently: why should she give him the satisfaction? Chase seemed to thrive on female attention. Why should she give him any more of it? She had a strong urge to call Jessica, to show female solidarity and to warn her not to get back into bed with Chase. What was it she had said at the bar? '*If he calls I come running, I can't help myself.*' Elodie felt an unpleasant cocktail bubble inside her: hurt, with a dash of anger, a splash of humiliation and garnished with a wedge of shame.

She heard Chase's glass clink as it was set down on the bar and his footsteps fade as he left. She waited a few moments, her heart beating fast. She didn't know what to do. Should she phone Jess and warn her? Should she mind her own business? There were pros and cons to both. She stood up and, picking up a new glass, poured herself a measure of whisky before knocking it back. She was going to need a little Dutch courage to break the news to Jessica.

The phone call with Jess didn't go well. At first, Jess had

denied any involvement with Chase; she'd laughed it off and told Elodie she was being crazy. Then, when Elodie pressed her, she retracted her earlier sentiments and said that it was none of Elodie's business and finally resorted to telling her that Chase had told Jess everything. About how Elodie was practically stalking him, gate-crashing private dinners and turning up to his house with a suitcase. By the end of it, Jess had painted Elodie as some tragic woman, obsessed with an older man and whose jealousy had led her down a dark path where she was determined to slander Chase to anyone who would listen.

Elodie had been in total shock. How could he twist things so much and, moreover, how could Jess believe him? Elodie had tried to explain, but Jess just wouldn't listen. Eventually, Jess had hung up the phone and Elodie had stared at hers in disbelief.

She let out a low sigh. She had less than twenty-four hours in Mexico and she would be damned if Chase was going to spoil them. Elodie felt very alone as she disembarked. She wanted to tell Carla and Steph what she had overheard but she just couldn't. Her stupid pride had been hurt and she was still smarting from it. Elodie thought that maybe being on her own wouldn't be that bad. Some alone time might be just what she needed. She headed off to her hotel; she was going to use this time to think things through, to really try and figure out what she wanted. She spent the night completely by herself: she switched her phone off and made the most of the hotels fabulous facilities. She took herself swimming, choosing the indoor pool as there was less chance of bumping into anyone there, and had an in-room facial provided by the spa team, which was nothing but heavenly. She enjoyed a quiet bubble bath in absolute silence and later watched an old black and white Hollywood film that made her cry. She went to bed that night feeling that she may have squandered the opportunity to see Mexico, but she had made the most of her chance to spend some time with herself. As Elodie fell to sleep she couldn't stop her mind from wandering to Jessica. She really hoped that Jess wouldn't fall into Chase's mantrap again.

'Why wouldn't she listen to me. God, it's so annoying when

311

someone won't let you explain yourself,' she mused as she let sleep claim her.

Elodie managed to successfully avoid everyone the following day – everyone, apart from Mr Walker, who was walking behind her when he saw her dive behind a large cactus-laden plant pot in the main concourse of Mexico City Airport in order to avoid a run-in with Chase.

"What are we hiding from?" he asked sidling up next to her, a bemused smile on his face.

"Mr Walker! Oh, nothing. I was just, errr, I was just getting something from my shoe, a pebble," she said lamely, standing up and wiggling her foot about as though she had just relieved herself of some discomfort. "What are you doing here? I thought you were staying in Mexico."

"I was." Mr Walker looked at her as though maybe she had overstepped her mark, but continued anyway. "Something's come up and I need to get back home, so I'm hitching a ride with you guys – if that's OK with you, that is?"

Elodie blushed; she hadn't meant to sound impertinent, she was just shocked to see him especially since he'd discovered her crouching behind a plant pot. Elodie watched him disappear towards the private lounge area. Once he was out of sight she gave the place one last look around and, when she was sure it was clear, headed off to security so she could board the plane. Gareth was already on board, clipboard in hand checking off all the jobs that needed to be done before passengers could board.

"OK, we're almost ready. You can retrieve Mr Walker now, hun," Gareth said, smoothing down his uniform. His voice was strangely tense.

"You OK?" Elodie asked, putting her hand on his shoulder. Gareth looked at her and shrugged her off.

"I'm fine. It's just that, well, this could be it, couldn't it? You know, Mr Walker seeing how valuable I am, finally. I think he's flying back on purpose, to give me a ticket to the gala."

Elodie smiled uncertainly. How could she tell Gareth that she'd already been given one? She decided that she wouldn't and instead wished him luck and left to escort Mr Walker onto the flight.

Feeling a touch guilty about being given one of the much-coveted tickets, Elodie went above and beyond: anything Gareth wanted she did without question and anything he needed she sought to find and, to top it all off, she even managed to big him up a little bit to Mr Walker. She hoped Gareth would get a ticket, she really did, and was going to help in any way she could to make his wish come true.

The flight passed without incident and Elodie found that Mr Walker, when flying solo, was even more pleasant to be around. He chatted with them jovially between bouts of work and seemed to really take an interest in their well-being. Elodie felt extremely lucky to have a boss like him. Midway through the flight, he caught her stifling a yawn and suggested she make use of the bedroom. Elodie must have given him a look because he immediately burst out laughing, apologised and clarified that if she needed to rest, she was more than welcome to. The rest of the flight passed and before long Chase had announced that they were in descent. Elodie had managed to keep him from her thoughts up until that moment, but couldn't help reacting when his smooth voice rang over the address system. Elodie had gained some perspective in the short time she'd been away. She knew she needed to make things up with Carla and Steph. She knew that Chase was bad news, and the sneaking suspicion that she needed to apologise to Aaron had begun to plague her in the back of her mind. The way Jess had reacted to her had mirrored how she had reacted to Aaron, and the frustration she had felt would have been only a fraction of what Aaron had experienced. It was then that Elodie was struck with an idea. It was a long shot, but it might go some way to making things right between them all.

Alpha Whiskey's Boeing Business Jet touched down at Langley late afternoon. Elodie left feeling extremely pleased with herself. Her plan hadn't exactly gone off without a hitch. Alex Walker had reacted with incredulity at first and even after much explaining and a touch of begging was still firmly stuck on *'no'* as the answer to her question.

"You don't want much, do you?" he had asked. "I'm sorry Elodie, but I don't just hand out tickets at random."

"OK, well how about just one more? That way I can give

them both to my friends. They won't hate me anymore and I'll just stay at home."

Mr Walker looked at her quizzically and cocked his head to the side as he ran a hand down the side of his face.

"I would love to help, but there are other people more deserving. I'm sorry." He gave her an apologetic glance before leaving the plane.

Elodie stood there at a loss. She had been so sure his good nature would bend in her favour. She sighed, knowing of course that he was right. It was completely unfair to ask for three tickets to the gala, especially since she'd been downright lucky to secure one in the first place. She realised then and there that she must have appeared so ungrateful. Elodie disembarked feeling diminished. She was concerned that her request bordered on impertinence and worried that maybe it would have ramifications of a negative persuasion.

'Why can't you just keep your big mouth shut?' she scolded herself.

Inside the terminal, Mr Walker was chatting to someone that Elodie didn't recognise. She hung back, desperate to make amends and put herself back in his good books. The two men shook hands and parted, this was it, so Elodie took her chance.

"Mr Walker?" she said as she paced over to him, "I want to apologise, I should never have asked. It was so rude and entitled and I just want to say sorry."

"You shouldn't be sorry for looking out for your friends, but you need to be a bit careful about people taking advantage. They're not the first pals to try and get a free ticket."

"Oh no, they haven't asked," Elodie said with surprise. She thought she'd explained everything back on the plane but realised that in her desperation, her story had come out as more of a jumble than a cohesive tale. "I did something terrible and I want to make it up to them. I'd do anything to make it up to them."

Alex Walker surveyed her and rubbed his chin, but said nothing. All Elodie could do was wait. She hoped he could feel how sincere she was, how much she wanted this and not for herself but for her friends.

"Alright then, but this might make you unpopular." He

opened up his jacket and retrieved another two tickets. "Now promise me you won't go shouting about this, I don't want to get accused of favouritism but, I'm a sucker for a person in need, plus anyone who'd be willing to forgo the event for her friends is either a very good person or crazy... and I don't think you're crazy."

Elodie couldn't believe it: the tickets were in her hand. She stared at them. The gold lettering glinted as she turned them over, hardly able to believe her luck.

"I don't know what to say," she began.

Mr Walker put a hand on her shoulder and smiled.

"You don't need to say anything, I can see how much they mean to you."

"Thank you," Elodie managed, "I can't believe it."

She stood there, completely dumbstruck as Alex Walker bade her farewell and, with a warm smile, walked off.

Elodie was thunderstruck. She floated through Langley, eager to get home and share her news. She was so thankful that after some explaining, negotiation and perhaps a touch of desperation, she had managed to pull it off. Her suspicions about Mr Walker had been right: he was a *very* nice man.

On her journey home she rang both of them, twice, wanting to make sure they were both together and waiting when she got back. Neither of them answered her call so she left them voicemails as a last resort and just hoped that they would pick them up before her homeward journey came to an end. She walked through the door with a giant smile on her face, unable to hide just how happy she was. Her smile didn't last long; the flat was empty. She called for both of them, but they weren't there.

"Shit, they're not here," Elodie said aloud to her empty flat.

She tried them both again but neither picked up when she had tried phoning. A horrible feeling began to creep over Elodie that maybe things wouldn't just go back to normal as easily as she wished.

'But they're my best friends, they have to forgive me,' she hoped.

Elodie poured herself a glass of wine and spent the

evening watching telly. She flicked through the channels aimlessly without taking in any of what she viewed, her attention divided. The time ticked by and Elodie couldn't help but wonder where on earth they were. She got the feeling they were purposefully avoiding and ignoring her and dodging her calls. Elodie sighed: had her actions really been that bad? Elodie knew deep down that her words had been really hurtful, and that they had cut the pair deeply. But more than anything, she knew that abandoning Steph on her birthday, or rather not even thinking about her whilst she was with Chase, had been a really, really shitty thing to do. She had every intention of thoroughly apologising; she needed to say the words to them and for them to hear how truly sorry she was. She had an idea that it might take an extra-special something to make it up to them, a grand gesture of sorts, Elodie cast her eye to the envelope Mr Walker had given her.

'*Well, if this doesn't do it, nothing will.*' All she needed to do now was to get them all together, offer a heartfelt apology and unveil her surprise.

To Elodie's dismay, she was called in to work. Gareth was sick and there was no one else to cover at such short notice. Elodie, still keen to impress, agreed to go in without hesitation. The deal was sweetened slightly by the fact that their destination was Bermuda, a place Elodie had longed to visit since she was a child. She knew Chase wouldn't be there; she had overheard him tell Jessica, or had it been Tara, that he had the next fortnight off work. She shuddered as she remembered the creepy way in which he'd tried to entice both of them, one after the other, with the same line. Elodie would be away for a week; her plan was going to have to be put on hold. She wanted to do this face-to-face. A text or call simply wouldn't suffice.

Elodie boarded the flight to Bermuda feeling uneasy. Time was slipping through her fingers like sand. As much as she was looking forward to this trip, she couldn't shake the feeling that she would enjoy it so much more knowing that she, Steph and Carla were back on good terms.

"So, do you know what's the matter with Gareth?" Elodie asked after a couple of hours. Grace turned to her and told her that it wasn't professional to gossip about other crew member's health. "I wasn't," Elodie said, a little flustered. "I was just asking after him, he's my friend and I just…"

"Sorry," Grace said suddenly, "I've just had a rough few weeks. It's not your fault. I know you didn't mean anything by it."

Elodie stared. She opened her mouth to say something but couldn't find any words. Had Grace just apologised to her? Was this the olive branch that Elodie craved? Elodie didn't know what to say, so she did the only thing she could think of, she smiled.

Elodie stepped off the plane and onto the tarmac at Bermuda's L. F. Wade International Airport feeling good. She was sure Grace was beginning to warm to her and that feeling put a spring in her step. Elodie had been the last of the plane, relieving Grace so she could leave a little earlier.

Elodie headed outside to wait for her car. They were staying in the Clear View Hotel and Elodie couldn't wait to get there, unpack and enjoy a little luxury for a few days. The sliding doors opened and Elodie smiled as she felt the sun on her skin. She was surprised to see Grace still standing outside, a stony look on her face. Her arms were crossed over her chest and her foot tapped impatiently.

"Everything OK?" Elodie asked.

"Fine," Grace said curtly, "There's been a mix-up and I don't have a car, so now I'm waiting for a taxi but they've said it'll be at least half an hour. I've done back-to-backs non-stop and I'm shattered. Ugh! All I want to do is go and lie down."

"You can share my car if you like?" Elodie offered.

Grace looked at her, a curious expression on her face. It was as though Elodie had just done her a great kindness and she couldn't quite believe it.

"If you're sure?" Grace asked. Elodie nodded enthusiastically.

The two women waited for a few moments before the car arrived. Elodie climbed into the back alongside Grace and the car set off. Elodie marvelled as they drove: Clear View was only a short drive away but it was the best short drive of Elodie's life. They traversed a beautiful stone bridge, which took them from the airport to the main part of the island. Elodie gasped at the view. The calm sea looked to Elodie like a glistening sapphire, so rich in colour that it almost didn't look real. She dug around in her bag and took out her phone: she absolutely needed pictures of this.

"Do you always act like a tourist wherever you go?" Grace asked.

"I am a tourist," Elodie replied, grinning. "Oh come on, even if I saw this every single day I'd never tire of it."

"It *is* pretty spectacular." Grace conceded.

Elodie took several pictures before setting her phone down. She didn't want to be one of those people who only experienced things through the eye of a lens. She wanted memories of her own, to be able to close her eyes and recall the feeling of experiencing these things with her own eyes.

"Aaron really liked you, you know," Grace said suddenly.

Elodie turned her head sharply and stared at her, wondering where on earth that had come from.

"And I really liked him," Elodie said carefully, "when I thought he was single. Look, I know things between the two of us have always been a bit rocky and I know that's my fault in a way, but I genuinely didn't go after him. I didn't know he was seeing someone and if I did, well, I wouldn't have gone anywhere near him. I'm genuinely not that kind of girl."

"Seeing someone?" Grace quizzed.

"OK, sorry, had a girlfriend. More than seeing someone, I don't know. Sorry… you, you just make me nervous," Elodie said defensively.

Grace raised her eyebrow and turned to look out of the window. Elodie sighed. *'Just when I thought things were starting to go well,'* she thought mournfully.

The car pulled to a stop outside Clear View and Elodie got out. The air was thick and warm outside of the car, but even so Elodie suddenly felt as though she could breathe far easier. Grace grabbed her suitcase in record time and was off to check in before Elodie had time to blink.

The car journey had been a confusing one. If Grace and Aaron were a couple, then why would Grace say that he had liked her? Was it a sort of trap? A way to see what had really happened between them on their ill-fated date? Elodie couldn't make head nor tail of it – it just didn't make sense.

She checked in, was given her key card and headed up to her room. The room was simply furnished, clean and entirely unremarkable. What took Elodie's breath away was what was outside. She pulled the balcony doors open and let out a low, impressed sigh. The view was spectacular. She cast her eyes down towards the white sandy beach and calm turquoise waters; above was crystal-clear blue sky that stretched as far as the eye could see. It was incredibly hot. Elodie stripped out of her work uniform; the cream pencil dress fell to the floor and she stepped out of it. She was desperate for a shower, as the flight had been almost eight hours and the passengers had definitely erred on the more demanding side.

Elodie had just stepped out of the bathroom when there was a knock at the door.

"Just a second," she called, as she roughly dried herself before slipping into a large cotton robe that had been hanging on the bathroom door. She padded across the room and opened the door.

"Can I come in?" It was Grace, stood there with a bottle of bubbly in one hand and two glasses in the other. "I wasn't sure what to bring and figured that everyone likes a bottle of bubbly."

Elodie stepped aside to let her in. She was in shock: Grace was the last person she had expected to pay her a visit.

"Hi. Errr, is everything OK?' Elodie managed.

"I think we need to talk, and I think you'll want a glass of this whilst we do." Grace handed the bottle to Elodie and marched herself across the room. She lifted the latch on the door to the balcony and settled herself on the balcony. "Come on then," she called from outside, "I don't have all evening."

Elodie poured the Champagne into two tumblers she found in the bathroom and the two women sat out on the balcony together in complete silence for several long moments.

"So what is it we need to talk about?" Elodie asked, taking a sip of the crisp Champagne and savouring the taste.

"The whole sordid affair," Grace said curtly. Elodie wasn't entirely sure what she was getting at but thought she better let Grace speak; she wasn't exactly famed for her long fuse. "Your little love triangle, you know… you and Aaron, you and Chase."

"Look, it's like I said before, I'm sorry, I…"

"Didn't know. Yes, yes, I know you didn't know, because there was nothing *to* know. Aaron and I aren't together, we never have been. Christ, Elodie, don't be so naïve. Aaron is a lovely guy who I've known for a really long time and if you'd only listened to him and treated him with a bit more respect you could have had something really good. But instead, you binned him off and went for Chase. God knows where you got the idea that we were together."

"Well, I saw you guys laughing and then Chase told me, well as good as. He said that Aaron was a bit of a lad's lad, that he didn't so much have a girlfriend, more like girl-friends. He…"

"And you believed him? What reason on God's green earth could he possibly have to lie to you? Elodie, *he's* the lad's lad, he's the one with the girlfriends, and he thought that if he poisoned you against Aaron you would be free for the taking. It's all a competition for him and you were the prize." Grace took a deep breath. "Look, I don't want to carry on this weird tension. It's doing neither of us any good and, as I've gotten to know you better, I can see that you're not like the other women he's been with, you're not an idiot, you're not money-grabbing or trying to sleep your way to the top. You're just naïve. You actually liked him, didn't you?"

Elodie said nothing: this was a lot to take in in a short space of time. She looked out to sea, the horizon suddenly looking like a very inviting place.

"But… it's not just Chase's version of events that made me think that Aaron was no good, there was a picture too," Elodie said, her mind racing back to the two shadows cosied up to one another.

"What picture?" Grace asked as she furrowed her brow.

Elodie explained to Grace how she and Carla had done a bit of online detective work, albeit it with slightly flushed cheeks. When she had finished Grace inhaled and, taking out her phone, said nothing. She tapped at the screen; her eyes narrowed and she wore a look of dogged determination on her face.

"Ah! here," she said, brandishing the phone towards Elodie. Elodie took it from her and felt a little wave of sadness as her eyes fell onto the very picture that had sown the seeds of doubt in the first place. "Elodie, look at the next photo."

Elodie swiped and saw that the next upload was one of a delicious-looking fry-up, posted the following day.

"I don't understand..." Elodie said, utterly perplexed. How was a picture of beans and bacon proof of anything?

"Oh, Jesus, read the post," Grace said, impatience creeping into her voice. Elodie's eyes drifted downwards and as they did so her stomach lurched.

Great couple of days with my sister, one of the most amazing women I know. Breakfast, courtesy of The Pig and Bear pub, was amazing!

"So, Aaron was telling me the truth, the entire time?" Elodie asked with dawning comprehension. "Oh, I feel so awful. I'd never let him speak. Ugh, and Chase was lying to me, about everything?"

Grace nodded.

"Chase wouldn't know the truth if it hit him in the face. It's who he is, Elodie, he's a user. He thrives on new and shiny things, women included. He tricks you, uses you and then when he's done, acts like you never even existed, like you're the one with the problem, like you're crazy." Elodie noted a touch of sadness in Grace's voice.

"Grace, did you and Chase...?"

Grace nodded again.

"We got together a long time ago now, long enough for me to be over it, not long enough for me to be happy about it still happening right under my nose. I was naïve; it was my first proper relationship, at least that's what I thought it was. Months and months he kept me hanging on. By the end of it, I didn't know whether I was coming or going. I almost handed my notice in, you know? But something about it wasn't right. Why should I go? Why should he get to win? So I decided to stay, to remain professional and to learn a lesson. When I saw, or rather sensed, things going on between the two of you, I couldn't take it. Not because I was jealous, don't labour under that illusion. It was because I couldn't stand to see it happening again, and then when you treated Aaron so badly, I figured that *'you deserve what you get'*. Like I said, Aaron's a good friend and my loyalties lie firmly with him. But, as time went on and I got to know you, well… I figured you weren't the type of girl who used and abused people, and judging by the look on your face right now, I was right."

Elodie was shaken. She felt really silly, stupid even. She had been so certain Chase was the good guy in all of this. She knew he was a player, the conversations she'd overheard had proved that, but never had she had him down as someone who would poison her mind. She wondered just how many other women he had done this to, how many others there were feeling bad about themselves and not understanding why. He was a master of manipulation. Elodie felt a wave of rage swell within; she slammed her glass down and stalked back towards the bedroom.

"You can't do anything about it, Elodie, he's too clever for that. Besides, going off the handle only makes you look bad. Trust me, I've learnt the hard way that it's better to leave some things, and some people, well alone. You should take comfort in the fact that he's the one suffering. He's miserable, Elodie: he hates himself and uses women like us in an attempt to distract himself from that. So, take my advice and leave it."

"Like you did, you mean?" Elodie whipped around, staring at Grace. "Leave it so that the next girl gets humiliated, gets her heart broken? I'm not like you, Grace, I can't do that. You may have kept your distance from me because of how I treated Aaron and, to be honest, I don't blame you, but part of you must have known that you should say something."

"Elodie," Grace said calmly, "if I had, would you have believed me? Or, do you think Chase would have told you about me and him, said that I still had a thing for him and that I was trying to turn you against him?"

Elodie tried to think, but her mind was foggy. She felt as though the last few months had been totally wasted, that she had ruined any chance she had had with Aaron and that above and beyond anything else, she had ruined things with her two best friends, over a worthless guy. She slumped down and rubbed her temples. She was going to ring him, she wanted to hear it from the horse's mouth, she should have confronted him when she'd overheard him trying to line up women, but she didn't. She couldn't let this slide, she had to have her say. If anything, just telling him what she thought of him would be cathartic.

"You're right, I know you are," Elodie said, lifting her gaze to meet Grace's. "I just can't let it go, I've got to say something to him. He needs to know that what he does to people has consequences."

"Not so meek and mild as you'd have people believe, eh?" Grace said, solemnly pouring two more glasses from the bottle. "There's nothing you, or I, can do about him. I tried once before. He has, well, I guess you'd call it evidence against me. He's threatened to show the world if I make things difficult for him. So I have no choice but to leave it, be the bigger person."

"What an absolute pig," Elodie replied, knowing full well exactly what it was Grace meant by *'evidence'*. They sipped their drinks in silence for some time, the steady, unrelenting wash of the ocean the only sound to mar the disquiet.

"To answer your earlier question, Gareth's fine. Well, he's not but he will be," Grace said finally.

"What do you mean?" Elodie asked confusedly, "he's either ill or he isn't."

"He's taken some time off, had a bit of a meltdown. He had his hopes pinned on going to Mr Walker's gala. They're these big, posh parties, you see. Packed with famous people, models, film stars, photographers, that kind of thing. They have art exhibitions and instalments. I've never been, but I've seen pictures. They do look pretty spectacular, and if I got invited, of course I'd go, but I'm not about to go and throw myself off a bridge because I didn't get a golden ticket.

Gareth has been hankering after an invitation for years, but it's never happened. I think he's just too keen. He's never taken it quite as badly before, though. I think he really felt like he'd paid his dues and deserved a reward of some kind. But no, he practically begged Mr Walker but he wasn't budging, he said there were only a certain number of invites and that maybe next time he'd get one."

Elodie felt a pang of guilt,

'Poor Gareth,' she thought sadly, feeling incredibly guilty that she had not one, not two, but three of them at home.

"So he rang in sick?" Elodie asked, unable to believe it of Gareth; he was a staunch professional through and through.

"I just think he's very hurt and felt as though he'd show them how valuable he really is through his absence. Don't say anything, though: the official line is that he has the flu."

Elodie agreed to keep it to herself, although somewhat absentmindedly as she couldn't shake the unsettling feeling creeping over her that she'd had one huge load of information dumped on her and taking it all in was proving to be easier said than done.

"Thanks, Elodie, it's been nice getting to know you properly and I'm sorry for the way I behaved. There I was, mad at you for not hearing Aaron out, when I didn't extend you the same courtesy," Grace said as the dregs of their glasses were emptied.

Elodie shook her head and waved Grace's apology away: she would have done the exact same thing if it were someone treating one of her friends badly. The thought of them made her wince. She still had that problem to deal with as well.

Elodie went to bed that night feeling as though she had the weight of the world on her shoulders. As she lay her head down, her mind raced. If she hadn't been so naïve, so headstrong and so stubborn things could have been so different. She had been so determined to be her own woman after her break-up with Tom that she turned a blind eye to all the warning signs. She had convinced herself that they were challenges to overcome, not reasons to turn and run. She argued with herself for most of the night, swinging back and forth between what she'd done and what she should have done. She toyed with the idea of quitting her job, of finding something else, something with better people. She sighed, knowing full well that even if the people were better, the prospects wouldn't be. Alpha Whiskey offered her everything she ever wanted: a great wage, great places and great perks. She thought about the gala, about poor Gareth, who'd been so excited to go and who had been so sure that this time he would secure an invitation. A knot tightened in the pit of Elodie's stomach.

She rolled over and tried to get to sleep, but no matter how exhausted her body was her mind wouldn't let her drift, each time dragging her back to consciousness. Questions plagued her. Should she call Chase? Should she speak to Aaron? Before any of this, should she make amends with her friends? Eventually, the gentle grip of sleep tightened and she found herself in the middle of a dream. Fractured memories plagued her latent thoughts: it would seem that no matter her conscious state, she couldn't escape her recent past.

Elodie awoke the next morning feeling far from refreshed. She looked in the mirror and could swear she'd aged ten years overnight. Her eyes looked puffy and her brow furrowed. Never before had she felt so bad about herself. It was as though Grace's words had been a form of slow poison: the longer they had been said, the stronger Elodie felt them.

After washing, Elodie slung her hair into a low ponytail, lathered on sunscreen, packed a beach bag and took two Paracetamol; she'd woken up with a bad head and didn't want it to spoil her day. Heading out to sunbathe Elodie figured that wallowing on the beach was a far better option than wallowing in her bed, so she settled herself in a quiet spot next to a parasol. The beach wasn't overly populated. The majority of tourists had packed up and gone home; October was technically out of season, after all. Elodie was grateful for it. The last thing she felt like doing was navigating a beach packed full of pasty sun-seekers, even though she was technically one of them. She held the corners of her beach towel, a bright blue one she had bought in the airport whilst working for Zip Air, and unravelled it with the flick of her wrists. She climbed on top and closed her eyes. The sun, although it was barely mid-morning, beat down heavily, and Elodie let out a contented sigh as she felt the previous evenings disquiet begin to ebb as the sound of the sea lapped soothingly in the background.

Elodie opened her eyes. Judging by the tingling she felt all over, she knew that the protective shade in which she had lain had long gone, and the ache in her head told her that she had had too much sun and not enough water. She dragged herself up, rummaged in her bag for the bottle of water she'd stowed earlier and downed it in one. Gazing around the beach through squinted eyes, she saw that the majority of its inhabitants were couples, all of whom were enthralled in each other's company. Elodie suddenly felt as though she stuck out like a sore thumb: she was the only person as far as she could see flying solo. She moved the parasol round so that she was once again in its welcoming shade, catching the eye of a tanned woman rubbing sunscreen onto her partner's back as she did so. Elodie thought that there was a look of pity on the woman's face. Elodie looked away and, although it should have been impossible, felt her cheeks flush pink. Deciding that she'd had enough sun for one day, she gathered up her belongings and headed back to the hotel, not entirely sure as to what she should do for the rest of the afternoon.

'The rest of the week, even,' Elodie thought to herself solemnly. Here she was in absolute paradise, and all she could think about was how lonely she felt and how she wished more than anything to be back at her flat and on good terms again with Carla and Steph. There was something else as well: a small something, deep in the recess of her mind. This something was named Aaron. She still felt terrible about how she had treated him; even more so now. She kicked herself, not for the first time, about the whole situation. Looking back on it now, she felt foolish, immature and a little desperate. How on earth had she allowed Chase to lead her on like that? She thought back on everything that had happened between them, on how he had run hot, then cold, then bloody freezing, time and time again. Each and every time Elodie would excuse his behaviour. Letting out a low, discontented groan, she vowed never again to ignore the advice of her friends, ever again. With her head thick from the sun and feelings of nausea beginning to wash over her Elodie decided that a cool shower and a nap were exactly what she needed.

She climbed on top of the crisp white sheets, her hair still wet from the shower, and closed her eyes. Her headache had intensified: her temples throbbed and the late afternoon light stung her eyes. She pulled the duvet over her head and found that she had drifted into a deep sleep before the cover had fully settled over her.

Elodie cracked one eye open and squinted. Her head still throbbed, but now her bladder did too. She dragged herself from her bed and went to the bathroom. She had left her watch on the side of the sink when she had taken her shower; she picked it up and checked the time. Puzzled, Elodie wiped her eyes and looked again. That couldn't be right. The watch's face showed the time to be seven pm, but it couldn't be: Elodie felt as though she'd been asleep for hours, plural. She set the watch back down, climbed back into bed and tried to commit to memory the fact that she would need a new watch battery sorting upon her return.

A loud banging awoke Elodie from her slumber, she groaned – someone was at the door. Cursing, Elodie extricated herself from the tangle of bed sheets and went to see what all the fuss was about.

"Grace?" she asked in a voice thick from sleep. Grace stood at the threshold, hands on her hips and a furrow in her brow.

"Are you alright?" she asked, surveying Elodie with a look somewhere between concern and apprehension.

Elodie rubbed her eyes and nodded.

"Why wouldn't I be?" she asked confusedly, although she had to admit she really didn't feel that good.

"Because you've not been seen for an entire day, you haven't been answering your phone and I've knocked at your door twice. If you hadn't answered this time I was going to have to knock the damn thing down."

It took Elodie a moment to reconcile with what Grace was saying: she'd been asleep for longer than she'd thought, a lot longer in fact.

"I don't know. I had a horrible headache and just went

to bed. I did feel a bit sick but didn't think anything of it. I woke up once, just thought that my watch had stopped or something."

Grace let out a sigh of relief and walked inside. She poured Elodie a large glass of water, handed it over to her and instructed her to drink.

"I think you've got sunstroke. Come on, Elodie, you've been doing this long enough now to know that you stay hydrated, stay in the shade and if you're pale, wear factor fifty. Jesus, I'm half Nigerian and even I wear sunscreen," she scolded.

Elodie downed the cool water, not realising how thirsty she was until the liquid hit the back of her throat. She never thought she'd ever be grateful for Grace, and marvelled at how much could change in such a short space of time.

"I think I better stay inside today," Elodie said as she set the empty glass down on the side. "I'm still not feeling one hundred per cent."

To Elodie's surprise, Grace erupted in a broad grin.

"I thought that might be the case," she said, reaching into her bag and pulling out a pack of playing cards, a couple of magazines and a sharing-size bag of salt and vinegar crisps. "Fancy it?"

Elodie nodded, not entirely sure that she did fancy it, but not wanting to offend Grace, especially since it had only been a matter of days since they'd made amends and become friends.

It was amazing how quickly time flew. Grace taught Elodie several card games and Elodie discovered that she had a natural talent for a little known Israeli card game called Yaniv, which Grace had learned on her travels. The two women chatted amiably and Elodie quickly found that the topic of conversation, as she suspected it might, turned to Chase. Elodie knew they were covering old ground but still couldn't help herself from going over it all again and again. Elodie found herself sharing with Grace details of her home life, of Carla and Steph and how they had helped her career change and generally been there for her from the word go.

"They sound like great friends," Grace said, as the evening drew to a close.

"The best," Elodie concurred. A wave of guilt, furnished with sadness, washed over her.

The day had drawn to a close and Grace got up and collected her things. Elodie gave her new friend a hug and thanked her for the day. She readied herself for bed and Grace's final phrase echoed in her head. Carla and Steph really were the best, and yet Elodie hadn't spoken to them properly in what seemed like forever. They had left things on such a sour note and Elodie knew that the blame for that lay squarely at her door. She had been so wrapped up in Chase, so adamant that he was the one for her that she hadn't been able to bear the truth of it all, no matter how plain it was to see and no matter how gently Steph and Carla had tried to open her eyes. Elodie vowed to make it up to them. She still had one card up her sleeve; and hopefully, this card would see her win the game.

CHAPTER 18

TOUCHING DOWN ON HOME SOIL, ELODIE WON-
dered if her plan would work, if everything would go back
to how it was. Or, if the things she had said and the way she
had acted had done irreparable damage. She whole-heartedly hoped for the former. Her last few days in Bermuda
had been exquisite: she had visited the Crystal Caves, the
museums and had spent a lot of time relaxing in Horseshoe
Bay. Grace had accompanied her on a few excursions but for
some reason wasn't as enthused about sightseeing as Elodie
was.

"Ladies and gentlemen, this is your captain speaking.
Thank you for choosing Alpha Whiskey Air, we wish you
a safe onward journey. You are now free to disembark the
aircraft at your leisure."

Elodie felt her stomach lurch. There was no going back
now. She was going to have to face the music and just hope
that Steph and Carla would see how truly sorry she was. The
jet would be grounded for just a few hours. After that, it
was bound for New York, as Alex Walker had a huge fashion
campaign to shoot. She decided to give it a quick once-over
and started with the bedroom. It was practically perfect, but
that didn't stop Elodie from checking. She re-emerged and
stopped in her tracks. Aaron was there peering into a brown
envelope that, as Elodie got closer, appeared to be addressed
to none other than their boss, Mr Walker.

"Elodie?" he said with a start, moving the envelope
behind him and mumbling an apology.

"Aaron?" she said uncertainly. "What... what are you
doing?"

"Oh, nothing. I was just..." He trailed off and took a step

backwards, his eyes flitting to the gangway door momentarily.

"Give it here," she said, holding out her hand.

"Elodie you've got it wrong, this is mine, it's..." Aaron began, shifting his weight from one foot to the other.

"Give it to me or I'll have no choice but to report you. I can see that isn't for you. I mean, what are you thinking? You could be fired for this!"

She held out her hand expectantly but Aaron didn't move, his eyes darted towards the open door again and Elodie could see that he was weighing up his options. As he paused thoughtfully, envelope turning slowly in his hands, Elodie saw her chance and took it. She shot towards him and in one swift movement stole the envelope from his hands. She turned it over: she had been right, the envelope was addressed to Mr Walker. She shot Aaron a look and swept off the plane, completely at a loss as to what Aaron could want with a letter addressed to the owner of Alpha Whiskey Air.

Elodie trudged back into the flat a little after five pm that afternoon, although she felt as though the time should have been midnight considering how tired she was. She hadn't phoned Carla to announce her arrival; she wasn't sure why, but she just couldn't bring herself to do it. Carla was there, on the sofa, painting her fingernails. She had reams of toilet tissue crammed between her toes and had her feet hanging over the arm of the sofa. Clearly, these had been painted earlier and were now being left to dry.

"Carla, look I...." Elodie stammered, as Steph entered the living area from the bathroom. Elodie hadn't expected to see them both together.

"I'm glad you're here," Steph said without emotion. "Today's a big day for me and despite the past couple of weeks being a bit shitty, I'd love for you to be there. So what do you say?"

Elodie looked confused. She wasn't sure what to say. She knew she needed to say something, though: both Carla and Steph were staring at her, strange expressions on their faces as if they were scientists examining some strange findings.

"Big day?" Elodie managed. Despite racking her brain, she was none the wiser.

"I knew she wouldn't remember," Steph said to Carla, her voice clipped and matronly.

"Guys, this isn't fair. Remember what?" Elodie pleaded.

"This evening is when Betty hands over the keys to Steph. She asked us to be there for a little celebration. We both said yes," Carla explained icily.

Suddenly the memory flooded back and Elodie was overwhelmed with guilt. This was not how she wanted her peace talks with them to go.

"Oh Steph, I'm so sorry," Elodie said, her voice genuine and thin. Steph looked at her reproachfully but said nothing.

"You need to get your priorities sorted, El. You've been a really weak friend lately," Carla added sternly.

Elodie opened her mouth to argue, but found no rebuttal in her arsenal.

"You forgot my birthday, you had such a go about me not liking Chase, you didn't listen to me about Tom or take notice once with the whole Aaron drama. You haven't even tried to make it up with Carla or me, and now you can't even remember this. Tonight might mean nothing to you and your super high-flying life with celebs and pilot-shagging, but it's a really big deal to me," Steph said, her tone as fiery as her hair. Elodie had never seen Steph upset like this. She looked dejected, as though she had just suffered a great loss.

"I, I…" Elodie stammered, "I'm really sorry," she said, getting up and walking over to Steph. "I know now might not be the exact right time. I had planned to give you this surprise tomorrow, but I think now might be better."

"I don't want a surprise, El, I just want you to be a good friend again," Steph said, fixing Elodie with a resolute stare.

Elodie nodded. Perhaps now wasn't the best time for gift-giving, even if it was meant to prove how sorry she was.

"If you'll still have me I'd love to come," Elodie offered. "That goes for you too, Carla. I am so sorry for being so shitty to you both. I guess I was just a bit obsessed and selfish. I promise to never, ever put a guy ahead of my girls again."

Carla was silent for a moment, she looked from Steph to Elodie with a glazed expression that Elodie wasn't sure how to read.

"We've all been there, I guess. Well, apart from me, obviously," she said with a half-smile after a few, long moments. "If you promise to never, ever let it happen again, then we're cool."

Elodie nodded enthusiastically and then found herself in the midst of an enormous group hug.

"I can't believe how twisted you can get over a guy," Elodie surmised.

The others nodded, finally glad that she could see him for what he was.

"OK, so we've got an hour or so until we're meant to leave. Think you can get ready in that time?" Steph asked.

Elodie said that she could and, dragging her suitcase into her bedroom, shut the door and began to get ready. She suddenly felt lighter than she had done in days, happier and extremely grateful to both of her friends. She pulled herself together in record time; the fatigue she had felt when she'd walked through the door had now been replaced by excitement and gratitude. She was excited for Steph, excited to give them their surprise at a later date and thankful that they had both given her another chance. To some, what had happened might seem small, insignificant in fact; but their bond of friendship hadn't been tested in many years, and when things were usually smooth sailing even the most minuscule crest was felt firmly by the boat.

Considering there would only be the four of them at Steph's honorary inauguration, everyone had made a pretty decent effort. Carla stepped out wearing a cool grey outfit, complete with heeled boots and a dazzlingly bright clutch bag. Steph looked, as usual, effortlessly sophisticated in cream, and Elodie had opted for a blue playsuit with wedged tan sandals that she felt elongated her legs to epic proportions, when in reality she was still the shortest of the group by some margin. Elodie was just about to close the door behind her when she remembered something.

"Won't be a minute," she said, darting back inside the flat. She heard Carla and Steph both chime together that she should hurry up. "Sorry, forgot my phone," Elodie said, reappearing and patting her bag.

"Whatever, come on, I'm starving and my feet hurt already. Damn the price of perfection," Carla said in a mock-whine. She stuck her hand out into the street and shifted her weight from one foot to the other. Steph reached out and pushed her hand downwards. "We're not getting a cab?" Carla moaned when she realised that Steph intended to take public transport, any hint of humour disappearing from her voice.

"Of course not. I'm not made of money, plus with all the changes I'm planning on making, I need to save every penny I've got. You should be doing the same, you know. I know modelling is well paid but only when you're actually book-ing the jobs. You said you've missed out on the last three." Steph quipped.

"Thanks for reminding me," Carla said glumly. "Fine, we'll get public transport like peasants, then."

"As opposed to taxis like tourists?" Steph argued. "You know they're a waste of money and they're not even quicker. Do you know the average city taxi speed is seven miles per hour?"

"I'll pay for a taxi for us," Elodie offered, prepared to do anything to end this petty squabble. "I'm making good money now. Come on, it'll be my treat."

She held her hand out and flagged down a passing cab. Elodie opened the door for them and waited as first Carla climbed in, followed by Steph. Elodie was just about to follow when she heard her name being called by an unmis-takable voice that stopped her in her tracks.

"Elodie, wait," Chase said, striding across the road, his hand raised. Elodie felt her tongue tie and, despite desper-ately searching for some words, any words, found herself at a complete loss. "You've not answered my calls."

"This isn't a good time," she said crossing her arms over her chest, the face of her watch turned towards the setting sun and glinting in the light. Chase glanced at the taxi and saw both Steph and Carla inside. Instead of looking beaten, he took on a grandiose swell and smiled.

"Off out?" he stated. "Why don't you let *me* take you

out instead? I want to explain, you just caught me at a bad time. Please let me wine and dine you. Come on, El?" Elodie felt herself begin to soften, she unfolded her arms and then crossed them again, her fingertips tapping gently on her forearm.

"Oh you've got to be kidding," Carla said from within the taxi, she had wound down the window and was surveying the pair of them. "She wants nothing to do with you, Chase. Come on Elodie, ignore him. He's a dick –" The last of her words were muffled, because Steph, in her infinite wisdom, had decided to wind the window back up.

"Come with me, Elodie. I'm only here for one night and I want to show you how sorry I am."

Elodie paused. He did seem genuinely sincere and whole-heartedly sorry.

"I can't," she said finally.

"Well how about this, give me an hour of your time and I'll make sure you get to your friends safely?" Elodie looked at Carla who was, in turn, looking back, her eyes ablaze.

"I, I…" She trailed off wondering why this was such a difficult decision. She knew she should tell him where to go, to dismiss him as he had dismissed her. But, there was something about him, something in the way he carried himself, something in the way he looked at her that filled her with uncertainty. She looked to Carla again, imploring her to help. She opened the car door and leaned in.

"Guys, I'm not bailing, but I need to do this. I'm going to hear him out and then tell him what I think."

"Do what you need to do, Elodie, but remember, you're worth ten of him," Carla said as she pulled the door shut. It closed with a resounding thud.

Elodie could see Carla's eyes blazing like fire through the glass. She turned to Chase and did her best to erase all emotion from her face; she wanted to appear completely indifferent. The taxi pulled away and even though Elodie no longer had backup, she felt a sense of power settle over her.

"Well, now Thelma and Louise are gone, we can get reacquainted," he said. "What do you say? This is your place, isn't it?" He nodded to the old Victorian building, which housed Carla's flat. He took Elodie's hand but she pulled it away, rooted to the spot.

"I thought you wanted to take me out. *'Wine and dine,'* you said."

"We can go out after, gorgeous. Come on, I'm here for one night only and I've missed you, so let's make the most of it, shall we?" he said, grinning. He reached out for Elodie again but she stepped back. Chase retracted his hand and looked at her, a sort of dumb expression on his face. "What is it with women lately?" he muttered under his breath.

Everything anyone had ever said about Chase echoed in her mind. No longer would she give him the benefit of the doubt; she was done with him full stop. She knew that she was just a plaything to him, a coveted toy that he only wanted because it had been confiscated. *'And he has the nerve to call me immature,'* she thought angrily. She had once again made a bad decision and once again it had been because of Chase. *'No.'* She couldn't lay the blame at his door. He did have a certain hold over her, but she was after all her own person and the sooner she took responsibility for herself, the sooner she could break free from his spell. *'This just isn't right,'* she thought to herself, and thought about Carla's words once more: *'If it isn't right it's wrong.'*

"This has all been a mistake," she said, rummaging in her bag for her phone.

She now realised that she didn't need to give him a piece of her mind: telling him what she thought of him was wasted energy, energy that she should be spending on her friends. She pulled out her phone and to her surprise saw not one, two or even three missed calls from Chase, but dozens. It would seem that he had been trying to get hold of her ever since she stepped off the plane, but in her rush to get home and ready for the party she'd missed them all.

"I'm the one who's made the mistake, Elodie, I never should have…" He trailed off, the sound of ringing coming from his jacket pocket. He whipped his phone out and cancelled the call.

Normally Elodie would have felt privileged by this action, as though he were putting her first, but something told her that she hadn't been the only one he'd called that evening.

336

She'd borne witness to how he tried to line up women when he had nothing better to do.

"Chase, what are you doing?" Elodie asked.

Chase looked at her with uncertainty, as though she were a puzzle he just couldn't crack.

"I just wanted to spend some time with you," he said, his voice faltering ever so slightly. That was all Elodie needed: it was only now she could see how insincere his words were.

"Was that your friend, Aaron?" Elodie said evenly; she watched him carefully now. Aaron had been playing on her mind more and more now since Grace had explained a few things.

"Elodie. You know I don't actually know Aaron," Chase sighed. "You should be flattered, though: I didn't want you seeing anyone else, I wanted you to myself. Come on, it's a compliment if anything."

Elodie took a step backwards, a look of total disdain etched on her face.

"I've got to go," Elodie said numbly. "Bye, Chase."

"Oh come on, don't be like this, you should be nice to me. Remember the little keepsake I've got? Well, we wouldn't want that surfacing, would we?" Chase said, an altogether stonier tone in his voice now.

Elodie looked at him, hardly daring to breathe. How could he? She couldn't believe that he would stoop so low. She wondered if he'd ever been the man that she thought he was, or if, more likely, she had made that man up.

"Chase, I…"

"Of course, there's one way to make sure it never sees the light of day," he said as his hand wandered to the nape of her neck. He stared at her, his eyes scanning her face intently.

"Chase, no. I can't. I don't want to," Elodie said without malice.

Suddenly she felt very differently about him. She was no longer angry or hurt, she felt something strange towards him now and she realised, as her eyes drifted over him, that it was pity. He appeared so much lesser now, smaller somehow and uglier. It was as if for the first time she was seeing him for what he was, rather than what she wanted him to be.

As the taxi pulled away Steph turned to Carla, a forlorn expression on her face.

"She's not going to come, is she?" Steph asked glumly. "I really can't believe she'd choose him over me again."

"Give her a chance Steph, you don't know that. I think she's going to tell him to fuck off once and for all," Carla said, placing her hand on Steph's knee and giving it a squeeze. "Don't worry, this is a great night for you and with or without El, I'm going to make sure you have the best time ever."

Steph managed a wan smile and looked out of the window.

"I just wish Andy was here," she added in a small voice. Carla didn't reply. There was nothing she could say that would change the fact that he wasn't. Instead, she asked the driver if she could connect her phone and started a playlist that she knew Steph would love.

The taxi pulled up outside Betty's Book Café and Carla handed the driver a crisp twenty-pound note.

"Are you going to change the name?" Carla asked, gesturing towards the sign above.

"I hadn't thought," Steph replied, casting her gaze upwards. "I don't think so, 'Steph's Book Café' just doesn't have the same ring to it. Plus it's not as though I'd actually own it. I'm just taking the reins while Mum chills out. She reckons every year running a café is like ten sat behind a desk."

Carla held back as Steph opened the café's door. Steph expected to see only her mum; she had, after all, insisted that she only wanted her nearest and dearest there and that she most certainly did not want to make a big deal of it. Much like the surprise gathering for Elodie a few months ago, there were balloons placed around the café, a large banner hung with the words 'Congratulations Steph' and an assortment of party food had been laid out. All of the staff were there, as well as a few of Steph's old friends, some family members and on the counter right next to the till stood a large TV screen.

"Ahhh, guys, this is… Well, it's just amazing. Thanks so much," Steph managed when she was finally able to get some words out.

"No Elodie?" Betty asked looking around the room.

"She's on her way," Carla replied, confidence in her voice, but not in her eyes.

"What's that for?" Steph said, interrupting and pointing to the TV by the till.

"That's the best part," Betty said mysteriously. She took Steph by the shoulders and with a flourish of her wrist pressed the on button. Andy's face lit up the screen: he was in full army gear and looked very smart. Steph squealed when she saw his face.

"It's a video message from your Andy."

Betty hit play and Andy began to speak.

"Hey babe," he started. He looked a little nervous, as though he wasn't entirely comfortable talking on camera. "I'm so sorry I can't be there for your big day, but I want you to know that I love you with all my heart and I'm so happy for you. You're going to totally smash being the boss. I can't wait to see what this next chapter brings for you, and us. Love ya, babe, always have, always will."

Carla looked at Steph, she was surprised to see a tear running down her cheek. Steph wasn't exactly one for displays of emotion, even when they were well and truly called for. She wrapped her arm around Steph and gave her a squeeze.

"You really miss him, don't you?" Carla said.

Steph turned away from her friend, nodded and wiped the tear from her cheek.

"But this is a happy day, so no tears," she said, closing her eyes and taking a deep, steadying breath.

"Well, I think your day's about to get a whole lot happier," Carla said furtively, her glance flicking from Steph's eyes to something behind her. Steph wheeled around, hardly daring to believe it; but stood there, still in his uniform, was none other than her Andy. She flew to him, and wrapped him in a huge embrace. He showered her with kisses and Carla saw him whisper something in her ear. Whatever it was it had the desired effect: Steph simply couldn't stop smiling.

Elodie marched down the street, leaving Chase in her

wake. She had thought he might follow her, but when she turned to give him one last glance she could see that he was on his phone. Elodie imagined that his next port of call would be Jessica, or Tara, or whoever else was in his little black book. His black book made her think of his black box, or rather what was housed within it. She felt sick, and sicker still that he would use it as a way to keep her quiet. Elodie marvelled at how she had been taken in and wondered just how many women had been led down the same path. Elodie understood, that for her, it all boiled down to flattery. She had been unable to imagine what Chase saw in her and as a result had been so taken aback that she had been blind to him. Steph and Carla had seen though him; they had never taken to him, not really. They had been right about Tom and right about Chase. Elodie promised herself that from now on they could be in charge of her love life. Inhaling deeply, Elodie quickened her pace. All she wanted to do now was to see Betty hand over the keys to Steph, to celebrate with her friends and to forget about Chase completely.

"Taxi!" she exclaimed holding out her hand and feeling very much as though she was in an episode of *Sex and the City*, especially when teamed with the warm evening air, the hustle and bustle of the streets and the fact that she was turned out in her most stylish ensemble.

She stepped out of the cab a little while later having had time to mull things over. She was thankful that she would have Steph and Carla to vent her frustrations to. Of course, she would save her negativity for a later time. Elodie just wished Chase had been different. She was ready to be swept off her feet…

Something about that thought seemed familiar. It was the ghost of a memory, a flicker in her subconscious that someone at some time had offered that to her, at least she thought they had. When it came to the opposite sex, Elodie wasn't all too sure of anything anymore.

Elodie walked into Betty's amidst a throng of excitement. Unsure as to what was happening, she immediately sought the first familiar face she knew. Carla was busy pouring Champagne; Elodie pushed her way through the crowd and knew that she'd missed the main event as her ears filled with cries of congratulations and the clinking of glasses.

"Is she mad?" Elodie asked Carla in a quiet voice.

"Mad? She's over the moon!" Carla said excitedly. "Take it things with Chase didn't go well?"

Elodie shook her head.

"It's over, completely over. I should have listened to you guys; no, I should have listened to myself. He was never interested in me, he just wanted someone to pass the time with. He's a user, I should have seen, should have known, but I guess he just managed to work me," Elodie said resolutely before turning her gaze to Steph. "But this evening's all about Steph and her new business."

"Well it was, but now it's all about Steph and her engagement," Carla replied with a grin.

"Her what?!" Elodie said, a half-puzzled, half-amazed expression on her face. "Her what?!" she repeated.

Carla pointed to the corner of the room where Elodie saw Steph and Andy talking animatedly to a group of people Elodie knew to be Steph's old school friends. She tore her way through the guests and flung her arms around Steph, apologising profusely for missing her moment but exclaiming how happy she was for them all the same. Steph dutifully held out her hand for Elodie to examine the ring. It was a simple solitaire diamond on a plain platinum band: understated, elegant and extremely Steph. Elodie was ecstatic for her and listened eagerly to Andy's story of how he had planned the proposal. Betty had been in on it from the very beginning and couldn't have looked happier with the news. She beamed from ear to ear and on the odd occasion looked as though she may even shed a tear.

As the evening went on Elodie had hoped to give them the tickets this evening, but knew that now was definitely not the time. She placed her hand on her bag, conscious of what was inside but understanding that it would just have to wait: tonight was all about Steph. As the last partygoers left the café, Elodie began to clear up. It felt good to slip back into her old role, if only for an hour or two.

CHAPTER 19

THE GALA WAS ONLY A FEW DAYS AWAY AND Elodie still hadn't broken the news to Carla and Steph that they were going. Steph had been busy with Andy, and Carla had barely spent five minutes in the flat at any one time. Elodie had passed the time with housework and dreaming of gowns. She'd done a bit of research online and from the previous events' photographs, it looked as though the only rule for the dress code was full-length and fabulous, which worried her as she was more a 'function over fashion' type of girl.

'Ugh, it's so easy for guys. Shall I wear my black tuxedo, my black tuxedo, or maybe I should wear… my black tuxedo?' she thought to herself as she slammed Carla's laptop shut and decided that dress dilemmas were the least of her worries. She needed to get Steph and Carla together. Elodie sat on her bed for a few long moments, her gaze resting on the hand-quilted blanket her grandmother had given her. *'Oh what a simpler time it was back then: no love triangles, no arguments, no feeling like absolute crap because everything is just so damn complicated,'* she mused, knowing full well that it wasn't true and thought that people have been having relationship problems since the beginning of time.

Elodie spent most of the day wallowing. Something was gnawing away at her and she felt decidedly unsettled about whatever it was. She tried everything to distract herself: she ran a bath, watched a film and even went so far as to put a load of washing on. It seemed as though nothing was going to work.

"You've been busy," Carla called to her when she arrived back home a little after seven that evening.

"I've been bored," Elodie countered. "Where have you been? I've called you like a bazillion times."

"I know, I've been so busy. Spent the day traipsing around the city for castings and meetings. Think I'm going to try and switch agents, the ones I'm with are a bit shit, really. They keep sending me for jobs that I'll never get in a million years. I need management that are going to really try and help me with my career. Anyway, I'm knackered now. I need a shower, I swear London gets grimier by the day. God, I'm starving, you haven't by any chance made anything, have you, my lovely little housewife?" Carla grinned.

"Paella is on the hob, will be ready in about twenty minutes," Elodie replied distractedly.

"Wow, you really *have* been bored!" Carla called as she disappeared off into the bathroom, only to reappear to add a 'thank you.'

"Do you think Steph might pop over if we invite her?" Elodie asked, trying to sound nonchalant, but failing because Carla called her on it immediately.

"Why? What do you want?" she asked suspiciously.

"Nothing, I just all want us all to hang out," and then added weakly, "it'll be nice."

"Well if you ask me you're up to something. You usually want an early night before work and you're all twitchy and you never cook! Look at you! What's up? Tell me, El?" Carla demanded.

Elodie said nothing, figuring that it was better to remain silent than to risk getting caught out in a lie.

"It's nothing, OK, not nothing, it's something but I want you both together and tonight's kinda the last chance I'm going to get to tell you." Elodie eventually said.

Carla folded her arms in front of her chest and Elodie shirked away as she felt her friend's critical gaze wash over her.

"OK, you got me. I'll tell her to come over and then you can tell us what all this is about, but if you tell me that you're pregnant with Chase's bastard child then I'll screw," Carla said, only half-joking.

It was over an hour before Steph arrived. She walked in to find Carla sat on the sofa flicking through one of Elodie's scrapbooks of travel destinations and Elodie sat on the arm-chair, staring into space and chewing her fingernails nervously.

"Is someone going to tell me what's going on?" she asked as she settled herself on the sofa next to Carla. She fixed Elodie with a look that said: *'This better be good.'* Elodie reached inside her bag and produced a crisp white envelope, which she promptly opened up, turned upside down and emptied the contents out onto the coffee table. Three pristine, white envelopes lay there. Each envelope bore one of their names, written in Elodie's hand.

"What's this?" Carla asked, giving Elodie a puzzled look. She picked up the envelope with her name on and opened it up. She pulled out an equally crisp white card with embossed gold leaf lettering on one side and read. Steph followed suit but had barely opened her envelope when Carla began to scream.

"Are you kidding? Oh my God, Elodie, this is incredible! How did you? Where? I mean who…? Jesus, it doesn't matter. Is this for real? Am I dreaming? Please tell me I'm not dreaming. Oh my God, Steph, do you know what this means?" Carla babbled, her voice getting higher and higher with each word until Elodie was pretty sure only the neighbours' dog would be able to hear her.

"I don't understand, are these invitations for us?" Steph asked. "To Alex Walker's gala, this weekend?"

Elodie nodded enthusiastically. She was unable to speak for fear that she'd cry with happiness. The look on their faces was absolutely priceless and made Elodie's heart soar. Carla was grinning from ear to ear, still babbling and at various intervals clapping her hand over her mouth and squealing. Elodie turned to Steph, who was, to her dismay, frowning.

"I can't go," Steph said bluntly, handing the invitation back to Elodie. "I'm sorry, El, but Andy and I are away seeing his parents. He goes back next week and this is the first time we'll see them since the engagement. I wish I could go, really I do, but…" she trailed off.

Elodie understood, of course she did, but that didn't stop her from feeling irritated.

'Stupid old Andy coming here and ruining my surprise,' she

thought, before giving herself an internal slap and scolding herself for being so self-centred. Steph was right: she should have asked them weeks ago, the fault was entirely her own.

"Is there no way you can get out of it?" Elodie asked tentatively.

"Oh, El, it's not about that. I don't *want* to get out of it. I'm really excited and I'm sorry but there's just no competition. I don't get see Andy as much as I'd like to and we see his folks even less. I really appreciate the gesture though, honestly I do." Steph gave Elodie a smile that dictated that there really was no way she was going to change her mind and stood up.

"You're not going already are you?" Carla asked. "We should have a drink. You can have one small one, can't you, El? It's not like you're the one flying the plane, and Steph, come on, we've not raised a glass to you and Andy yet, just the three of us."

Steph declined, albeit politely, and Elodie flat out refused, telling them that she absolutely couldn't touch a drop the night before a flight. Steph picked up her things and gave an apologetic look. She clearly wanted to spend as much time with Andy as possible and there was nothing, not even VIP tickets to one of the most coveted social events in the world, that could change her mind. Steph gave Elodie then Carla hugs before leaving. The door closed firmly behind her and suddenly Elodie felt as though she'd been hit by a freight train. Carla had thrown herself across the room and had pinned her down in an almighty hug.

"So, what are you wearing? I've got some old dresses that'd do but I think this calls for something a little more extravagant. Ooooh, let's go shopping!" Carla said excitedly.

"I'm going to have to, I've not planned this well at all. I've literally got nothing. But when? I'm working up until the day of the gala and I can't very well go then. What if I can't find anything? They're only stupid domestic flights but when the shops are open I'll be ten thousand feet in the air, ugh…"

"Shop online?" Carla suggested.

"You know I hate internet shopping. Nothing ever fits and it's such a pain in the arse having to send things back. You just end up with loads of clothes that don't fit and that you can't return, stuck in the back of your wardrobe for years until you eventually take them to the charity shop. No, I need to physically go shopping."

"You could always pull a sickie?" Carla said mischievously.

Elodie shook her head, although the thought did sound quite appealing and it wasn't as though other people didn't do it. *'Christ, Gareth had called in sick just because he didn't get a ticket to the gala,'* Elodie thought, before dismissing the idea.

"No, I'm still in my probation period. I can't phone in sick and, besides, I'm a terrible liar."

"OK, how about this? I've got nothing on tomorrow. Give me your credit card, I'll go and shop for you. I know your size and I know what looks good. I'll get you all kitted out and anything you don't like I will return for you."

Elodie mulled the idea over. It was certainly more appealing than airport shopping – she didn't think that the gala was the place for bikinis and bathing suits – and she really did hate online shopping.

"OK," she agreed as she rummaged in her bag and took out her credit card. "On one condition. You treat yourself to a little something too, my way of saying thanks," Elodie said.

Carla didn't need telling twice, she grabbed the card from Elodie's outstretched hand and flashed her a big grin.

"Great, you're the best. Elodie, this is amazing. You really are one in a million, you know. Now, off to bed with you, Grandma, we can't have you late for work, you need to stay in their good books!"

Elodie agreed that she did and, after bidding Carla goodnight, took herself off to bed. She lay there trying to sleep for what seemed like an eternity, fighting the negative feeling that Steph hadn't been grateful enough. She knew that feeling this way was entirely ridiculous but couldn't help it, all the same. There was a niggling feeling, an ugly feeling inside of her that she knew, but wouldn't admit, was jealousy. She was still angry with Chase, still sad and still hurt; none of which was Steph's fault. She drifted into a restless slumber and when her alarm rang out the following morning she felt as though she'd only just closed her eyes.

'*What a way to start the day,*' she grumbled to herself as she trudged to the bathroom, concentrating hard on just putting one foot in front of the other, knowing full well that this was going to be a long day. Still, there was one thing that would brighten it: getting home to Carla and her haul later that evening.

Elodie's flight to France and back was as dull as dull could be. The passengers were four women, all dripping in diamonds and heading to Paris for a spot of shopping. They weren't exactly the nicest people and treated Elodie as more of a dogsbody than an actual human being, but sometimes that was just part of the job description; it was a sort of 'like it or lump it' situation. Gareth was now back at work but was still far from his usual cheery self. Gone were the quick-witted comments, the broad smile and general happy demeanour; they had been replaced with a dour expression that Elodie's gran would have said could turn milk sour.

"Still bummed about the gala?" Elodie asked once they had landed and the passengers disembarked.

"I don't know what you mean," Gareth managed, "I'm absolutely fine, just concentrating on the job in hand. I'm not petty, Elodie. Alex has chosen those he deems worthy. Sadly, I'm not one of them. I hope you have a fabulous time." Elodie managed a very small, very guilty smile and wiped the back of her neck feeling suddenly very hot. She hadn't told Gareth she'd been given a ticket, but clearly, someone had. "Why you felt the need to hide it from me is beyond me, still, I guess that comes with being so young."

"I, I wasn't sure how you'd take it," she replied carefully. "I know you've wanted to go for..."

"Years. I've wanted to go for years," Gareth answered quickly, "as many years as I've worked here in fact, which is five by the way. Tell me, how many years is it you've worked here? How many years have you grafted, shed blood, dripped sweat and cried tears for this airline? It's not even six months, let alone six years. But, Alex's word is final, and he only has a certain number of tickets. He can't hand them out to just anyone now, can he? To think, I even bought a

tuxedo for it, I was convinced that this would be my year."
Gareth's voice weakened and he turned away from Elodie.
"Would you be a love and finish up here? I'm suddenly not
feeling very well again."

Elodie agreed at once, wanting nothing more than this
conversation to be over. She felt extremely sorry for Gareth
and guilty for causing his pain all at the same time. Gareth
thanked her and left looking extremely forlorn, his eyes
sparkling with the threat of tears.

'He really isn't taking this well,' Elodie thought to herself,
wishing wholeheartedly that there was some way in which
she could help. It was then she realised, in one sweeping
moment, that she could: she could give him exactly what
he wanted. Without thinking, she rushed off the plane,
descending the steps two at a time in an effort to catch
Gareth before he made it to the terminal. He had and was
now nowhere to be seen. Elodie let out a great sigh of irritation and wheeled back around: she wanted to make his
day as soon as possible. It all made perfect sense. She had a
spare ticket and Gareth wanted one. She only wished she'd
thought of it sooner instead of spending the daydreaming of
what Carla would pick out for her on her shopping trip.

The journey home was smooth and uninterrupted. Mr
Bosworth was his usual affable self and could tell at once
when something wasn't quite right. He asked her what was
going on and without hesitation Elodie reeled off everything
that had happened, from start to finish in one long, rambling and increasingly emotional tale.

"So I guess to top it off, I threw away something potentially great, I wasted a lot of time and energy on an absolute
prick and pissed my friends off whilst doing it. I've made
Gareth feel awful, and even though I know how to fix it,
I've got no way of getting hold of him before the event and,
judging by the speech he just gave me, he wouldn't take my
call even if I had his number."

"I have both," Mr Bosford said after some time, clearly
mulling over whether this would be a breach of trust or not.

"You do?" Elodie asked hopefully. Mr Bosford nodded
and, when he pulled the car to a standstill at some traffic

lights, handed Elodie his phone. She copied Gareth's number down quickly and dialled the number.

"Ugh, his phone's off," she griped as Gareth's voice-mail kicked in. Can you take me there instead?" she asked imploringly.

"Oh, I don't know about that. I've had a long day and he lives miles from you."

Elodie nodded; she understood. She would just have to find some other way.

"I'm kidding, you're my last drop off of the day. I'll take you to Gareth's place, have a quick spin around the block then drop you back home. It's practically on my way anyway."

"Really?" Elodie asked, unable to believe her luck. "You don't mind? I'll pay you…"

Mr Bosford waved his hand, and her offer, away.

"No you won't, it's no bother at all. In fact – I insist."

Mr Bosford snapped on the indicator and expertly manoeuvred from one lane to the other, making the turning towards Gareth's home just in time.

"Oh, it's you," Gareth said as he opened the door.

Elodie had never seen Gareth out of work and was utterly surprised by his relaxed appearance: he wore faded jogging bottoms and an old vest top, which were an absolute world away from his usual smart attire.

"I have something for you," Elodie began fumbling in her bag. Steph's ticket was still tucked safely in its back pocket.

"Elodie, I don't mean to be rude, but can this wait? I'm not feeling great and…" He trailed off as Elodie pulled the crisp white ticket out of her bag.

"Here," Elodie said, holding out the ticket to Gareth.

"Is that a ticket to the gala? Wait, you're giving me your ticket?" he asked, stunned.

"It was for my friend, but I think you deserve it more anyway." She winced and wondered if Gareth would take umbrage with the fact that it was originally intended for someone else.

Gareth remained silent, frozen to the spot with an odd expression on his face.

"I couldn't…" he began.

"Go on, just take it. You deserve to go more than anyone, and so what if it's not from Mr Walker himself? It doesn't matter. You should go." Still Gareth stood there, completely mute. "Say something, will you?" Elodie said when the silence became too much to bear.

"I don't know what to say," Gareth began. "Thank you, but I don't think I can, I wanted to earn it, you know. To get to go off my own merit."

"Screw that!" Elodie said. "You *have* earned it, a million times over in fact. Just take the ticket, Gareth, go, have fun. It doesn't matter who gave it to you, all that matters is that you go."

Gareth reached out and took the ticket gingerly as though it were made of fine china that might break at the slightest touch.

"Thanks, Elodie. I don't know what else to say."

Elodie gave him a warm smile, which he returned; and it was in that moment that she knew she had done the right thing.

"See you there then," she said, leaning in and giving him a kiss on the cheek. Gareth stood there, still staring at his invitation as if it were a jackpot-winning lottery ticket. She left feeling as though she could walk on air; the sky seemed bluer somehow and she became overwhelmed by a deep sense of wellbeing.

Elodie returned home much later than she had intended. Carla was in the bath belting out a 'nineties power ballad. Elodie smiled to herself, knowing that most people would feel embarrassed to know they'd been overheard warbling En Vogue to themselves, but not Carla. She'd probably up the ante and put on even more of a show. Pacing across the living room to her bedroom, Elodie was forced to stop in her tracks. She took a couple of steps back and positively recoiled at just how many bags were on the sofa. She stood there, mouth agog for several long minutes.

'*There have to be twenty bags here at least,*' she marvelled, wondering just how bad the damage to her credit card was going to be.

"Oh the wanderer returns, about bloody time too," Carla said, fastening the belt of her robe as she emerged fresh from the shower. "So what are you waiting for, let's get this show on the road."

"Is all this for me?" Elodie asked.

"No, don't be crazy, of course it isn't," Carla replied as she leaned into the pile and pulled free the smallest of all the bags. "This one's mine." Elodie rolled her eyes as Carla pulled out a deep plum-coloured lipstick from the bag. "I didn't use your card though, didn't want to take the piss. This little bad boy was almost thirty quid," Carla said, popping the lipstick back into the bag and loading Elodie up with as many bags as she could carry.

"OK, you know what goes with what, so hand me things and I'll try them on?" Elodie suggested. She needn't have bothered though: Carla was already on it. Before Elodie could utter another word, she had been handed a heavily-laced burgundy gown with black chiffon puff sleeves and black chunky heels to match.

"Isn't this a bit gothic?" Elodie asked sceptically. Carla rolled her eyes and told her to live a little. Elodie stepped out of her work ensemble and into the dress. It was nice, but just not very her.

"Don't you think it's a bit...?" Elodie said, surveying herself in the mirror.

"Fucking hideous? Yeah, I do, take it off. Sorry, my bad."

Elodie laughed at Carla's brutal honesty and slipped out of the dress, which Carla folded neatly and returned to the bag from which it came. Next was a full-skirted, beaded black number. Elodie marvelled at how heavy it was but tried it on nonetheless. The black dress was little improvement; if anything, it was worse.

Three more dresses came and went, all of them looking positively awful. Finally, there was just one outfit remaining. Elodie had little hope that this would be any better. Carla had great taste but had missed the mark considerably on this occasion.

"It's a good job I saved the best for last," Carla said, grinning. She removed a stunning, gold fishtail dress from the final bag.

Elodie let out a little noise of admiration and stretched out her hand for it greedily. It was faultless, elegantly detailed and had a satin finish to die for. It was something she never would have picked out for herself, but somehow that made it even better. She stepped into the dress and pulled the straps over her shoulders. Admiring how it looked in the mirror, she slipped on the shoes that Carla had selected to go with it, a pair of sparkling heels that caught the light beautifully with every turn of her heel.

"Carla, I love it," Elodie managed, unable to drag her gaze from her own reflection. "It's perfect, absolutely perfect."

"I know, right?" Carla said. "Sorry about all the others. I guess you could call them red herrings, I just couldn't help myself. That lavender one was hilarious. I don't know how I kept a straight face."

"You cow! I thought you'd gone mad or something!" Elodie howled with laughter and threw one of the shopping bags at her friend, "I should have known something was up when you gave me those bloody cork wedges."

"Sorry," Carla laughed, wiping a tear from her eye. "You should have given me a budget."

The mention of money made Elodie reach for the label: a dress like this wouldn't be cheap and it wouldn't matter how perfect it was if it meant she couldn't pay her rent or feed herself because of it.

"Carla, I don't know, it's an awful lot of money for a dress," Elodie began.

"It isn't just a dress though, it's a 'Pierre Du Cabine'. Have a look online, the second-hand ones are almost as much as a brand-new one. If you're ever skint, just sell it."

Elodie let herself be swayed: the dress was just too damn good.

The following twenty-four hours positively dragged by. The more Elodie looked at her watch, the slower time seemed to go. Had this been any other day, the flight would have been something Elodie would have been excited for. A six-piece girl band, having just won a massive talent show, were using the jet to fly out to Munich to record their debut album, their single having just gone platinum. But this wasn't any ordinary day, and even when they started practising harmonies, dance moves and talking about things Elodie would never experience, she still couldn't manage to get excited. Instead, her mind wandered to what the following evening might be like. She imagined movie stars, designers and so much Champagne you could sink a battleship. Each second that ticked past seemed longer than its predecessor, and by early afternoon Elodie felt as though the day were made up of twenty-four years, instead of hours.

"Elodie, one more thing," Grace said, a distinctly stony edge to her voice.

Elodie looked up. She had thought that she and Grace were on pretty good terms now, but judging by Grace's dead an expression maybe she had thought wrong.

"I need you to do a full inventory, all three aircraft and the lounge's bar."

"But I..." Elodie trailed off. Grace had begun to laugh. "For God's sake Grace, I thought you were serious."

"How could I keep you behind? You've been neither use nor ornament all day. Go on, have a good time. Oh, and Gareth told me about what you did. That was really good of you. You could have got decent money for that ticket if you'd sold it instead."

Elodie told Grace that there was no way on earth she'd have sold the ticket ahead of gifting it to Gareth, although not without wondering exactly just how much she might have been able to sell it for.

"Go on then, what are you waiting for? I'll finish up here, go on! I won't tell you again."

Elodie flashed Grace a thankful smile and with a flurry of excitement made her way off the plane. Anticipation built with each and every step that she took, so much so that by the time she arrived home she could barely contain herself.

Carla let out a low groan as she checked the time for the one-hundredth time that day and wondered where on earth Elodie could be. The last thing she had said before heading out the door was that she'd be back by six. It was now quarter past and she still wasn't home. Pacing up and down the flat didn't have the effect Carla had hoped for, so instead of waiting by the door like an impatient toddler she decided to run herself a bath. After all, she didn't need Elodie there to start getting ready herself. Once the bath was drawn, the wine poured and the music on, Carla climbed into the tub.

The heat was almost too much to bear, and she stood there shifting her weight from one leg to the other as she became used to the temperature. After a few minutes, she lowered herself into the water and let out a low, content sigh as the suds washed over her shoulders. Truth be told, Carla didn't need a bath: she'd showered that morning and hadn't been out of the house all day. She was simply trying to pass the time before zero-hundred hours. She reached over for her wine, a dry white she had found at the very back of the fridge, and took a sip. She set the glass down and as she did so heard the unmistakable sound of Elodie's key in the door.

"Honey, I'm home," Carla heard Elodie call from the kitchen. She quickly rinsed the suds, jumped out of the bath and wrapped herself in a large fluffy towel.

"You're late," she began as she pushed the bathroom door open before stopping mid-sentence to ask, "What are they?" as Elodie held up a pair of glinting bejewelled earrings.

"They're the ones you wanted. I asked Mr Bosford to take a detour and got them for you, you deserve them."

"Oh Elodie, you shouldn't have…" Carla began.

"Oh, OK, well I'll just take them back then," Elodie said, slipping them back into the gift bag from which they came.

"No, no, no, gimme! I'm sorry, you should have, you totally should."

Carla held out her hand and Elodie dropped the earrings into her outstretched palm, watching Carla admire them in the fading sunlight and feeling so happy that Carla now had the earrings she'd dreamt of owning for so long.

"Right, our car is coming in t-minus two hours, so it's all systems go. I need a shower and a nap before we go, I'm shattered."

"Less of that. You need a glass of wine and some Ariana on full," Carla replied as she slid over to the speakers and cranked the volume up. Elodie couldn't help but smile, she couldn't remember the last time she had seen Carla this excited. As one song ended and the next began Elodie became aware of a banging at the door,

'Jesus, who could that be?' she wondered as she padded towards the door.

"Miss Taylor?" a man dressed head to toe in beige asked.

Elodie nodded and a box was thrust into her hands. She scribbled her signature on the delivery guy's pad and closed the door. The package was addressed to her and Carla.

"Hey, come here, we've got something."

"What is it?" Carla asked, appearing from her bedroom and sidling up beside Elodie. Elodie shook her head and shrugged.

Carla took the box from her and tore into the packaging and pulled out a bottle of Champagne. Elodie recognised it at once as being the same brand Chase and his friends had bought for them all those moons ago and her heart sank. *'Please don't let it be from him,'* she begged silently. There was a little gift card inside. Carla opened it up and read aloud.

To my two favourite girls, enjoy tonight. Love always, Steph x

Elodie felt relief wash over her and Carla squealed with excitement. The Champagne was cracked open immediately and the half-drunk glasses of wine were discarded into the sink. They raised their glasses to Steph and drank deeply, then, with an almost frenzied realisation that time was quickly slipping past, they continued to ready themselves. Waves of anticipation fell over the room and when the final adjustments were made and it was time to step into her dress, Elodie practically shook with excitement. Carla wore a simple black, backless dress accessorised with the glittering earrings Elodie had gifted her and a simple silver bangle that had been a gift from her father on her twenty-first birthday. She had pulled her hair back into an elegant slick ponytail, which showed off her high cheekbones beautifully. Elodie had never seen Carla looking so refined and took every opportunity to tell her so.

"Jesus, El, it's like you've never seen me in a dress before," Carla exclaimed, placing one hand on her chest in mock offence.

Elodie laughed. She'd seen Carla in plenty of dresses, just none of them past the knee.

"OK, let's get you into your dress, I'll give you a hand."

Elodie stepped into her glittering gown as Carla played dress maid.

"What do you think?" Elodie asked, feeling uncertain. Now that her hair and makeup were done, and the dress and heels were on, she wondered whether or not it was all a bit too much.

"You look sensational. Now we look the part, let's just hope we can act the part too." Elodie raised her eyebrow: there was only one of them that might fall foul of propriety and it wasn't her. "OK, I know, I know, best behaviour, no excessive drinking and no sleeping with your boss," Carla said, laughing. "Okay, quick selfie and then we're outta here!"

Carla held her phone high enough to capture the perfect shot and after a couple of seconds of tapping declared that she was done and that they should go. Elodie grabbed her small gold clutch from the side, slipped on her heels and took one last look in the mirror. Her hair, which had been arranged in romantic waves, fell loosely over her shoulders; she ran her fingertips through the ends and thanked her lucky stars that she had someone like Carla by her side.

A long, low whistle escaped Elodie's lips as their car pulled up to the imposing stone steps of the Grand Royale, the hotel that had the honour of hosting the gala. A barrier had been set up between the guests and the public; photographers, journalists and fans beckoned the more famous amongst them over and flashbulbs went off every few seconds. Elodie stepped out of the car and onto a deep mulberry-coloured carpet, barely able to take in her surroundings. Her fear that her ensemble might be a bit over the top was soon quashed as she saw that everyone was dressed to the nines. Equally fabulous dresses were donned by the elite, and Elodie was pleased to see, as she was given an appreciative glance, that she didn't stand out for all the wrong reasons.

"What do we do?" Elodie asked, a low note of nerves creeping into her voice. She realised that she may not stand out, but she sure as hell didn't fit in.

"I guess what everyone else is doing," Carla said.

She hitched up her dress and began to climb the steps but not before giving the excited crowd a gentle sort of wave and sincere smile that wouldn't look out of place on a royal. Elodie followed in her wake, keeping her eyes set firmly on the ground in front of her; the last thing she wanted to do was trip in front of all these people, especially since about ninety per cent of them held cameras.

A burley-looking man in a tux admitted them into the building; he reminded Elodie of a James Bond villain. Once inside, the opulence continued, as a white-gloved hand offered Elodie a glass of Champagne, which she gratefully accepted.

"Where to start?" she asked.

The hotel seemed to be reserved exclusively for the gala. There were formally-dressed waiting staff floating from guest to guest, all with trays laden with either Champagne or canapés. Elodie's stomach growled and she realised that she hadn't eaten anything all day. She reached out for the canapés and took two, popping one then the other straight into her mouth. They were delicious, little drops of heaven and Elodie just had to have one more. The waiter offered her a wan smile and extended the tray once more. Elodie's hand hovered over it as she decided which one would be next. She felt the sharp point of Carla's index finger jab her in the ribs. Elodie turned round to defend herself, knowing full well that Carla would be telling her off for being uncouth at the gala.

"Alright, alright, that's the last one I swear..." she began before trailing off.

Over on the other side of the room, chatting animatedly with two very dapper-looking gentlemen, was Chase. Elodie felt her heart stall and lurch within her chest: Chase wasn't alone. A tall, leggy woman in a full-length, backless red gown stood opposite him. She flicked her long blonde hair over her bare shoulder, placed an elegant hand on his arm and leaned into him, in an attempt to join in with the conversation, Elodie thought.

"You OK?" Carla asked. "Look, just don't worry about him. You were bound to see him at some point and it's better now, when you're looking like this, than just bumping into him after work or something. Who's that he's with?" Carla strained to try and catch a glimpse of the woman's face.

Elodie didn't need to see to know exactly who that was: the words '*he calls and I go running*' echoed through her mind.

"It's Jess, from my course. The one from the bar, remember, she turned up to the surprise party."

"Because I invited her…" Carla said, realising that she had inadvertently introduced them, "I'm sorry, El. But look at it this way: now he's messing her around instead of you. I mean, fuck that guy. He's clearly a massive dick. Come on, let's get another drink and find something more interesting to do. El, come on, please don't let him spoil this," Carla begged as she practically dragged Elodie away.

Elodie stole one last look as she walked away. Jessica still had her back to them but Chase had glanced over and now fixed Elodie with a very definite stare accompanied by one raised eyebrow. Elodie felt the hairs on the back of her neck stand to attention and felt an overwhelming urge to scream. She wanted to shout at Jessica for being so stupid, to tell her to have a bit of self-respect and that she was worth ten of him. But more than anything she wanted every single individual at the event to know what kind of person Chase was, how cruel and manipulative he was. But that would mean admitting to their relationship, facing a firing and risking the whole world seeing a photo she'd rather didn't exist. She seethed at the unfairness of it all: what would happen to him, a slap on the wrist perhaps?

'*No, more like a pat on the back,*' she thought indignantly.

"You're right, I know you're right. Still, it's not nice to see…" she started, but Carla held her hand up to silence her.

"No, it's not nice, but it's also not your problem and just look at what you're missing out on, or should I say *who* you're missing out on. There are loads of eligible bachelors here, probably twice as rich and ten times as nice."

Elodie nodded in agreement but couldn't help herself from adding:

"I don't care about the rich part, I really don't. Money means nothing if it's all you've got," and for a brief moment Elodie felt as though the lustrous shine of the gala was dulled.

"Yeh, but it helps," Carla added cheekily. "Check out that

358

guy. Obviously hot: just look how many women are fawning after him and he's got to be loaded, everyone here is."

"*We're* not," Elodie interjected.

"We're the exception, he's the rule," Carla said knowingly.

Elodie glanced at the guy. He had his back to them, but even facing away Elodie couldn't help but admire his form. He was tall and broad and wore a suit incredibly well. A bevy of women seemed to have encircled him; Elodie saw him take a step backwards and for an instant felt sorry for him. He seemed uncomfortable, he kept running his hands down the back of his trousers and shifting his weight from one foot to the other. She thought about going to save him, swooping in and pretending he was needed elsewhere or that he and she were old friends and needed a catch up at once. But that was the kind of thing that worked in films, the kind of thing that on the big screen would result in a torrid love affair and probably marriage. In real life it would end in an awkward silence and many judgemental stares, Elodie scarpering with her tail between her legs and the sound of mocking laughter following her as she went. Her reverie was broken by one of the staff: a small man, dressed head to toe in immaculate liveries, extended an antique silver tray laden with Champagne saucers. Elodie took one and thanked him. Carla took one, paused then grabbed another.

"For our friend," she lied as the waiter looked at her with a raised eyebrow.

After a couple of glasses of Champagne and plenty of speculation about what the rest of the evening would hold, Elodie and Carla decided to have a good look around the venue. The hotel was truly stunning, with exceptionally high ceilings, wooden panelled walls, crystal chandeliers and enormous arrangements of flowers in ornate vases everywhere the eye could see. A beautifully framed sign listed the running order of the evening. Carla pointed to the line that read that at nine pm the gallery would open for perusal and an hour later the auction would begin for the pieces within.

"Last year a painting done by Dwayne Glover sold for almost half a million pounds," Carla informed Elodie sagely.

"Who on earth is Dwayne Glover?" Elodie asked dumbly.

"Only the greatest rapper alive, apparently. Not the

greatest artist, though. I saw a picture of his painting in a magazine, looked like Betty had done it after a few too many gins," Carla said.

Elodie snorted and her hand flew to her mouth in embarrassment, her eyes darting around to make sure no one had heard.

"Very elegant," said a voice from behind. She wheeled around embarrassedly and was relieved and very pleased to see that it was Gareth.

"Well, don't you look dapper?" Elodie said, admiring Gareth's plush velvet tuxedo jacket. "You look like a movie star."

"Darling, tonight I *am* a movie star," Gareth quipped before doing something wholly unexpected: he leant over and planted a very sincere and very soft kiss on Elodie's cheek. "Thank you so much for this, darling, you've no idea how much this means to me."

Elodie gave Gareth a warm smile without knowing what to say. As it turned out she didn't need to say anything: Gareth was able to do the talking for both of them. He went on to give them a blow-by-blow account of his evening so far, including the 'little bit of stuff' he'd met in the ballroom.

"We were both admiring this gorgeous sculpture at first, but then we started admiring each other. His name's Glenn and he's getting me a drink as we speak," he motioned to the heavy-set and ornately gilded bar in the far corner. "Oooh, look who he's with. I know it's not professional to say, but our Captain certainly does a well-tailored suit justice, doesn't he?"

Elodie knew of course who he was talking about but couldn't stop herself from turning to see all the same. Chase was stood, feet from the bar, listening to a fellow guest with apparent interest. His gaze flicked from his companion to Gareth, whom he nodded to. Elodie sensed, rather than saw, Chase begin to move; he must be coming over to speak with Gareth and hadn't realised from across the room who else he was with.

"Elodie, I think I just felt my zip break, I need you to check it for me," Carla said without hesitation, clearly sensing Elodie's panic and not wanting her to suffer for it. They said a quick farewell to a bemused Gareth before Carla grabbed Elodie's arm and hauled her in the direction of the restroom. They slid through a heavy oak door and slipped out of sight. The door closed behind them with a satisfyingly safe thud.

"Thanks for that. I just went into meltdown mode and froze," Elodie sighed, leaning against the wall, her hands on her hips and head tilted back in annoyance. "Why do I turn into a wreck around him?"

"Because you liked him and he treated you like shit and we've got an inbuilt programme that makes us want to win men like that back, just so we can have the pleasure of dumping them. It's like getting the last laugh or something. But, that's what I'm here for. I wasn't about to stand there and let him have the satisfaction of making you feel awkward. Screw him, he's a knob," Carla said as they stepped inside.

"My God, these toilets are bigger than our entire flat!" Elodie gasped once they had walked through the entrance corridor and into the main part of the toilets.

"And probably cost twice as much too. I mean, look at these," Carla added, pointing at two enormous gold gilded mirrors.

The toilets were, in keeping with the rest of the building, spectacular. They boasted a spacious circular waiting area, complete with velvet chaises longues, glittering chandeliers and a plush cream carpet that felt heavenly underfoot.

"I can't believe he brought her here!" Elodie groaned once they had settled themselves in a quiet corner.

"Well if it's any consolation, you look banging and she looks like he just hauled her off a street corner."

Elodie laughed, appreciating Carla's cattiness but knowing that it wasn't true all the same. Elodie opened her mouth to add something, but found that she had nothing else to say. It was what it was, and no amount of slating Jess was going to change that. Two flamboyantly dressed women entered the bathroom and without hesitation made their way straight over to the mirror nearest Carla and Elodie.

"Do rich people have no sense of personal space?" Carla whispered only half-jokingly. "Come on, let's get out of here.

We can't hide all evening. Let's just try to avoid him and try to have a good night."

Elodie nodded her agreement and made to leave; she pushed the heavy wooden door of the restroom open and stopped in her tracks. Jessica was stood, mere inches from her with a look of absolute disgust on her face.

"Oh, you've got to be kidding, are you actually following him?" she said. "He said you were obsessed. You can't just leave him alone, can you? He's made his choice and it's me. It's like feeding a stray dog or something, he just can't be nice to you without you hanging around like a bad smell."

Elodie opened her mouth to reply and closed it again feeling completely wounded. She averted her gaze and wished more than anything that the ground would swallow her whole.

"Oh, hell no," Carla said, appearing from behind Elodie with something akin to absolute rage etched on her face. "Chase didn't choose you, he's settled for you. Chase is an absolute fuckwit and anyone who thinks otherwise is too, and how dare you speak to her like that? She's done nothing but try to be a friend to you. You know what, you two deserve one another: you're vain, shallow and you're going to find yourself all alone when he moves on to someone else, and trust me, he will do that. Come on, Elodie, let's go, you're better than this."

For a moment Jessica looked torn, as though a war between what was easy and what was right waged inside her. If such a quandary had existed within her, it seemed to pass quickly. Carla pushed past, her eyes flashing with anger and Elodie followed, still unable to look at Jessica and unable to believe what had just happened. She still couldn't believe the colours Jessica now showed. *'I guess that's just what being with people like Chase does to you,'* Elodie thought glumly, remembering some of the things she had thought and said to her best friends. The two of them walked back to the gala and Elodie's heartbeat returned to what would be considered a normal rate.

"You OK?" Carla asked when they were far away from the restrooms. Elodie nodded. She was OK. Of course, the confrontation had been far from enjoyable but Elodie was pleasantly surprised to find that she didn't care all that much now that the dust was beginning to settle. She didn't care that Chase was here with Jessica, she didn't care that Jessica had turned into a bit of a bitch and that she'd allowed herself to be taken in by Chase.

"Come on, let's get a drink and have a look round the auction, it's almost time. Who knows, maybe Wayne Glover's done another painting?" Elodie said, making her way towards the exhibition at the back of the building.

"Dwayne, it's Dwayne Glover," Carla said, laughing.

Glasses charged, Elodie and Carla made their way into the auction room. It was a vast expanse of polished floor and high ceilings, not too dissimilar from the Eason Art Space. The glittering light cascaded down onto the pieces up for auction. A couple of them already had red dots placed next to them, which Elodie knew from her date with Aaron meant that they had been sold already. The auction room dictated that patrons be respectful, or in other words quiet. Well-positioned staff had been placed around the gallery and offered the necessary shushes whenever a guest became too raucous.

"Some of this stuff's incredible," Carla whispered, pointing to a huge bronze statue of two people embracing.

"And some of it really isn't," Elodie added, motioning to what looked like an old, mangled bicycle mounted within a giant cloche. They turned the corner, giggling as quietly as they could, not wanting to be reprimanded, or worse, thrown out.

"Now, something I can get on board with!" Carla said as they reached the photography part.

Giant photos of famous people in candid shots, beautiful locations, and cool street photography hung on the walls. Elodie and Carla took their time perusing the pictures, stopping every now and then to appreciate them fully. At the very end was a concealed piece, hung behind draped velvet curtains with heavy-looking ropes either side. Elodie leaned forward to try and get a better look, the only part visible was a small gold plated placard that read:

'Title: Hidden Delights. Artist: B. Nash'

"So what do you say, shall we have a peek at the hidden delights of 'Hidden Delights'?" Carla said, glancing around, her hand hovering mid-air as if she meant to whip the curtain back. Elodie grabbed her arm and pulled her away.

"No, we shall not," she reprimanded, as a member of staff eyed them suspiciously. "That's it, no more booze for you. You're a bloody liability sometimes."

Carla shot Elodie a wicked grin and took a step backwards, her hands above her head in mock-surrender.

"OK, no sneak peek. Bet it's shit anyway," Carla laughed and was promptly shushed by the nearby staff member.

Elodie turned to face her, her eyebrows raised in an *'I told you so'* sort of way but Carla seemed to be staring straight through her, as if Elodie was made from nothing but fresh air. Carla's gaze seemed to stretch down the entire length of the room and Elodie turned to see what it was she was looking at with such fascination. She realised with a jolt that it was Jenna Broderick, her husband Sven, a model Elodie recognised as being Kiri Kingston and several other celebrities all following in their wake. The group were admiring the artwork and through the quiet of the room Elodie heard one of them say, quite loudly, that they had bought one of the pieces already.

"Total steal, thirty grand for this one, it's a DuMour. I'm going to have it hung in the downstairs loo," the voice echoed.

A hush fell over the guests as a gong sounded, and from the distance of the ballroom Elodie heard the auction being announced.

"Ladies and gentlemen, anyone wishing to take part in the auction need only make their way through these doors to the gallery. Proceedings will begin in five minutes," a voice boomed over them.

Elodie looked at Carla with something akin to panic on her face: they were still in the gallery and now, with seemingly every single guest making their way in, they were trapped there.

"Relax," Carla whispered. "Just because we're here doesn't mean we have to bid on anything."

Elodie let out a low sigh. From their vantage point they

had a pretty decent view of the gallery and could see just about everyone gathering around the small stage awaiting the auctioneer, who was at that precise moment flicking through some papers, obviously in a last-ditch attempt to remember as much as he could about each item.

The gong sounded once more and the auction began. Elodie saw several paintings go for several thousand and was amazed at the amount that the old, crumpled bike fetched. She glanced at Carla who was rolling her eyes unsubtly.

"Next we have a bust of Lady Nicola Bradley cast in bronze. A beautiful piece here, ladies and gentlemen. Who'd like to open the bidding at, say, three thousand pounds?"

Carla's hand shot in the air immediately and Elodie spun round to stare at her.

"What are you doing?" she hissed under her breath. Carla just looked at her with a wicked smile on her face and shrugged nonchalantly.

"Do I see any more for any more?"

"Five thousand," a gentleman at the back of the room shouted. The auction went back and forth for a few moments before a lady in a green gown at the very front of the room silenced all other bidders with an offer of ten thousand pounds.

"Sold, to the lady in green," the auctioneer said as he slammed his hammer down and moved on to the next piece.

"Damn, so close," Elodie heard Carla whisper through stifled giggles.

The auction came to a close just thirty minutes later with absolutely every single piece being sold. The auctioneer brought the hammer down on the last item and thanked them all for attending. Elodie nudged Carla and gestured towards the painting behind the curtain; no one had made any mention of it at all.

"Maybe it's already been sold?" Carla murmured.

Elodie shook her head: if it had already been sold, then why was it still behind its curtain? Why had no one mentioned it and why didn't it have a tell-tale red dot next to it?

"That concludes this evening's proceedings," the auctioneer said, "but before I let you all leave, may I welcome Mr

Alex Walker to the stage, without whom none of this would be possible?"

Elodie, who had already begun for the door, stopped in her tracks, unaware but pleasantly surprised to find Mr Walker on stage with a smile on his face and a little note card in his hands. He cleared his throat twice and waited for the applause to die down.

"Well, this evening has been one of the best so far and I'd like to thank each and every one of you for turning up. Without your support, none of this would be possible, and so many good causes would go without." He paused briefly to glance at the card. "Now, this is a first for the annual gala, but I felt it only right to honour some lesser-known, but equally talented, artists. Success is a funny thing: we chase it for so long and when it arrives it's never what we thought. Attainment isn't absolute; neither is failure. They are not at polar ends of the scale, but merely a sidestep from one another with nothing but courage, conviction and confidence connecting them. The winner of the first-ever 'New Talent' award has all three in spades. I've known him for years, but we'd never truly met until an envelope was left for me, containing a single image and a note, which I will read an excerpt from now.

"'I hope you can feel my passion and dedication through the picture I enclose. It cost me a lot and is what I consider to be the greatest example of who I am as an artist and what I have to offer.'

"Now it just so happens that I *could* feel his passion and dedication. Not only that but I could see his talent and after spending just one evening with this person I knew, almost at once, that he was passionate and committed to his craft, and to making a success of himself. Ladies and gentlemen, please put your hands together for Mr Bernard Nash, Alpha Whiskey's first winner of the New Talent Award with his debut piece, 'Hidden Delights'."

The group burst into tumultuous applause as the heavy-looking ropes were pulled and the red velvet drapes were opened. Elodie was struck dumb: the photograph displayed was indeed beautiful, but it was not that which occupied her thoughts. It was the man stepping up, the man shaking hands with Mr Walker, the man accepting the ornately carved award, the man she knew to be Aaron.

The next few minutes passed in an instant, she felt Carla's hand clasp around her arm and she allowed herself to be pulled away, but not before stealing one last look at Aaron. He was surrounded by society's finest, all of them clad in expensive clothes and huge smiles. She wondered exactly how many of them would have given him the time of day a few weeks ago, when overalls and a greying cap had replaced his smart tuxedo and instead of an award he held a mop and bucket. Elodie could not make out for the life of her how this had come to be. The sights and sounds of the gala melted into one and seemed to move past her like ribbons of colour all tangling together. They emerged into the main hall, the commotion of the auction behind them. Elodie felt herself breathe for the first time since Aaron's, no Bernard's, name had been called.

"What the hell...?" Carla started but trailed off when she saw Elodie's face.

"I'm so confused. His name's Aaron, he's a cleaner, for Christ's sake," Elodie said, snatching up a glass of Champagne and downing half the contents in one go.

"He's also a photographer," Carla surmised.

"Yeh and a bloody good one, too. Did you see the picture?" Elodie asked. Carla nodded her reply.

"You should go and talk to him," Carla said. "Go and clear the air, congratulate him or something."

Elodie stood there and stared into the contents of her glass, as if the answer was somehow swirling about in there. Slowly, and with a dogged look of determination, she nodded.

"Take this," she said, handing Carla the glass. "I'm going to go and talk to him."

Carla gave her a little squeeze and wished her luck. Elodie retraced her steps back into the auction room and made her way towards the back where she knew Aaron would be, still surrounded by his new friends.

CHAPTER 20

AARON WAS DEEP IN CONVERSATION WITH A petite, elfin woman when Elodie spotted him. Her auburn hair had been twisted into an elegant chignon, which had been accessorised with crystals that glinted handsomely in the warmly-lit room. Aaron's gaze was not fixed on his companion; instead, his eyes seemed to wander from one side of the room to the other, as though he were watching a very slow pendulum. Elodie thought that maybe he was taking in the beauty of the artwork but knew deep down that those nomadic eyes meant only one thing: he was bored.

"I'm so sorry to interrupt, but do you mind if I have a word?" Elodie managed, her voice quivering slightly as the petite woman cast her a scowl.

"Actually, we were just in the middle of something," the minute woman began but trailed off when she saw Aaron's expression change.

"Elodie," Aaron managed. Elodie noticed with a small wave of delight that he didn't recoil in horror at the sight of her. "I wondered if we'd bump into one another."

"You knew I was here?" Elodie asked dumbly.

Aaron nodded and produced his phone. After a couple of seconds, he held it out and on the screen for all to see was the photo Carla had taken of them earlier, shared on her social media.

"She followed me a few months ago, I followed back because she's a model and, you know, always helps to know people in the business. I don't go on very often but this evening I did and there you were. I almost thought about not coming, about skipping the whole thing. I've been so nervous for days now and this seemed like some kind of sign, but I had to come. For my career and the future. I've already spoken to people I had never even dreamt of meeting, I've even been given a commission..." he trailed off, blushing slightly.

"I don't get it, though. How did Mr Walker know? Was there a competition or something?"

"That day you caught me going through that envelope addressed to him. It wasn't a letter, it was a print of that." He nodded towards the image of 'Hidden Delights'. "I was actually having second thoughts. I'd sneaked back on to recover it, give it up as a bad job and just stick to what I'm good at, but then you appeared."

"God, I took it and handed it in to be delivered. I'm sorry, I thought one of the passengers left it..."

Aaron waved her apology away.

"There's nothing to be sorry about. If you hadn't been so pig-headed, so utterly infuriating, all this would have never happened."

"So, he saw the picture and then what?" Elodie asked.

"He wanted to help; he really is a good guy, you know."

Elodie nodded; she did know. After all, without his generosity she wouldn't be there, Carla wouldn't be there and probably, maybe more importantly, Gareth wouldn't be there either.

"He wanted to create an opportunity where I could build myself up and he'd had an idea about some sort of award a while ago, so it was perfect really. Next year it'll be a competition where young photographers can submit their work. One piece will be chosen and put to auction, and the person behind it gets to network at the event and keeps fifty per cent of the sale value," Aaron explained.

Elodie couldn't help but feel a connection to Aaron; his passion was really attractive and it didn't hurt that in his tuxedo he looked every inch the A-lister. Elodie realised that she hadn't spoken for several moments and instead had been staring at Aaron, lost in her own thoughts.

"So you're here with Chase?" Aaron asked, his voice steady despite the look of disdain on his face,

"No, absolutely not." Elodie shook her head violently. "I'm here with my friend. There were meant to be three

369

of us but I ended up giving a ticket to Gareth. He's always wanted to go and…"

"That was really kind of you," Aaron interrupted, smiling at her.

Elodie had neither the heart nor the inclination to correct him. For some reason she wanted Aaron to see her in the best light possible. The two of them chatted somewhat awkwardly for a few moments. Elodie glanced around and saw that Carla was animatedly talking to an extremely tall, extremely broad man. He was a good foot and a half taller than her and was practically bending double, presumably to hear her over all clamour of the guests, who as the evening wore on were leaving their airs and graces behind and embracing an entirely more raucous approach to proceedings.

"So Bernard Nash, eh? I thought you were Aaron Ber-*nard*?" Elodie asked, twisting a loose strand of hair around her fingertips.

"Bernard's my middle name. Nash is my surname," he answered, somewhat bewildered. "How did you know that?"

Elodie could only respond by blushing: she knew that because she had, once upon a time, done a little bit of digging. What was it Carla had said, 'social stalking' or something? Well, whatever it was, she had done it, and now she had been caught out.

"Just, when we first, you know, met…."

"It's fine, relax. Everyone does it. You really think I didn't look you up?"

Elodie breathed a sigh of relief, and found herself wondering just what it was that Aaron had seen of her.

"Look, Aaron, there's something I need to say. I, well I wanted to apologise. For how I acted, for the things I said; well, for being me, really. I don't know what I was thinking, maybe that's just it, I wasn't thinking at all. I got caught up in everything, Chase made me think that you were something you're not and I believed him. I'm sorry for that, and for generally being a complete bitch to you. You were nothing but nice to me and I just let myself get carried away," Elodie said, staring at the floor; she couldn't bring herself to look Aaron in the eye. Apologising wasn't something she was used to: Elodie's policy in life had always been to try not to do anything that you'd later need to apologise for and up until recently she'd been pretty good at it. "If we could just go back to being friends I'd really like that."

Elodie held her breath. She felt the air stagnate in her chest but held it there anyway, as if somehow Aaron's words would be less damaging this way.

"Elodie, I'm sorry, that's just not going to work for me."

Aaron shook his head. Elodie looked up and saw that he had fixed her with a look that she couldn't quite place. She shifted uncomfortably from one foot to the other and smoothed down the front of her dress.

"Oh OK, I just thought…"

"That's not going to work for me because, honestly, I want more than that, a lot more than that. I think I'm ready for you, for us. I'm not one for denying myself, especially when it feels so right. I know it was a rocky start and I know that you were hurting from your ex. I don't blame you for any of it. I don't entirely understand it, but I don't need to. The short amount of time I spent with you was enough for me to know that I really like you. You're sweet and charming and your laugh makes me laugh." He paused and took a step closer to her. Elodie's breath caught in her throat. She wasn't entirely sure what she had been expecting but this certainly wasn't it.

"Aaron, what are you saying?" she asked, her voice small.

"Let's try again, start afresh, however you want to put it. Look, this might be a crazy idea, but you've always wanted to travel, right?" Elodie nodded. "And let's face it, your job's great but it's not the freedom you wanted, is it?" Elodie nodded, again without any idea where he was going with this. "Well, with the award comes a bit of money, to start me off. I'm going to Australia next week and," he paused and swallowed audibly, "I think you should come with me. We don't have to label this and you can do what you want but think about it. You and me, a million miles away, with so much to explore."

Elodie stared at him, wondering if she had heard him right. She must have misunderstood; there was no way on earth that he'd just proposed their second date as a trip halfway around the world.

"Come again?" she said, cocking her head to one side and fixing Aaron with the kind of look usually reserved for a particularly hard Maths equation.

"I," Aaron said, pointing at himself, "want you," he pointed at Elodie, "to fly," he outstretched his arms, "to Australia with me." He pointed back to himself. "So what do you say?"

Elodie blinked twice in quick succession, unable to process this information with the necessary speed that the situation required.

"But," she began, hoping that something sensible would come from her mouth, "I... I mean, Aaron, that's crazy... totally nuts. I can't just drop everything and jump on a plane with you. We hardly know each other."

"I know enough, and sure you can. Take a sabbatical or jump ship, I dunno, but what I do know is that life's too short, I've been wasting my days cleaning up other people's mess instead of chasing my dream. It was you, your story of jacking it all in and going after something you really wanted that got me thinking. Without you I'd still be there, unhappy and unfulfilled." He looked at Elodie and in his eyes she saw desperation and a pleading look that married hope and desire. "Look, the way I see it is that in the grand scheme of things our life is just one day. We're all born with the sunrise and we die with the sunset and every second is precious, each and every one of them. Each minute and hour between is ours for the taking, ours to make memories, to love, to live and to be happy. I feel taken over by you, Elodie. The more I see you, even just brief glimpses of you have invaded me. The fleeting moments we share aren't enough; I want you to be happy and I think I can make that happen."

There was a moment between them, where time ceased to move forward, where it seemed as though all sound had quieted and, as it had been in that hidden park the night they had kissed, there was only the two of them. Elodie looked at Aaron and saw something deeper there than she'd ever seen before; his blue eyes bore into her and she found herself unable to tear herself away from his gaze. Aaron took a step closer to Elodie; there was nothing between them now. His body pressed against hers and she felt his hands tentatively snake around her lower back, he pulled her into him and she found herself completely willing to be led. Her heartbeat quickened and she was sure that Aaron would be able to feel the thud in her chest beating against his.

"Aaron, I don't know what to say..." Elodie managed in a whisper.

"Say yes," Aaron said as he leant in closer still. Elodie closed her eyes and in that instant felt an alignment. Things seemed to be in place now, as though she had known the answer all along, she just hadn't understood the question. Aaron's lips softly brushed hers and although it was the faintest touch it provoked the strongest of reactions. Elodie felt as though she were spiralling towards utter bliss. Her lips parted as he pressed against hers, more firmly this time and their breath became one. His mouth was so warm and his lips so soft that Elodie felt sure she could sleep on them. She felt his hand trail up her back and as his fingertips grazed her bare skin Elodie sensed that this could be the start of something wonderful.

"So what do you say?" Aaron said as they broke apart. He smiled wanly, clearly hoping for the best, but preparing for the worst.

"I don't know," she said truthfully. Elodie's head was spinning. This was the type of offer that happened in the movies that Carla loved, the type of offer that followed a torrid love affair embarked upon by two Hollywood A-listers. Not something that happened after one date, a couple of arguments and a whole host of ill-feeling. But had it been ill-feeling? Elodie thought. Perhaps not; maybe all of her anger and frustration hadn't been because of Aaron. She thought that maybe she had misdirected her annoyance. Suddenly images of both Tom and Chase entered her mind and an uneasy feeling began to settle over her. Maybe all of it had been a sort of rebound; maybe she hadn't given herself time to heal and as a result had totally lost it at the very hint of things going wrong; after all, it had taken one stupid picture, one word from Chase and one knee-jerk reaction to ruin things between her and Aaron.

'*How could I have been so foolish?*' Elodie thought to herself, realising that a lot of heartache could have been avoided if she'd only given herself some time. She looked at Aaron and despite her desire to say yes found herself incapable of doing so.

"OK, well I want you to come with me. You want to see the world and I want to capture it: what could be more perfect than that?" Aaron said, simultaneously touching her shoulder and breaking her reverie.

"I don't know what to say…" Elodie began.

"Okay, don't say anything," Aaron said, cutting across her. He reached into his breast pocket and retrieved a slim envelope. "Here's your ticket, take it. I'm flying out in a few days but I thought that might be too soon for you, your flight leaves a couple of days later. I'll be on the other side waiting, or not… Whatever you decide."

He leaned towards her once more and, bending down, gave her a soft kiss on the forehead. They broke apart and Elodie felt an overwhelming urge to kiss him again, she could sense their meeting drawing to a close and now wanted more than anything to prolong it for as long as possible. She opened her mouth to say something, anything that might make him stay just a little bit longer, but felt she was at a loss for words.

Aaron gave her wrist a gentle squeeze and looked at her. "I really hope you come," he said before calling over a nearby waiter. "I think a top-up for the lady might be in order," he said.

"Of course," the waiter replied before dutifully filling Elodie's Champagne glass. Elodie took her eyes off Aaron for just a moment as the waiter topped up her glass and in that instant he disappeared into the crowd. Elodie stood there, dumbstruck; she was vaguely aware of the waiter bidding her farewell but the exact words he uttered would never be known to her. All she could do was stare. The freshly-filled glass suddenly seemed very heavy. She lifted it to her lips, her fingers trembling as Aaron's words echoed in her head. She had been in shock, unable to think properly, but now the dust that clouded her mind's eye began to settle and shock gave way to utter disbelief.

"Penny for them," a familiar voice slurred into her ear. Elodie wiped at the nape of her neck as the perpetrator's hot breath lingered there. She turned around and was unsurprised to see Chase standing there.

"You can keep your money," Elodie said flatly, picking up her Champagne and taking a deep drink. She felt very much as though occupying her mouth was the best course of action; it would prevent her from saying something she might later regret.

"Oh come on, El, I'm only joking with you. So, what did Cinderella in a suit want? Cleaning tips?" Chase said, chuckling mirthlessly.

Elodie rolled her eyes. Comparing Aaron to Cinderella wasn't funny; it was cruel.

"Aaron is ten times the man you are," Elodie said, her temper beginning to flare. "If it wasn't for you lying…"

"Hey! Can I help it if that's what I thought at the time? And let's be honest, you didn't take much convincing. The way I see it is that you wanted a real man and you still do." Chase inhaled deeply. "By the way, you look really good tonight, you know." He leaned in towards her and added, "And you smell sensational," before fixing her with a look that she knew far too well. There was a time when she would have seen desire in his eyes, but now they just seemed predatory and shallow.

"You'll have to excuse me," Elodie began.

She turned herself away from him, intent on leaving the conversation there and then. She didn't think she could stand to hear anything else come from his mouth. She began to walk away but Chase grabbed her by the wrist and pulled her back to him.

"Don't be rude now, I only want a friendly chat, to see how you are," he paused for a second and leaned in closer. Elodie could smell pungent alcohol on his breath. "You know, there are lots of dark corners in a place like this; I wonder if there's an unused store cupboard kicking about?"

Elodie twisted her wrist from him and felt the flesh where he had made contact burn.

"Chase, we're not friends and that's not happening.

Where's Jess? Nipped to the loo, so you thought you'd kill five minutes?"

Chase wrinkled his nose as if he had suddenly smelt something rather unpleasant.

"She's gone, too immature, she can't handle being with someone like me."

Elodie felt a strange sense of happiness at his words; Jessica appeared to have seen the light after all.

"Well, you'd better call one of your other women because I'm not interested," Elodie quipped, thinking back to the phone calls she had overheard back on the jet. She saw a fleeting look of embarrassment sweep across Chase's dark features and knew in that instant that there *were* no other women. "Oh, I get it. Exhausted all your options, have you?"

"Not at all," Chase said recovering quickly. "El, I've missed you and need to be honest with you, I know I played you terribly but honestly, it's you that I want. Things were just so much better when you were by my side, come on, what do you say?" his voice dropping.

He now looked at nothing but his hands, which he wrung nervously. Elodie surveyed him closely and sipped at her Champagne thoughtfully. She gave Chase a sweet, saccharine smile and watched as his demeanour changed in an instant. He transmogrified from shy schoolboy to the cat that got the cream in less than a nano-second.

"You've made the right choice," he said reaching out for her again eagerly.

"Chase. I wouldn't go near you if you were the last man on earth," she said, snapping her hand backwards and almost spilling her drink as she did so. "Do you really think that recycling the same, old, tired lines will work on me?" Elodie said in a commanding voice that made Chase take a step backwards. He stammered something about not knowing what she meant, which made Elodie smile,

'He knows exactly what I mean,' she thought to herself.

"Well, let me educate you then. I have heard you use those lines before, not something similar, not in the same vein, but those exact words... to Tara and then to Jess. I was there that day, on the plane. The day you phoned every single woman that had ever given you the time of day to try and get them back into bed with you."

Elodie finished, noting with something akin to pride that Chase looked taken aback. He recovered quickly and cleared his throat.

"So you've been spying on me?" he said, raising one eyebrow in mock-horror. "Can't keep away eh?"

"You're pathetic, you know that?" Elodie said, unable to believe the sheer nerve of the man.

"I thought you were supposed to be nice to me, any more nastiness and that picture might see the light of day…"

"Do what you want Chase, you will anyway," Elodie said, cutting him off. She gave him one last look, unable to believe he had taken her in, or that he could stoop so low, before spinning on her heel and leaving him behind and feeling his eyes boring into her as she went.

Elodie found Carla leaning casually against the bar. The gentlemen she had been with had gone and she was just stood there drinking in her surroundings with a half-cocked smile on her face.

"So how did it go with Aaron?" she asked.

"Oh, fine," Elodie managed. "I need a drink."

Carla leaned over the bar and placed her order with a waitress who looked as though she would rather be anywhere else. Carla handed Elodie a short tumbler, filled with ice and housing barely an inch of amber liquid in the bottom.

"Whisky? Really?" Elodie asked, eyeing the glass suspiciously.

"Sure, why not. It's expensive stuff, for free and besides, you look like you need a good nerve tonic." Elodie took the glass and, looking Carla in the eye, knocked it back in one. The liquid slid down her throat far easier than she had expected and Elodie thought that maybe she could get used to it after all. She waited a moment anticipating the usual burn that came with whisky but found that it never appeared; instead, she felt a pleasant warming sensation, like gently licking flames dancing at the back of her throat.

"Another?" Carla asked, but Elodie shook her head.

"I think I'm going to get off," she said glancing around

the room. She couldn't concentrate and wanted, more than anything, for a just little bit of quiet to think.

"Oh no, let's stay longer!" Carla pleaded.

"You stay. I think I'm done for the night," Elodie said tonelessly, the shock of Aaron's offer still fresh.

Carla nodded and gave Elodie a kiss on the cheek.

"Only if you're sure?" she checked.

"Totally, you stay. Have a good time. Go find that tall guy again, he looked very interested," Elodie said grinning.

"He's a model scout, gave me his card. This place is great; it's like I'm wearing my CV," Carla laughed.

Elodie bade her a fond farewell and made her way outside, suddenly feeling absolutely exhausted.

CHAPTER 21

THREE DAYS HAD PASSED SINCE ALEX WALKER'S famous Gala. Carla had had a fabulous time; she had used her evening to network with industry professionals and had taken no fewer than six business cards home with her. Since then she had been updating her portfolio and working on her online presence, so that when she did eventually follow them up she would have the best shot of making the right impression. Elodie had gone home in a daze and had spent the days since either in autopilot at work, or keeping to herself at home. She felt unable to articulate what had happened, not the run-in with Chase, nor the offer from Aaron – one far more important than the other.

'I'm not one for holding back, for denying myself what feels right.' Aaron's words whirled around in her head, echoing each and every time she had a quiet moment. She had hidden herself away in her room feigning a headache. Carla had laughed at her for getting old and joked that a three-day hangover was only to be expected from people of a great age. Elodie had managed a weak smile before closing the door and settling herself down. She drew her old patchwork blanket over her head and shut her eyes, hoping that the answer would be easier to see in the dark.

Later that evening Elodie found herself traipsing up and down the flat, repeating the same steps over and over again. She ran her fingers through her hair and tugged at her sleeve as she mulled over the outcome to each and every scenario she could imagine. If she went with Aaron she would lose her job, leave her friends and there would just be so much pressure on them to become a thing. She would also be unable to pay Betty back as quickly as she had hoped. What if she discovered that their connection had been false, that they weren't suited and that she didn't want to be with him? If that happened it would mean she'd have left everything behind for nothing, she'd have to come home, tail between her legs and start from scratch. The other option was to stay, to let him leave, possibly never see him again and carry on working for Alpha Whiskey. She'd have to forget all about him, an idea that seemed to go hand in hand with a heaviness in her heart.

"Will you pack that in?" Carla said, looking up from her phone. "You're wearing a hole in the floor."

"Sorry," Elodie said. "Carla, can I talk to you?"

"About bloody time! I've been waiting for this since we came home the other night," she said, setting her phone down on the arm of the sofa and turning to her friend.

"You have?" Elodie asked with surprise.

"Of course, I can read you like a book. Now, sit down and tell me what's going on in that little head of yours. Oh, and grab me a wine while you're at it, I'm parched."

Elodie poured two large glasses of wine, finishing the bottle off between the two.

"Here you go," she said, sitting down opposite Carla and handing her the over-filled glass.

"Good job we never served wine at Betty's," Carla chortled, steadily relieving Elodie of one of the glasses. "So go on then. Not that I need to ask really, I saw you two together." Elodie looked at Carla with one raised eyebrow, unsure exactly how Carla could be so intuitive. "Chase has somehow managed to say the right things or look at you in a certain way and now you're all dithery because you want to go for it but you know we'll all have kittens if you do?"

Elodie, who was taking a sip of wine, struggled not to spit it out through laughter.

"No, no, no," she managed after she'd swallowed awkwardly, "it's nothing to do with Chase. Yes I spoke to him, yes he did try it on with me, but no, I'm never going back there again – ever."

"So what is it then?" Carla asked suspiciously.

"It's Aaron," Elodie began.

She explained the whole situation to Carla, who sat there

patiently, only breaking her concentration to occasionally take a sip of wine. It took Elodie so long to relay the story, how she felt and to ask for advice that condensation from her own glass ran down the side and dripped onto her lap.

"You know what you need to do?" Carla said authoritatively.

"No, what?" Elodie said, taking a sip of her now lukewarm wine.

"You need to come with me. Drink up, we're going out." Elodie began to protest but the steely look on Carla's face told her that any words of objection would fall on deaf ears. She drank her wine, placed the glass in the sink and without a word of hesitation followed Carla out the door.

The bell above the door of Betty's Book Café rang softly as they entered. Sat at the table in the corner, the one by the large window, were Betty and Steph.

"I feel like I haven't seen you guys in so long," Steph said, getting up to hug each of them in turn. She sat back down and Carla and Elodie followed suit, sitting at the chairs designated by their trademark coffees. At Elodie's place sat a milky latte and at Carla's a shot of espresso; Steph was already halfway through her flat white and Betty had opted for a pot of tea, served in one of her floral vintage teapots.

"Go on then," Steph said gently, "what's the matter?"

Elodie gave them all a solemn look and relayed the story to them. Carla listened patiently, even though this was the second time in as many hours that she'd heard it. When Elodie had finished a long and arduous silence fell over them all.

"Brilliant," Elodie said sarcastically. "Thanks for your help, guys."

"Well, what do you want us to say?" Betty asked, "It's mad, absolutely mad. Going off with a boy like that. He could be a murderer for all you know."

"He's not a murderer, Mum. He's just jumping the gun a bit," Steph placated.

"A bit?" Betty laughed cynically. "The only way he could jump the gun further would be if he'd proposed. Besides, even if you knew him really well it's still so last-minute. People spend months planning this sort of thing, not days."

Betty crossed her arms in front of her heaving chest, her eyes narrowing and mouth upturned in a frown.

"I have been planning, and for more than a few months," Elodie said defensively. "I've kept notes and pictures and bits of information in a book for years. I've got everywhere in there. I call it my personalised travel guide."

"Even so, Elodie, it's a big risk," Betty replied.

"Well, I think it's romantic," Carla said effusively. "You should go for it El. Wish I hadn't bloody brought you here now, what with Patty and Selma raining on your parade. I expected more from you two. This is a once in a lifetime opportunity and let's face it, Aaron's hot," Carla said. "I can't see what the big deal is, personally."

"It's not once in a lifetime, the world isn't going anywhere and it's not like you don't get to visit some lovely places anyway. If you want to go, go, but let it be on your own terms. Not when someone tells you you should." Steph offered helpfully.

"Yes, listen to Steph. I knew I could trust you to talk sense," Betty said animatedly, giving her daughter an approving look. "It doesn't matter that he's hot, he's practically a stranger and hot won't save you when he's left you stranded or worse…" Betty trailed off, a look of genuine concern on her face. "I just think you should play it safe, love. Don't do anything risky, you're too precious."

"It isn't risky. If it all goes tits up, she comes home. Where's the risk in that? Look, millions of people go travelling every year and hardly any of them die, do they?" Carla said hotly. Betty gave her a stern look and pursed her lips together tightly, as though she were trying her very best not to say what was on her mind.

"Guys, I appreciate your input," Elodie said. Tempers were becoming fraught and she didn't want anyone falling out on her account. "Look, I know the risks. I know it's mad. I know I don't know him well." She paused and fidgeted with her coffee cup. Did none of them see the irony in telling her she shouldn't just do what Aaron wanted but she should do what they wanted? "But I also know that I want to go. I mean, it's Australia and it's an amazing opportunity. Carla's right: if it goes wrong, I come home. That's not to say

I'm definitely going to go, though. I don't know what I'm going to do. All I do know is that I'm running out of time to make a decision," Elodie said, unable to look at anyone, her eyes remaining fixed on her cup. She twisted her fingers together awkwardly and felt tears of frustration beginning to prickle in the corners of her eyes.

'Pull yourself together, for God's sake. Crying over this! Don't be an idiot and get a grip,' she commanded herself. She felt a hand on her shoulder and looked up. It was Betty, standing over her with a kind smile on her lips but concern in her eyes.

"I'm a lot older, and wiser, than the three of you. It's not a good idea, love, but I can't tell you how to live your life. You've got to do what will make you happy and what you think is the right thing to do. Don't listen to any of us in particular; think about what we've all said and then make a decision that's right for you. Promise me you'll at least do that?" Betty said.

Elodie nodded and let out a sigh.

"First world problems, eh?" she said half-heartedly. She stood up in preparation to leave but found that Betty had caught her in a huge bear-like hug. It was a simple gesture that spoke volumes; Elodie folded her arms around Betty to return the gesture and squeezed her tightly. Elodie felt another pair of arms enter the mix and then another. The four women stood, in the middle of the book café, in an embrace that lasted for several long moments.

When they broke apart all four of them wore solemn looks. Elodie and Carla began to say their goodbyes but just as Elodie reached the door Betty called them back.

"I almost forgot," she said. "I have news of my own."

Betty went on to tell them that she was handing the reins over to Steph a little earlier than expected.

"Next week?" Elodie said, stunned. "But how? I thought the sale of the cottage wasn't going through until..."

"I thought the same," Carla interrupted.

"Sometimes things just go your way a little easier than you thought they would. Doesn't happen often, but when it does you've got to make the most of it," Betty said. "Besides,

Steph knows what she's doing and I'll always be on hand to help."

"So when's the leaving do?" Carla asked.

"I wasn't going to have one…" Betty began, to cries of protest, "but seeing you girls here now has made me change my mind. I should really say goodbye to everyone and what better way to do it than in the place where it all started? So what do you say, how's Friday, seven pm for everyone?"

All three of them nodded enthusiastically.

"Sounds like a great idea, Mum," Steph said. She draped her arm around Betty's shoulders and bent down to give her a kiss.

"Go on, be off with you. You'll have me crying if you carry on like that. No, this is a good thing. It's a happy time for me. Finally, I'm going to get to put my feet up and enjoy some peace and quiet," Betty smiled warmly at her, and with Steph's arm still wrapped around her, both mother and daughter retired upstairs.

Elodie and Carla were very quiet as they made their way home, each wrapped up in their own thoughts. They arrived back at the flat, Elodie's half-drunk glass of wine still on the side. She grabbed some ice out of the freezer and dropped it into the glass.

"What?" she asked when she saw Carla giving her a reproachful glance. "Waste not, want not. Did Betty teach you nothing?"

"Everything's so different now, isn't it?" Carla said with a hint of uncertainty. "Like, really different."

"Yeh, it is," Elodie said, nodding her head and taking a sip of her wine and musing on Carla's words.

She cast her mind back to where she had been this time last year and shuddered: so many parts of her life had been wrong and yet she'd been completely unaware.

"So do you still have no idea what you're going to do?" Carla asked hesitantly.

"Oh no, I know," Elodie said with certainty. "I'm not going."

"You're not?" Carla gasped. "I was so sure you'd go."

"Well, I couldn't even if I wanted to. Betty's leaving do and the flight are sort of at the same time and there's no way I could ever not send Betty off on her way," Elodie said resolutely.

"She wouldn't mind, you know, if it was what you wanted."

Elodie knew that Carla was right: Betty would do her best to understand. Betty had given her sage advice earlier when she'd said, *"Do what makes you happy, do what is right."* Elodie knew that going to Betty's leaving do was right. Betty had been like a mother to her for so long and Elodie figured that she owed her that much at least. This was definitely a sign and one that she shouldn't ignore. She felt as though the universe wanted her to stay, so that's exactly what she would do – and besides, Steph was right, the world wasn't going anywhere.

Friday seemed to roll around in the blink of an eye. Elodie flew to Geneva and back in the space of a few hours. She really loved her job, well, aspects of it anyway. She'd had only one flight with Chase. He'd the good sense to give her a wide birth, most likely the only decent thing he had ever done in his life, although Elodie felt it probably had more to do with knowing when he was wasting his time than from any real sense of decency. He had kept their exchanges brief, professional and hadn't even had the balls to look her in the eye. Elodie was just about to disembark the place when she noticed a black box sat neatly next to an overnight bag and a laptop case. Elodie's breath caught in her throat. She remembered that box all too well. The sound of it thudding shut after Chase had thrown a Polaroid picture of her in there echoed in her mind. She looked around, hardly able to believe that the only thing separating her from it was a locked box. There was no sign of anyone on the plane as she had offered to do last checks. Although that didn't explain why Chase's bags had been left; surely he was either still hanging about or he'd be back any moment to collect them. Feeling a hot wave of nausea began to wash over her, she decided then and there that action must be taken. She knelt down, taking care to touch nothing but the box and made to open it.

'*Goddamn, it's locked,*' Elodie thought angrily. Heat rose

up inside her and caused her fingers to shake. She steadied herself and thought hard. *'What would Chase's code be?'* She didn't know his birthday or any numbers that might be significant to him. She tried 'one two three four' but to no avail. She scratched her head and furrowed her brow. This was going to be hard, especially since the code could be anything, anything at all. Next, she tried all zeros, but again the padlock wouldn't budge. She racked her brain and somewhere, in a far corner, deep inside her mind she felt she knew the answer, or at least part of it. She scrolled the first numbered wheel to six, the second to nine and the third to six again. She stared at the padlock, wondering what the last number could be. She decided that she would have to quickly try every combination on offer by trialling the last number, starting with one. The second her finger touched the last numbered wheel she knew the answer: it came at her from nowhere. *'No, it can't be. But of course it can, it is Chase after all,'* she thought to herself. Somewhere between amusement and disdain she dialled the fourth and final wheel to the number nine and heard a small, but certain little clunk. She rolled her eyes upon the realisation that Chase's passcode was sixty-nine, sixty-nine. *'What is he, fifteen?'* she asked herself.

The lock opened and Elodie lifted the lid, her eyes wide. Inside was a black cloth, which Elodie pulled back; she gasped, underneath there were twenty, maybe even thirty or so Polaroid pictures of women in varying states of undress. Elodie paused, wondering if she should dispose of them all or if she should just search through and find her own. The box also contained the camera, a pair of silver handcuffs that Elodie recognised far too well, a blindfold, a vibrator and several condoms of different varieties.

'Looks like Chase's travel pleasure chest,' Elodie thought grimly. She was shocked at the fact that he took it out and about with him, as though he never knew where or when he might need it. Without warning, images of Grace and Jess flooded her mind, and Elodie decided then and there that she would destroy all of the pictures: she wouldn't look at them, she would just pick them up, cut them up or burn them and then throw them away. She collected them

up one by one and shoved them all, face down into the bottom of her bag. She reached back towards the box and grabbed the lid, but before she had the chance to shut it was struck by another idea. She looked over her shoulder hastily, just to double-check the coast was clear, then picked up the camera, which up until then had lain redundant at the bottom of the box. She turned it on, turned it to face her and gave a wide, wicked grin before holding up her middle finger and clicking the button. The camera went off and a second later spat out a small sheet of Polaroid paper, still undeveloped and blank. She snatched it out of the camera and shook it a couple of times just like she'd seen it done in the movies and then threw the camera back in. She waited for just a moment, then as soon as she saw the blank photograph begin to show colour she neatly folded the cloth back over the contents and placed the picture on top, bang in the middle and obvious to see.

She closed the lid and secured the padlock, then with one last furtive glance she heaved her overnight case from the overhead compartment, pulled out the handle and took off. She had already been cutting it fine to get home, ready and to Betty's party, now she was going to be late. Elodie was looking forward to giving Betty a good send-off but in the back of her mind was a niggling feeling that just wouldn't settle. Uneasiness seemed to roil inside her, as though she were on particularly choppy waters in a particularly flimsy boat.

Mr Bosford was waiting in his usual spot, with his usual smile and usual friendly small talk. Only today, and most days, it wasn't that small. Elodie had found herself really enjoying and often looking forward to their chats. His impartial ear was always available to bend and he seemed to appreciate her confidence and revelled in the times she sought his advice. This was one of those times; she relayed her predicament to Mr Bosworth.

"So will she stay or will she go now?" he asked, a half-smile visible to Elodie from the rear-view mirror.

"Well, it's not really a question worth asking now," she said, "that ship has sailed, or plane has flown. The flight's tonight and I'm not even ready to attend a party, let alone go travelling."

"I see," Mr Bosford said thoughtfully. "Elodie, I'm going to give you some advice. Now whether or not you take it is entirely your choice. Life is short, really short and you are young. Don't settle; you've tried that once before and look how it turned out. As for having a steady job and a regular wage, let me tell you that when you get to my age you'd trade most of that security for a few memories and some experiences. I guess what I'm trying to say is that it's OK to follow your heart; you just have to remember to take your head with you too."

Elodie pondered his words carefully, asking herself over and over again if he was right. The problem, aside from the obvious, was that she now had too many pearls of wisdom from too many people.

"Mr Bosford?" she said suddenly. "Could you take me straight to Betty's Book Café?"

The two made eye contact in the mirror and Elodie saw the corners of his eyes crease.

"Your wish is my command," he said before flicking on his indicator and switching lanes.

Instead of arriving late to the party, Elodie was early. Steph and Carla were both pleased to see her, especially since an extra pair of hands would mean that they would be set up and ready to enjoy themselves sooner than expected.

"Pour us a glass of fizz will you, El?" Carla said as she balanced precariously on a chair whilst attempting to hang up some brightly-coloured bunting.

"Where's Betty?" Elodie asked, fidgeting with the plum-coloured belt around her waist. She still wore her uniform, having not had enough time to change after her secret mission with the photos.

"She's upstairs, I've told her not to come down until I call her," Steph said as she arranged cupcakes onto a three-tiered cake stand.

"OK, well I need to talk to you guys," Elodie began.

"Talk and work, hun," Carla said. "We've got a lot to do and not a lot of time to do it in. Here, blow these up, will you?" A pack of vividly coloured balloons came flying her way. She caught them and immediately set them back down.

"Girls, I really need to talk to you," she repeated.

Something in her tone made both Carla and Steph stop what they were doing and turn to face her.

"OK, you're worrying me now," Carla said, stepping down from the chair.

"Me too," Steph agreed. "Is everything OK?"

Elodie closed her eyes and took a deep breath inwards.

"OK, well I've made a decision," Elodie began. She went on to tell them, in as much detail as possible but without wasting time, what she had decided in the car. "Once I'd made my mind up I had to come straight here and tell you guys. I know it's crazy and last-minute but it's right, you know? I just feel it, right in here." She pointed to her chest, a move she felt might have been cheesy in any other situation, but in this one felt very much called-for. Carla and Steph told her that they understood and hugged her, Steph a little more loosely than Carla.

"When will you be back?" Carla said, and Elodie was surprised to hear that her voice was strained. She pulled back from her and saw that her eyes were glassy.

"Why? Are you going to miss me?" Elodie asked, a thin smile on her lips.

"Nah, I'm just wondering if I need to rent out your room," Carla said, stifling a sob. The last thing Elodie had expected from Carla were tears, she felt completely taken aback by them, and although she'd never admit it, a little touched.

"Oh don't cry. I'm not planning on being away forever and I've got enough money saved to keep my room going for a little while yet. It'll take more than this to get rid of me." Elodie wrapped her arms around Carla and squeezed her tight.

"Are you sure you know what you're doing?" Steph asked, unable to help herself from asking the sensible questions.

"Nope," Elodie said, "but that's what makes it all so exciting."

"Well I guess all that's left to do is tell my mum, then," Steph replied.

"That, and pack," Carla added.

Elodie nodded. For some reason, she felt even more trepidation about telling Betty than she had done her friends. Perhaps it was the fact that Betty had been like a mum to her for so many years, or maybe she was worried that Betty would see her investment as being squandered. Perhaps it was a combination of both, but whatever it was, it wouldn't stop the fact that it was happening. She checked her watch and noted with grim resignation that she had very little time to spare: she needed to get home, get packed and get herself to the airport. She gave Carla and Steph a warm smile, told them she'd keep them updated before making her way through the back of Betty's and up the little staircase that led to the flat. She knocked on the door tentatively, somehow hoping that maybe if Betty never heard her she wouldn't have to have this conversation. However, Betty did hear and opened the door after just a few seconds.

"Elodie my love, come in, come in," Betty exclaimed.

Elodie had assumed that she would interrupt Betty getting ready for the party but was surprised to see that this wasn't the case at all. She still wore her flour-dusted apron and messy bun that Elodie had come to know as Betty's uniform. "I didn't think you'd be here till much later. Do you want a cuppa?"

Elodie shook her head as she walked into the flat Betty shared with Steph. Boxes were piled high and bore words such as 'Bedroom' and 'Kitchen' written in large, loopy letters on them. Elodie perched on top of one of them and wondered just what words she should use to start with. After a brief moment, she settled on the same words she had used downstairs. Betty turned to face her and fixed her with a stern expression; her firmness was fleeting, and as quickly as it had come, the frown had turned into a small smile.

"I've made a decision…" Elodie began but couldn't get any further because Betty had engulfed her in an almost suffocating hug.

"I know what you're going to say, love. Truth be told, I think I've known it all along. I told Steph you would go. It's this evening. isn't it? I take it you've told both the girls?" Elodie nodded, amazed at how this woman knew her even better than she knew herself.

"But how did you know?" she found herself unable to keep from asking.

"You get good at reading between the lines when you're a mum. That, and you're a terrible liar," Betty answered with a grin.

Elodie caught a glance at the kitchen clock. No longer hung on the wall, it now rested on the kitchen table ready to be packed.

"I've got to go, I'll miss my flight otherwise," Elodie said. "I'll miss you, you know."

"And I'll miss you too. I guess we've both got our own little adventures to go on now, haven't we? You go, have fun, and be safe," Betty said, fixing Elodie with a fierce stare. "I meant what I said the other day: you, Elodie Taylor, are very, very precious. Now you remember, you can call me any time, day or night."

Elodie promised that she would and then demanded the same from Betty, who laughed and said that she didn't think that she would be at too much risk in the Derbyshire Dales.

"There's just one more thing..." Elodie began.

"Oh, you pay me back when you can, love. There's more to life than money, you know," Betty replied, once again knowing Elodie almost better than she knew herself. Elodie gave Betty a tight squeeze and sniffed, she could feel the onset of tears and tried to abate them.

"Now go on, you'll miss your flight."

"Thank you," Elodie said. "I mean it, thank you so much."

Betty gave Elodie a warm smile and shooed her out the door. Elodie blew Betty a kiss from the hallway as she made to leave, she felt that another word, no matter how jovial, might break what little resolve she had left. Betty caught the kiss in an overly exaggerated manner and popped it in the front pocket of her floral apron before patting it gently. It was a sweet gesture that Elodie knew would remain in her memory for many years to come.

Elodie said her final goodbyes to the girls. They had clearly been talking whilst she had been upstairs because not so much as a single balloon had been blown, nor bunting hung. They hugged, Carla cried and they both repeated the same mantra Betty had: *"Look after yourself, stay safe and be careful.*" Elodie promised to do all three and added that she'd be in touch all the time and that they'd probably not even notice she was gone. She was about to leave when an odd sensation settled over, a memory of sorts: Carla's words, *'If you're ever skint, sell it.'* She had been referring to the Pierre Du Cabine dress Elodie had worn to the gala.

"Carla, my dress. Sell it for me, would you? Don't tell Betty just yet but use the money to pay her back, and treat yourself and Steph to something nice with the rest?" Carla promised that she would. Steph looked very happy with the idea and gave Elodie one last hug, this time squeezing her just as tightly as Carla had.

Elodie had made an enemy out of time, so it was with one last hug and a deep breath that she walked out of Betty's Book Café and out onto the street, hearing the little bell above the door tinkle for the last time. She quickened her pace, knowing that she really was cutting things fine. A taxi approached with its light on; she held out her hand and was thankful to see its indicator flick on. The car slowed to a halt beside her and she got in.

"Fitzjohns Avenue," she said as soon as her seatbelt was fastened. The driver nodded and set off, trying his best to make polite small talk but giving up when he saw that his passenger's mind was clearly elsewhere.

Elodie's key turned in the lock and she darted inside, vaguely aware at the back of her mind that this would be the last time in a long while that she would come home. She had asked the taxi driver to wait for her, he had said he would and was clearly delighted at the fact that he could keep the meter running at the same time. She kicked off her heels and stepped out of her dress in record time, hoping that Carla would be good-natured enough not to begrudge her leaving it in the washing basket. She pulled on a pair of dark blue jeans and a white vest top before extricating her large suitcase from the back of her wardrobe and began throwing things in at random, unsure exactly what it was that those who travelled the world packed. When the suitcase was full to bursting she zipped it up and hauled it off the bed.

She was almost out of the door when a thought struck her. She wasn't going on holiday, she was going travelling.

She didn't need three pairs of heels, ten dresses and an entire bag full of makeup – she needed only necessities. She unzipped the suitcase and took out the basics, shoving each essential item into a rucksack and pausing only for breath when she was satisfied with her haul. She slung the rucksack on her back; it was neither too heavy nor too light.

'In the words of Goldilocks, it was just right,' she mused. Her passport, which nowadays barely left her side, was nestled securely in the inside pocket of her bag. Elodie double-checked it, a habit she had become used to and after a quick check realised, with a sense of exhilaration peppered with maybe the teensiest bit of dread, that she was all ready to go. She stood in the living room looking around, wanting to commit as much of the flat to memory as possible. It was there, in the middle of the living room, that Elodie felt silent tears track down her cheeks. She couldn't believe she was going to do this; suddenly her mind was plagued with doubt. What if every single worry everyone had ever expressed came true? She fought with herself for a moment, knowing that it was thoughts like these that would help to keep her safe, and realising that if she had no reservations in the slightest then she would be a very stupid girl. She wiped at her cheeks, determined to have only positive memories of this. Everything that had happened before this was all for a reason. Without everything aligning as it had, she wouldn't be where she was now: about to embark on an adventure she had yearned for since she had been ten years old. She gave the flat one last look, knowing that feeling sad was silly; she would be back soon enough, and with better experiences, and better stories, than before.

The taxi driver had stayed true to his word and was waiting patiently outside her front door. Elodie climbed in and winced when she saw the meter running at almost sixty pounds already. This was going to be one expensive taxi ride, but she was sure that it would all be worth it in the end. Elodie instructed him to take her to the airport and he set off.

"Going anywhere nice?" he asked.

"I hope so," Elodie replied, smiling.

The taxi driver looked at her confusedly through the

reflection in the rear-view mirror and chose not to question her further. Instead, he turned his attention to the road, which was thankfully rather quiet.

Elodie was dropped off right outside the airport. She strode in and ground to a halt in front of the departures board, scanned the information displayed excitedly. There were flights to Geneva, Australia, Mexico, Thailand and Canada and more besides, all leaving within the next few hours. Elodie looked around. She hadn't been to this airport since she'd quit Zip Air; she was half-expecting to see Vanessa striding up to her about to yell at her for being late or for some task that she had failed to complete to her exacting standards. But happily, neither Vanessa nor anyone else she had ever worked with were in sight.

She got in the queue to check in and waited patiently as everyone in front of her got their tickets and passports checked. Second-naturedly she slipped a hand into her bag and fingered the outer edge of her passport, just to make sure she had it. Elodie was not used to waiting in queues; usually, she would be fast-tracked in order to get on with her duties as quickly as possible. Her mind wandered to the private jet; she certainly wouldn't be seeing that kind of luxury again for quite some time. It was in that moment when her head was filled with images of high-flyers, Champagne and luxurious surroundings, that a thought struck her. She had told everyone she was leaving – everyone, apart from the one person who she should have told first: her boss. She glanced towards the front of the queue and counted the passengers still waiting, there were six ahead of her and Elodie guessed that she still had at least fifteen minutes to wait. She pulled out her phone and scrolled down to Gareth's name.

"Elodie? To what do I owe the pleasure?" came Gareth's northern lilt down the phone. Elodie took a deep breath and began to explain.

When she had explained herself to the hilt she paused, and prepared to move the phone from her ear. She fully expected Gareth to go crazy at her. How could she have forgotten to do this? She could have kicked herself for being so stupid.

"Gareth, say something, Please." Elodie managed when the palpable silence had gone on for too long.

"I don't know what *to* say," Gareth said. "You could have given me a bit more notice." Elodie agreed with him on that. She apologised profusely making sure that Gareth knew just how sorry she truly was.

"It just all happened so fast, I literally made the decision today and then it's been a massive whirlwind. I am so, so sorry. You know I wouldn't have done this to you on purpose."

"I do know that," Gareth said, "and there's nothing I can do to make you change your mind and not board that flight?"

Elodie told him that there wasn't and that now her mind was set.

"I've made up my mind," she said. "I need to do this, Gareth. I won't be able to settle until I've travelled and seen more of the world than just nice hotels and tourist traps." Gareth was silent again; Elodie bit her bottom lip and waited for his judgement.

"Well," he sighed, "I'm going to miss you. I'll file the paperwork tomorrow and email you anything you need. It's a good job Alex Walker insists on such a long probation period."

"Why's that?" Elodie asked.

"Because he can be funny about re-hiring people that leave. You, my little lovely, have managed to find a loophole. I hope you'll reapply when you've finished seeing the world? You know I'd make sure you went to the top of the pile," Gareth said, laughing.

Elodie thanked him and, after one more attempt to get her to change her mind, Gareth signed off and the phone call was ended. Elodie stood there with her heart thumping: a rhythm she had never felt before, it was an excited thud that Elodie was sure could be heard by the person at the back of the queue. She stepped forward as she reached the front of the queue and handed over her paperwork and passport.

"Any luggage to check in?" a red-lipped woman asked her.

Elodie shook her head.

"Just hand luggage," she answered.

"And did you pack the bag yourself?"

Again Elodie nodded, a little more fervently this time. The woman opened up the passport and looked from the picture to Elodie and back again.

"Before you scan it, can I just check something?" Elodie asked as the woman picked up her ticket. She had long red nails that matched her lips perfectly.

"Of course," she replied through a smile. Elodie tapped her own nails on the top of the desk and lowered her eyes. Was she really doing the right thing? She was running out of precious time to make that decision. She hovered there for a moment or two, wavering from one decision to the next. Elodie asked her questions and the woman behind the desk listened. When she had finished speaking the woman tapped a few keys on her keyboard, furrowed her brow and after some more tapping printed her boarding card. She extended it towards Elodie, whose hand was ready and waiting. The woman withdrew quickly and looked at the card.

"Is there a problem?" Elodie asked, thinking, or perhaps hoping, that for a brief moment that there had been some sort of mistake.

"No, you're all good to go," the woman replied, handing her ticket and passport back to her along with the newly printed boarding card. She offered Elodie a final, crimson-capped smile and gestured in the direction of the boarding gates. Elodie thanked her, picked up her rucksack and paper-work and made her way through security. Elodie was well practised in the art of airport security and passed through without incident. She couldn't help but roll her eyes at the travellers being stopped with bottles of shampoo, nail scissors or some other contraband. One woman was moaning loudly that she absolutely needed her tweezers and that she simply couldn't manage a fortnight without them. The airport staff member charged with confiscating them told her, with a deadpan expression, that she would just have to buy another pair on the other side.

Once through security Elodie felt as though she could relax. She bought herself a couple of travel magazines in one of the airport shops and settled herself in a quiet corner of the lounge. She rolled the magazines up and slotted them in one of the spare compartments of her rucksack; they nestled there, wedged snugly against her own travel companion, the scrapbook she had been working on for so many years. Elodie felt as though she could feel its beating heart inside her bag, as though the act of travel had bought it to life somehow.

She sat there for a few moments, taking in her surroundings: there were families off on holiday, solo travellers heading off on business and a couple of hen and stag parties off for long weekend city breaks or a boozy week in the sun. She took out her phone. It lay there idle in her hands for a few moments: she needed to contact one more person, someone that up until that very moment she hadn't been able to. She scrolled down to Aaron's name and typed out a lengthy message, which she laboured over for some time. She deleted whole sentences then re-wrote them several times over. When she was finally satisfied, she hit 'send' just as a loud voice over the PA system sounded, announcing final boarding for flight BA7005 at gate 16. Elodie checked her ticket.

'Well this is it,' she thought as her pulse quickened, 'I guess it's now or never.'

She stood up and made her way to the gate. With each step, her feet felt heavier and heavier and by the time she reached the walkway that connected airport to plane, she felt as though she were wading through tar. Elodie knew she was doing the right thing; she just hadn't been aware that doing the right thing would be so difficult.

Elodie found her seat with ease, she was now completely fluent in the ways of air travel and could have got herself seated, belted and navigated the inflight magazine blindfolded. She had stowed her bag in the compartment overhead but not before taking out her magazines. The flight would be long and she would need some form of entertainment of a less mind-numbing persuasion than the crappy comedies and slushy rom-coms available on the inbuilt TVs. Elodie had been lucky and had managed to get a window seat. Sure, it was slightly inconvenient when you needed the bathroom, especially on long-haul flights, but in the run-up to landing, it would all be worth it just for the view she knew would be waiting outside.

"Ladies and gentlemen, the captain has turned on the seatbelt sign, if you haven't done so, please stow your luggage and take your seat ready for take-off. Please turn your attention to the screen in front of you, our inflight safety demonstration video is about to start."

Elodie saw that a svelte-looking blond guy with azure-coloured eyes headed up the cabin crew. He walked the length of the aircraft, checking everyone's seatbelts were fastened, and as he got closer Elodie saw that his name badge read: 'Ryan.' He offered her a warm smile as he reached her and, when satisfied that she was securely strapped in, made his way to the row behind.

The plane began to taxi, picking up speed as it traversed the runway. Elodie looked out of her window and bade a fond farewell to the land below. She let out a low, satisfied breath as the wheels left the ground and the plane took flight. Elodie looked down and saw that the passenger seated next to her, an older man with hair greying at the temples, had gripped the armrest so tightly that his knuckles had turned white. Elodie found herself surprised at this; she was so used to flying that the mere idea of someone finding the experience anything less than pleasant hadn't crossed her mind. She placed her hand on the armrest too and patted this arm in a manner that she hoped came across as kind rather than over-familiar.

"Are you OK?" she asked kindly.

"Fine… thanks, I just hate take-off and landings," he said his voice shaking, "but, my daughter lives in Australia so I'm afraid needs must, it wouldn't be so bad if the flight was nonstop, but the layover means double the trouble for me."

"Don't worry, it'll be over soon," Elodie placated, and sure enough, it was. Within a few minutes the aeroplane had levelled out and her new neighbour had released his grip and looked a whole lot more relaxed than he had done just a few moments before.

Elodie had tucked her travel magazines down the side of her chair for take-off. Now they were in the air and cruising she retrieved one of them and opened it up on her lap. She had barely had time to read the front page when the captain's voice echoed throughout the cabin.

"Ladies and gentlemen, I'd like to welcome you onboard flight BA7005 to Bangkok. My name is Captain John Thompson and accompanying me is Captain Carter. Ryan, Rebecca and Amber are your cabin crew today and will be taking care of you. If you have any questions please don't hesitate to ask. We'll be reaching a cruising altitude of thirty-five thousand feet and steadily maintaining for the duration of the flight. The weather in Bangkok is temperate; we're just coming out of monsoon season so you folks have picked a great time to visit. Flight time today of eleven hours and thirty minutes. We hope you enjoy your visit to Thailand, or if you're carrying onward we wish you a safe journey," Co-Pilot Thompson signed off and the cabin was quiet again.

Elodie felt a rush of excitement settle over her. Hearing the captain's announcement had really bought it all home: she was heading off, on her own. A lot of the passengers would be staying in Thailand for just a few hours, using Bangkok as a pit stop to further-flung destinations, but not her. No, Elodie was tired of dreaming; she wanted all those sun-drenched, exciting daydreams to become her reality.

If the past few months had taught her anything it was that she was far more capable than she gave herself credit for. She had realised that she didn't need to be with anyone: the answer was never a guy, and if it was then she had been asking herself the wrong question. Elodie knew that in order to open her eyes to the future she would need to close the door to the past. She had thought she had done that: she had moved on from Tom, she had moved on from Betty's, but in the process she hadn't moved on at all. She'd merely side-stepped, side-stepped to another bad man and another job that didn't fulfil her. Aaron had opened her eyes to what she really wanted, to see the word. He had been right about that; he had just been wrong about whom she should do it with. Elodie did really like Aaron and found that she cared for him a great deal more than their fleeting romance should have allowed for. But he would be there when she got back; and maybe she would fly out to see him one day, when she had scratched her own itch for adventure. If it didn't work for them, then it would just be another thing that she could add to the list of *'wasn't meant to be.'*

Reclining in her seat, Elodie found herself unable to stop from smiling: she felt a powerful sense of self-worth and control. But, more than anything, she felt very, truly, happy with the choice she had made.

"Excuse me, any refreshments?" Ryan asked. Elodie began to shake her head but changed her mind almost at once.

"I'll have a rosé wine please," she said, figuring that she may as well start enjoying herself right then and there. She took a sip: the wine was cool, refreshing and crisp, it was exactly what she wanted. Elodie gazed down at the magazine, which now lay open in her lap, and lazily flicked through it, wine still in hand. She sipped occasionally as she turned the pages, devouring each and every article with the same enthusiasm as she had the first. The beautiful white sands of secluded beaches, bustling city streets and little-known restaurants off the beaten track, all looked out at her from the pages. Electricity coursed through her veins as she realised that for the first time in her entire life, she was the one in control of her destiny, and for once it didn't feel like a pipe dream. It was there for the taking and Elodie simply couldn't wait.

Elodie closed her eyes, happy in the knowledge that soon enough she would actually be able to feel the sand between her toes, hear the noise of the busy streets and taste the food at those hidden restaurants. No longer would she settle for the picture; she would now get the real thing. No longer would she live a safe life; she wouldn't settle and she wouldn't put things off. She decided there and then that life was for living and, if Aaron were right and each lifetime was a day, then she had already wasted so many minutes. From now on, she would try to make each and every single one count; she didn't want the sun to set on her day and for her to have regrets. She would live her life to the fullest, and she was going to make sure she had a goddamn fantastic time doing it, too.

THE END

400